ALSO BY EMILY MCINTIRE

Be Still My Heart: A Romantic Suspense

The Sugarlake Series

Beneath the Stars

Beneath the Stands

Beneath the Hood

Beneath the Surface

The Never After Series

Hooked: A Dark, Contemporary Romance

Scarred: A Dark, Royal Romance

Wretched: A Dark, Contemporary Romance

Twisted: A Dark, Contemporary Romance

Crossed: A Dark, Contemporary Romance

HEXED

A Never After Novel

EMILY MCINTIRE

Bloom books

Cover design by Cat at TRC Designs
Cover images © tolokonov/Depositphotos, alexraths/Depositphotos, ilya1993/Depositphotos, AntonMatyukha/Depositphotos, Cassandra Madsen/Shutterstock

Published by Bloom Books, an imprint of Sourcebooks
P.O. Box 4410, Naperville, Illinois 60567-4410
(630) 961-3900
sourcebooks.com

Cataloging-in-Publication data is on file with the Library of Congress.

The authorized representative in the EEA is Dorling Kindersley Verlag GmbH. Arnulfstr. 124, 80636 Munich, Germany

Printed and bound in the UK and distributed by
Dorling Kindersley Limited, London
001-345543-Nov/24
CPI 10 9 8 7 6 5 4 3 2 1

Playlist

"Poor Unfortunate Souls"–Pat Carroll, Disney

"Anti-Hero"–Taylor Swift

"What Was I Made For"–Billie Eilish

"Only Love Can Hurt Like This"–Paloma Faith

"Bring Me To Life"–Evanescence

"Kiss Me"–Sixpence None The Richer

"But Daddy I Love Him"–Taylor Swift

"The Loneliest"–Måneskin

"Who I Am"–Wyn Starks

"All Of Me"–John Legend

For anyone who's felt unseen.

But a mermaid has no tears, and therefore
she suffers so much more.
—Hans Christian Andersen, "The Little Mermaid"

Author's Note

Hexed is a dark contemporary romance. It is an adult fractured fairy tale. **It is not a fantasy or a literal retelling.**

The main character is a villain. If you're looking for a safe read, you will not find it in these pages.

Hexed contains mature and graphic content that is not suitable for all readers. **Reader discretion is advised.**

For a full list of trigger warnings, you can find it on EmilyMcIntire.com or by scanning the QR code below:

PROLOGUE

Venesa (Veh-neh-sah)

Twenty-One Years Old

"DO YOU EVER THINK ABOUT DEATH?"

It's a simple question, but the man sitting underneath me—tied to the hotel suite's wooden chair—doesn't answer. Instead, he shifts, the bulge in his pants jabbing between my thighs. I slip my fingers down his dress shirt collar and behind his skinny black tie, and my chest skims across his as I lean in, my breath ghosting against the shell of his ear.

His body shivers.

Mine tries to recoil in disgust.

My lips are almost touching him, but I don't bridge that last millimeter of space. After all, my lipstick is red, and I can't stain his skin with the proof I was here.

"What?"

"You heard me," I whisper. My grip tightens around his

tie until I'm making a fist, my other hand now resting on his shoulder.

"Do I think about...*death*?" His brown eyes drop, locking on to my tits. My dress is low-cut, my breasts are large, and I'm using both to distract him.

Men are so easy.

My hips shift, sinking the full weight of my body into his lap, and he groans, his head falling back in either torture or pleasure—I'm not sure which. I imagine if he hadn't asked for me to secure his hands behind him, he'd be gripping my waist so tightly, I'd bruise.

Luckily for me, Joey here has a thing for being tied up.

I glance around his presidential hotel suite.

We're in the center of the living room. I moved the chair as soon as I arrived, smiling as he asked me to take the black rope he brought and restrain him. Joey thinks I'm bought and paid for, but the reality is I'm so much more.

There's a large brown leather couch in front of us facing the flat-screen TV, and behind his back are french doors leading to the primary bedroom. They're open, showcasing a king bed with small foiled squares of mint chocolate on fluffy white pillows, the Marino hotel's logo emblazoned smack-dab in the middle.

Joey isn't *actually* spending the night here, and it shows in the pristine condition of the room we're in. This hotel is just a nice place to hide some of his darker desires.

Like me.

Although I doubt I'm an escapade he ever saw coming.

Smirking, I yank him forward as much as the rope allows. "That's right," I drawl. "Death."

"Not particularly." He hesitates. "Do you?"

"All the time."

It's the most honest thing I'll say to him tonight.

He frowns. "I didn't bring you here to talk about weird shit like this. Now put those lips to good use."

"Mmm," I murmur, loosening my grip on his tie so he drops against the chair. "And here I thought we'd be having an enjoyable time."

His body jerks so sharply beneath me, it makes me bounce.

A slow smile spreads across my face. "You all right? You seem a little agitated, sugar."

He turns his face to the side, his ruddy cheeks growing even more splotchy. "I'm fine."

"If you say so."

He's *not* fine, but I'll give him a few more minutes to come to that conclusion himself.

My fingers trace along my exposed collarbone and dip into my cleavage. There's a pocketknife stashed in my bra, and its presence is so heavy, the metal feels like it's vibrating against my pale skin. Normally, I'm a poison girl all the way to the end—it's more artistic, more *fun*—but the guidelines for this venture were straightforward.

"What are you doing?" He jerks again, his neck arching in a spasm this time. "*Fuck.*"

Turning his cheek back toward me, I tap it with my fingertips. "Shh. Don't speak, darlin'."

"Enough with the pet names," he snaps.

I smile.

He's really quite pitiful when he's agitated.

Trepidation flashes across his face, and his leg twitches, jostling me forward until my breasts press against his chest.

"Un-untie me," he stutters.

I drag out the knife and flip it open before running my bloodred nails across the sharp edge. "Joey, *honey*, you're hardly in the position to be making demands."

"Untie me, bitch," he repeats. "*Now.* Do you know who the fuck I a—"

His words drop off as another tremor hits, and I take the opportunity, brushing the metal blade down the side of his face and over his Adam's apple until it's resting at the base of his throat.

"Careful with that filthy mouth," I coo, putting pressure on the handle of the knife. "You're turning me on."

He pulls against his restraints, no doubt trying to escape, but he won't be able to. My uncle taught me how to tie those knots when I was fifteen, and I've had a lot of practice since then. Still, the movement changes the angle of the blade, and a deep red stream of blood drips down his neck.

His legs twitch with another convulsion, and I shake slightly on his lap.

"I'm afraid those little…muscle spasms of yours are only gonna get worse, honey."

"Wh-*what*?" Joey stammers.

I give him a pitying look. "On account of the strychnine

I laced your drink with when you were busy putting your face in my tits."

His breathing grows rapid until he's gasping for air.

Right on cue.

You can't ever count on a man, but you can always count on the poison that will kill him…or whatever that saying is.

"I don't know if you've ever studied the beauty of poison." My eyes peruse him. "Doubtful. Honestly, it's a lost art. One people don't take the time to truly appreciate. There's a beauty in my potions." I pause and give a self-satisfied grin. "That's what my best friend back home calls my little concoctions—*potions*, like I'm some witch here to steal your soul."

"Fuck… fu—"

"Technically, I guess he's not wrong," I say to myself and then look back at Joey, tilting my head. "The night goddess Nyx *has* been antsy for a sacrifice, and while she prefers animals burned and buried, I can never bring myself to harm them, so people have to do."

Now I'm just fucking with him. While I *do* practice baneful magick, I don't actually sacrifice living things to gods. Most witches don't.

"You're a fuck—fucking…psy…cho."

Sighing, I pull the knife back. "I told you, honey, don't waste your breath. If *I'm* here, it's because you made a deal with the devil, and there's nothing you can do to save yourself."

"I didn't d-do anything."

"Oh, sugar, I believe you, I do, but you know how it is in

this business." I wave my hand in the air. "It's better if I don't really know the specifics."

His entire body is shaking now, jerking uncontrollably while he struggles to take in air.

Honestly, this whole thing is getting a little tiresome for my taste, and I'm growing bored.

"Does it help to know that I wish I could? Save you, I mean. I'm trying to be better these days, you know? To help people instead of hurt them."

It's not the truth, not really. It's just something I say sometimes because it makes me more palatable.

"You're…hurt—hurting *me*…cunt."

My grin drops. "True. About the hurting you part anyway. The cunt part is debatable."

I reach out and grip his chin in my hand, digging my nails into his flesh and leaving crescent-shaped moons behind. "Unfortunately, you made a bargain with someone *besides* me. And a deal's a deal, darlin', no matter who you make it with." My face screws up as I look at how sallow his skin is turning, and I pat his cheek before shoving it away. "You understand."

His neck jerks back, and his mouth opens on a wide, pained gasp.

I lunge, plunging the metal deep into his carotid artery.

Joey's scream is loud but short, and he gurgles something through the liquid collecting in his throat. Truthfully, I can't understand a thing.

In my experience, it's better when men can't talk anyway.

Adrenaline is pumping so hard in my veins, my eardrums pulse in time with my heart.

Joey's twitches are strong enough that the chair wobbles, so I glide forward, hoping my added weight keeps it from toppling over. Blood continues to seep around the edges of the blade and down the crisp collar of his cream shirt, and I tighten my grip, blanching my knuckles a ghostly white.

I yank the knife out, jumping from his lap and backing away as red spurts from the wound like a fountain, not wanting to get any on my clothes. I wore black just in case—because I know myself—but it's a new dress, one I couldn't afford but *had* to have, and I'm really hoping to wear it again.

The chair *does* topple over now, thumping against the floor, and I watch with sick fascination as Joey's groans fade and he slumps lifelessly on the stained carpet.

Blowing out a steadying breath, I crouch until I can see his face. I cringe when I look at the mess.

Yeah, poison is *much* cleaner.

Joey's eyes are open and glossy, unblinking and empty.

The silence is so thick, it makes my ears ring.

He never screamed, save for that one short burst at the start. Probably too proud to appear weak, even in his last moments. So many men of his stature are.

"Thanks for the warm welcome, Joey," I say to his dead body, wiping off my blade with the corner of his shirt. "The Kingston family sends its regards."

CHAPTER 1

Venesa

Two Years Later

"WHAT THE *HELL* ARE YOU DOING HERE?" MY cousin's shrill voice pierces the air as I stand across from her on a secluded part of the Hudson River.

It's dark tonight, the clouds masking even the glow of the moon, so it took her a long time to notice me. She's lucky it's *just* me. Anyone could have found her, and she's so obtuse to her surroundings, she'd be dead before she could even scream.

"Hi, Aria. Nice to see you too." I grin sarcastically and scan her attire.

An emerald-green evening gown, her scarlet hair in a messy updo that's definitely seen better days, and two red-bottom shoes dangling from her fingers, one of them with a broken heel.

Always the pampered princess, even when she looks like a dumpster fire.

"Out for a midnight run?" I ask.

She pushes a strand of hair off her smooth forehead before leveling me with a glare. "What I'm doing is *none* of your business. How did you even know where to find me? And why are you in New York?"

"You're asking a lot of questions for a girl with broken shoes and a clear death wish." I gesture to our surroundings.

I found her the same way I always find her: the tracking device my uncle installed in not only her phone but also the bracelet she got for her sweet sixteenth.

Truthfully, the tracking tech is probably in everything he's ever given her, which is the whole caboodle. Aria doesn't exactly make her own money, and he's beyond overprotective of his only daughter, even after she up and skipped town years ago. Sometimes I wonder if she realizes that allowing him to bankroll her entire life means the whole "running away" thing doesn't hold any weight, but she seems happy enough, and she's always loved to live in the lap of luxury, so I'm not really surprised.

Aria crosses her arms. "Did Daddy send you again?"

I smirk.

She already knows the answer to that.

"I'm not a fucking kid! I can do things on my own. Make sure you remind him of that when you go back home." She stomps her foot and then winces before bringing it up to look at the sole. There's a thin stream of red, and she groans. "Great."

I quirk a brow, looking pointedly at the broken heel of the shoe she's carrying in her hand and then to the deserted area we're in. "Seriously, what are you doing traversing damp rocks and murky waters in a thousand-dollar gown?"

She doesn't answer right away. Instead, she gives me a curious look, like I should already *know* why she's out here being reckless.

"I was on a date," she finally says. "It didn't go well, and it's…peaceful on the water."

She moves then, stumbling along the rocky shoreline, her dainty fingers reaching for purchase on some of the larger boulders as she slips between them.

"Where the hell are you going, Aria? Don't you wanna know what dear ol' Daddy has to say?" Begrudgingly, I follow her.

She trips and lets out a sharp hiss.

"You're gonna cut up your feet and get them infected." I try again just to get her to slow down.

She looks back at me and stops moving. "You're so dramatic."

"Seems like high praise coming from you," I muse. "Maybe I should take my chances in New York, try out the whole singing thing, and *you* can go home and work for your daddy."

"Be serious."

"You don't think I'd have better luck getting auditions for Broadway?"

She snorts. "Please."

I'm not being serious. I enjoy working for my uncle, even more so now that Aria's been gone for years and I get his full attention. Besides, I'm confident Aria has no clue who her father actually is beyond being the wealthiest businessman in the South.

What *I* do for him is so much more than that. I help prop up that hollow legacy, making sure the truth of his power remains out of sight.

Corruption sings with shiny buildings and fancy suits, and the *truth* is that my uncle is not only a respected businessman but he's also the most powerful gangster in the South.

In any case, I don't blame Aria for leaving South Carolina. New York is something special. Across the Hudson, broken up by the thick cables of a bridge, is the city skyline, and when I see it, something warm expands in the center of my chest.

I love it here, although admitting that out loud would mean also admitting I have something in common with Aria.

She's been obsessed with Manhattan since we were kids. She would find pictures in magazines to cut out and hang on her wall like window dressing, and I guess her obsession rubbed off on me.

It's all farcical, though. Dreams are that for a reason. Just dreams.

Maybe one day she'll learn…or maybe she won't. What do I care?

"Well." She throws her hands out to her sides. "What is it, then? Spit it out, Urch. What's Daddy want now? Did he send you out here to try and help me?"

I snap out of my daze, glowering at Aria for the nickname as I move toward her, trying my best not to slip on the rocks. "What do you mean 'help you'? With *what?*" I look at her funny because what is she even talking about? "He just wants to make sure you're okay."

Aria blinks at me, that same confused look as earlier coasting across her face. "That's it?"

I shrug. "Yeah. You know how he is."

It's not like I want to admit my uncle, who *claims* I'm his most important asset, sent me out here to do an in-person, late-night checkup with his spoiled daughter and, because I'm desperate for his approval, I said yes.

My best friend, Fisher, says being so unwaveringly loyal is my biggest weakness, but I disagree.

"So you're all right? Barring whatever this is?" I wave my hand up and down her disastrous frame.

She shoots me a dark look. "Would you shut *up*? God, you're always so—"

A deep, low groan cuts off her sentence, and I reach out to grip her arm, shushing her, my heart ratcheting up in speed.

That sounded like a person.

And I don't know how Aria ended up here or what kind of trouble she might have gotten herself in to make her look so haggard, but hanging out at a deserted part of a river known for cement shoes attached to dead bodies isn't exactly high on my list of to-dos.

Aria looks around, arching a perfectly manicured brow. "Hear what?"

Another groan has me spinning, my vision skimming over the large damp rocks and the dark pockets of shadows that line the area.

"Seriously, you don't hear that?"

"Who cares?" Aria looks at her nails like she can't be bothered. "Listen, since you're here, tell Daddy I could use some more wiggle room with the monthly allowance."

I ignore her, walking toward the water to find the source of the noise.

Aria stumbles as she comes after me. "Hey! Are you listening to me?"

"With a voice like yours, who can ignore you?" I bite back.

"You're pathetic, you know that? I wish you'd go back to where you came—"

"Quiet," I snap, my eyes homing in on a figure in the distance.

There's a man laid out along the rocks, close enough to the water that it laps at his body like it's attempting to shove him awake. But his eyes stay closed, and every time the small waves hit him, he just moves like a limp rag doll.

Great. Dying men were not on my agenda tonight either.

Heaving a heavy sigh, I drop my head back and stare up at the sky. *Waxing crescent moon.* Fantastic for acting on new beginnings. I should have never claimed I wanted to be a better person. It's not like I meant it anyway. Being *good* is overrated.

Now the universe is *mocking* me.

"Venesa," Aria hisses.

I ignore her and take a step closer, cocking my head. He looks young, but not *too* young, and he's strangely familiar, although with how much dirt and blood covers his face, it's difficult to tell.

"Urch, what the hell are you…? Holy *shit*," Aria breathes as she comes to stand next to me.

"Mm-hmm." I nod, taking inventory.

He's definitely unconscious, at least partly, and there's no doubt in my mind he's injured. Probably some low-level gangbanger who got himself in trouble. Although with the way he's dressed in an expensive—and thoroughly ruined—suit, it could be worse. He could be a made man.

I shouldn't get involved.

"We should leave," Aria whispers, her blue eyes wide.

I shake my head. "We can't just leave him."

"What?!" she hisses. "Are you crazy?"

"I'm trying to be a decent person," I snap.

Aria huffs and mumbles, "Little late for that."

I blink at her.

Well, now she's just pissing me off.

Licking my lips, I stare at her for one more second before moving so I'm right next to the injured stranger.

Aria's footsteps crunch on the wet, muddy pebbles until she's behind me. "Jesus, he looks half-dead. Just leave him for the fish to find or whatever. Let's *go*."

She's right, I know she's right, but still…

Dropping to my knees, I touch his neck and check for

a pulse. It's there, but it's faint. Blood seeps onto the wet ground beneath him, pouring from a wound on his side.

He's definitely hurt. Pretty badly, from the looks of it. Stab wound? Gunshot? It's too difficult to tell in the dark.

The man groans again, his head shaking back and forth in a lazy motion, but his eyes stay closed.

My stomach jumps into my throat because I *really* shouldn't be here.

"Venesa, this isn't funny," Aria snarls, keeping her voice low. "Daddy will kill you if you get involved with this."

I cut her a glare before focusing back on the injured stranger. What does she know about what her father will or won't be mad about?

Although, in this scenario, she's not wrong.

Aria stomps her foot. "I'm leaving."

"Good *lord,* either shut the hell up or actually do what you keep threatening," I bark at her.

I take my black sweater off and jostle the man onto his side so I can slip it underneath him. I try to tie it around him to stem the bleeding, but he's *large* and slippery from the blood and grime, so it doesn't work. Blowing out a haggard breath, I settle for balling up the fabric and pressing it against him instead, applying as much pressure as I can.

If we were back home, I'd have some yarrow I could mix with water to spread on the wound like a paste, but of course, the urge to be a good person only happens when I have absolutely *nothing* on my side to help.

His eyes flutter, and it sends panic whirling through me like a tornado.

Aria's right; Uncle T will murder me if this guy is, in fact, part of the New York mob and I get involved without specific orders from him.

But for some reason, I can't just leave this stranger either.

"Listen," I say to Aria. "Stay here with him, okay?"

"Fuck. That." She crosses her arms, shaking her head.

Sighing, I run a hand through my hair. Aria's always been the most difficult person to walk the earth, but she's also shallow as hell and loves the limelight, so convincing her to do something is all about the angle.

I stare at her for a second, sinking my teeth into my lower lip while I work out what that angle is. "Everyone would probably laud you as a hero."

Her eyes flare, her fingers tapping against her inner elbow.

"Think about it. You know better than anyone how to spin a story in your favor, and I know you're desperate for some media attention like you used to get back home." I gesture down at the man. "So take the opportunity. *Give it a spin.*"

She glances at him again before looking at me, indecision warring in her wide-eyed blue gaze.

"Look." I reach into the right side of my bra and pull out a small vial I keep for emergencies.

Her face contorts. "What is *that*?"

"Ammonia-soaked cotton. It'll wake him up." I jerk my

head toward the guy on the ground, my right arm still draped over his body while my hand keeps pressure on his side.

"God, you're weird. You just…carry that around?"

I lift a shoulder because yeah, I do.

She hesitates but eventually walks over and takes it from me.

"You'll have to keep pressure on his wound until someone gets here to help. Otherwise, he might bleed out."

"Ew, that's disgusting. I'll get his blood all over me." Her nose scrunches. "You know what? No. I've already had a shitty night, so fuck this guy, and fuck you too."

She spins and walks away.

Annoyed, I look between her and the guy on the ground.

For whatever reason, my left hand brushes over his midnight-black hair. "What did they do to you?"

And then, although I'll never be able to explain *why*, I lean down and whisper in his ear, "Don't die. Don't let them win."

His body jerks and his eyes flutter open, bright ocean blues locking on to mine.

Panic spreads through my body, and I jump to my feet, backing away as quickly as I can.

Stupid, Venesa.

If he's some guy who's supposed to be dead and Uncle T finds out I interfered in *New York* business?

I might as well just kill myself.

The man closes his eyes again, passing out, and I'm gone, jogging all the way to the tree line and hiding behind it. I glance down at my blood-soaked hands. My teeth sink into my lower lip as I debate what to do, my thumbnail picking at the cuticle of my ring finger—but then, surprisingly, Aria's there again on the shoreline, so I watch her instead.

"Urch," she whisper-yells, glancing around.

I suck on my teeth to stay quiet.

She tries again. "Venesa!"

The man on the ground groans, and it draws her attention.

Aria moves closer to the stranger, dropping to his side and picking up my abandoned sweater, grimacing as she crouches over him. "You better be front-page worthy, you hear me?"

She releases the fabric for a moment, just long enough to uncork the vial I gave her and put it beneath his nose. She glances around one more time, presumably searching for me.

A large gasp, and the man is awake, his eyes flying open and his gaze tangling with hers.

And that's when Aria stops looking for me completely.

Instead, she runs her hand through his river-soaked hair, her other fingers pressing *my* sweater against his wound, and she starts to hum.

CHAPTER 2

Enzo (Ehn-zo)

One Year Later
Twenty-Nine Years Old

EVERYONE EXPECTS ME TO MARRY.

The "acceptable" next step for a man of my stature and family. Back when I was a kid, I looked forward to it. Dreamed of it, even.

When I was really young, I'd be kept awake at night by Ma giggling like a schoolgirl and Pops murmuring dirty words, muffled through the thin walls of our small two-bedroom apartment in Trillia, Brooklyn.

Usually, the next morning, I'd come out to a big breakfast of sausage and eggs and the smell of coffee, while Pops ignored everything and buried his nose in the day's paper. Back then, Ma always had a certain look. A flush to her cheeks and a sparkle in her blue eyes, identical to mine. Pops would wink and play grab ass when she walked by, and it would make her light up like a kid in a candy store. Warmth would suffuse my chest, providing a stable, dependable comfort.

In every other aspect of life, my pops was a hard-ass. When it came to my mother? He was the quintessential lovebird, and she was too. Watching them made me sure that true love was out there waiting for me, just like theirs.

But as I got older and Pops moved up in the ranks of the syndicate, Ma's giggles morphed into arguments punctuated by his yells and her screams. And then one day, she popped too many of those pills Pops brought home to "keep her calm," and those screams turned into silence.

My belief in love was tainted, like a scent evoking old emotions I'd rather forget.

Love equaled the pain of my mother's death.

So Pops arranging for me to get married to the girl I've been fucking for the past year? It's no big deal for me.

A piece of paper, really.

I glance down at my phone.

Giovanni: Your dad wants you to call him. Something about him being watched again.

Groaning, I debate what to say back. Pops has always had a hard time trusting people, but the past few years after my brother's death, he's been particularly unhinged, paranoid in a type of way where there's no calming him and no way of knowing how he'll react to any situation.

"Babe, are you even listening to me?"

I glance at my fiancée, Aria, who's sitting next to me in the car. I skim my gaze down her frame, past the ends of her brightly dyed red hair, over her small but perky chest, then to those killer legs flowing out of a pastel-pink skirt. Her skin is smooth as butter and pale as hell, despite her being half Italian and baking herself at my penthouse's rooftop pool back home. When I meet her baby-blue eyes, my irritation at her interruption fades.

She snaps her fingers, the thin gold bracelets on her wrist clanking together, and just like that, my soft feelings harden into stone.

I take her hand, moving it from in front of my face, and kiss the back of it. "Of course, princess."

Her pinched features smooth out, and she grins, one of her eyebrows arching. "Then what'd I say?"

My temples throb, and I drop her fingers to grip the inky-black strands of my hair, tugging on the roots to keep the burgeoning headache at bay. "Christ, Aria, what is this, twenty questions?"

She sinks into her seat, crossing her arms and giving me a sweet smile. "No need to be snippy. You know I'm not trying to upset you. I just wanted some attention, is all."

I tense my jaw and glance toward the front, locking eyes with my younger cousin, Scotty, in the rearview mirror. I don't think he really wants to be here, listening to domestic disputes and being my glorified chauffeur for the next couple of weeks, but he's a *cugine*, trying to make his bones while he waits for the books to open, so he came along for the trip.

He averts his gaze quickly, but I see the flash of *something* there, and I bite back the groan. Scotty's always been a fucking gossip, and the last thing I need is it getting back to Pops I'm being an asshole to Aria.

For some reason, he *loves* her. Enough that he demanded I marry her anyway. Not that Aria knows it's at his request. Or that her father approved the arrangement immediately.

Guilt worms its way through me when I remember I wouldn't even *be* here if it weren't for Aria. I owe her my life. Marrying her is the least I can do.

It's not like she's hard to look at.

Decent fuck too.

Aria's already-plushy demeanor softens even more when I angle my body toward her and cup her cheek. My thumb rubs against the smattering of freckles across her nose, and she leans into my palm like a kitten desperate for my touch. She looks beautiful, her skin dewy and the sharp angles of her face highlighted perfectly by the soft pastel-colored LED lighting that lines the interior of the Mercedes Maybach.

"Princess, let's not pretend you're with me for my listening skills," I say.

She scoffs. "Don't be a jerk, babe. I'm with you because I love you."

I don't know why I'm being such an asshole, especially when she's done nothing to deserve it. Maybe I'm hoping that for once, she'll bite back. Give me something to feel while I'm stuck in a stuffy thousand-dollar suit, pretending to be an upstanding citizen about to meet my bride's father.

It's been a long time since I've felt any type of *fire*.

I sit back and adjust my cuff links. "Come on, Aria. You knew who I was when you agreed to marry me."

She huffs, turning her face toward the tinted window, but she doesn't deny the statement. I know she thinks she's in love, but for me, this marriage is nothing more than a business deal. One that gives her what she wants and appeases my father.

I owe them both.

"Ah, come on, don't give me that." I point to the pout on her face. "What do you want me to do?"

"An apology would be a start." She lifts her chin and sniffs.

I chuckle. We both know she isn't getting one of those. "How about that new ring you've been drooling over for the past month instead?"

She peers at me from the corner of her eye. "The pink diamond?"

My phone vibrates in my lap, but I don't pick it up. Instead, I keep my gaze on Aria.

"How much was it again?" I ask.

She uncrosses her arms. "Does it matter?"

Yes. Money always matters, but I know the way to Aria's heart isn't through sweet words and apologies. "For you, princess? No."

And that's all it takes.

A bright smile crosses her face, and she turns toward me. It's the same solution every time: I offer a new trinket for her to add to her collection of gizmos and gadgets, and she melts.

"I'm just nervous about how everything will go," she says. "Daddy is... He and I haven't... Well, I just want you two to like each other."

In moments like this, it's painfully obvious she doesn't know me, even after a year together.

Originally, I hadn't intended for it to be anything more than a few satisfying nights of her tight little pussy clamping around my cock. A nice way to thank her for saving me out on the Hudson when I was left for dead by...well, I don't really know who.

I remember nothing from that night except waking up.

Turns out, Aria Kingston is a media darling, and when it hit the news that she'd saved my life, we became the "it" couple in New York. After my dad found out who her father was, it was game over.

Tying our family to the Kingstons in the South? That means more power and influence for him, and these days, it seems like that's all he cares about.

If he weren't so goddamn terrifying, the other families in the Cosa Nostra would be more vocal about how he's muddling this thing of ours.

Ruining it, if the whispers are to be believed.

However, nobody has the courage to stand up against him, especially after he sat behind his own consigliere in the back of a car and popped him in the head because he had a "feeling" he was about to be betrayed.

Never replaced him either. Instead, the duty of who he trusts falls solely on *my* shoulders, and every day, that trust thins simply because of his own paranoia.

Especially after the failed attempt on my life.

All trying to kill me did was prod at the beast, and despite his shift in mental faculties, I'm nothing if not loyal, so what Carlos Marino says goes. Besides, it's never been my job to speak reason back into my pops. That was always Peppino's thing, and after my brother's murder, I'm still not sure how to step into the role.

Forcing a smile, I grip Aria's thigh.

She covers my hand, her eyes fixed on our fingers, probably envisioning the exorbitantly expensive piece of jewelry she is about to gain for her collection.

A few seconds of blessed silence go by before Aria lets go of my hand to open the compact refrigerator hidden behind the rear seats, and pulls out a chilled bottle of champagne, then pours some of the bubbly into one of the crystal flutes before handing it to me.

"Liquid courage?" I bring the glass to my lips and take a sip, hiding the grimace that wants to cross my face. I don't actually *like* the taste of overpriced garbage, but after the past few years of sipping on champagne to appease the pompous fucks I do legitimate business with, it's become a tolerable taste.

"Something like that." She glances out of the window

and swirls her glass. "This trip will be good for you…for *us*. Atlantic Cove is slower in pace. We can relax, enjoy the engagement party, and you can get to know the area."

I take another sip. "We're not moving here."

"What? God no. I've been desperate to escape this place since the second I was old enough to walk."

"Yet you insist on going back," I reply.

"Daddy wants to throw us an engagement party, and I'm trying to mend some fences," she corrects, shrugging.

"Ah."

I couldn't give a fuck where we have the engagement party her family wants because everything worth a shit will happen back in New York. I drain the glass of champagne and reply to the text from my right-hand man, Giovanni.

Me: Tell him to pick up his phone and learn to use it like everyone else. Any news on the spot in Brooklyn?

We've known each other since we were kids, and after Peppino got himself clipped and I took over his businesses, becoming part of the Mafia's administration as the family's new underboss, I promoted Giovanni from *soldato* to *caporegime*. Now it's Gio who runs my crew while I'm stuck hiding behind bulletproof glass in fancy buildings, talking about real estate like a pussy.

Regardless, in this life, it's important to surround yourself with people you can trust, and he's the only one I do.

Honestly, I think real estate is boring as fuck.

I've always been more of the rough-and-tumble type. Having to legitimize myself to keep the Feds off our case doesn't interest me, but I learned early on that it's part of the gig. You have to at least *look* like your money is coming from aboveboard sources. And these days, a lot of it is. But not all of it.

And the way we get most of our contracts is questionable at best.

I brush my thumb over the knuckles of my opposite hand, remembering what it used to feel like when I could use them as an outlet, reveling in the fresh cuts and bruises that would sting long after I got whatever point I needed to get across.

Gio: About to handle that situation right now, actually. How's South Carolina?

I glance out of the window. Right now, we're driving through what looks like the heart of Atlantic Cove, passing by a large white Ferris wheel and some small shops lining the boardwalk and the ocean just beyond. They're surrounded by planted palm trees, hotels, and residential buildings; tall, glassy skyscrapers disappear into the low-hanging clouds that cover the sky. It's an odd mix of old and new here, a war between conserving history and gentrification. I wonder which part Trent Kingston handles: the tearing down of buildings or the preservation.

There's a long wooden bridge that disappears out into the water, with a wrought-iron arch that says "Atlantic Cove Boardwalk" in faded steel writing, a vibrant pink seashell at the very top. As we continue to drive, it's impossible to miss the kids running around the sandy beach with gigantic smiles on their snot-covered young faces.

My chest smarts, and I reach up to rub at the dull ache, then text Giovanni back.

Me: Kitschy.

Gio: What the fuck does kitschy mean?

Me: What am I, a dictionary? Look it up.

Gio: Stronzo

I smirk at him calling me an asshole.

Aria's foot bounces, and even though I can only see the rhythmic motion from my periphery, it's enough to irritate the fuck out of me.

"It'll be fine." I smile widely, trying to soothe her anxiety. "Parents love me."

Her posture relaxes, and she grins back. "*I* love you, and that's all that matters."

I don't respond.

We drive past the beach until the tourism thins, the crowds dying out until they don't exist. Skyscrapers change to small single-story houses with mobile homes sprinkled in, and not long after, I stop being able to see much at all. Eventually, we make it to a large gated entrance with a sweeping driveway.

Aria rolls down her window, showing her face to the camera, and then the fence is opening. Perfectly manicured trees line both sides of the windy pathway until we reach the circle drive in front of an old-school estate, which has big shutters on the windows and large white pillars that frame a wraparound porch. There's a stone fountain with a mermaid sculpture right in the center, her mouth and hands pouring water continuously into the pond below.

"This is where you grew up?" I ask Aria.

I'm not sure why I'm surprised. She was born into luxury, which is honestly just another glaring difference between us. My family built our fortune and power from the ground up, but it wasn't until I was in my twenties and Pops became *capo di tutti capi* that we really lived like kings. Before that, I was just a kid of a *soldato*, running loose around the streets of Brooklyn, causing trouble and using my pops's name to get out of it.

Aria hums, nodding.

I step from the car and take a second to stare at the mermaid fountain before walking around to meet Aria as Scotty helps her out.

"Bring our bags in," I tell him.

He nods, his thin fingers tapping against the side of his thigh as he glances around. "You got it, boss. You want me to just wait around after, or…?"

"Go grab a bite or whatever. Check into the bed-and-breakfast spot I hooked you up at." I wave him off. "Just keep your phone close."

"You ready, babe?" Aria asks, her eyes sparkling up at me as she grabs my hand.

I nod and escape the death grip she has on my fingers, placing my palm at the small of her back as we walk between the white pillars lining the wide concrete steps and up to the wrought-iron double doors.

My phone rings, and I pull it from my pocket, Giovanni's name flashing across the screen.

"E..." Aria starts.

"Don't. I'll be right behind you."

She stands still for a second, defiance flashing through her gaze, before she gives in and walks into the house without me. My jaw clenches as I watch her go, and then I'm swiping the screen of my phone and heading back down the stairs.

"Kitschy," Gio states before I even say hello. "'Considered to be in poor taste because of excessive garishness or sentimentality, but sometimes appreciated in an ironic or knowing way...' whatever the fuck that means."

"And your dad said you'd never amount to anything."

"Yeah, well, what's he know?" Gio replies.

"You'd better be calling to tell me good news."

"Do I ever call with *bad* news?"

He has a point. In our line of business, we can't handle bad news over the phone, especially in this day and age where everything is susceptible to tapping.

"They accepted our offer on that Brooklyn Heights spot," Gio continues.

"Excellent."

"And your pops is hounding me for you to call him."

"Yeah, yeah. I'll call him." I sigh, running a hand through my hair again. "As soon as I settle in here."

"Good. You know, it makes me nervous when he uses me to teach you a lesson."

"He's not *teaching* me a lesson, you fucking goon. He's just checking in."

"Oh!" Gio lets out a laugh. "I'm just saying, I don't like being the go-between. Your pops ain't all there these days, you know?"

"Careful," I warn.

"How's it going out there anyway?"

"Define 'it.'" I look up at the gaudy estate and cringe.

Small pebbles crunch beneath my shoes as I hit a gravel pathway that leads into the back. I squint, looking into the distance. There's a giant infinity pool that drops off with nothing but ocean beyond it, but to the left of that, there's what looks like a two-story mother-in-law suite bigger than any house in the neighborhood I grew up in.

"That *thing* you're marrying, for starters." There's a teasing lilt to his voice, but I hear the truth between the words. Giovanni's never been a fan of Aria, claims she's untrustworthy and shallow. Which, to be fair, she probably is. But she's a good person deep down. Bad people don't save strangers from bleeding out on riverbanks.

Besides, what do I care if she's shallow? I'm not marrying her for deep conversations; I just need her to keep her mouth shut and her legs open, let me put a couple of kids in her belly, and look good on my arm in public.

"Calm down," I retort.

"She's a vain bitch with a pretty voice and killer legs. What's there to calm down about?"

I grin. "You say that like it's a bad thing."

A snapping sound makes my heart jump. I glance up and twist around, looking back at the mansion. There's nothing there, but when I face forward again, there's a figure in the distance.

It's a woman, leaning against the brick of the mother-in-law suite, and she's staring directly at me. I lift a brow as I meet her gaze, and she straightens, running her nails down the front of her lengthy, *tight* black dress.

She's… I don't even know how to explain it. Her long hair is bright, so light blond that it's a silvery white, the ends of which kiss the top of her ample cleavage perfectly, and when she moves toward me, her saunter makes everything touching her skin seem like silk cascading down her fine-as-fuck body.

Jesus Christ.

Giovanni's mumbling something in my ear, but I'm definitely not listening.

The woman stops a few paces in front of me, and her bloodred lips spread into a slow smile, accentuating the dimples that crease the apples of her cheeks.

"Is there a point to your call, Gio?" I interrupt Giovanni's rambling.

"Listen, you rude motherfucker—"

"Reception's bad here," I reply, still keeping my gaze locked on the mystery woman. Her eyes spark like two swirling black whirlpools, sucking me down until I can't break for air.

She swipes her tongue along her bottom lip, and my stare drops to her mouth.

I hang up before Gio can say anything else.

And then we're both just standing there, silent, watching each other, and it's the strangest thing, but I swear every time one of us breathes, the air grows taut like a rubber band, pulling and stretching until it's about to snap.

"No need to rush off the phone for little ol' me," she finally says.

The way she enunciates every syllable in a slow, controlled way makes her voice trickle over me like a heat wave. Her Southern accent is strong, and I don't know why it surprises me, other than the fact Aria doesn't have one at all.

I slip my phone into my pocket. "Well, you seem like a woman who demands my full attention."

She grins.

My stomach lurches forward violently.

"Enzo Marino," she states.

Usually, I hate hearing my full first name. It reminds me of being a kid with my ma yelling that as long as I was under her roof, I'd have to follow her rules.

But the way *this* woman says it feels like honey dripping onto my skin.

"I think I'm at a disadvantage," I remark.

She takes a step closer, peering up at me from beneath long black lashes. "I can't imagine a man like you *ever* being at a disadvantage."

I'm not sure if she's stroking my ego or insulting my stature, so I tell her as much.

She shrugs. "Up for interpretation, I guess."

The corner of my lip twitches, and I take inventory of her again, soaking in the soft angles of her body and how even the breeze seems to cling to her plentiful curves.

"You're interesting," I voice.

"That's what they tell me," she replies.

"They?"

"That's right."

I slip my hands in my pockets and rock back on my heels. "Do you keep your name from them too, or am I special?"

She laughs, and it tugs me in like a scarf around my neck. "You're a man, honey. I'm afraid there's nothing special about any of you."

Grinning, I step closer, and the space between us hums like a string being plucked until it vibrates a deep, dark note. "Sounds like you haven't met the right man."

She smiles back, and her eyes dance with mirth. "Sounds like something the wrong man would say."

My grin grows wider, even as a pinch of guilt tries to weave its way into the moment. It's not like me to be so forward with a woman when I'm in a relationship with another, but there's something here…something about her that makes it impossible to resist. "Tell me your name, piccola sirena."

Her pupils flare, but the sound of tires crunching on loose gravel interrupts our moment, and her gaze slides past my shoulder, locking on something in the distance. The tension breaks, and I feel like I've been sucker punched in the chest by this woman who's robbed my breath and bruised my lungs.

"See you later, Lover Boy."

She walks past me.

I turn to watch her go, surprised she knows my nickname and irritated by the way it makes my mind fire with interest.

"Tell me your name," I call to her back.

She spins slightly and gives me a bright white smile, her eyes flashing with amusement.

And then she disappears around the corner and out of my sight.

CHAPTER 3

Venesa

THERE'S A CHIP IN MY NAIL POLISH. EVERYWHERE else, the red is smooth and perfect, but not there, not on my pinky. It's right by the cuticle too, the *worst* place for an imperfection. My mind races, as it's prone to doing, while I try to figure out when it happened. Was it before or after I combined that methyl bromide? Maybe it was post-preparation but pre-use. Or maybe it was when I hit my hand on the bus's seat while heading out here to my uncle's forty-acre estate.

Most likely, though, it was after running into Enzo Marino, just walking around the property like he owns it.

Picking at my cuticles when I'm nervous is a nasty habit I've never *quite* been able to break, and as much as I hate to admit it, Enzo being here makes me nervous.

For several reasons, although I'd never speak them out loud.

"You were supposed to make it look like an accident." Uncle T's rumbling voice floats through the air and snaps me back into reality.

Dropping my hand to my lap, I cross my legs and settle further into the bucket chair facing his desk. His sky-blue eyes are piercing as we lock gazes, and it's easy to see he's upset about the way I handled my latest project. He's always had a terrible poker face; that broad nose of his flares and those frown lines crease deeper whenever he's up in arms.

"Oops?" I shrug, flashing a wide smile.

Uncle T's fist drops against the cherrywood, rattling the small odds and ends scattered across the top of his desk: a crystal tumbler filled with Kentucky bourbon, a custom engraved case that holds his finest Cuban cigars. A framed picture of his late wife, Antonella, and their picture-perfect daughter.

"Damn it, Venesa, this isn't a game. When I say to make it seem like an overdose, you *make it seem like an overdose.*"

A jab of shame hits me, right in that space inside where I ache for his approval. "I know that, I just..." My words trail off because what's the point of wasting breath trying to explain something that shouldn't need an explanation? I did what he asked me to do, and that *should* be the end of it.

Clearly, he doesn't agree, and unfortunately for me, I *do* still give a damn about his approval. It's all I give a damn about, if I'm being honest with myself.

Still, I'm a Leo rising and sun sign, so the need to get my point across burns bright enough in the moment where I can't hold my tongue.

"This way was better," I argue. "He'll have permanent brain damage now, *severe* lifelong issues."

"If he survives."

I hesitate and then nod. "Correct."

His blunt fingernails tap, tap, tap against his desk as he watches me. "Did it ever occur to you maybe I didn't *want* him to survive?" He shakes his head, his thick salt-and-pepper brows drawing together. "Now I have to sit here and worry about whether that idiot district attorney will be all over my ass."

I snort. "Please, the district attorney couldn't give a rat's ass about the Atlantis Motorcycle Club *or* their extended family."

Truthfully, the law around these parts is upheld by a bunch of do-gooders, ones who wear their golden halos like badges of honor, but most of them have a price—one that I suss out easily enough when I barter deals to keep them quiet and looking in the other direction.

Shoving a needle in the arm of the brother-in-law to the newest MC president was a message: either continue working with us or people get hurt. Besides, if *we* don't keep them in line, then it's up to the law to do so, and its enforcers do a shit job.

The DA should thank us, honestly.

But a drug overdose? Talk about *uninspired*.

"I should have given the job to someone else," he murmurs.

I scoff. "Who?"

He lifts his hand in the air before dropping it back down. "Bas, probably."

It's a ridiculous suggestion to make. Bastien may be Uncle T's second-in-command in name, but his art lies in the brutality of torture, which is the opposite of subtle. I love Bastien like a brother, but he wouldn't have been the right choice for a job like this.

"Anyone else would have made more of a mess, and you know it."

"Anyone else would have *followed orders*, or they'd be dead," he snaps.

I open and close my mouth a few times because, technically, he's right. You don't disobey Trent Kingston and live to tell the tale. Being his niece has its advantages, but even the people who love you have their limits, and sometimes I wonder if one day I'll break through his unintentionally.

The thought makes my stomach cramp. I live life constantly worried about falling too far out of his favor because I push against him too hard, thus losing what little bits of him I've snagged.

"You always do this," he continues, running his fingers through his coiffed white hair.

"Do what?"

"You…" He waves his hand in the air. "Play with your food."

I cross my arms. "I do not *play* with my food, and frankly, I resent that analogy."

He quirks a brow.

My perfectly arched one cocks in return.

"You were sloppy," he states.

"I beg your pardon?" I've never been more offended in my life. "I'm impeccably precise. It's not like I left a trail. The man had a stroke. If he survives—"

My uncle scoffs.

"*If* he survives," I reiterate, "Johnston Miller will have to live every day staring at his wife's brother, knowing he caused this to happen, and a living reminder is always better than one buried somewhere in the dirt."

"That's not your call to make."

"What's it matter anyway?" The second the words leave my mouth, I regret them. I know my temper only pisses him off more, but in the moment, I'm not the best at biting my tongue.

"It matters because I say it matters." He picks up his bourbon, and his forefinger, weighed down by a thick golden ring, leaves the tumbler to point at me from around the glass. "One of these days, your luck will run out, little one, and you'll bring down this entire family with you."

My lips purse.

He's being dramatic, considering our family is the most powerful name this side of the Mason–Dixon line. Uncle T not only owns the largest construction company in the South but he's a major player in freight shipping, with hubs stretching throughout South Carolina and the bordering states.

The King of the Sea.

But there's an underworld, the same way there is everywhere else, and it's the true foundation that props up the Kingston legacy.

He always does this, though: gives me a task and then acts unhappy about how I handle it. He also frequently calls me "little one."

Little.

Even though I'm twenty-four and have been taking care of *his* messes just as long as he's taken care of mine.

I lean forward, grabbing one of his cigars and the stainless steel Zippo he keeps beside it. Puffing on the roll, I move the flame over the opposite end until thick smoke surrounds me, the taste of tobacco, earthy notes, and a hint of espresso dancing on my tongue. "What's a woman gotta do to get a little respect around here, Uncle T?"

"You want respect, Venesa? Then stop disappointing me."

My teeth bite into the cigar, and I puff one last time before dragging his ashtray to the corner of the desk and placing it down. "I'm sorry. I'll do better."

Empty words to appease him. Or maybe to appease the biggest part of myself that's desperate for his love.

There's a smaller piece, though, one that whispers in the back of my mind, saying he wanted a message sent, and the message *was* sent. Signed. Sealed. Delivered. It's not my fault if he can't see the vision.

Men. Their pride is always their downfall.

Uncle T blows out a breath, his eyes never leaving mine. I know better after all these years than to keep filling the silence with chatter, so instead I sink back and allow the quiet to surround us.

Classical music plays in the background, the soothing notes grating against my nerves.

When I was young, a few months after my momma died and I was sent here, I approached Uncle T and asked him why he always played that kind of music. He said it made him feel sophisticated, and although he didn't particularly enjoy the sound, "you have to *be* how you'd like to be perceived."

And Trent Kingston has always wanted to be seen as a cultured, elegant man. Says it's part of the family legacy.

I used to sneak into his office and curl up in his leather chair, the one that just sits there like a throne behind his big cherry oak desk, and I'd listen to Chopin or Pachelbel, imagining I wasn't alone in a fifteen-thousand-square-foot house with nobody but housekeepers and a nanny, while my uncle went on family trips with his wife and daughter.

The music was always comforting, like a soft blanket on a cool night.

Now I hate the noise.

Just another reminder of everything I *almost* have but don't.

"I can hear you thinking." Uncle T sighs.

My vision refocuses, and I look past him to where a large painting hangs, an ache blooming in my chest.

The painting has been passed down through the generations of Kingstons, from father to son, repeatedly, like a rite of passage.

It's not even an actual picture *of* the family. It's just seven empty marble chairs at the bottom of the ocean and a glowing trident floating in the middle. A representation of the seven kingdoms of Atlantis, which Kingston lore says we're descendants of.

But I don't care about any of that.

I just want it because it was my momma's favorite thing in the entire world, so much so that her daddy gave it to her instead of upholding tradition of passing it down to the son.

It's supposed to be mine now.

"You're just like your momma," Uncle T says.

My heart hurts the same way it does every time he brings her up.

How would you know? I want to ask. "So you always say," I murmur instead.

He gives me a pointed look but doesn't press the subject, taking another sip of his bourbon before setting it down. He grabs his own cigar, lighting it up and puffing until thick plumes of smoke curl into the air, clouding around him like a fog. "Your cousin's home, you know."

My stomach twists at the mention of Aria. "I guessed as much when I ran into her fiancé outside."

His jaw tenses as he rolls the tobacco between his fingers. “Don’t sound so disappointed.”

My mouth pops open. “I’m not.”

I am.

“I just…I’m surprised. It’s been what, six years?”

Uncle T nods. “People always come home to their roots. In the end, family’s the only thing that matters.”

Aria is the same age as me and a bona fide daddy’s girl. She’s the princess of the Kingston family and, as a result, the princess of Atlantic Cove.

I think everyone in town expected Uncle T to go to Manhattan himself and drag her back when she ran off, but he never did. Instead, he’d send me to “check up on her.”

Now there’s no need. Not with her engaged to a man like Enzo Marino.

“So why’s she back?” I ask nonchalantly, clicking my nails on the arm of the chair.

“I’m throwing them an engagement party.” He grins widely.

A short huff of breath escapes me. “You can’t be serious.”

“And why wouldn’t I be?”

“I don’t know…”

I *do* know.

Enzo’s reputation precedes him, even all the way down here in South Carolina. He’s the son of Carlos Marino, the man who is rumored to have singlehandedly usurped the Italian American Commission of the Mafia and brought back the *capo di tutti capi*, taking on the role of "boss of all bosses" for himself.

The thought of mixing our families makes my gut sour, and knowing Uncle T agreed to this marriage arrangement with Carlos puts me on edge.

Plus, Aria doesn't even realize it *is* an arranged marriage.

"Do you really think this is a good idea?" I prod.

"I don't keep you around to question me," he states plainly.

"I'm only looking out for us," I continue. "You know how messy this could get if things don't work out? Enzo's a powerful man, sure, but do you really want him with your *daughter*? When have our interests ever aligned with the Marinos'?"

Uncle T's head tilts. "And what would *you* know about our interests?"

I think I know a damn well decent amount considering everything he's had me do, but I swallow the words I really want to say and shake my head instead. "Never mind. I just thought because of our past—"

"Enough," he interrupts.

I can tell I'm irritating him because the corner of his mouth twitches in time with the clenching of his jaw. "This is *good* for the family, for our business. You understand?"

Apparently, I've got a death wish today because I can't help the next words from tumbling out. "I just think it's risky. Having a Marino around when we have so many secrets is—"

"Do I not provide for you?" he snips.

Guilt churns in my abdomen. "You do," I say carefully.

"When your momma died, may she rest in peace, did I not give you the world? Do I not continue to give you what you ask for, despite it not being the best option for *me*? Bringing you into the fold no matter how much trouble you cause. Buying you shitty Southside bars and letting you run them into the ground."

Ouch. That one stings. He's referencing the restaurant I manage: the Lair. It's dark and seedy and means absolutely everything to me.

I love my Lair, and I guess I love my uncle too.

But I hate it when he brings up my mother.

"All I ask is that you show your loyalty in return and keep your mouth shut unless I tell you to speak," he continues, his voice sharpening like a blade. "Everything will be fine, and we'll…"

"We'll what?"

"Become one big happy family."

I huff out a short laugh, but I'm not feeling joyful. If anything, I'm so annoyed that I can taste it on the back of my tongue like sour candy.

"Come on, little one, don't make me feel bad," he says. "You're my best asset, you know that."

I nod, the tendrils of my heart reaching out to grasp at his words like they're raindrops in the desert.

"You just need to learn to sit back and trust my decisions. I'm the king of this castle, not you. Now go on," he finishes.

"Check on the chef for me. Make sure dinner's almost ready. We have a lot to celebrate."

He shoos me away, and I oblige him, the same way I always do, standing up and making my way to the door. Right as my fingers grip the handle, his words stop me. "And, Venesa, I'll expect you to be on your best behavior."

CHAPTER 4

Enzo

WHEN I FINALLY MAKE IT INSIDE THE KINGSTON estate after calling Gio back, Aria's waiting in the foyer for me.

My footsteps echo off the tall, coffered ceilings, and the sparkles from Aria's five-karat oval ring ricochet off the marble floors.

There is *nothing* about this place that doesn't drip with wealth.

"Ready?" she asks.

I nod.

She beams at me and turns to walk down the hall, our fingers intertwining as she drags me behind her, passing by what looks like a chef's kitchen, until we reach an oversize chestnut door nestled in the back of a hallway.

"Daddy's office," she whispers before knocking twice. I take my hand from hers before we walk in.

Trent Kingston is across the room, surrounded by dark wooden bookshelves and a large desk, his attention focused solely on us.

"Daddy!" Aria squeals, racing over to him.

Trent stands, grabbing her up in a hug. It's been a while since they've seen each other, and I'm not sure they ended on good terms, so I hang back, allowing them their moment and taking in Trent's office.

It's nice. Classic. All oak wood and deep burgundy leather.

There's an interesting painting hanging on the back wall that doesn't quite mesh with anything else, though.

"Ah, Mr. Marino," Trent says, releasing Aria and nodding toward me.

I appreciate the respect he's giving me, and I walk forward and shake his outstretched palm. "Call me E."

"I thought you'd keep my girl away forever. I appreciate you finally bringing her back."

"Daddy," Aria complains.

I grin but don't reply.

"I hope the trip down was all right?" Trent continues.

"E has a private jet," Aria says. "You should get one, Daddy. It's as smooth a flight as you can get."

"Oh, I don't know," someone chimes in.

The hairs on my neck stand on end because *I know that voice*. My mystery woman from a few minutes earlier glides into the room, her footsteps slow and unrushed as she comes to stand next to Aria. She locks eyes with me for a brief second before glancing at my fiancée. "You can *always* crash and burn."

"Venesa," Aria greets, her tone flat. "How...unsurprising you're still here mooching off my family."

Venesa.

Satisfaction pours through me from learning her name.

"Well...someone had to stay behind and take over the job once you ran away," Venesa replies.

Aria scoffs. "Revisionist history at its finest."

"You really want to speak on revisionist history?" Venesa hits back.

Aria's lips thin. "I don't know *why* I'm surprised when all you've ever done is—"

"Girls, that's enough," Trent demands, narrowing his gaze on Venesa. "We have company."

She looks at me and allows her stare to linger, dragging it from my eyes down to my feet and back again. I feel every single inch of her perusal.

"Oh, I apologize," she says. "I hadn't even noticed you were there."

We both know that's a lie. "Don't worry about it."

She moves toward me, reaching out her hand. I grasp it in mine, pinpricks of heat lancing beneath my skin as I bring it to my mouth and brush my lips across the back. It's the same thing I've done with a thousand other women, but it sure as fuck feels different.

"What a gentleman," she murmurs.

"It's a pleasure, *Venesa.*" My thumb ghosts across the top of her knuckles.

"Is it?" She slips her fingers from mine.

I wrap an arm around Aria's waist, simply to offset the inappropriate interaction I just had with this other woman.

"It appears you have me at a disadvantage, Mister..." Venesa says.

"Marino." I play along.

"Marino," she repeats. "Italian, then?"

"Very."

"An important one?" Her lips curve up.

"Depends on who you ask."

"Hmm." She cocks her head, trailing her gaze slowly up and down my frame for a second time. "Can't say I've heard of you."

"Guess that makes two of us."

"*Venesa.*" Trent's voice is a thunderbolt, and it straightens her up immediately, her spine stiffening and grin dropping, an impenetrable mask falling over her face.

"I apologize for my niece's behavior," Trent says. "She's been with us for years, but her mother wasn't known for civility, and I'm sure you can imagine how *difficult* things like that are to train into a young woman once she's been taught another way."

That was kind of an asshole thing to say.

Aria leans into me and asks her father, "I'm starving. Is dinner ready yet?"

"Actually, I'd like to talk to E before we eat. You go on ahead. We'll meet you in there."

Aria nods like an obedient little mouse and pops up to kiss me before she prances out of the room.

For someone who claims to not enjoy it here, she sure seems spritely to be back.

I turn around, moving to sit in the chair. I'm not surprised Trent wants to chat. It's his power move to let me know we're on *his* turf, in *his* house, and it's *his* daughter. It's the same thing I would do in his position.

Unfortunately for him, I don't give a fuck.

My turf is wherever I decide it is.

The door clicks when it closes, and Trent plants himself down behind his desk.

I'm surprised when Venesa follows him and perches on the corner. She crosses one long leg over the other, the slit in her dress making the fabric fall to the side, putting every inch of that delicious thick thigh on display.

Blood rushes to my groin, and I shift in my seat, tearing my eyes away and willing myself to not get a hard-on. This is beyond inappropriate, and although cheating is a normal thing in the Mafia way of life, it's never something that's interested me.

I saw the way it tore my mother up from the inside out, and no one will ever convince me it wasn't the final nail in her coffin.

"I'm glad you finally made it down, E. Would have been nice to have received an earlier visit or at least a phone call before you popped the question, but I guess we can't have everything." Trent smiles around the cigar he just placed in his mouth.

I smirk. We both know he was in the marriage negotiations with my father. "I'm not really in the business of asking permission. You understand."

Trent's eyes narrow, his broad forehead creasing. "I knew your brother, you know."

His words are a punch to my gut, but I don't let the hurt show on my face. Giuseppe—or Peppino, as we called him—has been gone for a little over three years, but sometimes it still feels like yesterday.

That's the thing about grief, I guess. It steals the air from your lungs just as you've finally figured out how to breathe.

"Oh?" I cross my leg over my knee.

Venesa sighs, and I flick my eyes to her briefly, trying to ignore the buzzing between us. We're not even that close, and yet the energy zaps so strongly, it feels like her skin is rubbing against mine.

"He was planning on opening up a hotel down here, did you know that?" Trent continues.

"There are a lot of things Giuseppe did that I wasn't aware of." I keep my tone relaxed, even though I'm internally wondering how the fuck I *didn't* know that.

Growing up, I always let my brother and Pops do their own thing. I was never interested in the ins and outs of Peppino's business or the way he ran it. It was only after he passed away and I took his place that I realized maybe I never really knew him at all.

Almost immediately, I discovered his shady business deals—even by our standards—and illegitimate children with multiple women. None of them claimed publicly, of course, so none who are taken care of or get to see a cent of the fortune he left behind.

Peppino wasn't a good man, and I always knew that. I guess I just never paid attention to *how* shitty he was until after he was gone. There's a difference between a man who does bad things and a bad man. Not that it really matters. He may have been a shit human being, and we may not have been close, but he was still my brother.

Trent runs a bulky hand over his white beard. "I'd like you to consider doing the same now that you've taken over his company. Opening a hotel down here, I mean."

I nod toward his cigar case. "You don't mind?"

He waves his hand. "Please."

"Here, let me." Venesa reaches out before I can, grabbing a cigar and bringing it to her mouth, then flicking open the top of the Zippo and circling it over the end until it lights up cherry red.

I'm transfixed on the sight of her lips forming perfectly around the cigar, and visions of them leaving a red ring around my cock the same way make my dick twitch to life. I'm like a goddamn teenager around this chick, and a brief thought of her possibly doing it on purpose courses through my mind.

I wouldn't put it beyond Trent to be testing me.

She pulls the cigar from her mouth, blowing out a plume

of smoke before leaning forward and passing it to me with a wink. Our fingers brush as I take it, and the exhilarating feeling of being served by her rushes through me.

Trent clears his throat, and Venesa perches back on his desk.

I let the air stay pregnant with silence, a sharp jab of arousal hitting me when my mouth covers the same place Venesa's lips just touched. I shake off the feeling, trying to get my mind straight.

"I'll think about it," I finally say.

Trent frowns.

"You'd be silly not to do it," Venesa cuts in.

I flick my gaze toward her, amusement sparking in my chest. "And you're someone I should take business advice from because…?"

"We're about to be *family*. I hear that means a lot to you Italians."

My interest wanes, and I point my finger at her. "Don't get cute."

"Think about it, E," Trent interjects. "I know you've only been running your brother's business for the past few years, but it's a good choice to expand down here. We've got a hold on the unions, and I've got the construction company built right in. It can be a…mutually beneficial experience."

I purse my lips and stare at him because is he really lecturing *me* on racketeering? I'm from New York. I *am* racketeering. "Is that right?"

Trent smacks his palms together like he's dusting them

off. "One hand washes the other, you know? Together…we can rule the world."

Blowing out a ring of smoke, I lean forward, resting my elbows on my knees. "You seem to know a lot about my business, so let me make something clear: I'm not my brother, and I don't care what deals you may have been working on with him or how good your relationship was. *He* is not *me*." I jab my chest with my thumb.

Trent smiles like I'm throwing a tantrum instead of laying down a law, and honestly, it's a little condescending. My fingers twitch to curl into fists, but I shake off the urge.

"Sleep on it," he says. "After all, the important thing is that you're marrying my baby girl, yeah? And as long as she's happy, I'm happy." He cuts me a look. "And so is your father."

I take another puff of the cigar, hearing his words for exactly what they are: a thinly veiled threat. It's laughable, really, that he thinks he has the power to go against me in any capacity. His corn bread Cosa Nostra is *nothing* compared to the real thing. He should feel fucking honored he's even breathing the same air as me. And if he thinks Pops is someone firmly on his side, then…well, he hasn't experienced the many facets of my overly suspicious and trigger-happy father.

One thing is for sure after this, though, and that simple truth is this: I do not like Trent Kingston.

"All right," I agree. I point at Venesa, the smoke from my cigar swirling around her silhouette like even *it* can't resist her. "But *you'll* have to convince me."

"Pardon?" She tilts her head, blinking quickly.

"You were so confident a few seconds ago when you were telling me what to do. It's only fair you're the one who shows me why Atlantic Cove is worth my time. Business-wise, I mean."

Fire flashes behind Venesa's eyes, and her jaw stiffens. "Uh, no thanks. Ask your fiancée."

I grin like a Cheshire cat, standing up and placing the cigar on the ashtray. "There you go again, spitting orders like I'm your bitch."

A slight flush dusts her cheeks, and it makes my smile widen.

She crosses her arms. "Yeah, well, I'm not a tour guide."

I brush a piece of lint from my sleeve and move toward her until we're closer than what's socially acceptable. In my peripheral vision, I can see Trent frowning at us from his chair, but I don't give a damn. My words aren't meant for him. They're meant for Venesa alone. "You better brush up on your history, piccola sirena, because those are my terms."

Her eyes flare, and adrenaline pumps through my veins like a drug.

"Your terms suck. But I'll do it if it means you'll stop swinging your dick around, acting like you're the biggest man in the room." She slips off the corner of the desk, her gaze dropping to my belt before rising again. "Compensating for something?"

A laugh escapes me, and I step back to take her in fully.

Goddamn, she's interesting.

I don't know a single person in the world who would dare speak to me the way she just did. It's both refreshing and off-putting in equal measure. I definitely don't think I can trust her.

Venesa walks past me and leaves the room, and I follow, heading back to the woman I'm about to marry. But my thoughts are filled with *her*, and the realization that I can't get her out of my mind makes me sick to my stomach.

CHAPTER 5

Venesa

I HATE THIS SCHOOL. I MISS THE SMELL OF THE *hallways at Southside Elementary, as weird as that is.*

Like sneakers and microwaved lasagna.

Atlantic Cove Prep just smells like money. And they look at me like I'm some type of monster. Nobody's said it to my face yet, but earlier today, I heard one of the eighth graders call me a "shoulda been" when she passed me in the hall. I walked right up to her and asked her what it meant. If someone has something to say about me, they better have the nerve to say it to my face.

Turns out, a "shoulda been" is someone who should have been born into money but turned out poor. Like lost potential. They also whisper that I killed my own mother just to come live with Uncle T.

If only they knew the truth.

It was my no-good father who did it.

I thought maybe when I made it here, to middle school in a fancy place with a fancy family, it would feel different. That I'd fit in more. Still, I don't miss the small one-bedroom apartment with my momma, living paycheck to paycheck and having her vacillating between love bombing me and ignoring me entirely while my dad disappeared for weeks on end to gamble and drink away every single penny.

I never *want to go back to that.*

So they can call me whatever names they like, I guess.

I close my locker, spinning the lock, and then I'm down the hall and looking for Aria. She didn't tell me where to find her today, but I'm hoping she can help ease the transition.

"You're new."

My footsteps stutter as I twist to face the voice, only to see a blond guy towering over me, a chain dangling from his baggy pants and a ring hooped through his nose.

"And you're a genius, clearly." I pull on the strap of my backpack.

He laughs and then throws a long, gangly arm around me like we're old friends. "What's your name?"

He maneuvers us through the crowd and toward the cafeteria.

"I don't introduce myself to strangers," I tell him.

His clammy hands grip my upper arms as he stops us from walking and physically places me in front of him. Then he grins and puts out his palm, leaving it in midair. "I'm Fisher Engle."

He winks, and it's endearing, so I shake his hand. "Venesa Andersen."

"Now we're not strangers." He tugs on my fingers and I go flying into his chest. Before I can recover, he's tossed me again, his

arm back around my shoulders and me tucked into his side like I'm his newest pet project.

Maybe I am.

Or maybe this is a cruel joke.

"What grade are you in?" he asks while we make our way down the stark white halls.

"Sixth, you?"

"Seventh. Should be eighth, but they held me back a year."

"Why'd you get held back?" I adjust my backpack again, and he grabs it from me, swinging it over his shoulder.

"Because I'm too charismatic."

I snort a laugh. "Okay."

He winks at me again and tugs me harder into his side. "Come on, Short Stack, I'll show you where the cafeteria is."

"What'd you call me?"

He chuckles. "Short Stack. You know…because you're so short."

I look at him like he's got one too many screws loose because I'm the tallest girl in my grade, always have been.

Like every school cafeteria, the room is loud. The yells and chatter scratch across my eardrums like nails on a chalkboard, and the fluorescent lights burn my retinas. I glance around, looking for the bright red hair I helped Aria dye three days ago.

A fresh start for a fresh place, she said. A celebration of her becoming more of a woman. We're sixth graders now, after all. I wanted to dye mine too, because the chocolate brown just reminds me of my past, but Aria wouldn't help me, and I was too scared to do it myself. She said I was too young, like she isn't the exact same age.

My eyes immediately go to the center of the room because I know in my mind that's where Aria will be. That's where she always is: front and center and ready to shine.

Sure enough, that's where I find her, sitting on the top of a table, her legs dangling off the edge, about fifteen people surrounding her like minions waiting on their queen. She's laughing at something, her head thrown back and her mouth wide-open, that dyed hair swaying back and forth like soft waves on a shoreline, and I couldn't have pictured a more cliché scene than the one playing out in front of me right now.

But I guess clichés exist for a reason.

Relief swarms through me when I see her, though. I've lived with Uncle T and Aria for the past few months, and she's the only person who's been there for me. Sure, she's a little rough around the edges and gets her digs in when she can, but she's the closest thing I've ever had to a friend. To a sister.

"There's my cousin." I point to Aria.

Fisher looks in her direction, and his body stiffens.

"What?"

"Aria Kingston is your cousin?"

I lift a brow, feeling defensive. "Yeah, what about it?"

He grins down at me and pinches my cheek between his thumb and forefinger. "Not a thing, jelly bean. It was nice to meet you, Venesa, cousin of Aria. Don't be a stranger."

My brows draw in. "You're not gonna come sit with me?"

He hesitates, looking over at Aria's table and then me. "Not really my scene."

"Okay. See you later, I guess."

He turns around and leaves, and I stare after him for a second before spinning back to focus on Aria.

She's seen me. In fact, she's staring right at me with an odd expression on her face. I grin and wave, but she doesn't react.

Okay, then.

I stiffen my back and make my way through all the people. Crowds make me nervous. I've never been a popular person, and the more people there are, the more stares and whispers follow. It's hard not to feel like every single person is silently judging me, even though I know they aren't.

Everyone grows quiet when I stop in front of Aria, and she looks at me, leaning back on her hands so her chest is sticking out. She lifts her chin, peering down the bridge of her nose like I'm an ant that needs to be squashed.

"Hey." I look around, trying to find a place to sit.

Her brow lifts as she stares, and suddenly I'm feeling super awkward.

"I've been looking for you all day. Thought you were avoiding me." I tuck my dark hair behind my ears.

"Can I help you?" she sneers.

My body freezes up, and I glance around, not missing the way her minions are all stifling laughter behind their hands or looking at me like I'm the punch line of some secret joke.

My anxiety creeps back in like slime coating my insides, clogging up my confidence. My thumb picks at the cuticle of my ring finger, and I force a laugh. "Aria, come on."

"Come on, what?" she asks, adopting a bored expression.

"Well, I just…I—"

"Tuh-tuh-today, Venesa." Aria chuckles. "Jesus, you're so pathetic."

Her words slam into my chest, and I physically stumble a step. "What?" I don't even know what else to say.

I notice all the people hanging on her every word, and reality comes crashing down on me. Gone is the nice Aria from this summer, and in her place is this…she-devil.

I am not *welcome here.*

She rolls her eyes and leans forward, something dangerous glinting in her gaze. I'm not sure what's going on or what happened; I've never seen this side of her before.

Stupidly, perhaps, I thought we were friends. I found comfort in knowing I had a family member who actually cared.

"Are you deaf or just dumb?" Her eyes narrow as she trails them up and down my body with a disgusted look on her face. "All that extra weight blocking your ears?"

My stomach growls right on cue, loudly. Giggles burst from the girls sitting on either side of her.

"No, I…"

Is she calling me fat?

Heat rushes to my face, my cheeks flaring what I know will be a bright crimson.

"Look at her, she's blushing," some girl croons from Aria's side. "Go back and sit with that freak you walked in with, little piggy. You two are perfect for each other."

Aria's jaw clenches, and she shoots a dark look at her minion, but then she tilts her head to the side. "You didn't actually think…" She tsk-tsks, gazing at me with a self-satisfied smirk. "I would never be friends with a used-up piece of trash who was so desperate to be like us she killed her momma and even her daddy couldn't wait to get away from her."

Grief reaches through my chest and squeezes my heart until it splinters like a fractured bone.

Someone's standing behind me, and I run into them, my backpack flying from my shoulder and its contents spilling out on the floor.

I drop to the ground, scrambling to pick up the odds and ends, biting my tongue so hard, I taste blood.

No tears, though. My father trained those out of me years ago.

Aria scoots forward from the table, her cute aqua shoe with a purple bow on the top nudging me in the chest and making me fall over. My palms smack the linoleum floor hard, and anger ignites in the center of my chest.

"Look at you, on the floor cleaning, just like those bottom-feeders in the ocean. Get away from me, you fucking urchin, before your filth gets all over us."

"Aria never told me she grew up with her cousin," Enzo notes, taking a sip of wine from across the table.

His voice cuts through the memory, and my chest smarts. I reach up and rub at the ache, focusing my attention on him instead.

I've never seen a man exert power over Uncle T and live to tell the tale, but I guess I've never met a man like

Enzo Marino either. I still wish I hadn't. He puts me on edge.

We've made it through most of dinner, and it's been an awkward time, filled with small talk and everyone pretending like the prodigal daughter who defied her father and ran away *hasn't* been gone for the past six years.

The room itself is cold, filled with monochromatic colors and a glass chandelier that looks like icy raindrops falling from the fifteen-foot ceiling. The tension that always exists between Aria and me makes it feel like hell has frozen over entirely and made its new home right here in the Kingston formal dining room.

I finish chewing my piece of lamb before replying with a mocking tone, "Now, why wouldn't you want to talk about me with him, sweet Cousin? I'm hurt."

"In New York, it's easy to forget you exist, *Urch*," Aria says, a chilly warning in her stare. "Don't take it personally."

That nickname still stings like a papercut, even after all these years.

"No worries, Aria. You always *have* been a self-centered bitch, so it's not surprising you wouldn't want people to know about me."

Aria's lips pinch together until they form a tight white line.

"Yrsa Venesa Andersen, watch your tone," Uncle T snaps.

I widen my eyes innocently as I look over at him. When my uncle gets angry, a bluish vein throbs at his temple, pulsing in time with the grinding of his teeth. Right now,

I can see it beneath his skin like a living dragon, his lips pursed and eyes glacial as they cut across the room and sear into me.

I grab my water glass and take a sip to keep myself from saying something else.

Suddenly I feel like I'm nothing more than that insecure, damaged ten-year-old I was when he first took me in—lonely and broken and looking for someone who was proud enough of me to actually love me out loud.

Funny how something as simple as a memory brings up the old feelings.

"Yrsa? That's an interesting name." Enzo relaxes back in his chair.

My chest pulls with faint memories of my momma elongating the vowels "ehrrrr-saahhh" when we'd play hide-and-seek, one of the very sparse happy times I had with her, echoing on a loop in my brain.

I pick up the cloth napkin from my lap, then dab at the corners of my mouth before meeting Enzo's gaze. "It's Nordic. My father was from Denmark."

"Venesa doesn't enjoy talking about her past, babe," Aria says with a tight smile. "Her daddy was a drunk who liked to beat her momma."

"Aria," Trent laments.

"What?" Her eyes grow wide as she looks at him. "It's true, isn't it?"

She's not wrong. The last thing I want is to be sitting here talking about my dad and the name that's haunted me ever since he disappeared, but maybe if everyone else is as uncomfortable as I am, then I'll feel better about how the night's going.

Luckily for me, E asks no more questions. He just nods, his attention flicking to my water glass and then to everyone else's wine before he starts a conversation with Uncle T.

But I feel the phantom burn of his eyes on me.

I take the moment to soak up Enzo Marino in full. There's something about him, like an itch I can't scratch.

He's arguably the most attractive man I've ever seen, rugged in a way that can't be covered up by his polished appearance. The medium tan of his skin and midnight strands of his hair complement the crisp black of his cashmere sweater perfectly, and his jaw is so sharp, I'm surprised it doesn't cut through glass. He looks every inch the rich and powerful man in his tailored clothes and movie-star good looks, but there are hints of ink peeking out from the corners of his neckline when he moves certain ways, and I can't help but wish he'd drop the couture attire and let me see what he deems worthy enough to become art on his skin.

I bet he's a good fuck.

My phone vibrates on the table next to me, and I peer down, seeing a text from Fisher flash across the screen.

Fisher: Need me to come save you yet?

I can *always* count on him to come through. I pick up my cell and reply.

Me: How fast can you get here?

Fisher: I'm already down the street. How's the family reunion?

The knot that's been sitting in the middle of my chest loosens with the possibility of an early escape.

Me: Come find out for yourself.

"Venesa."

My head snaps up, everything in the room coming sharply into focus. Everyone's looking at me, and when I meet Uncle T's gaze, I shrink under his disappointed look. "E's asking you a question."

That knot tightens again like a vise, and I paste a wide smile on my face, gingerly setting my phone down next to me.

"I'm sorry," I reply, even though I'm not.

I'm so used to saying the words to Uncle T that they've lost all of their meaning, but they placate him either way.

"No need to rush off the phone for little ol' me," Enzo chimes in, amusement dancing across his face, mimicking what I told him when we first met outside. Aria gives him a funny look, but he ignores her, taking another bite of his meal instead, chewing slowly, his eyes cascading over me like he's cataloging every feature. "I was just asking what it is you do?"

"Oh," I reply, glancing at Uncle T and then back. "This

and that. Mainly, I run a restaurant for Uncle T, but I'm his go-to girl." I force a smile.

Aria laughs, and I glower at her, feeling every inch the teenager I was when she used to live here.

Ugh, I *can't stand* how she makes me feel. "Something funny?"

"Not the *Lair*," she guesses.

I tilt my head. "Actually, that's exactly what it is."

She harrumphs and lifts her shoulders in a careless way. "Guess I'm not surprised you're back where your momma used to run herself ragged. You can take the girl out of the ghetto, but you can't take the ghetto out of the girl."

Enzo cuts a sharp glare at Aria. "Watch your mouth. What's wrong with you?"

Her jabs hit where they're supposed to, but like I've always done with her, I don't let it show. "I'm thrilled you're back, Aria." I grin widely. "It will be so *fun* getting to know each other again."

Her face flashes with confusion.

Footsteps from the hallway interrupt the moment, and for the first time all night, a genuine smile takes over my face.

"Fisher," I say as he comes into view.

Fisher Engle is larger than life, at least in personality. He's not physically bulky, but he's tall and has a wiry frame. His height isn't what sets him apart, though. It's that bright blue mohawk of his and the tattoos that cover almost every inch of his skin, from his fingertips to his neck.

To me, he's the best. A ride or die who's more like a brother than a friend.

Aria stiffens in her seat when Fisher walks around the large dining table and leans down to kiss my cheek. "Short Stack."

My smile grows. "Hey, Gup."

"Sorry I'm late," he says loudly, plopping in the chair next to me.

"Hello, Fisher," Uncle T says dryly.

"Daddy T," he replies, ignoring the obvious tension streaming from across the table. "Aria, long time."

"Fisher," Aria greets, her voice stiff. "Not long enough."

His smile widens, but I can tell it's heavy and dripping with condescension. There's a lot of history between them, some of which even I don't know.

"You're looking as beautiful as ever," he says. "That dress on you is fantastic. I just *love* how you don't care what anyone else thinks."

The air grows still, a heavy pause making everyone visibly uncomfortable, but Fisher doesn't mind. He lives to put people on edge. It's part of why we get along so well. Besides, he has years of hurt from Aria, and when someone hides that kind of pain for so long, the ache turns bitter.

He reaches to the center of the table and grabs a croissant from the basket before leaning back in his chair and popping a piece into his mouth.

I bask in Aria's discomfort.

Fisher's brows rise. "Ran off to New York and lost your

accent, I see. So the country bumpkin *can* become a city girl."

"Some of us have aspirations besides wasting our entire life in Atlantic Cove, dealing drugs and being degenerates," she bites out.

Fisher chuckles, throwing his arm around the back of my chair. "Don't be a hater."

Suddenly, the energy shifts, tingles of awareness prodding at my spine, and I know without looking that Enzo is staring at me. Again. I glance over, and his eyes narrow with a frosty glare that douses me like ice.

What's his problem?

"And you are?" Fisher homes in on Enzo, and that makes me nervous.

Fisher doesn't have a filter, and he might like to stir up drama, but he's not built to withstand terrifying things, which is why although he does some of the grunt work for Uncle T and me—an easy transition from when he used to deal drugs to the high school kids around town—he's not involved in the darkest parts of the business. And despite Enzo looking like a proper gentleman, I know he's the monster that goes bump in the night, just like me.

Energy attracts energy, so when two people have a similar vibration, it's easy to feel.

Enzo's brow rises, and he lounges back in his chair. "I'm the *fiancé*."

I laugh at the possessive note in his tone. "Don't worry, E. Fisher's got no interest in your woman."

Aria smiles thinly. "That's right. Fisher's never wanted anything except *Venesa*."

Enzo throws an arm around the top of Aria's shoulders, mimicking Fisher's earlier move, his dark brow lifting as he watches his future wife and my best friend interact.

"You know me," Fisher says. "Can't get enough of that Kingston love."

She scoffs. "Venesa's hardly a Kingston."

A quick jab, but it does the job. My stomach drops when nobody at the table comes to my defense.

I am a Kingston. My momma was *the* Kingston before she gave it all up for my father. She was the apple of my granddaddy's eye, the same way Aria is for Uncle T. Even after she chose my father over her family, she still got gifts and letters from my granddaddy. Percius Kingston never gave up on her, not until the day his house burned down with him inside it.

Enzo's fingers skim across Aria's shoulder, his gaze coming back to me.

I shift in my seat. *I wish he'd stop staring at me like that.*

"Probably why I like her," Fisher replies.

"Fisher, not that we aren't all thrilled by your company, but why exactly are you here?" Uncle T interrupts, sighing like Fisher's the biggest pain in his ass.

"I came for my girl, of course."

"Ouch, babe," Aria squeaks. She rubs her shoulder and glares at Enzo.

He doesn't reply or move his eyes from me, but his

thumb smooths over where he obviously gripped her too tightly.

I grin up at Fisher, leaning closer to his side.

"You ready, sugar?" he asks.

I glance at Uncle T, and he gives a slight nod, dismissing me.

"You're leaving?" Aria's voice is incredulous. "We haven't even talked about the engagement party."

A laugh escapes me as I stand up and brush down the front of my dress. "I'm sure you'll manage. You should really come by the Lair sometime." I let a slow grin spread across my face. "If you ask real nice, maybe I'll let you host your little party there, but you'll have to promise not to mess with anything. I know how you like to play with things you think are beneath your stature and then leave them out to rot."

My eyes flick to Fisher and back to her.

She frowns, her features twisting into something sinister, and I wink before saying my goodbyes and heading out the door.

CHAPTER 6

Enzo

THERE'S NOTHING MORE UNCOMFORTABLE than being a guest in somebody else's home, but there's also no better way to learn about someone than being immersed in their environment, and my goal is to find out everything there is to know about Trent Kingston and his ragtag gang of criminals. The way he threw around Peppino's name just doesn't sit right with me.

The fuck was Peppino doing, making business deals in the South without telling anyone?

When we first found out my brother had been murdered, I was determined to uncover who exactly it was that put the hit out on him. But every place I looked was a dead end. Nobody knew anything. Or at least nothing I could force out of them. And then my pops went off the deep end, the fists of power chipping away at his reason one knuckle at a time until he became so volatile, even I couldn't predict his moods.

Now Pops is almost impossible to control, and that's dangerous for someone in his position. One misstep and it's all over.

The past few years, I've been spending so much time trying to protect our family, I barely have time to *breathe*. But if I don't do it, we're toast. There are plenty of guys who would love to reinstate the commission my pops so violently tore apart. To keep the old laws of the land in place in a way that my father doesn't seem to care about.

If anyone actually asked me, I'd agree with the fact Pops is disrespecting both our history and tradition. But no one ever does, assuming I'm the mouthpiece for my father through and through. Technically, they're not wrong.

He's tarnishing what it means to be Mafia, but it's not my place to question him—not unless I want him to kill me for the disrespect. I'm barely hanging on to his approval as it is, the less feathers I ruffle, the better.

Still, weirdly, finding out Peppino was doing business deals with shady people outside of the family—maybe even without my pops's permission—makes me feel a little less like the Marino fuckup.

I breathe out a heavy sigh and crack my neck, looking around the room. Much to my dismay, Aria and I are staying in her childhood bedroom and *not* in the mother-in-law suite. I wonder if Venesa lives in the guesthouse and that's why we're in the main one instead. Or maybe Trent wanted to keep a close eye on me. I know if the situation were reversed, I'd do the same.

There's a canopy-style queen-size bed with baby-pink sheets in here and so many things everywhere that they're overflowing from the shelves lining the peach-colored walls. French doors lead to a small balcony overlooking the private beach, and it's very obvious no one has touched this room since Aria left.

It's outdated. A time capsule filled to the brim with *stuff*. Aria loves to collect things, that's for sure. There's no way I'm letting her clutter up my penthouse back home, though, so she'll need to get a handle on that before she moves in.

Maybe we can live separately.

Aria fell asleep shortly after we settled in a few hours ago, but not me. I don't sleep well when I'm in a place that isn't my own. Lowering your guard is a quick way to get a bullet in your dome, and I didn't get to where I am by being comfortable in my surroundings.

I send a text to Scotty, whom I had my assistant, Jessica, set up at a little bed-and-breakfast a few miles down the road, telling him to be here in the morning at nine, and then I glance at Aria while she burrows deep under the comforter. I head to the left side of the bed, staring down at the small space beside her. Aria likes to cling to me in her sleep, and when she does, I feel suffocated, like the walls are closing in, so she doesn't spend the night with me often.

I've never been a cuddler. Makes me itch.

Grimacing, I slip beneath the covers and blow out another breath, my mind racing like it always does when the world goes quiet. Before I can stop myself, my thoughts turn to Venesa. She's just…I'm not sure what she is exactly, but I do know guilt drips like a steady leak every time I try to push her from my brain and she drops back in.

Especially when I'm picturing her while lying next to my fiancée.

Aria shifts and murmurs something before opening her sleepy gaze and locking it on me. She grins softly, and I close my own eyes, pretending to be asleep.

It doesn't fool her.

"You're not still mad, are you?" she asks, her voice thick.

I blink slowly, then stare at the top of the canopy. "Who says I was mad?"

She giggles, scooting over and placing her head on my shoulder. Immediately I feel stifled, but then I think of the way Ma used to get, after Pops started staying out late at night and coming home in the morning smelling like other women's perfume. How she'd cry in their bedroom, trying to stifle the noise so I wouldn't hear her break apart through the thin walls. How she'd walk around the house looking so goddamn lonely, so broken from his betrayals.

That memory is all it takes to finally push Venesa from my thoughts and focus on the woman next to me instead.

"Please, E, you practically choked the life out of my arm when Fisher and I were interacting."

Ah.

"You're sexy when you're jealous," she murmurs, her lashes fluttering as she gazes up at me.

I hold back my laugh. *Jealous?* That's not an emotion

I've ever felt in my life. Simply put, there's nothing for me to be jealous of. Wanting things you can't have does nothing beneficial. It only muddles the mind and keeps people from achieving greatness.

Besides, if I really need something, I simply take it.

"You're mine, aren't you?" I peer over at her.

"That's the deal." She yawns. "For better or for worse. Forever."

The words grate against my skin, but I push the feeling away. "Right," I say, "so what's there to be jealous of?"

She moves quickly, rolling on top of me, her warm cunt pressing on my lap. My hands fly to her hips instinctively, and when she grinds down, my body reacts.

"My macho man," she croons. "Pretending you're not upset at me getting attention from another guy."

I'm not really in the mood to get my dick greased, but the tension I've been feeling all day needs some sort of release, so if she wants me to fuck her, I won't argue.

I grin. "Why don't you show me how sorry you are, princess?"

"You have nothing to worry about with him, you know that, right? He's vermin. Literally the town's drug dealer since we were kids. I would *never* stoop so low."

She smiles lazily, and something about it makes my stomach turn, so I grip her hips tighter and lift her off me, flipping her around until she's face down and ass up.

Much better.

I spend the rest of the night buried balls deep inside her,

but it's the vision of her cousin underneath me that has me coming so hard, I black out from the pleasure.

The next morning, I'm at the Grotto, a well-known bed-and-breakfast two miles down the road from the Kingston estate.

Like everything else in Atlantic Cove, it's not to my liking.

It's too flowery.

Too bright.

Too…sunshiny.

Right now, I'm sitting in a quaint kitchen off the main living area, watching the owner, Betty, dance around and pamper Scotty like he's her long-lost son.

There's no one else staying here. I paid a pretty penny to ensure it. There's a forest-green door off the kitchen that opens to a small paved patio with white metal chairs circling a round table, a strip of ocean just beyond. If I were someone who liked to relax by hearing birds chirp and bees buzz, I'd probably find it soothing.

But I'm not.

The level of calm here makes me uncomfortable, like I'm just waiting for the other shoe to drop.

Scotty, however, has made himself right at home.

Betty plops down a steaming plate of biscuits and gravy in front of him, and Scotty, the fucking kiss ass, beams at her like she hung the moon.

"So, Betty, what's the news today?" he asks, shoveling a giant bite of food into his mouth.

I flip down the corner of the *Atlantic Cove Gazette* I'm skimming. "Aye, don't talk with your mouth full."

He grins at me, his cheeks bulging.

"Now, why would I know that?" Betty drawls.

"Ah, come on, Betty Boop, don't be shy just because E's here. He's my guy. You can trust him." Scotty takes another bite and then chugs a bit of orange juice. "Everyone excited about the big engagement party?"

Betty swipes a strand of curly gray hair from her forehead. "Trent Kingston's prodigal daughter come home at last? Of course. It's the talk of the town."

"Interesting." Scotty elongates the word like it's a song. "You really picked a popular princess, huh, Cuz?"

I roll my eyes. "Eat your food."

"Hey, how come she left here anyway?" he asks.

I shrug and look over at Betty because fuck if I know why. Aria told me once she didn't like it here, and I never thought to push for more. Never really cared, if I'm being honest.

Betty raises a thick brow at me and then shakes her head. "Now, I would never talk about a neighbor." She throws a blue towel over her shoulder and picks up a fresh pot of coffee to fill up mine first and then pour a cup for herself. "But when I was younger, I used to enjoy sitting out front and watching the sunrise with a fresh mug of caffeine." Betty sighs and leans against the counter. "Nothing like watching the world wake up, you know? And sometimes, in those early mornings, I'd see things."

Scotty leans in, enraptured by Betty's tale. I flip a page of the newspaper, pretending I'm not listening.

"What things?" he asks.

"Aria had a habit of sneaking out, and I'd see that *rat*... Fisher Engle? That boy was no good from the beginning. No parents around to keep him in line. He'd drop her off right at the corner in that Chevelle of his, and she'd slip out with flushed cheeks and messy hair, running up the road back to her place."

I'm not surprised Aria used to fuck around with him. Neither of them was good at hiding it last night.

"What about her cousin?" I pipe up, because honestly, I don't give a fuck who Aria used to screw around with when she lived here. This entire conversation is tiring.

Betty straightens. "Her cousin?"

I fold the paper, placing it on the table. "Yeah, Venesa."

She tilts her head, something flashing in her face as she looks to Scotty and then back to me. "Speaking about that girl is none of my business. She could use a good church, though, always walking around doing her witchy spells and wearing all those crystals. Girl needs Jesus, if you ask me."

Scotty whistles. "Betty's no gossip, E. I don't know what to tell you."

"Yeah, I can see that." Clearing my throat, I grab my phone and stand. "You two, behave."

I give Scotty a look and then step onto the back patio to call my pops.

My hair rustles from the slight breeze, and my face scrunches when the smell of salt and sunshine hits my nose.

"*Ciao, figlio mio*," my father answers gruffly, his Italian accent strong and sure.

"*Ciao*, Papá."

"How are things?"

"Warm," I reply.

"And your fiancée? How's her *famiglia*? *Bene?*"

My father is direct. He also frequently goes back and forth between Italian and English, something he's done since he moved to Brooklyn with my nonna as a boy from Sicily.

"Did you know Trent was talking shop with Peppino?" I ask, something still not sitting right in my gut about how Trent revealed that information like it was a hidden ace up his sleeve.

My father sighs deeply, the absence of his immediate reply crackling through the phone. "He may have mentioned it."

My forehead creases. *The fuck?* "And you didn't think to mention it to me?"

He chuckles, dark and deep, and it makes my spine bristle. I can't tell if he's about to threaten me for speaking my mind or answer my question.

I shouldn't have phrased it so harshly.

It's eerie, the way he can do that—put you on edge simply because you never know how he'll react.

"You never cared about things like this. Too busy with getting your hands dirty in the streets and fighting in those ridiculous cage fights."

The cage fights that make you a shit ton of money. I don't say it out loud because I'm too relieved he's having a conversation about it instead of flying off the rails.

"You know how many people your brother was in 'talks' with?" he continues. "Peppino knew enough about this life to know when to involve me and when to handle it himself. Too many questions make me think you're planning something you shouldn't be. *Are* you planning something, *figlio mio*?"

My stomach tenses. "Of course not, Papá."

Pops's voice is soft and lacking intonation. "There's a reason for everything we do."

"And what's the reason for a hotel down here?" I ask.

"Careful," Papá replies. "Even if I *did* want to share, I can't right now. They're always watching. I think someone tapped the house."

"Gio sends someone every morning to check, Papá. Everything's good."

"And how can I trust *Gio*?" he questions. "I taught you better than this."

My jaw clenches, but I know better than to talk back.

"Say yes to the hotel, Enzo. Don't disappoint me, or you won't like the outcome."

"Okay, Papá."

This *is* bullshit, though. I've never wanted to be part of Marino Enterprises. That was always Peppino's thing. He was the businessman, and I was the muscle. Sure, I had a few things going—a drywall company that got the bids on my brother's projects and a few clubs throughout the city—but I was where I liked it, being immersed in the true foundation of my family's legacy, out on the streets and with my guys instead of suffocating in boardrooms and staring at dried-up pussy in pencil skirts.

Back then, I was a capo, and my crew was *the* work crew of the family. I was the one who got the contracts for the kills and did the shakedowns for people who didn't remember to send us our cut. But when Peppino got himself clipped, the books opened, and my pops called for me to be the new underboss. I had no choice but to settle into place. It's my duty to *la famiglia*.

I stare out over the garden of flowers, watching the sun sparkle off the water just beyond it. "Well, I've found Trent's respect…lacking."

Pops chuckles. "Then you remind him whose son you are. But you *will* build a hotel down there. It's good for business. For expansion. Do your part for this family, you understand?"

"Yes, Papá, I understand."

"There's a van that's been driving by every day, and I know they're trying to see in my windows and listen to my conversations. Don't call me again on this line."

Click.

He hangs up before I can respond, and a hit of annoyance stabs the middle of my chest because his paranoia is always taking my best guys off the streets and having them watch for nothing, just to soothe his panicked brain. Irritation vibrates through me, and I tap the phone against my palm before brushing down the front of my suit.

Christ, it's hot here.

Aria's busy today meeting with some party planner, so I have the afternoon to do what I wish. She tried to convince me to go with her, but I'm not wasting my time doing froufrou shit like smelling flowers and tasting pastries.

And suddenly, all I want is to see that firecracker Venesa again. I try to push it down because it's dangerous wanting something so badly when there's no rhyme or reason, and she's something I need to purge from my system before it devours me whole. But if I don't solve the mystery of why she's so appealing, then she'll never leave my head.

So I call Trent and let him know I expect her to meet me at the boardwalk in an hour.

CHAPTER 7

Venesa

STEAM BILLOWS AROUND ME AS I EXIT THE bathroom. Rubbing a towel on my soaked hair, I make my way into the main area of my studio apartment before glancing at my ends, hoping I didn't leave the purple shampoo in for too long.

Icy white. Perfect.

I look over to the left and smirk when I see Athena, one of my regular hookups, lounging in my bed with her delicious body on full display, the thin cream sheet barely covering her tits.

Sighing, I continue into the room. "You're still here."

Athena smiles, her bright white teeth sparkling, and my gaze traverses her smooth, dark brown skin. She stretches her arms above her head, and her grin grows when she notices my lingering perusal. "Don't sound so excited."

I blink, shaking myself out of my stupor. "You can go now."

She sits up farther, the sheet slipping down her body, and a shot of arousal hits me because *damn* if she isn't gorgeous.

Fantastic at eating pussy too.

But I'm really not in the mood for this, especially after waking up to the text from Uncle T telling me to meet Enzo at the boardwalk in an hour.

There's nothing I want less than to be around Enzo Marino. Just like the first time I saw him, when he was unconscious and on the shore of the Hudson, there's this connection there. One that has me wanting to tell him things. True things, things he can't know.

Athena saunters over to me and tugs at the corner of my towel until it drops off my body.

"God, you're so fucking hot," she mewls, her dainty hands gripping my hips and pulling me into her.

Well, maybe a quickie. I'm already calculating whether I actually have the time, though, which means the mood is severely lacking.

When she leans in toward my lips, I turn my head.

She sighs into my ear before dropping her face against mine. "You're so irritating sometimes, Venesa."

"Sorry, honey, but you know the rules." I push her back, and she releases me without a fight.

She huffs, ambling to where her clothes are in a pile on the floor, right next to the edge of the bed, where I stripped them off her last night. "You and your stupid rules. Kissing someone on the lips isn't going to *kill* you, V. It's called intimacy."

I blink at her.

She laughs quietly, tugging on her pants. "But why would you know anything about that?"

My thumb rubs against the nail on my ring finger. "Listen, this was fun, but I've—"

"Let me guess," she interrupts, buttoning up her shirt. "You've got things to do?"

"And people say you don't pay attention." I wink. "Yet you know me so well."

"We *could* know each other better." She moves back toward me.

"Any better and we'd end up killing each other. Now out." I point toward the door leading to the Lair downstairs.

It's early, so it's not open yet, but if she waits any longer, the staff will have arrived, and I'd rather they not see her sneaking from my apartment. I'm gossiped about enough around here.

She walks to the door, pausing with her hand on the knob. "You know, you could take a chance and give us a real shot."

"I could," I say carefully as I trek to my makeshift closet and run my fingers along the rack of clothes I have against the far wall. "I just don't want to, darlin'."

She mutters something in reply, but I ignore her, keeping my eyes on my garments, cocking my head like picking an outfit needs intense concentration.

Finally, I hear the door click shut as she leaves, and my shoulders drop, the knot in my stomach untangling as I blow out a deep breath.

I walk from the rack and to my bedside table before opening the drawer and grabbing my gratitude journal and the meditation pillow underneath, and then I make my way to the center of the room. Manifestation is something I've believed in since I was struggling in high school and started writing down that Uncle T had let me drop out and come work for him instead. Two months later, those words became reality.

At that point, I had already delved into the world of witchcraft—although in the beginning, it was more curiosity and less spiritual devotion—so manifestation fell in line with raising my frequency and manipulating energy to my benefit, and even though Fisher makes fun of me for the practice, I know it works. There are too many things the universe has opened for me, too many ways my life has changed for the better since starting.

Mentally, I make a note to do a cord-breaking ritual for Athena the next time the sun is in Aquarius, and then I wipe the thought entirely from my head and focus on my breathing.

Thirty minutes later, I'm back at my clothing rack, grabbing an off-the-shoulder top I picked up from Goodwill and my favorite shorts before tossing them to the side, scrunching up my nose at the lack of options.

I miss designer clothes and the walk-in closet I had at the mansion. But that was a long time ago, when Uncle T was legally responsible for providing for me. The day I turned eighteen, Aunt Elle wasted no time kicking me to the curb, and my "loving" uncle stood beside her, watching silently as I packed my bags.

Bitterness fills my throat, making the back of my mouth turn sour.

I'm glad she's dead now, at least.

My phone rings, Uncle T's name flashing on the screen.

"Morning," I answer, putting a bit of extra pep in my tone to cover the guilt from what I was just feeling.

"Hey, little one," he replies in a soft voice. "You got my message earlier?"

"About meeting E? Of course." I nod to myself as I continue picking out an outfit for the day. I hold up an option and walk to my floor-length mirror, which sits kitty-corner to my bed, before tossing it to the side and going to grab another one. "I don't know. This is all just a little ridiculous. The vibes are off."

Uncle T chuckles. "If we ran the world based on your vibes, everything would burn to the ground."

"Well…" I toss another shirt on the bed. "Sometimes you've gotta burn things so you can start fresh."

"I want that Marino hotel I was promised years ago, and he's going to give it to me whether he wants to or not."

Putting my phone between my shoulder and ear, I hold it there while I take a deep purple shirt off the hanger and lay it out on the bed. "So that's the angle, manipulate him into doing what we want?"

"If that's what it takes."

"And you're so sure he *can* be manipulated? Because I'm not. And this is—"

"He's marrying *my* damn daughter, so if I want to make sure he's under my thumb, even just a little, then that's what I'll do."

"He's about to be family," I retort.

"Sometimes family fucks you over."

Well, he's got me there.

"Want me to cast a spell?" I joke, knowing he avoids anything to do with my practice. Uncle T is a Protestant through and through. Not a very good one, but who am I to judge?

"Don't even *speak* about that devil worship, girl."

I roll my eyes because that's *not* what it is, but I don't argue with him. I learned a long time ago that it's easier to gain his affection if he can pretend I fit into his narrow-minded box, so I let him believe what he wants to believe.

But sometimes, when I focus on the way he doesn't accept me for who I am, resentment drizzles on my insides like an acid, slowly eating away at my resolve, and I can't help but let the little barbs fly.

"Can't we just have Aria show him around?" I ask. "This feels an awful lot like I'm on babysitting duty."

"Just do it, Venesa."

Click.

I stick out my tongue at the phone like a child and then text Bas.

Me: Heads up, boss man is being extra today. Put on your big girl panties before you see him.

I toss the phone on my bed and finish getting ready, completing my look with my favorite bloodred lipstick and an obsidian necklace.

There's nothing a good red lip and a protection stone can't cure.

Heading out of my apartment and down the spiral staircase that leads into the back hallway of the Lair, the first person I'm looking for is Fisher.

I'm satisfied with the few employees prancing around the place, setting everything up for the lunch rush. We aren't known for our food, and we don't get truly busy until the sun sets, but there are always a few stragglers who make their way to the south side of Atlantic Cove during the day, desperate to escape their miserable existences and drown themselves enough to forget their woes.

Our liquor sales keep us in business, and it makes me *sick* if I think about it for too long.

But who am I to judge someone else and their life choices? Who cares if they come and spend all their money here, then go home to ruin their child's life?

My stomach churns, and I push the thought away.

Not everyone has a problem with alcohol, Venesa. You're projecting.

Gothic-style windows line the far-right wall, arched and iced out so no one can see in. The walls themselves are a dark mossy green, and low purple and blue lights line the perimeter, creating a dark and intimate atmosphere. Saltwater fish tanks are interspersed throughout the decor, filled with polyps that sway from the soft wake of the swimming angelfish and eels.

A dozen round tables with mismatched chairs are dotted around the room, facing a stage at the front. It's made from old wood, worn with age, and deep-purple velvet curtains frame it.

The bar runs along the left side wall, open to the tables, and Fisher is currently behind it, cutting fresh limes for the day shift. The citrusy scent slams into me as I walk up to him and run my fingers along the copper bar top.

Fisher grins and pulls out a coffee from our favorite place down the street.

"My hero," I drawl, grabbing the cup from his hand and taking a sip. The bitter notes of the coffee complement my mood perfectly, and I immediately start drooling like Pavlov's dog when he hears a bell.

"Long night?" he questions with an arched brow.

I lift a shoulder and take another sip.

"Which one of your lackeys was it? Jason or Athena?"

"They're not my *lackeys*." I laugh.

"Way to avoid the question."

I tilt my head, watching as he places a lime in the metal cutter and pushes down, slicing the fruit into several perfect pieces.

"Does it really matter?"

He shrugs, moving the wedges into a clear plastic bin. "Just gauging your mood for the day."

"And you can do that based on who I fucked the night before?"

"Definitely." He nods and then waggles his eyebrows. "Athena actually makes you come, which makes you a much nicer person to be around."

He's not wrong. She's *definitely* the better lover, but I scoff anyway.

"Your hair looks ridiculous," I say, pointing at his freshly dyed blue tips that he's styled into a spiky mohawk.

"So do your tits."

I glance down at my cleavage, offended.

He laughs. "Are you here for the day, or busy again being your uncle's bitch?"

"Don't call me a bitch, *bitch.*" I set my coffee cup down.

He pulls Saran Wrap from its case and rips it. "If it walks like a duck and talks like a duck…"

"I'm headed to the boardwalk, actually."

Fisher grimaces. "Yuck. What for?"

"Gotta show my new cousin-in-law the town."

"Enzo Marino," Fisher proclaims with an exaggerated Italian accent. "He's hotter than I thought he'd be."

"Leave him alone." I point at him.

His eyes sparkle. "What did I do?"

"Nothing, and it needs to stay that way, you hear me? The last thing I need is to worry about you getting yourself into trouble with Aria's man. I don't have time to clean up one of your messes."

He smirks. "So it was Jason, then."

I glare at him, but the corners of my lips turn up. "Athena, actually. I'm leaving. Try not to burn the place down while I'm gone."

"Yeah, yeah." He waves me off.

"And, Fisher…stay away from Aria too, okay?"

The humor leaves his eyes, and he nods, swallowing heavily. "No worries on that front. I can promise you."

CHAPTER 8

Venesa

MY MOMMA DROVE A MUSTANG CONVERTIBLE. A sparkly blue-green one that changed tints in the sun depending on how the rays hit the paint. It was her pride and joy, and she spent more time loving that thing than she ever did loving me.

Ironically, most of my best memories of her were in that car. Whenever she'd cover that curly brown hair of hers in a silk scarf and smile in that blinding way she was known for—one that stopped hearts and made a mess of a man—I'd know she was about to take me on a ride.

We'd giggle like schoolgirls and pile into that convertible, and if it was my birthday, she'd make an extra stop to get shaved ice from Morgan's Ice Shack on the boardwalk before we'd ride down the coast without a care in the world.

I'll never forget the feel of the wind blowing in my dark

hair or the grin that split my face, my lips stained a cherry red, sticky with sweet joy.

Back then, I used to think it was her way of apologizing for ignoring me in virtually every other aspect of life, but now I realize it was just her way of escaping reality. My father was not a kind man, and I have a begrudging respect for my momma, knowing she did her best to hide the ugliest truths about her life from my view. It's just buried beneath the mountains of animosity from how badly she failed at it.

I step off the city bus that stops right in front of the boardwalk, pushing away the memories that cause old wounds to rip open and bleed from the center of my chest.

It's humid today, the smell of city and salt water mixing in the air and lying like a thin coat against my skin. The familiar feeling makes my insides crawl.

The Atlantic Cove Boardwalk is a landmark of South Carolina. First built in the 1930s, it spans over two miles of beach, filled with tourist attractions and overpriced food and drink. It's been reconstructed several times, usually under my family's hand, but there's one area that's original, where the wrought iron arch with the pretty pink seashell sits like a beacon, drawing people to the bridge on stilts that extends out into the water.

That's where I find Enzo.

He's leaning against the railing as if he doesn't have a care in the world, his ocean-blue eyes already trained on me as I walk up to greet him.

"Lover Boy." I nod, slipping my hands into the back pockets of my frayed black shorts.

He lifts his chin in reply, his gaze stripping me bare as he peruses my body, from the top of my bleached head, over my exposed shoulders in my purple top, to the tips of my black Nikes. He looks laughably out of place in his tailored suit, and I know he *has* to be sweltering, but he doesn't seem to mind. If anything, it makes him look even more powerful, as though even the South Carolina heat can't touch him.

People are laughing around us, lounging in their tiny bikinis and tropical board shorts, kids building castles in the sand or running away from the waves as they lap at the shore. Couples walk between us, some aged with leathered skin and some young with puppy love in their eyes.

The boardwalk is good for that, setting a beautiful backdrop to a first date or a proposal that promises the fairy tale of a forever kind of love.

But Enzo acts as though none of that exists, his stare trained on me like I'm the only thing he can see.

It's unnerving.

He frowns, and somehow even *that's* attractive.

"You're late," he states.

I hit back. "And you're overdressed."

"It's sweet you care." He straightens off the ledge and takes a step closer to me. "Do you always take the bus by yourself, looking the way you do?"

I glance down at my outfit. *What's wrong with it?* "I'm sure I don't know what you mean."

His lips twitch as though he's about to smile, and he reaches out, tugging lightly on one of the large silver hoops dangling from my ear.

"My earrings?" I question. "Well, you know what they say."

He tilts his head. "No, what do they say?"

I grin. "The bigger the hoop, the bigger the wh—"

His finger presses against my lips, and the feel of him touching any part of me makes me squirm with unease, like static electricity is sparking through my body.

"Watch your mouth," he says slowly, his New York accent coming through strong, dropping the r and elongating the vowels. "You won't disrespect yourself to me."

Surprise at his words makes me feel off-kilter, and I reach up, my heart tripping in its rhythm as I grab his wrist and pull his hand away. "I was just joking, Enzo."

He stands there and stares at me for a moment, the muscle in his jaw ticking before he grins. "I like the way you say my name."

My brow furrows. "You know, you don't have to be nice to me just because I'm Aria's cousin. It'll probably work against you, actually."

"You think I'm being nice for Aria's sake?" His smile widens.

"Aren't you?"

He steps back, glancing around us instead of answering. "What's on the agenda for the day?"

I shrug. "You dragged me out here. Why don't you tell me?"

Uncle T told me to make sure he sees what Atlantic Cove offers, but honestly, I think the area speaks for itself. Overpriced and oversaturated.

"Give me the authentic Atlantic Cove experience." He waves his hand around us.

"Well, this is it." I put my hands out to my sides. "Welcome to the Atlantic Cove Boardwalk, where the drinks are expensive and the attractions are made for tourists. Perfect for a Marino hotel."

He looks at me. "Have you *been* to a Marino hotel?"

Suddenly uncomfortable, I shift on my feet. "Once…a few years ago."

Enzo blinks, most likely waiting for me to elaborate, but the last thing I'm going to do is tell him about how I committed *murder* in a Marino penthouse suite, so I let the quiet linger until he finally chuckles and gives a short bob of his head.

I hate that I like the sound of his laugh.

We walk down the promenade, and I point out some places that have been here for years, skipping the newer shops because I know nothing about them, and what's it really matter anyway? The quicker we get through this, the better.

I also skip any of the places that remind me of my past, hoping he doesn't notice. I think I've gotten away with it until he stops walking abruptly.

"What's up with you?"

"Nothing," I lie.

He points to Morgan's Ice Shack behind us. "You don't see that place to tell me about it?"

I glance over at it, nausea hitting me strong and sure, curdling in my throat and sticking along the edges of my mouth like thick mucus. "I do."

He crosses his arms.

Throwing my head back until I'm staring at the blue sky, I think about how to handle the situation. Uncle T made it clear I'm supposed to convince him to trust me. To listen to me. To *want* to go into business down here. My stomach cramps when I realize honesty is the best policy. Being difficult is only going to cause problems I'll have to fix later, and being dodgy will only make Enzo suspicious.

"Listen, there are just some things I don't like to talk about, and *that*"—I point to the Ice Shack—"is one of them."

He makes a face, but I don't elaborate any more. Who does he think he is anyway, cocking a brow like I'll just vomit pieces of myself at his command? He must notice my reluctance because he steps in close, his hand twitching like he wants to reach out and cup my cheek. Or maybe that's my imagination. Either way, he doesn't, though. Thankfully.

"I'm not playing any angles to get information or trying to test your knowledge," he says.

Obviously. *I'm* the one doing that to him. "Right."

"I've always been honest with you," he continues.

I snort. "You've known me for two minutes."

"And?" he replies with a wry grin. "What's that gotta do with honesty?"

As I lick my lips, my gaze flits away from his.

He dips his head down and captures my stare again, lowering his voice. "I don't have to know you to see the same thing in your eyes that lives in mine, and I get the distrust, and the walls, and the being constantly on guard. I respect it. But I promise you don't have to do that with me. Just be real, okay?"

My mouth parts, and my heart speeds at his words because he's right. I *don't* trust anyone, and the fact he called it out so plainly is a little shocking.

But I can't give him what he wants.

Being fully honest with him isn't a luxury I can afford.

"And you're being real with me?" I retort, because come on. He barely knows me, and yet here he is spouting off words like we're supposed to have a layer of trust and reciprocity.

He gives me a questioning look. "Why would you think I'm not?"

"It's just a little suspect that you're dragging me, a stranger, out here to show you around town when you have a perfectly healthy fiancée who was born and raised here."

He side-eyes me, a brief flash of what looks like guilt coasting through his gaze before he smirks. "Have you *met* your cousin?"

I laugh because he's not wrong. Aria isn't really the "take you out on the town and show you the sights for your benefit" kind of gal. Not unless there's a photo-op at the end.

"Unfortunately," I murmur.

He stops walking, and I wait for him to reprimand me

for talking down about his precious Aria, the same way everyone always does, but he doesn't.

"You know I had never even heard about you until I got here?" he says instead. "Don't you think that's weird?"

"Not really."

Why would Aria want to talk about the person who *actually* saved his life?

He continues to stare at me, and it's still unnerving, but I also kind of like the way it feels. His attention is all-consuming.

My teeth sink into my lower lip. "There's not much to tell."

He shakes his head. "I don't believe that."

"Okay," I acquiesce. "Being here? It reminds me of my past."

"Your past," he repeats.

My heart stutters. "Of my momma. She used to bring me down here. Rarely. She wasn't…well, she just wasn't up to it much. But once a year, on my birthday, she'd wake me up early and make it a big production. We'd get shaved ice right there." I point to Morgan's Ice Shack. "And then she'd walk with me down the line of shops and tell me I could pick my favorite thing to buy."

"Just one?" Enzo jokes.

"Things were hard. We didn't—she didn't—take money from the family, so yeah…just one." I swallow over the sudden knot forming in my throat. "It was my favorite day of the year, though."

"Because it was your birthday?"

"Because for that one day, my momma loved me out loud."

His jaw clenches, but then he nods, a blinding smile taking over his face. "Loving you out loud. I like that."

"Yeah, well..." I shift on my feet, my cuticle tearing from how badly I'm picking at it.

He slips his hands into his pockets and glances around, and then he places his palm on the small of my back and steers us toward a pop-up stand right next to the Sea Wheel, the two-hundred-foot Ferris wheel that defines the Atlantic Cove Boardwalk. I let him prod me forward, too stunned by this entire interaction to argue.

We walk up to the stand, pieces of jewelry hanging from the end caps and shirts that say things like "In My Mermaid Era" overflowing off the sides. He jerks his head toward the display. "Pick something."

"What?" I laugh.

He steps toward me until he's so close, he has to physically look down to peer into my eyes. "You heard me. Pick something."

I frown at him, confused as to why he's doing this and why he seems to care, but oddly touched by the gesture. "Why?"

"Because I said so."

"Does that normally work for you? The whole 'because I said so' schtick?"

"Yes."

I walk around the pop-up shop and take one of the seashell necklaces into my palm, inspecting it. "Well, I don't know if you know this, but people like an explanation of why they should do something before they do it. Makes them feel like you're treating them equally instead of talking down to them."

A loud laugh escapes him as he comes to stand next to me. "You're right. I want you to pick something because I can tell that memory of you and your mom, it's a good one. And I want to be a good one, too."

Surprise flickers in my chest like a candle.

"Do you like that?" He looks down at the seashell necklace in my hand.

"Sure, it's pretty." I place it back on the stand.

"Do you want it?" he presses.

My brows shoot to my hairline. "Uh…no thanks. I'm good."

"I'd like to get it for you."

"If I wanted it, I'd get it myself."

My eyes scan the price tag, because it really *is* pretty. But I don't have the money to spend on trivial things, and I'll be damned if I let him get it for me out of pity.

"*Christ*, you're difficult. Can't you accept a gift?" He nods toward the merchandise.

"When it's from the man marrying my cousin? I don't think so." I shake my head. "You don't have to do this, you know?"

His tongue swipes along his bottom lip, and my stomach

clenches tight, heat flaring between my legs. He leans down, his voice dropping an octave. "I don't do anything I don't want to."

The timbre of his words skates across my flesh like a knife.

"How about I pick something for you instead?" I bargain.

He considers it. "Is that the best I'll get?"

"Most likely."

He grins and straightens. "It's a deal."

"That's it?" I cross my arms. "You folded just like that?"

He shrugs. "Sure, if it will make you happy."

A smile breaks across my face unbidden.

If it will make you happy.

I don't know if anyone has ever said those words to me. It's dangerous how much I like the way it feels.

CHAPTER 9

Enzo

TEN MINUTES LATER, I'M THE LESS-THAN-enthusiastic owner of a T-shirt that says "Mariner of the Seas," with a sailboat against a rainbow backdrop.

"It's rude you're not wearing your gift." Venesa points at the shirt, which she picked out, that I now have tucked under my arm. "Do you not like it?"

I look at her, amused. "Is it a gift if I paid?"

She lifts her shoulders and smiles. "It's the thought that counts. Besides, did you know your last name in Latin means 'of the sea'? It's basically your namesake on a shirt."

My footsteps stutter, and I eyeball her because I'm still not sure whether I can trust her or not. For all I know, her specialty could be to make people feel comfortable before she fucks them over. "And what do you know about my *namesake*?"

Her mouth pops open to answer, and honestly, despite

the fact I'm having trouble gauging her level of sincerity, I'm enjoying the back and forth, but before she can say anything, her stomach growls so loudly, I wonder if she's eaten at all.

"You're hungry."

"I was ordered to come straight here and convince you to invest in the area. I didn't really have time to eat."

Humming, I move my hand until I'm *just* hovering around the small of her back to steer her.

It's harder than I thought it would be to not touch her when I'm this close—my fingers centimeters away from knowing what she feels like—but I resist, because I'm *engaged*, and even worse, to her cousin. One wrong step and Venesa could run to her uncle, bringing the whole house of cards down.

Trent made a deal with my father, and if word gets back to Pops... Unease churns deep in my gut because I'm not sure *what* my pops would do.

Besides, I didn't get to where I am by giving in to things just because I want them.

This could be a tactic. *Most likely is.*

"What are you doing?" she asks.

I glance down at her while I move us toward the front of a restaurant on the water called the Sharkbait. "Feeding you."

She huffs out a small laugh and takes a step away, turning around until she's facing me, her back toward the black double doors. "You *really* don't need to do that. I'm fine."

"I didn't ask if you were fine. In fact…" I move closer to her. "I don't remember asking for your opinion at all."

"That's true, actually." She crosses her arms. "Pretty rude of you to not take my feelings into consideration, then."

My lips purse. "Do you always do this? Disagree with *anything* someone says? It's pretty fucking annoying, I'll be honest."

I take another step, and she moves until she's pressed to the glass of the entrance like she can't wait to get away from me. Her lashes flutter as my arm brushes against her exposed shoulder, my palm flattening on the door behind her.

She smells like salt water and a hint of cherry, and I… think I like it?

"Don't stand so close," she breathes out.

I bend my head farther just so I can take another hit of her. "Tell me what to do again."

Goose bumps sprout down her neck and disappear beneath her shirt, and satisfaction spirals through me at the sight.

She can pretend I don't affect her, but the proof is right there on her pretty skin. I'm not sure why that makes it better, knowing this attraction isn't one-sided. Maybe because it makes me feel less like a piece of shit for having a wandering eye when clearly this thing between us goes both ways.

It's not just me.

I push on the door and hold it open, inclining my head, gesturing for her to walk inside.

I'm half-convinced she'll argue with me again, and

the thought of it makes blood pulse through my veins, a hit of anticipation lighting me up. I wish she would. It's… something, to have someone in my company who doesn't seem afraid of me and isn't trying to constantly kiss my ass. Exhilarating, even.

But she doesn't argue with this, at least. She just lifts her chin as she saunters through the front door and inside the restaurant.

When we walk in, *everyone* turns to look at her, but I don't think she even realizes it.

We're seated quickly, and when the hostess disappears, Venesa laughs, bringing the menu up to hide her face.

I reach across the small circular table and push it back down so I can see her. "What's so funny?"

She grins, tilting her head toward the hostess. "Just seeing the Enzo Marino effect in action, I guess."

"The Enzo Marino effect?"

"Yeah, you know…you're all big and bad and *manly*. It… *affects* people." Her elbows lean on the table when she speaks, her hand waving in my direction, and it pushes her cleavage until it's *right* there in my face, begging me to glance down and soak in every inch of her while I can.

But I'm not an amateur, so I resist the temptation.

My grin widens, and I rest my chin on my hand as I watch her. "That's the nicest thing anyone's ever said to me."

The server comes by, and Venesa orders a bowl of she-crab soup while I pick a shrimp po'boy with two Cokes, and neither of us really says much else until the food arrives.

I expect it to be awkward, the way it usually is with people you hardly know, but it feels like there's a level of camaraderie between us already, and I lean into the feeling.

It *should* make me want to run the other way.

Comfort with someone is a red flag, in my experience, especially with someone I've only just met. I can't afford to let my guard down in a regular situation, let alone with a woman who's about to be family.

"You surprise me," she blurts suddenly when we're almost done with our meals. "I thought you'd have your minions here following your every move."

The corner of my lip curls up, amusement filling my chest. "My *minions*?"

"Yeah. You know." She waves her hand through the air again. I notice she does that a lot, talks with her hands. The gestures are big and swooping, and if she's really trying to get her point across, they're even more pronounced.

"Your guys or whatever," she continues. "Uncle T won't go anywhere without his. He never used to let Aunt Ella or Aria out of their sight either."

I frown. "Yet you show up unaccompanied and on a city bus."

She smirks, but not before a hint of sadness flashes across her face, one I unfortunately recognize easily because I see it in my mirrors.

"I can take care of myself," she says.

"Hmm." I take a sip of my drink.

"What's that mean?" she asks, her eyes flitting around

the room before landing back on mine. "Listen, you don't get to judge me, okay?"

I smile at her. "Are you always so defensive?"

"I..." She tilts her head. "I'm not defensive. I'm just..."

My brows lift as I wait for her to come up with a word.

"Overcompensating?" I throw in, remembering her jab at me from last night.

She scoffs, gesturing to her body. "Please, what do *I* need to overcompensate for? I'm *very* generous with my gifts."

I chuckle and shake my head. "Generous with your modesty too."

A small grin touches her lips, those dimples making the apples of her cheeks even more pronounced.

My heart jumps.

"So how did you and Aria meet anyway?" Her eyes aren't on me; they're on the spoon she's slowly pushing through her half-eaten bowl of soup.

The reminder of Aria is like a wet blanket on chilled skin, dousing the moment in reality.

Doesn't she already know?

I can't imagine she doesn't. Everyone knows how Aria and I met because it was all over the news. New York's prince saved by a Southern shipping princess. The closest thing to American royalty, they call us.

The whole thing gives me a fucking headache.

I shouldn't *want* to be in the spotlight; it makes it that much harder to do the things necessary for the family. But of course, Pops didn't see it that way, so I ignored how uncomfortable it made me feel. And eventually, things you ignore grow roots too strong, their weeds all but impossible to dig out.

I've already accepted that this boredom—this monotony—is going to be the rest of my life.

"You don't know?" I test her.

She shrugs. "So what if I do? Maybe I want to hear about it from you."

"It's not an interesting story." I wipe my mouth with the cloth napkin on my lap and then place it on the red-and-white-checkered tablecloth.

"So make it interesting," she replies.

I stare at her, rubbing my chin. "She was a singer in one of my clubs."

Venesa huffs out an amused laugh.

"What?" I prod, trying to bite back the smirk.

"It's just kind of cliché, don't you think?"

I lean back, spreading my legs out wide until my calf brushes against hers. A shock runs through my body at the unintentional touch, but neither of us moves away.

"Us sitting here, eating overpriced seafood and buying thirty-dollar souvenirs is a bit cliché, but it doesn't make it any less enjoyable…or true," I retort.

"Mm-hmm. So you fell in love with her voice and that was that?" She snaps her fingers.

I pop a fry in my mouth. "Something like that."

She rolls her eyes and chuckles before standing up partway from her chair and bending over the table, swiping a fry from my plate, and slipping it between her gorgeous lips.

My throat dries, and I swallow harder than I should, heat blazing in my lower abdomen. *That fucking mouth.*

"You're not a very good storyteller, Enzo," she says after chewing. "I thought you'd be better at lying."

Enzo.

There she goes with my name again, and fuck, it sounds good rolling off her tongue.

I want to hear her say it again.

Moan it.

Scream it.

But that's a dangerous thought, so I clear my throat and turn my face to the side.

Clearly, I have control issues around her.

"Why don't you tell me what *really* happened?" she asks.

I run a hand through my hair. "Because that story's been beaten to death."

"Tell me anyway."

I shrug, a weird tightening sensation spreading across my chest. "Someone tried to gut me like a fish, and Aria dragged me onto shore and saved my life. Then she just… never really left. She was by my side every day. *Every day* in the hospital, making sure I was taken care of. Not many people would do that, you know? See a dying man and stick around to make sure he lives."

Venesa gives a sad smile.

"Anyway, I felt like I owed her, so when I was all healed

up, my pops suggested I take her out, and then…" I shrug again.

"The rest is history," Venesa finishes.

My gaze flicks up to hers, my chest feeling heavy. "Something like that."

She nods, sucking on her teeth. "So who was it, then?"

I cock my head. "Who was what?"

"The person who tried to kill you."

It's a bold question. And one that not a single person has asked me other than my pops, and even he doesn't seem to give a damn, too worried that everyone's out to get *him* instead.

I shake my head. "No clue. I've got a lot of enemies, so it could've be anyone, really."

That delicious-looking mouth of hers pops open. "You didn't try to figure it out?"

Embarrassment fills me. "I did. I just couldn't fucking find them."

I push my plate away, my appetite entirely gone now. *This is why I don't like talking about this shit.*

"Well, no offense," Venesa says. "But the actual story's way more interesting than that bullshit one you tried to sell me."

"She really sang at my club, though, after everything." I laugh. "I wasn't lying about that."

"How generous of you," Venesa deadpans. "She always wanted to be a singer, even though, if you ask me, she isn't much of one. Uncle T used to pay off the school so she'd get the leads."

"She ain't so bad."

Venesa gives me a knowing look. "Such a gentleman."

"You're right. I liked her voice, but I got tired of hearing it, so I took her back to my office and fucked her until she couldn't speak. How's *that* for a gentleman?"

I'm not sure why I say it or why I'm watching her like a hawk to see how she reacts, but when her eyes heat instead of turn cold, like maybe she's imagining me fucking *her*, well… that makes the tension ramp until the base of my neck goes hot and my dick grows hard.

My vision skims across her face and down her body, and I picture what it would be like to have *her* bent over an office desk with that silvery-white hair wrapped around my fist like a leash.

Christ.

She grabs her Coke, pulling the straw between her pillowy red lips, and now I'm picturing what it would be like to slip my fingers between them, to feel her teeth indent my skin the same way they tear up that mouth of hers.

She takes a sip and rubs her neck before smirking. "Just like a man."

I smile back because she's right. I am *very* much a man right now, a *dog* even. One who can't keep it together enough around her to lock away the most basic, primal parts of me.

"It was the start of a beautiful relationship." I say it mainly to remind myself, and my libido, that I am, in fact, in a relationship.

"So…tell me something else, Lover Boy."

My brows lift. "What'd you want to know?"

"I don't know. Something real. Something *no one* else knows. Like…how'd you get your nickname?"

My stomach cramps. She's out of her mind if she thinks we're talking about me like that. I paste on a cocky grin. "I'd think that's pretty obvious."

A challenge lights up her gorgeous dark brown eyes, and she stares at me for a few moments, her fingers tapping on the table. Then she shakes her head. "No, I don't think so. It can't be that easy."

I don't respond because she's right. It isn't.

"This is hardly fair." She crosses her arms and leans back in her chair. "I gave you that whole sob story about my momma, and you won't even give me a small, little, insignificant thing?"

After standing up, I throw a couple of hundreds on the table and walk around to her side, then lean down until my nose brushes against her hair. "Well, that's your first mistake, piccola sirena. Who ever said I was fair?"

She inhales sharply, and I straighten, placing my hand in front of her to help her stand.

I lift her by the fingers, and her body twists until she's facing me. She's a tall woman, her head level with my shoulders, but she still has to crane her neck to look me in the eye.

When our gazes lock, my stomach drops out and my chest kicks.

Damn it.

She licks her lips. "Noted."

Once we're outside, I face her again, slipping my hands into my pockets because now that I've touched her, I'm finding it hard to think about doing anything else. "So, where to next?"

My original plan wasn't to spend the entire day with her, if I'm being honest. I just wanted to know more about the mystery of Aria's cousin. The woman who sits in on Trent Kingston's business meetings and makes Aria so mad, she turns into a hissing, immature teenager.

But…I'm enjoying Venesa's company. And I need to know if I can trust her or if this is all a ploy on her uncle's orders.

Her face drops.

"What?" I step into her, and she throws her hands up, hovering above my chest.

"Seriously, what is *with* you and personal boundaries?"

"If you don't like it, then push me away," I challenge.

Her palms continue to hover, so close that I can feel the energy sparking off her fingers. But not close enough.

She drops them and sighs. "All right, just tell me where you want to go."

I smile like I'm satisfied, but I can't deny the disappointment settling inside me at her giving in so easily.

"Take me to the Lair."

CHAPTER 10

Venesa

IN THE LAIR'S HEYDAY, AT THE HEIGHT OF THE Prohibition era, it was the hotspot of the Southside. People loved going there for the "music," which really meant the hidden speakeasy in the basement.

When I saw it was up for sale, I knew it was perfect to pitch to Uncle T. I had been waiting for the moment for years, to be honest. Another arm to add to his arsenal, both for washing his money, and because the built-in speakeasy was perfect for an illegal gambling ring.

When you live the formative years of your life being the product of someone's vices, you know how to extrapolate them. Liquor and gambling: my father's downfall and my way of making Uncle T money.

I never told Uncle T I spent every weekend there as a kid while my momma waited tables, but I'm sure he knew, despite him not having talked to her since they were teenagers. Even at my granddaddy's funeral, they ignored each other, probably because my uncle was too busy with the family office manager, handling how best he'd utilize taking over the Kingston fortune, since no one could find a trace of a will.

But then again, before Aria had become an enemy, I'd told her all about my momma and the Lair, so no doubt word got around.

Running it now gives me a sense of belonging; it ties me to my roots and allows me to claim some of Momma's history as my own, as lackluster as that history may be.

It's important to me.

Almost as important as that painting hanging in Uncle T's office.

Apparently, Granddaddy used to preach to him and Momma about how whoever held the painting held the power, and I think Uncle T may have taken that phrase too literally.

Even though Momma chose my father over the family, that painting showed up on our doorstep, and I'll never forget how serious she was when she told me it was her most prized possession. That if anything ever happened to her, she wanted me to have it. Made me pinky promise right then and there. It's the only promise I ever made her, and it burns something fierce knowing I can't keep it.

At the time, I didn't understand why she hid it away behind a loose panel in the bedroom closet if she loved it so much, but after Uncle T swiped it before she was even buried in the dirt, I started to get the gist.

Enzo's driver, Scotty, glances at us from the rearview mirror, his eyes eating me up when he thinks I'm not looking. I send him a wink, enjoying the way a blush rises to his angular cheeks.

He's a cute kid. Young, probably a few years younger than me, but still...*cute*.

"Keep your eyes on the road." Enzo's voice is sharp.

Scotty jumps, his gaze swinging back to the street and his grip tightening on the steering wheel.

"Definitely one of your *minions*," I tease.

Enzo stares at me with a blank expression, his hand coming up to rub at his jaw. "He's my cousin. How much longer until we're there?"

I try not to react to the sudden coldness in his tone, and I glance out the window. "A couple of minutes."

"Not the best area," he notes, following my gaze.

I shrug. "I like it here."

He looks at me then. "Because you like overcoming adversity?"

"Because I like to put money back into the community that raised me."

He looks surprised, adopting a thoughtful expression. "This is where you grew up?"

"About three blocks down that way and to the left." I point out the window. "A small apartment with smoke-stained walls and roaches that loved to hide in our dishwasher, but it was home."

"Until it wasn't."

I nod in agreement, a pang of grief hitting me in the chest. "Until it wasn't."

It surprises me he doesn't ask more questions about why I grew up with nothing, why my momma wouldn't take any money from her family when the Kingstons are the backbone of Atlantic Cove. But then again, maybe my saying just that much was enough. I'm sure Aria has plenty to say on the matter if he asks.

We pull into the Lair's parking lot, the purple neon sign gleaming against the darkening sky. By the time I've gotten my seat belt off, Scotty is already opening my door, his hand gripping mine to help me stand.

"What a gentleman," I purr.

"Only when I see a lady." He winks. His black hair is slicked back with so much gel, the streetlights reflect off the top.

"You should teach your cousin some of those manners, cutie."

"Please, I taught this kid everything he knows." Enzo appears at my side a second later and prods me toward the entrance. "The Lair," he muses. "So, this is all yours?"

"My baby, and the only one I'll ever have, God willing," I say.

His brows lift. "You don't want kids?"

"You do?"

He slips his hands into his pockets. "Never thought about it any other way. In my life, it's expected."

"Ah." I nod, my stomach souring at the thought of Aria bearing his children.

A reminder I need, to be honest—since my vagina has apparently decided Enzo is her ideal mate and he's literally the most off-limits person to me in the world.

I'm not sure why the thought of that makes my stomach drop.

"Gotta get those heirs, right?" I joke, shaking off the weird feeling.

His jaw tightens, but he doesn't reply, twisting his upper body to glance around. "Where's your security?"

I grin, gesturing to myself. "You're looking at it, darlin'."

He frowns, and I don't like it, so I walk over to him, then reach up and smooth out the crease between his brows before I realize what I'm doing. He stares down at me, and it's only when our eyes lock that I realize how close we're standing, how I just touched him without a second thought, and how my fingers are tingling to do it again.

I suck in a quick breath, my hand hanging in the air between us, frozen in space.

A throat clears, and I snap out of it, taking a giant step back, a flush creeping onto my cheeks as I glance at Scotty, who has a goofy grin on his face.

"You two gonna just stand there with stars in your eyes all night, or are we gonna go inside and get a drink?" he says.

"I'm gonna run upstairs and change, okay?" I dip my face down to hide the way touching Enzo affected me. "Go in and make yourselves comfortable."

Enzo looks up to the second floor of the building. "What's upstairs, the offices?"

"My apartment."

His brows rise. "You *live* here?"

"Yep," I say, popping the *p*. "You got an issue with that?"

He shakes his head, but that line is back again, creasing between his brows. "Is it safe?"

"How many times do I have to tell you I can take care of myself before you believe me?"

I make my tone light, but he doesn't take the bait, his brows dropping like he's genuinely concerned for my safety. He runs a hand through his hair and tugs on the roots, sighing. "Yeah, whateva."

I've realized that when he's trying to hide an emotion, his accent gets thicker, and I wish I didn't find it endearing, but I do.

"Okay. Whateva," I mimic with a grin.

He chuckles, dark and husky, hitting me right between the legs. "Real cute." And then he steps closer, because apparently invading my space is his favorite thing to do, and his gaze drops to my mouth.

My stomach tightens.

Enzo shouldn't be looking at me like this, and I shouldn't like it when he does.

"Yo, it's fucking *buggy* out here. Can we go inside?" Scotty complains, smacking at his arm.

Enzo groans and runs his fingers through his hair, looking over at him. "Would you shut the fuck up?"

Scotty puts his hands up in surrender. "My bad, E. It's not my fault mosquitoes love me. I've got sweet blood, you know?"

"You've got sweet blood," Enzo repeats in a bland tone.

"That's what I said." Scotty's eyes widen. "Imagine if vampires were real? I'd be fucked. Or maybe *fucked*, which wouldn't be so bad."

Enzo cuts him a sharp look.

"What'd I do?" Scotty asks, throwing his thumb toward Enzo. "This guy, like a brother to me, but treats me like this. Can you believe it?"

"Like a brother?" Enzo laughs, pointing a finger back at him. "More like you're my *mother.* Always on my ass, ever since you were a kid."

"Well, where else am I supposed to go?" Scotty looks around, his arms out to his sides.

"Christ, go *inside*."

A giggle bursts out of me, my hand slapping against my mouth to stop it, but it's too late. It's cute to see Enzo interact with his family, even if it is him acting like he's annoyed. I can tell there's love between them, and it's charming.

It also makes a pang hit my sternum because that love is something I've always dreamed of having. I've never had that dynamic with anyone, and it's so easy when watching them to imagine a giant table filled with laughter and lighthearted jokes. A family.

A *real* one. Like you see in the movies.

I've never experienced anything even close to that.

"Scotty, I hear there are *very* cute servers inside who you can flirt with." I smile at him. "Use that 'lady' line on them. They'll eat it up."

Enzo's still standing *so* close, and I need to get away for a second, if only so I can take a breath.

"You better go with him," I say. "Make sure he stays out of trouble."

"Yeah, E. Let's go look at the *ladies*." Scotty wags his brows when Enzo walks toward him, reaching out and patting him on the back of the shoulder as they finally disappear inside.

I let out a wavering breath and stare down at my hands, realizing I've curled them so tightly into fists, my nails are cutting crescent moons into my palms. Shaking them out, I roll my neck and make my way inside too.

Twenty minutes later, my attempts at recentering myself have all been for naught because I'm standing in front of my vanity, rubbing my loose black tourmaline crystal for protection until my fingers feel raw, working up the motivation to go back downstairs.

I've reapplied my makeup, making the lipstick extra red like a coat of arms, and slid into my favorite slinky silk dress. Every step of putting myself together feels like a puzzle piece clicking into place, but I'm still off my game, and I know it has everything to do with the dark, dangerous, and completely off-limits man downstairs in my restaurant.

The one who belongs to my cousin.

I texted Fisher to meet me up here, and he's leaning against the doorframe of my studio, watching me as I continue to pet my crystal in front of my full-length mirror like it will solve all my problems.

"What's wrong?" he asks.

I glance at him through the reflection. "What makes you think something's wrong?"

He straightens and moves into the room until he's standing just behind me, looking over my shoulder with a pinched brow and a slight frown on his face. He reaches out and takes the crystal from my hand before placing it on top of my dresser. "Your energy is off."

"My energy's fine." I grab my quartz ring while I say it, though, and slip it on my finger. *Just in case.*

Fisher chuckles, and his arms wrap around my waist, hugging me to him while he trails his hand down my side until he's holding my palm in his, his gaze falling on my jewelry. "Whatever you say, Short Stack."

I lean into his chest before smirking at him in our reflection. "You can never be too careful."

"Well, that's good, because we've got a situation," he says.

Relief pours through me at finding a reason to put off going back and being in Enzo's presence. I nod and push away from him, leaning forward to fluff out my hair. "Good."

Fisher moves and plops down on the edge of my bed, resting back on his elbows. "What do you mean, 'good'?"

"I've been Lover Boy's lapdog all day long, and I need something else to do for a while. So, 'good' because now I get to play." I spin around and face him, running my hands down my sides. "What do you think?"

He whistles. "I'd do you."

"You'd do anyone."

"What can I say?" He grins. "I'm an equal opportunist."

I brush my hair from my face and sit down next to him. "So, what's up?"

"There's some idiot downstairs counting cards in the game room. He's pissing people off."

"Is he good at it?"

Fisher's brow quirks. "At cheating us out of money? Yeah, he's not bad. Not from around here, I think."

My mind immediately goes to Enzo. "Yeah, that seems to be a theme right now."

Fisher's face drops into something more serious, and he tilts his head. "You want me to get rid of E? He doesn't have to be here right now."

I give him a sharp look. "Don't be ridiculous. Just…keep an eye on him while I go handle things, okay?"

"What if he asks where you are?"

"He probably will," I relent, sinking my teeth into my bottom lip and chewing. "Bring him down, then, I guess."

Fisher's brows shoot up to his hairline. "Bring him *down*? To the card room?"

I shrug. "Why not? He's about to be family, right?"

"Yeah but, V…it's—"

"It is what it is," I say, cutting him off. "Don't be stupid and get on his bad side trying to protect me, okay? Especially when I'm not asking for it."

Fisher blows out a breath. "Don't ask me to do that, Short Stack. I'll always protect you."

My chest warms at his words, and I grip his hands,

bringing him in for a hug. I sink into his hold, letting his embrace comfort me in a way that I never let anyone else.

"I don't want you to be involved in anything to do with him. Or *Aria*." I pull back slightly to look him in the eyes, and even now I can see the pain lingering in them. Years of heartbreak that he's covered up and tried to bury. "I *really* don't want to have to kill her for hurting you again."

He laughs, but it's shaky. "She can't hurt me."

"She can, Gup. You can lie to everyone else, but not to me. I know you loved her, and I know she hid you away like her dirty little secret for years, so if you're tempted, just remember if I have to murder her, then Uncle T will probably murder *me*, and if he doesn't, the Marinos definitely will, and you'll have to live with that on your conscience for the rest of your life."

"I'd replace you pretty easily."

I scoff and shove his shoulder. "Worst best friend *ever*."

"You *are* my best friend, Short Stack," he murmurs. "You know that, right?"

I smile and pull back, reaching up to pat his head. "And you're a good little guppy."

CHAPTER 11

Enzo

I'VE BEEN TRYING TO FIGURE OUT VENESA since the second I laid eyes on her, but after a day of being beside her, I'm just more intrigued.

She's clever. Confident. Kind of a smart-ass. And today, I saw another side, one where she was so goddamn real, it made me forget who she is—who she's related to—and why I'm out with her.

Now that I've been sitting here in this booth for the past hour with no Venesa in sight, feeling like I'm swimming underwater from all the goddamn fish around me, I'm remembering.

I glance down at my phone, sucking on my teeth, when I see another missed call and a text from Aria.

Aria: I miss you! xoxox

She's been blowing up my phone for the past few hours, and I'm sure she's wondering where I am since I never told her, but she knows better than to ask. It's not in her nature to push; she just accepts open and willingly. It's a trait my pops says is perfect for me, and honestly, he's probably right. A mob wife isn't supposed to speak out of turn. They keep their mouths closed and their eyes shut to anything other than what we decide to tell them.

Aria *is* a perfect fit for that. It's just starting to feel like she's not the perfect fit for me, and that's unacceptable. I won't chain her to a life like the one my ma had.

Another night of Pops coming home and losing his temper.

He's always been a harsh man, but it's only been in the past couple of years that he's started to bring his work home with him, taking it out on Ma and anyone else who's in his way.

In a few years, I'll be right behind him and Peppino, doing my part for the family, but I'll never be like him: A man who prefers fear over respect. A husband who sticks his dick in anything that walks and then flaunts it in front of the woman he promised his forever to.

He's stolen the light from Ma. She's a fucking disaster, if I'm being completely honest.

Peppino, the selfish motherfucker, stopped coming around the second he turned eighteen and moved out, no matter how many times I try to tell him that she needs help. That Pops is slowly killing her by coming home smelling like cheap perfume and tossing benzos in her lap to keep her sedated and pliable.

Tonight's bad though. She drank three vodka martinis at dinner alone, and even when I tried to get her to stop, she waved me off.

Vodka makes her handsy, and Pops doesn't like it when Ma punches back.

Eventually, like every other time, the yelling stops, ending with Pops storming out the front door, slamming it behind him. My ma's soft sobs are all that's left behind, filtering through the cracks of the walls and painting themselves on my chest and in my psyche.

Some nights, even my dreams are filled with nothing but that sound.

Sighing, I stand up from my bed and make my way down the hallway and into their bedroom, knowing exactly what I'll find before I find it.

Ma's sitting at her white leather vanity, a half-drunk bottle of vodka at her side and a bottle of pills open and splayed out on the table in front of her. She's hunched over, her black hair fanning across her arms and her head resting on her hands, her back heaving from the cries.

"Ma," I whisper, moving toward her.

She stiffens, straightening up, her mascara-streaked face staring at me in the mirror as she quickly wipes her cheeks. "Hi, baby boy, I didn't mean…"

Her words are sloppy, stringing together and tripping over each other, and my heart squeezes as I take her in.

Fuck Pops for making her this way. I tried once to stand up to him about it, but all it got me was a busted lip, a black eye, and a gun to my temple.

"Shhh," I soothe, coming to stand next to her and brushing her hair off her face. "You okay?"

Her bottom lip trembles, and she shakes her head, another sob pouring from her mouth.

"Come on, Ma. He ain't worth it."

"Don't speak about your father like that," she hisses. "He does his best."

I grit my teeth, not wanting to argue.

Silently, I watch as she grabs the bottle and tips it back, swallowing. I want to take it from her, but who am I to take away the only source of her comfort on the lonely nights?

"That bastard!" she suddenly yells, slamming the liquor down until it sloshes out of the top.

"What can I do?" I ask.

"Go find that puttana your father's fucking and put a bullet in her head." She looks to me with big eyes. "Can you do that?"

I swallow because we both know I can't.

She goes to tip the bottle back again, and this time I do grab it from her. "Come on, Ma. You're killing yourself with this."

"No, stop," she slurs, trying to yank it back.

"Don't make me be the bad guy," I plead, a vise wrapping around my middle and constricting. "Let's go watch a movie. I'll even let you put on that one you love. What's it called?"

*More tears roll down her face. "*Casablanca.*"*

"Yeah." I roll my eyes playfully. "The things I do for you, honestly."

She sighs and nods, gripping my forearm as she stands. Suddenly, she covers her mouth and keels over, vomiting at my feet. The stench is enough to make me want to throw up, but I bite it back.

This isn't the first time it's happened.

"I'm sorry, Enzo," she cries, dropping to her knees, gripping my arms like I'm her lifeline. "He just… I'm so…"

"It's okay, Ma." A knot lodges itself in my throat. "Do you want to just lie down?"

She nods, whimpering, and I maneuver us around the mess and take her to her bed. Gingerly, I help change her into fresh pajamas and then slip her under the covers, brushing her hair back and pressing a kiss to her head.

"I should kill him for doing this to you," I whisper.

Her eyes widen, and her voice is clearer than it's been all night. "Don't you ever say that again out loud."

"Ma…"

"You promise me right now you won't ever, ever go against your father. He's dangerous, and he's your family. You hear me? You don't step out of line, and you don't give him any reason to hurt you."

Her words settle in my gut like a boulder.

"Promise me," she repeats, her words slurring again.

"Okay, Ma. I promise."

That was the last promise I ever made her because the next morning she was dead. Swallowed a bottle of pills and ended her own misery.

A fresh drink is placed on the table and snaps me out of

the memory, even though I didn't order one, and I glance up at the server who set it down, nodding my thanks. She smiles, a cute little sprite of a thing, most likely an attempt to keep me distracted from the fact Venesa is nowhere to be found.

But clearly, I can't forget Venesa, no matter how much I wish I could. I'd *love* to get her out of my goddamn brain for a single second.

"This place is nicer than it looks from the outside," Scotty notes, sipping from his club soda and bobbing his head to the live singer. "Good jams too."

I hum my agreement, although I'm not a big music guy—so what would I know about if it sounds good?—but I keep my eyes on the stage, where some dude with a guitar croons anyway.

Where the fuck is Venesa?

I should never have let her disappear, but it didn't cross my mind she might ditch me.

She should know there's no place she can hide, especially since she told me there's virtually no security keeping people away from where she works *and* where she lives.

Although maybe she was lying about that. I'm still not sure what her game is.

I sip my drink, focusing on the burn as it sears down my throat instead of the anxiety scraping at my insides. She's got about five more minutes before I tear the place down to find her.

"So this is Venesa's, or is it a Kingston spot?" Scotty asks, looking around the room.

"Kingston, I think."

My eyes ghost over the patrons again. It's about half-full, which isn't that surprising since it's a Wednesday night, but you'd think Trent, being the actual owner of the joint, would try harder to bring in more business.

"You know, all Betty talks about is how much she hates that motherfucker," Scotty says.

I huff out a breath and lean back in the booth, glancing around for Venesa again.

"Fascinating," I intone.

"I *know.*" Scotty's eyes light up, thinking I actually want to hear about it. "Never shuts up about him and how all he does is bring in those 'New Jersey Italians' to the area."

My head snaps to him.

He lets out a chortle. "Says it right to my face. Can you believe that? Like she doesn't realize *I'm* Italian. And I tell her, 'Hey, lady, you gotta watch your mouth around me,' you know? I'm getting offended."

"What do you mean, 'New Jersey Italians'?"

I'm curious because the De Lucas, a New Jersey family, are under our control, but I've never heard a single peep about any of them coming down here or dealing with Trent Kingston.

Scotty shrugs. "Just what I said, I guess. I didn't ask, because once Betty yaps, you can never shut her up. And you know what else? She's always shoving food down my throat. Every time I walk in the front door of the fucking place, she's trying to feed me."

I smirk. "You could use some meat on your bones, kid."

Scotty puffs out his chest. "I work out."

"Listen, I want you to keep an ear out, and if she says anything else about New Jersey, you let me know, understand?"

He nods. "I can do that."

I cock a brow and lean in. "And stop listening to so much gossip, or you'll end up in the kitchen cooking Sunday dinners with your mother instead of on the streets for me."

"It's not my fault everyone likes to tell me their business." He waves me off and then looks around. "I *am* surprised Kingston lets a bitch run this place for him, though."

"*Stai zitto*," I snap, the word *bitch* grazing across my skin like a razor and putting me back in my bad mood.

Scotty's eyes widen, and his back hits the booth in surprise. "*Jesus*, what crawled up your ass?"

"Buh, buh, buh." I open and close my hand like it's a mouth. "You're like a bird, always chirping about *nothing*. I didn't bring you here to talk my fucking ear off."

Scotty mimics zipping his lips closed, then throws his hands in the air like I've got him at gunpoint. "Just trying to make conversation. You know, you're a real grump lately."

"You're telling me you like being here?"

He sits back in the booth. "It ain't so bad. Little hot, but that just means the girls wear fewer clothes."

I chuckle when he waggles his eyebrows. Scotty may annoy me, but I remember ten years ago when I was nineteen and ready to take on the world. "Yeah, well, if you want to have any hope of ever getting a girl to go from fewer clothes to *no* clothes? You gotta stop calling them bitches. They don't really like that, you know?"

Suddenly, I see Fisher, his ridiculous blue-tipped hair sticking straight up and shiny like it's got a glass coat locking the mohawk in place.

"You see that guy over there?" I jerk my chin toward Fisher.

"Yeah," Scotty replies.

"I want to talk to him."

Scotty salutes me dramatically and slips from the booth, buttoning up the front of his suit jacket and maneuvering through the room until he's standing next to Fisher.

I'm not sure what it is about this guy, but he makes my skin crawl, and seeing him *here*? I don't like it.

Are he and Venesa really together?

My chest burns at the thought.

Fisher straightens off the wall when Scotty approaches, crossing his arms and frowning. Scotty leans in and says something, and then they both look my way.

Is he going to make things difficult? I'll be forced to make an example out of him for the disrespect, and the thought of it makes me hum with anticipation. It's been a long time since my knuckles have felt the sting of flesh hitting flesh.

I wish the motherfucker would.

That hum fizzles quickly into disappointment when Fisher makes his way over without a fight before stopping in front of my booth.

"Look what the cat dragged in," he says in singsong

when he reaches me, slipping his hands in the back pockets of his ripped jeans. "You here for the entertainment?"

I take a slow sip of my drink. "Where's Venesa?"

Fisher tilts his head, like he's assessing me. "If she didn't tell you, then maybe she doesn't want you to know."

I give him a blank look. "I didn't ask what *she* wants. This is about what *I* want, and what I want is to know where Venesa is and why she's wasting my time making me look like a fool sitting out here for nothing."

Fisher grins. "She *has* always been good at knowing exactly what someone is."

I smile thinly. "Scotty." I look toward my little cousin while he leans up against the edge of the booth. "We're being rude, don't you think?"

He crosses his arms. "Starting to think so, E."

Fisher's confidence deflates, and he fidgets, shifting on his feet. "It's all good."

"Nah, see…where I come from, we introduce ourselves properly." I slide out of the booth until I'm towering over him and place my hand on his shoulder, squeezing until he flinches. "I apologize I haven't done that. Now, take me to Venesa, or I'll make sure you know exactly who I am. You get me?"

Fisher's nostrils flare, and he grits his teeth as he jerks his head up and down in a short stiff movement. "She's downstairs."

I release his shoulder and wave my arm. "Lead the way, sweetheart."

Scotty shakes his head and laughs, straightening up and slapping Fisher on the back. "You'll get used to E's sweet nothings. It's how he got his nickname, you know? He likes to kiss you a bit before he fucks ya."

We follow Fisher around the tables scattered throughout the room, past the bar and the main stage, and into a corridor that's lined with wooden walls. It's dark and narrow and smells like stale air, and I assume it's where the offices and storage areas are. Maybe the coolers too.

Fisher doesn't stop until we're at the back of the building, the exit sign casting a dim red glow across the darkened hallway. There's a small spiral staircase to the left of us that winds up to a door.

"I thought you said she was downstairs."

"She is," Fisher replies. He presses on one of the wooden panels lining the wall, and it opens, revealing a staircase leading down and disappearing into the shadows.

Interesting.

I turn to Scotty. "Stay here, and if you don't hear from me in ten minutes, you know what to do."

He eyes the basement and slicks his fingers through his dark hair before leaning back, his left foot kicking up and resting against the wall.

Fisher grins. "Nervous?"

I don't reply.

Our footsteps echo off the concrete as we make our way down the stairs, and then we're in a large hallway, closed rooms lining each side. We pass by all of them, heading straight to the back, where a large steel door set in the wall. Fisher knocks twice, and someone slides a small panel open, their eyes peering out before they unlock it from the other side.

When we walk into the space, it's like we've been transported into another world.

The walls are a deep-brown wood, with coffered ceilings and crystal chandeliers drench the room in a soft yellow glow. There's a bar that lines the far side with high-end liquors on glass shelving against a mirror backdrop, and gambling tables are interspersed throughout with burgundy chairs and felt tabletops, dealers perched behind every single one.

It's busy, much busier than upstairs, with groups of people huddled around the tables. Some are in suits, others in button-downs with rolled-up sleeves, and all of them are doing one thing.

Gambling.

My eyes coast over the area, taking inventory.

"There's our girl." Fisher nods toward the back of the room.

My eyes zoom in on where he's gesturing, finding Venesa immediately, and when I do, I almost wish I hadn't. She's sitting at the far table, sidled up next to a young guy in a black polo, wearing sunglasses like a douchebag. She's changed since I saw her, those casual cutoff shorts that stuck to her ass like a second skin gone, but she's in something just as devastating: a thin black silk dress that flows to her ankles. Her legs are crossed, and the fabric is split, just like it was the first time I met her, framing the smooth skin of her thigh.

An irrational anger rips through my chest, as I realize she's down here fucking around with other men instead of upstairs with me.

I don't appreciate how the entire Kingston family thinks it's okay to waste my time.

Flat-screen TVs line the walls, the buzz of a fight ringing from their speakers and into my ears, but I don't pay attention to it, and as soon as Venesa throws her head back and laughs, every man turns *their* attention toward her too. She reaches out and grasps the forearm of the guy sitting next to her. And I've had just about enough of being ignored.

"You can go," I dismiss Fisher.

Fisher inhales, his eyes bouncing back and forth between where Venesa sits and where I am before he acquiesces and leaves, the way I knew he would. He may walk around here like he's a big dog, but I can spot a coward a mile away.

There's an empty chair perched against the far wall, directly in front of where Venesa's sitting, and I take my time crossing the room toward it.

I brush *just* behind her, so close that her hair rustles as I walk by. Her body stiffens, but she doesn't look at me.

When I reach the wall, I unbutton my suit jacket and then take it off entirely, placing it on the back of the chair, going for slow and relaxed, like I don't have a care in the world.

Now she looks, and my eyes lock on hers immediately and don't let go.

I sit down and roll up the sleeve of my shirt until it's just above the elbow, my ink making its full appearance from beneath the fabric.

Her gaze drops to watch the movement, skimming along my body and resting on where my gun is on display, holstered at my side. I repeat the motion of rolling up my other shirtsleeve until both my forearms are exposed, and then I lean forward, resting my elbows on my knees. A lock of my hair falls on my forehead with the motion, and I run my fingers through the strands, pushing it back into place. Then I quirk a brow at her.

She licks her lips, and then, just like that, her attention is back on whoever the guy is next to her. But I see through her mask, and I know she's rattled because I'm down here, the same way *I'm* rattled whenever I see her.

I can't remember a single time Aria's looked at me with that kind of heat. Or maybe she has and I've just never felt it.

My chest twists with self-condemnation, and I tear my gaze away from Venesa, pulling out my phone to text Scotty that he can go wait in the car.

Venesa leans in and whispers something into the guy's ear, and he reaches out to grip her thigh possessively. A spark of irritation ignites in my stomach.

Still, I sit and wait patiently while they continue the hand of poker.

The longer I watch them interact, the more I'm sure she's playing him. It isn't the woman I've been with all day. This is someone else entirely.

She's just as striking to watch, though. Like I'm seeing another layer of her, uninterrupted.

Truthfully, I could stare at her all night in all her forms and never get sick of it.

The man she's with wins the poker hand, and as soon as he does, Venesa pulls him from the table, linking her fingers with his and dragging him from the room. She looks back once, flashing me a warning glare before she returns her attention to the guy. She stumbles in her heels like she's drunk, and that confirms it to me, because I may have only known her for two days, but every time there's been alcohol for everyone else, she hasn't taken a sip.

Definitely playing him.

And even though I know that, even though I can logically rationalize that I've walked into something she's probably trying to handle without me, it doesn't stop me from standing and following them out of the room.

Because fuck her if she thinks I'll allow her to disappear with another man on her arm when she came here with me.

CHAPTER 12

Venesa

ENZO MARINO IS THE WORST KIND OF DISTRACTION.

His presence down here isn't a surprise. It's just…more of a disturbance than I expected.

Luckily, I had already hooked the card-counting thief Fisher told me about—Sean—with a bit of cleavage and dirty, slurred words whispered in his ear.

The number one reason I have Fisher be the face of so many things for me here is because anonymity is a superpower, especially when you're a woman in a male-dominated world. Every weapon in your arsenal is important.

And everyone in Atlantic Cove already knows Fisher as the town fuckup. Emancipated from his folks when he was fifteen, he's been on his own since then, running the streets and making a general mess of things until I started having him work for my family.

"What are you gonna do with me?" Sean asks, his voice thick with lust as I lead him down the dark hallway.

Fisher's right; he isn't from around here.

I giggle, stumbling into him. "Oh, honey, what am I *not* gonna do with you?"

He groans, his disgusting hand gripping my ass, and I let out a whimper, pretending I like the feel of his meaty paw on me.

"My car's out front." He grunts.

I shake my head and run my fingers up his chest. "I don't think I can wait."

Looking around, I feign ignorance to the layout of the basement, widening my eyes as I point at the door on his left. "You think it's unlocked?"

He follows my gaze and grins, pulling me behind him. "Only one way to find out."

It *is* unlocked, but I already know that because I'm the one who unlocked it.

As soon as we're inside, he spins us around, shutting the door and slamming me against it. It hurts, and I wince at the stab of pain radiating up my spine. *Jerk.*

He trails sloppy kisses along the side of my neck, and I bite back the urge to gag from how moist his breath is against my skin.

I push him away, prodding him with my fingertips across the darkened room and toward the stainless steel table bolted to the ground in the center.

Sean jolts when his legs hit the edge, and he finally takes

inventory of where we are. His head flicks from side to side, no doubt looking at the floor-to-ceiling saltwater tank that spans the entire left wall, and then glances over to the metal storage units on the other side.

"Damn, it's huge back here. Are those *fish*?" He squints.

I grip his chin and physically twist his face until he's focused on me. "I'm more interested in how big *you* are, darlin'."

He falls back onto the table with the smallest push, and then I climb on top of him, straddling his hips and dropping until I'm pinning him by the lap.

The trick with seduction is to move too fast for their silly little brains to keep up. I don't want him to have time to formulate questions. Like why I showed up out of nowhere and led him into this room or why there's an empty table sitting in the middle of it.

I just want him to think he's about to get fucked.

Weak men always let their dicks do the thinking, and strong women know how to take advantage of that.

Sean's hands grip my hips, and I cover his fingers with mine, moving his arms until they're above his head, and press firmly while I simultaneously grind down onto his erection.

"*Fuck* yeah," he groans.

"You ever let a woman take control, honey?" I whisper in his ear, leaning over him until my breasts brush across his face. "Keep your arms there."

I'm hoping my words will distract him enough while I grab at the chains affixed to the underside of the table.

Bas had this design custom made. He loves to strap people down so they can't defend themselves because he's twisted and sadistic.

The door to the room swings open and cracks against the concrete wall just as I get the metal cuff above the lip of the table. Sean tries to sit up, but I shove him back down with my free hand and quickly secure both his wrists, tightening the chains just enough so every movement will dig into his skin.

He jerks violently. "What the *hell*?"

When he pulls against the restraints, the chains clank loudly, and I cringe.

It's a distinct noise, one that drives me up a wall. I make a mental note to ask Bas if we can change them out for a different material because I can't *stand* the metal on metal.

"Well, isn't this cozy?"

I sigh loudly at Enzo's deep and raspy voice, then jump off the table.

Sean continues to spit profanities and kick his legs in the air until his entire body is flopping on the surface like a fish desperate for water.

"I just *knew* you'd show up," I say, turning to face Enzo.

He beams at me. "Let's not waste time pretending you didn't want me in here."

"Please," I scoff.

"You didn't even lock the door."

I shrug, looking at my nails like I can't be bothered. "An oversight."

"What the *hell* is going on?" Sean spits.

Clack. Clack. Clack.

I roll my neck, trying to ignore the clanking noise of Sean's chains, and look down at him with a grin. "Shhh." I pat his cheek. "Adults are talking, sugar."

"Fuck you."

"Hey," Enzo snaps, his eyes narrowing. "Watch your mouth."

"Do you mind?" I ask, scowling at him. "I can handle this."

His lips twitch like he's fighting back a smile, but he leans against the wall and crosses his ankles, waving his hand at the room like he's giving me permission to continue. The muscles of his forearm flex with the motion, and a shot of arousal hits me.

Not the time, Venesa.

"Listen, I don't know what kind of kinky shit you're into, but I'm *not* here for this," Sean says, pulling at his restraints again and hissing as the metal digs into his skin.

A laugh bubbles out of me because how can he possibly still think I brought him back here for sex?

"You hear that, Lover Boy?" I pout, flicking my gaze to Enzo. "He thinks we're kinky."

Enzo's eyes spark. "He's got no idea."

Butterflies explode in my stomach, and I feel my cheeks heating, so I drop my head and focus on Sean again to hide my reaction.

"Honestly, I find it a little rude to presume." I move

closer to the edge of the table, staring down at Sean's face, enjoying the way reality is settling into his features. All the classic signs are there: the widening of the eyes, his forehead lines creasing deeper, sweat forming at his temples as panic sets in and triggers that pesky fight-or-flight instinct.

"I'm curious, Sean. If you're not here for *this,* then what are you here for?"

He doesn't reply, but his eyes flick to Enzo and back nervously.

"You need me to teach you some manners?"

"Let me go, you crazy bitch," he grits out. "And keep *him* away from me."

"If you don't teach him some, I will," Enzo cuts in. His voice is smooth and dark, like glassy water beneath a stormy sky. A shiver rolls down my spine.

"And they say chivalry is dead." I grin widely at Sean.

I run one of my nails along the side of his face, digging in just enough to leave a red line on his pasty cheek.

He jerks from my touch, and my smile grows. "You never said where you were from, darlin'."

His thin lips tighten, and a flash of panic coasts across his gaze.

Oh. I don't like that at all.

My grin drops, and I grip his chin harshly until his lips mash together from the force.

Originally, I assumed he was here to cheat me out of money, but that face he just made? That reeks of secrets he'd rather I didn't know.

I release him with a sneer, his head smacking against the table as I do, and then I walk to the other side of the room, near the shelving units where Bastien likes to keep his favorite tools.

The third drawer down has a line of different knives placed strategically from largest to smallest, and I pick up the meat cleaver, enjoying the weight of it in my hand.

Sean's voice is still in the background, spitting profanities left and right, his feet banging against the table and that ever-constant *clank*, *clank*, *clank* of metal on metal reverberating through the room. But it's all muted to me now. There's a pleasant buzzing in my ears, adrenaline pumping through my veins and muffling the outside noise. I'm in the zone. Focused. *Happy*.

When I spin around, Enzo's gaze sears into me, snapping from the cleaver in my hand to Sean and then to my face. There's a flicker of surprise, his features lifting and his eyes growing wider, but it only lasts for a millisecond, and then something else takes over. Something darker.

It feels like approval.

Satisfaction whips through me, sending my heart racing, because that's what I'm *constantly* craving from Uncle T but rarely getting. Right here with Enzo, it's like he's giving it freely and unrestrainedly.

It's a heady rush.

I take my time walking back to Sean, and then I look up at Enzo. "The least you can do is make yourself useful. Be a dear and come lock his legs down for me. Cuffs are on the underside of the table." I run my fingertip along the edge of the blade and glance at Sean. "Cleavers are fun, aren't they?"

Sean's eyes flick up to me and widen, but then his attention goes back to Enzo, who's got a gun pointed at his shins while he secures them to the table.

"Cat got your tongue, honey?" I continue. "Couldn't get you to shut up to save my life when you thought you were getting laid, and now suddenly you've got nothing to say?"

He stays quiet now, not even fighting against his restraints. I walk toward my aquarium, my heels clicking on the slick flooring, and place the cleaver down on a rolling table sitting next to a cabinet. I open the cupboard, skimming my fingers along the glass vials until I find the two I'm looking for.

"Something you should know about me is I *really* don't enjoy when people won't answer my questions." I move the glass bottles over to the rolling table and then grab disposable latex gloves and two separate syringes before placing them side by side. Spinning around, I smile at my little captive, feeling the burn of Enzo's stare.

Having him here while I do this is oddly erotic, like he's witnessing me in a vulnerable state, and it makes the euphoria coating my veins spark like fireworks.

I push the table over until it's next to Sean's head and pick up the gloves, slowly pulling them onto my hands with a satisfying pop against my skin when they're fitted. "I like it even less when people lie."

"I didn't lie!" Sean blurts.

"Well, you surely aren't telling me the truth." I pick up the glass vial labeled *verrucotoxin* and flip it upside down until it fills the syringe. "I noticed you watching my pookies in the aquarium over there when you first came in. They're beautiful, aren't they? My favorites are the two stonefish right there." I point to one of my babies that's lying on the ground. "It's hard to see them because they're masters of camouflage. Similar to what you tried and failed to do tonight. You could learn a lot about flying under the radar from them, honestly."

He grunts.

"*This*"—I flick the side of the syringe—"is the venom extracted from their dorsal fins. I'm afraid it's incredibly toxic to humans. Quite painful, actually, the way it works. For example, if I injected you here..."

I press the needle into the hollow point between his fingertips.

He jerks, trying to move away, but since he's chained by his wrists and ankles, the most he accomplishes is a subtle shift and some nasty scrapes from where the metal digs into his skin.

"It would cause intense pain, spreading all the way up your arm in a matter of minutes. If left alone, your skin would bleed and deteriorate in front of our very eyes. And then, of course, the venom would spread into your lungs, constricting your airways, making you choke on nothing while your nervous system seizes. Beautiful, really. Like art." I remove the needle from his skin. "But I'm fair, darlin'. So you tell me why you're here trying to steal from me, and I'll use the meat cleaver instead, chopping off one of your greedy little hands instead of injecting you with my pookie's poison. What do you say?" I lean over until his eyes are staring up into mine. "Do we have a deal?"

He doesn't reply, and that just irritates me. I'm being more than fair here, all things considered.

I sigh. "Is it because I'm a woman?"

"It's because you're a cunt," Sean forces out through gritted teeth.

I roll my eyes at the tired slur, but before I can say anything else, Enzo is there, gripping Sean's face so tightly, I can see the indentations of his teeth through his cheeks. "How many times do I have to tell you to watch your fucking mouth?"

My stomach flips.

I've never had somebody defend me like this before.

The veins on the back of Enzo's hands run up his sinewy forearms and disappear under the rolled sleeves of his button-down, and I swear to God, I really, *really* want to not be affected, but I'm also not dead, and I can't help the way heat floods through my body at the sight of him.

"You ever sucked a cock?" Enzo continues. "Say another word about her and I'll cut off yours and shove it down your throat. Give you some practice. You understand?"

I beam over at him. Now *that's* inspired.

He looks up at me and winks before releasing Sean's face.

Sean clearly doesn't value his life, or maybe he just is severely underestimating who he's in the room with, because he turns his head and *spits* on me.

My body physically vibrates from the anger rushing through me, and Enzo backhands him so hard, his jaw cracks as it hits the table.

"The fuck is wrong with you?" Enzo asks, incredulous. "Did you not hear what I just said?"

Sean groans, his cheek still pressed against the metal of the table.

Enzo tenses, and I'm a little nervous he *will* shove something down his throat, which would be detrimental because if he's choking on a dick then he can't tell us what I want to know. So I rest my hand on Enzo's forearm, ignoring the way it makes my palm tingle and my heart skip a beat.

"How come you get to have all the fun?" I say.

My words wash away the fury covering his face, and something soft takes its place. A piece of his hair has fallen just over his left eyebrow, and I reach out, smoothing it back into place. He licks his lips, gives a curt nod, and takes a step back.

And now I'm even more turned on.

Inappropriate, Venesa.

Turns out Lover Boy looks pretty good when he's a little unhinged.

I smile appreciatively before clearing my throat and focusing on Sean.

"I'm sure even a guy like you gets the precarious situation you've found yourself in. You come into my place of business and try to cheat me out of money? Surely you understand how I can't just let you walk away from that."

"Counting cards isn't illegal, you dumb bitch," he says.

Enzo sighs loudly and cracks his knuckles, but I shoot him a look, and he stays leaned against the wall, crossing his arms with a frown.

I put the tip of the needle in the hollow between Sean's first two fingers and press until it slips under his skin. He hisses and jerks.

"You know, normally I like a dirty mouth, but your repetition is *exhausting*. Where's the creativity? I don't like lazy people."

Silence.

Bending over until my hair brushes against his cheek, I whisper, "Where are you from, sugar?"

"I'm…fuck!"

"I don't *want* to hurt you." I press closer. "Last chance, Sean."

No reply.

I inject the venom and stand back, placing the syringe on the rolling tray.

Sean's body shakes almost immediately, making the chains rattle even more against the steel table, and he grunts.

"Yeah, I know that hurts."

I grab the other vial and show it to him, although his eyes are glossing over, most likely from the pain spreading through his body.

"This is the antidote, and I'll be honest, even though it sounds like a reprieve, I know how to use it to *my* advantage. I can inject you with this just so I can start the process over again. Over and over and over, until you're begging for death."

Sean lets out a yelp, his left arm growing pink.

"My deal's still on the table, Sean. Words will set you free, darlin'." I smile softly and run the back of my gloved hand over his cheek.

He mumbles something I can't understand.

I lean in. "What was that?"

"Ne-New Jersey," he stutters. "I'm from New Jersey."

From the corner of my eye, I see Enzo straighten off the wall.

"What are you doing in South Carolina?" he asks.

I cut him a look but wait for Sean's answer.

Sean's hyperventilating now, sweat pouring down the sides of his forehead and dripping onto the table beneath him. "You," he manages to get out. But his eyes are on Enzo. "I was sent to keep an eye on *you*."

Shock spirals through me, and my widened gaze meets Enzo's narrowed one. I'm not sure why someone is here for him, but having anything or anyone from the Northeast in these parts makes anxiety claw at my insides like a locked-up beast.

There are things my uncle does out there no one can know about. Things Enzo can *never* know.

I pat Sean's cheek. "Good boy."

And then I place the antidote down and pick up the cleaver. Sean's eyes grow wide, and he thrashes against the chains, his body flopping.

“I thought we had a deal!” he screams.

“Are you implying I’m not holding up my end?” I ask, affronted. “You tried to steal from me, Sean. And even worse, you’re here to *spy* on someone who’s about to be my family. You can’t possibly think I’d let you walk away with no repercussions?”

I lift the cleaver and then slam it down on his wrist, gliding it back and forth like a seesaw and smiling when he screams.

CHAPTER 13

Enzo

GODDAMN.

She's unhinged in a visceral way that makes her ruthlessness look like art, and I'm hypnotized by the sight of her.

I've always known *I* was depraved, but it's not until this very moment I see how deep that depravity runs because watching Venesa cut off someone's hand has me realizing that violence does, in fact, turn me on.

It was hard to not intervene after the man wouldn't stop disrespecting her, but I'm glad she stepped in when she did because I probably would have lost control and killed him, after torturing answers out of him, and that would raise too many issues back home.

In the Cosa Nostra, you're not allowed to kill freely. There's a system in place, one that's been there since the old country, and it works for a reason. The boss—in this case, my pops—gives his approval on every single contracted hit. Unsanctioned killings just don't happen, and if they do, there are grave consequences, meaning a bullet in the back of the head. My being the underboss doesn't change that fact, and neither does being in an unfamiliar state with different people.

There's a code. An honor system.

It freaks me out how quickly I would have let all that slip away because I couldn't control my emotions over someone treating Venesa like trash.

And then he says someone sent him to South Carolina for *me*, and it took every ounce of self-control to keep from taking over everything. From shoving her out of the way and torturing the answers out of him myself, but I'm not sure I want Venesa to hear the answers I'd get.

If he's from New Jersey, I have to assume it's the De Luca family who sent him, and if they have a message for me, they can say it to *me* directly.

I glance over.

Venesa's breathing heavily, her arms at her sides and the meat cleaver she just used on the man dangling from her fingers. There are blood spatters decorating her skin and a pool of red beneath the guy's sawed-off hand, leaking over the side of the table and onto the concrete floors. He's passed out, most likely from the stonefish venom she injected him with earlier, and my eyes flick back and forth between her and the gruesome scene.

"Well, now he definitely won't say anything," I joke.

Her lips twitch, her shoulders relaxing. "He will."

I nod, kicking off the wall and taking a few steps toward her. "So what now?"

"Now I inject him with the antivenom so he doesn't die, and I call Bas to make sure our little thief here tells him everything he knows."

"He'll get him to talk?"

Venesa nods, and a few strands of her icy-white hair fall onto her forehead. She swipes them away with the back of her hand, leaving behind a smear of red. "He always does… I'll tell you if he says anything, you know? About why he was here following you."

Good. Hopefully I can find out who he was because I'm finding it increasingly difficult to believe that New Jersey popping up again is a coincidence. Usually, we let the De Luca family do their own thing, as long as they understand it's still *us* they answer to, but if they're down here causing issues unsanctioned, then…

I should tell Pops immediately, but something holds me back. I'm not sure how he'll respond, and the last thing I need is for him to learn information that could make him volatile when I'm not there to try and keep him in check. Besides, if I call him again, he might take it as a personal insult, considering he's convinced we're being tapped.

There's a small rolling table at Venesa's side with two glass bottles and a couple of syringes, and she picks up one of each, flipping the bottle upside down and inserting the needle's tip until the liquid moves into the empty tube. Then she injects it into the man's remaining hand, right between his first two fingers, the same way she originally injected the poison.

Watching her question him felt oddly carnal, like I was witnessing her purge the blackest parts of her soul. It was invigorating and something I've never experienced before—intimate in a toxic type of way, her darkness enabling my own and making it vibrate beneath my skin, desperate to come out and play.

She walks toward the door and gestures for me to follow. "You coming, Lover Boy?"

I'm not sure where we're headed, but after what just happened, I think I'd follow her anywhere.

"Anywhere" ends up being out of the basement of the Lair and up a narrow spiral staircase that leads to her studio apartment.

Right now, she's in her bathroom with the door wide-open, standing in front of a small porcelain sink, gripping the edges, her hair draping over the sides of her face like a cloak while she regulates her breathing.

I say nothing, just lean against the doorframe with my arms crossed and watch her reflection, those dark irises swirling as she stares down at her hands.

"You okay?" I ask.

Her gaze flicks up to mine. "Yeah, fine. You just...weren't supposed to see that."

She turns on the faucet.

I take a step and then another one, putting our bodies so close that I can feel the adrenaline bleeding off her skin and sinking into mine.

Our eyes lock in the mirror.

"I'm glad I did," I say.

She grins, those dimples of hers appearing and dotting the apples of her porcelain cheeks. "Why, so you can use it to blackmail me?"

What she's saying isn't wrong; it *is* beneficial for me to know things like this about the underworld of the Kingstons, but her thinking that's what I'll do bothers me.

I move even closer, my heart kicking my chest when I brush against her.

Her breath hitches, and it pushes that phenomenal cleavage out in a way that has me biting back a curse, because *fuck*. Slowly, I reach around her until she's caged in by my frame, the energy between us dancing like tiny electric shocks along my body.

But I make sure not to touch her.

I *can't* keep touching her. Not right now, not when I'm feeling like this.

Instead, my hands surround hers on the edge of the sink, my thumbs centimeters away from meeting her pinkies.

She looks down at them and shifts on her feet.

When she moves, her ass pushes into me, and I bite the inside of my cheek so hard, I taste blood. I exhale slowly, gritting my teeth so I don't do something crazy like reach out and dig my fingers into the meat of her hips while I drop to my knees, rip off her skirt, and put my mouth on her cunt.

The visual alone...*Christ.*

Self-loathing mixes into the lust I'm feeling like a volatile cocktail; it's an internal war where I'm both the savior and the villain.

I grab a hand towel from where it's hanging on the wall, hyperaware of how she's tracking my every movement. I swear it feels like she's lighting me on fire, and it's fucking torture because I can't give in to the feeling, I don't *want* to give into it...but I can't pull away either.

Placing the cloth under the running water, I find myself wishing the tepid temperature would douse the fervor blanketing the air, but I know better than to assume it will. Instead, we just exist in this vortex of energy until it's physically painful to keep my body from falling into hers, and I have to remind myself she's more off-limits to me than any other woman in the world.

When I take the damp fabric and move it to her right hand, wiping away the specks of blood dotting her skin in slow, methodical motions, my stomach tightens with every pass.

"What are you doing?" Venesa asks in a hushed tone.

"Helping," I reply, although my voice comes out so low and raspy, I'm not positive she hears me.

"You don't have to—"

"Shut up," I snap, squeezing my eyes closed. "Just...stop talking."

When I look at her again, she's staring at me through the mirror, biting the lower corner of that plump red lip, and my heart jumps into my throat because fuck if I don't want to know what that feels like—what it *tastes* like to have her mouth beneath my teeth.

My hand shoots out and grips her hip as I spin her around.

Off-limits.

Her ass bumps into the sink, and I lean in close, making her breasts press against me. It's barely even a graze, but my heart backflips and dives like it's careening off a cliff anyway. I swallow and pray she can't feel how wildly it's beating.

After bringing the towel up to her cheek, I wipe away the specks of blood that dot her face like splatters of paint on a canvas.

That's what she is to me: a work of art.

I wish like hell she weren't.

Her hand flies to my wrist, holding me in place.

She blows out a shaky breath, and I suck in every tremble, over and over, our mouths so close that the heat of her lips warms mine. But I don't bridge that last millimeter of space; instead, I swim in the torture of almost touching, convincing myself that if I try, *almost* will be enough.

I've never experienced an immediate attraction to anyone like this before, and I don't know how to navigate it.

Pain radiates up my cheek from how tightly I'm clenching my jaw, and I use it to ground myself. To distract me from how badly I want to swing her around, bend her over, and sink so deep inside her, I drown.

Off-limits.

Off-limits.

Off-limits.

Finally, I tear myself away, ripping my hand from her hip and dropping the washcloth in the basin.

"All done," I murmur.

"Yeah," she whispers.

I clear my throat. "I should go."

She glances at me from under her long dark lashes, and lust scorches through my chest and up my esophagus until my mouth runs dry. I take a giant step back and then another, pulling at the collar of my shirt, because when the fuck did it get so hard to *breathe*?

After whirling around, I walk away.

"See ya later, Lover Boy," she calls to my back.

I'm in the room again and on her before I can think twice, pushing until she's flush against the sink, and I lean down so my lips skim along the shell of her ear.

"It's Enzo."

And then I turn and leave before I'll do something that both of us will regret.

Because it isn't *her* I'm supposed to want.

The beaches of South Carolina are *not* the same as the Northeast coast.

"Where were you again?" Aria asks me, her floppy sun hat casting a shadow over her face as she leans back in one of the lounge chairs on the Kingstons' private beach.

I toss my head until it hits my own lounger. "How many times do we have to go over this?"

Aria narrows her eyes. "I just don't understand what you could have possibly been doing for *work* while you're here."

Her voice has an edge to it, and it's the first time I've ever heard her be anything other than docile and sweet, at least when she's speaking to *me*.

"Your cousin showed me around." I speak slowly, hoping if I say it clearly enough, it will sink into her head. "Your dad wants me to open up a spot down here. A hotel or whatever."

She pulls down her sunglasses just enough to look at me over the rim. "My cousin."

"Don't do that."

"Do what?"

"Look at me like that, all puppy-eyed and disappointed. You should be happy your family and I are getting along."

A tendril of excitement blossoms in my chest, thinking she's going to argue, going to give me something other than the same monotonous agreement, but she just frowns and pushes her sunglasses back onto her face.

"Just be careful around her...Venesa, I mean." She leans over and brushes her fingertips along my forearm, squeezing. "She likes to take things that don't belong to her. And she's a liar."

"You worried about me, princess?"

She grins, and she looks so damn innocent that guilt slams into my middle and makes me queasy. I lean forward and kiss her, both because I'm getting a headache from her constant questions and also because if I think too hard about what this weird feeling is in my solar plexus, I'll have to come to terms with the fact I'm thinking about Venesa more than I should, even though we just met.

"I just know my cousin is all," she murmurs, running her fingers through the hairs at the nape of my neck before letting go.

She reaches behind her and adjusts the chair until it's flat, then rolls onto her stomach.

"What's with you two anyway?" I ask, both because it's weird, this animosity between them, but also because I can't stop myself from wanting to find out more about Venesa.

Her glossy lips purse into a frown. "She's a bitch."

There's an immediate urge to lash out and tell her to watch her mouth, but instead I laugh, because how am I going to explain telling my *fiancée* not to give some random woman a bad name. Besides, I don't know if I've ever heard Aria call someone a bitch before. "The mouth on you. Where'd that come from?"

"What do you mean?"

"You're different here."

"I'm not different, babe. I'm just…stifled. It makes me cranky."

I look around at the private beach and then back at the

mansion. "Yeah, you grew up in a real prison, princess. I feel sorry for you, truly."

She rolls her eyes. "Just because something looks like freedom doesn't mean it's not a cage."

"And your cousin has something to do with this how? She didn't put you in there." I point to the estate.

"No, she just treats it like it's all supposed to belong to her."

"Sounds a little dramatic."

Aria sighs heavily. "Venesa's mom was the jewel of the Kingston family, but then she chose some deadbeat, alcoholic gambling addict instead of her own flesh and blood. And look how that turned out—the man killed her and then disappeared."

Surprise trickles through me because I didn't realize Venesa's dad was the reason her mother died. "Her husband killed her?"

"Either that, or it was Venesa herself. They never caught the guy."

I give her a look. "But your uncle took Venesa in when her mom died, so she *is* a Kingston, technically."

"Semantics. He should have let the state keep her."

"Aria," I chastise.

"What? It's not *my* daddy's fault his sister gave up her right to everything, and I don't appreciate Venesa thinking she's owed it just because of who she is."

It just doesn't sit right with me how badly she's talking about Venesa. The woman I spent the day with yesterday? She doesn't deserve the disrespect.

My stomach churns from the story and the blasé way Aria tells me about it, like it's just some joke, and for the first time when I look at her, I don't think she's pretty.

"You have any other family members you need to warn me about?" I side-eye her.

She laughs and reaches into her bag, pulling out a magazine. "I don't think so."

"No aunts or uncles or anything like that?" I press.

"I mean, I've got an uncle, but we're not close."

"Oh, yeah?"

"Yeah, Uncle Frankie, but I've only met him a couple of times. He's out in New Jersey, I think." She flips a page in her magazine. "Why?"

My heart stops in my chest. *New Jersey.* "Just curious. You don't talk about your family much."

She giggles. "Well, after we're married, what's yours is mine anyway."

Her words feel like a noose around my neck, but I shove the feeling away because it isn't Aria's fault I suddenly can't keep my shit together.

"So this uncle of yours, Frankie…what's his last name? How come I've never heard of him?"

She gives me a weird look. "Why would you have heard of him?"

I lift a shoulder. "I thought I knew everyone in Jersey."

"Bianchi."

My hackles rise.

There's only one Frankie Bianchi I know of, and he's a

low-grade loan shark who calls himself "Shark Daddy." He's not a made guy, but if we were in a room together, he'd be introduced as a friend of mine, meaning he's connected but not part of the family.

I've never met him myself, but I'm wondering if that needs to change immediately.

Especially if he's *related* to my future wife.

I pick up my phone and shoot off a text to Giovanni.

Me: Find out what you can about Frankie Bianchi and why the fuck we didn't know he was related to Aria.

CHAPTER 14

Venesa

HIS HANDS ARE ROUGHER THAN I THOUGHT they'd be. Larger too, and when they skim up my sides, heat flares deep in my stomach and spreads until it's pooled between my legs.

I'm nothing more than a marionette, dangling from strings he's controlling.

I moan when he reaches beneath my shirt, those calloused fingers skating up the length of my stomach until he's cupping one of my heavy breasts in his palm, creating a friction that has me seeing stars as he manipulates my flesh.

There's no guesswork, no hesitation. Only strong, sure caresses.

It's been *so* long since a man has touched me this well.

His mouth follows the trajectory of his hands, brushing kisses up my abdomen and then along my collarbone, and as he moves, a piece of his black hair falls forward, tickling my skin. I laugh, and when he nips my flesh, that laugh turns into a moan, my own hands reaching out now, grappling to find purchase somewhere on *him*.

I'm not sure how we got to this point, but I don't really care.

The roots of his hair are just as soft as I always imagined, my fingertips running through the silky strands and tugging harshly when his teeth sink into a sensitive spot on me. He groans, and the sound resonates—vibrates—like my body was made to be a conductor for the noise.

"Enzo," I moan, trying to physically force his head down.

The scruff of his jaw grazes the side of my neck, and his hands slip farther until his fingers tangle with mine. He maneuvers my arms above my head, pressing them firmly into the bed. "I love the way you say my name."

His breath is hot against my neck, and then his tongue swipes out like he's desperate to drink me up. His mouth follows with a sensual kiss. And then another. And another, until he's all the way down my body and his lips are skimming against the waistband of my sleep shorts.

I shift, and one of his hands leaves mine, his broad arm locking across my stomach until I'm pinned and unable to move.

A shot of arousal hits me, and I'm so wet, I wonder if it's dripping onto the sheets and whether my thighs would get stuck together if he let them get close enough to touch.

They're not, of course. Enzo's frame is nestled between

them, forcing them to spread so wide, the stretch causes an ache.

His tongue swipes out against the crease of my leg, and my toes curl. I try to stay still because even though he hasn't told me to, it *feels* like there's a silent command in the air, and he's so good at manipulating my body, I just want to relax and let him do whatever he wants.

I'm wound so tight, I'm trembling, and when his nose brushes against the damp fabric of my shorts, right on top of my clit, my thighs slam shut around his head. He chuckles, and his hands shoot out, his fingers pressing into the muscle as he forces my legs back apart.

His nose brushes against my pussy again, and then he sits back and looks at me with a devilish grin before *blowing* on the fabric.

"Enzo, *please*," I beg.

He hums and continues his torture, pressing featherlight kisses—so soft that I question if they're real—right next to where I really need him.

He's driving me crazy.

Those hands of his move from my inner thighs and slip beneath the hem of my shorts, fingertips gliding through the wetness *he*'s causing, like he knows it's there just for him. My insides contract, and my spine stiffens as a shot of pleasure curls through me.

He makes a fist around my shorts with his other hand, right on top of my cunt, and then he leans in—

Bzzzzz.

I shoot up in bed, strands of hair sticking to my clammy face from the perspiration beading along my scalp, my chest heaving from the breaths caused by my dream.

My clit is literally pulsing, I'm so close to coming.

Glancing around, I get my bearings. Small purple-and-black vanity in the corner, refurbished dresser by the door, bathroom to my right.

I'm at home, in my apartment, and the throbbing between my legs is from a damn *dream*.

Groaning, I fall until my back bounces off the mattress, sinking into the Tencel sheets, and I run my hands over my face.

A sex dream about your cousin's fiancé. Great, Venesa.

The worst part is, this isn't the first time it's happened. It's been three days since Enzo was actually here, invading my space and wiping blood from my skin like I was something to be cherished, and dreams like this have happened every. Single. Night. Since.

I wish I could get him the hell out of my system, because this is dangerous. There are so many things he doesn't know, so many things I'll *never* tell him, and even if that weren't the case, I don't *do* things like this.

Attachments. *Liking* someone. I've seen what happens when you latch on to someone else, when you make them your entire personality and let them slowly chip away at who you are until you'd do anything for them…even if it's at the expense of yourself.

Or the kid you're supposed to love more than anything.

Men like Enzo—dangerous, charismatic, intoxicating men—only drag you down, whip you around, and tear you apart until you're nothing but crumpled pieces of paper being blown by the wind.

Getting emotionally attached is a death sentence, and while no one can outrun death, I plan to evade it for as long as possible. Besides, despite my dislike for Aria, I don't actually want to steal her man.

It's beneath me.

But alas, here we are.

Flashes of the dream parade through my memory, making the tension in my body wind tighter and tighter until I'm about to snap.

I'm not going to get anything done until I take care of this problem, so I give in to the images, closing my eyes and gliding my hand down my stomach slowly, trying to recreate the feel of my fantasy. But my fingers are too soft, too practiced, too comfortable.

Still, my clit's pulsing in time with my heartbeats, already on edge from the eroticism of my imagination, so it feels good as hell when I slip the tips of my fingers through my folds, picking up some of the wetness that's pooled between my legs and spreading it around as I start a circular motion against my clit.

My free hand moves to my breast, grabbing it roughly over my shirt, imagining Enzo's fingers pulling at my nipples, manipulating my own flesh as though I were under his hands. It doesn't feel the same—of course it doesn't—but

I let my imagination run wild, and if I try hard enough, I can still pretend.

His hands on my sides, gripping, grabbing, pulling.

His mouth on my skin, wet, hot, soft.

His voice in my ear, moaning because he can't control how badly he wants me.

And there's something about *that*, about him losing control, that has me at my peak within seconds.

My touch leaves my breast, and I move it down, pushing one finger inside myself and curling until I feel that spongy spot that sends bright lights flashing behind my eyes.

"Oh God," I moan, my back arching off the bed. My other hand speeds up its circular motion against my clit.

"Piccola sirena."

His imaginary voice in my ear is all it takes, and my body smashes into a thousand bits as I explode, coming so hard that my vision goes black and my ears go numb.

Immediately, guilt tears me up from the inside out.

Fuck.

I have got to get it together.

Two hours later and I'm thinking the same thing but for different reasons.

Seven Seas Construction sits at the corner of Eighty-Third and Arista Avenue in downtown Atlantic Cove. It's a smaller building than one would expect, but its architecture is solid and stunning. It's made almost entirely of reflective glass, and the sun shines off the surface like a mirror and sparkles along the water, making the building look like a thousand tiny diamonds glimmering in the middle of the city.

It's where Uncle T spends most of his days when he isn't at his home or on his yacht in the middle of the ocean.

I, however, can count the number of times I've been here on one hand.

Today is five, and I wonder why he asked me to meet him here when he's spent so many years making sure I stay away.

The sun is hot, the warmth of the rays soaking into my skin while I stand indecisively on the sidewalk just outside the front, getting lost in thought as I stare at the SS Construction decal plastered across the glass door.

Part of me is grappling with the thought of him finally allowing me into this part of his life, his business. But the other side of me feels suspicion, which is something I'm not used to feeling when it comes to Uncle T.

I'm not sure how long I've been standing here, but it must have been some time, because the door opens and Bastien walks out, a look of concern etched on his umber-brown features as he walks up to me and stands at my side. He slips his hands into his pockets and rocks on his heels as he stares at the building.

"Nice day," he muses.

I purse my lips. "Little hot."

"Sun is shining at least," he continues.

"I hate the sun."

He glances at me, reaching out and pressing a thumb

into my pale skin, watching as it turns white, then darkens back to a slight pink. "I think it hates you, too."

I smirk at him.

"You planning to stand out here all day?" He turns to face me.

"He sent you out here to get me, didn't he?" I sigh, running my fingers through my hair, wincing when one catches on a tangle.

Bastien nods. "You know how it is."

"How'd he even know I was here?"

He turns to look at me now, his face void of humor. "Your uncle sees *everything*, V. Never forget that."

"I won't." I give him a funny look because why is he saying it like that?

Truthfully, I don't even know why I'm debating walking in there. It's just…things have felt different these past few days, is all.

I've felt more like an afterthought that gets brought out from time to time when it suits his fancy instead of an essential part of his team.

It's probably just because Aria's back and she's sucking up all his time and attention. As soon as she and Enzo are gone, things will go back to normal.

They *have* to.

"Come on, V," Bastien says. "Just get it over with."

I follow Bastien into the building, and as soon as we make it through the doors, the smell of vanilla and freshly brewed coffee hits me in the face. There aren't many people here, but there's a receptionist behind a large U-shaped desk, *Seven Seas Construction* written in metallic lettering on the wall behind her that has water cascading from the bottom and rushing down into a small basin.

The woman smiles at me as we walk by...or maybe she's smiling at Bastien. I glance at him and see him studiously ignoring her, the way he does with everyone.

He's really quite the enigma, and even though we've been around each other for years, I still find him quite mysterious. I look up to him in a way because I wish I could shield myself from everyone, even the ones I'm closest to, as well as he does.

Neither of us talk as we enter the elevator and head to the top floor, and it's something I've always appreciated about Bastien: his quiet demeanor. So many people feel the need to fill the air with noise because they're uncomfortable in the silence, but not Bastien. If you ask him why he is the way he is, he'll either grunt and ignore the question or weave an elaborate tale, but you'll never know if what he tells you is fiction or fact.

But somehow, despite all that, he's the one I'd trust with my life. He's been around since the day my uncle took me in, and when I was trying with everything inside me to figure out where I belonged and how to navigate my momma's death, he was there. Sitting next to me. Picking me up from the seedy areas I'd sneak off to just to get away. Reminding me that things didn't have to be as shitty as I was making them. I owe Bastien a lot for that time in my life.

I glance at him again, my chest filling with warmth.

"What?" he asks, looking at me with a brow raised.

"Can't I just look at you?"

He blinks at me. "No."

I scoff. "You can't control where someone looks."

"I can control whatever I want to."

My mouth pops open. "You're so arrogant. What are you gonna do, dig out my eyes?"

He smirks. "Maybe if I did, you'd stop being such a judgmental bitch."

"Oh, that's *rich* coming from you."

The elevator dings, and Bastien heads straight to Uncle T's office. I follow him.

Just like at home, there's an oversize desk, and Uncle T is perched behind it, his hands resting on his stomach while he leans back in his throne-like chair. Bastien and I step in front of him and sit down in the two seats facing his direction.

Uncle T raises a brow as he looks at me.

"You didn't have to send Bas out to get me." I break the silence. "I was about to come up."

"You were standing out there for ten minutes, staring at the door like it was about to bite you," he replies.

"So? Maybe I was lost in thought."

"About?"

"Life."

It's as honest an answer as he's going to get, because I don't know *why* I was just standing out there other than I didn't want to see him. Didn't feel like walking inside. Not when he's doing a 180 on inviting me places he never has and is sending me on babysitting missions instead of having me do important things. If I think about it for too long, I'll start to spiral, worry that things are changing and I'm being shut out or that maybe it's *me* who's changing.

I've never *not* wanted to see Uncle T before.

He gives me a look. "I don't pay you to think about life."

You don't really pay me much at all.

"I disagree." I pick at the invisible lint on the arm of the chair. "You *frequently* pay me to think about life."

"Actually, he pays you to think about death," Bastien retorts. "If we're being technical."

"We're not," I say blandly.

"I was." Bas grins cheekily.

"You *both* do whatever I tell you," Uncle T interrupts.

I lean back in the chair, rubbing my thumb against my ring finger. "Can't argue with that. So what's up? Got a big bad man not wanting to play by your rules and you need me to go burn their whole house down?" I grin, excitement filling me at the thought. "It's been a while since I've gotten to do something like that."

Bastien laughs and shakes his head.

I glare over at him. "What is *with* you today?"

"Me?" His brows rise. "What's with *you*?"

Uncle T cuts in: "Actually, we've got a gun drop with the Atlantis MC in a couple of days, and I need you to handle it."

I sit up straighter and try to school my expression because

while I don't mind doing whatever it is he needs me to do, I cannot stand working with the local MC chapter. Especially after having recently taken the president's brother-in-law out of commission.

"So the warning worked, I take it?" I ask.

Uncle T nods, brushing his hand over his beard. "Of course it did. That's why I had you do it."

I'm nervous about it because I'm not naive enough to think the president of the MC, Johnston Miller, doesn't at least suspect I was the one behind his brother-in-law's recent loss of faculties, but if Uncle T thinks it will be okay, then I trust him.

He's always looked out for me.

Uncle T takes a sip of coffee from a mug on his desk that says *#1 Boss*, which was a gag gift Bas and I bought him for his forty-fifth birthday, and then he leans back, interlocking his thick fingers and crossing them over his slightly bulging belly. "So how'd it go with my future son-in-law?"

Images of "how it went" with Enzo flash behind my eyes and send shots of arousal through my system, followed quickly by guilt and a rare lack of something to say.

But what *can* I say?

I shrug. "Fine."

Uncle T's brow quirks, and he leans forward, his elbows coming to rest on the edge of his desk, and a deep, hearty chuckle pours out of him. "That's it?"

Bastien laughs and reaches over, pressing the back of

his big hand against my forehead. "You feeling all right, V? Modesty isn't your strong suit."

I smack his hand away.

Uncle T laughs. "Well, whatever you did, I'm proud of you."

Warmth infuses my chest, and I sit up straighter. *He's proud?* I don't think he's ever said those words to me before. Actually, now that I'm thinking about it, I'm not sure anyone has ever said those words to me before, and the way they make me feel is a brand-new sensation.

Like I'm floating above the earth and nothing can bring me down.

He's *proud* of me.

"Thanks." I clear my throat because the word comes out choppy. "Thank you."

"E's agreed to think about opening a Marino hotel down here in Atlantic Cove." Uncle T's smile is bright and wide, his eyes glimmering as he looks at me.

I slump back in my chair, relieved because maybe that means I won't have to interact with Enzo anymore, at least beyond the superficial hellos we'll share in passing leading up to the engagement party. "He told you that?"

"Aria mentioned it."

"Oh."

Images of Enzo and Aria cuddling in bed—his arm around her with a postcoital glow, him telling her about his business plans and asking her opinion—flow through my head.

My chest burns, and the feeling scorches up my throat.

"I didn't really do much," I say, shaking off my vivid—and very unwelcome—imagination. "I just showed him around—which I still don't know why I was put on babysitting the big bad mafioso. I'm sure Aria's pissed you let it happen."

Uncle T grumbles, his beard twitching. "She doesn't know."

"What do you mean she doesn't know? She's not curious about where her man is while they're in town?"

Uncle T sniffs. "I don't want her anywhere near this business."

I laugh, because surely he's joking. "She's marrying him. She's in it whether or not you want her to be."

"The women don't touch that life. They stay happy at home," Uncle T says.

I look at Bas, widening my eyes. He shrugs in return.

Men are fucking delusional.

Uncle T waves me off. "If she *insists* on staying gone from South Carolina, I need to know she'll be protected, and that's the last I'm gonna say about it. And don't either of you get any ideas and bring things up to her. She'll know what I want her to know, and that's final."

"Shouldn't that be something she gets to decide?"

I don't know why I'm defending her or pushing Uncle T's buttons, other than for some reason, it feels different today, almost like having the freedom to speak with Enzo opened up a new world, one I'm having trouble closing even though I know biting my tongue is the best way to stay in Uncle T's favor.

Besides, I may not like Aria, but I don't wish the chains of a man on anyone, not even her.

Uncle T leans forward. "Aria's never known what's best for her. And you're asking a hell of a lot of questions for a girl who can't afford the answers."

Ouch. That brings me back down to earth real quick.

That feeling from when he was proud a moment ago pops like a balloon stuck with a needle.

"Hey, what happened to that Sean guy?" I look at Bastien, trying to change the subject.

Uncle T frowns. "Bas handled it."

"And?" I sit up straighter.

"And nothing. He handled it. It's done."

My back falls against the chair with an audible smack.

"Does Enzo know?" Uncle T asks.

My forehead creases, something uneasy winding its way through me like vines. "Know what?"

"About what happened that night. I know you were with him, so I'm just trying to figure out *how* with him you were when everything with that little rat Sean went down."

My spine tingles with awareness because why would *that* matter? Uncle T is the one who made me spend the day with Enzo anyway, so this line of questioning is weird, especially since both my uncle and Bastien are being cagey as hell. It puts me on edge, something else I'm not used to feeling when it comes to Uncle T.

The truth of that night—of Enzo being in the room with me when I tortured Sean, and Sean admitting he was there *because* of him—vibrates at the base of my throat, but I swallow it and shake my head. "Why would he?"

It's an odd sensation, omitting the truth to the man I've spent my entire life looking up to, but my intuition has always been my guide, and in this situation, it's whispering to hold my cards close to my chest.

Uncle T casts a glance to Bastien, then back to me. "New Jersey isn't far from where he lives. Maybe he sent him."

"That seems like a question for your daughter, not for me. I barely know the guy."

Uncle T's eyes narrow. "Well, *get* to know the guy."

Bastien clears his throat. "So how'd you get Enzo to agree to the hotel?" He quirks a brow, and I mask the way my insides churn violently, like I'm a ship in the North Sea.

My fingernails pick at the wooden arm of the chair. "My sparkling personality, probably."

Uncle T smiles, his white teeth glinting at me the same way I imagine a shark's would right before it'd dive in to tear me apart. "Exactly, and we can use that to our advantage."

My stomach drops like a lead weight. "What do you mean?"

"I mean, I want you to keep him close while he's here. Get to know him, like I just said."

Hesitating, I reply, "You know I'll do anything you want,

but…his *fiancée* is here, first of all. And I want nothing to do with it or him. Honestly, after everything we've done, you shouldn't want me near him either."

"It's not up for discussion."

I lick my lips, casting a quick glance to Bastien before focusing on my uncle again. "So you want me to, what…spy on him?"

"Call it whatever you want." He waves his hand through the air.

"Boss," Bastien cuts in, his voice cautious. "You sure you want to send Venesa into the fire like this?"

"What *fire*?" I snap. "This is a glorified babysitting job for the freaking *underboss* of the Mafia." I point at Uncle T. "My talents are being wasted, and you know it."

He grunts. "Watch your mouth, little one. What's gotten into you?"

I shrink back from his sharp tone, chastised like he's physically cast a whip out and smacked me with it. *I don't know what's gotten into me.*

"Can we make a deal?" I grin, trying to dispel this weird teeter-totter of emotions.

Uncle T chuckles. "There's the Venesa I know, always wheeling and dealing. What're your terms?"

"The family painting." I hold my breath.

Uncle T lets out a boisterous laugh. "You know I can't do that, little one. It belongs to me, the same way it was always supposed to. What kind of man—what kind of Kingston—would I be if I just gave it to someone else?"

I drop back in my seat and exhale my disappointment. *It belonged to my mother, actually.*

Shaking off the gloomy feeling, I agree to keep tabs on Enzo.

The same way I always give in and do whatever my uncle asks.

CHAPTER 15

Enzo

GROANING, I LEAN BACK IN MY CHAIR, TRYING to curb the annoyance that is my fucking life.

I've been here at some florist called A Rose by Any Other Name for the past hour, staring at thirteen different flowers that all look the same, smell the same, and make me want to kill myself the same.

"Do you think white for this, E? Or, ooooh, maybe blue since Daddy wants to do a Lost City of Atlantis theme?" Aria's eyes light up, and she bounces in her seat at the small table set up in the middle of the area. Suddenly, I feel like a complete asshole. She's *so* excited, wanting me to be a part of things, and here I am, wishing I could be literally anywhere else.

"Whatever you want, princess." I reach over and grab her hand, then lift it to my mouth and press a chaste kiss to the back before setting it down.

There's an audible sigh next to me, and I roll my neck to the side, trying to ignore who I know it's coming from: Jenny, Aria's *very* annoying party planner.

"Can I help you?" Aria bites at her, her eyes narrowing.

Jenny snaps out of whatever daze she was in, staring at me like a vapid doll, and clears her throat, her vision dropping to the gigantic pastel-pink binder she has sitting in front of her. "Nope, I, uh…just ignore me. I just love seeing two people in love, you know?" She mumbles the last bit while clicking her pen repeatedly.

"Yeah, well—" Aria's hand strokes down the front of my chest, and she presses against my shoulder. "*That* I can't blame you for. But a word of advice, Jenny?" She crosses her legs and leans in slightly. "Stop eye fucking my man."

I lift a brow and finally look over at the party planner, who has turned such a tomato red that she could blend with the walls of roses lined up behind her.

"So-sorry, Miss Kingston," she stutters. "Mr. Marino."

This time, Jenny *doesn't* look at me, and I feel sorry for the girl. I've seen minor hints of a different Aria in the past few days, one who's a little mean and a little insecure. She's always been jealous, but I've never paid it much mind, assuming it was just a general chick thing. Being in Atlantic Cove is highlighting it even more than usual, and it's putting me on edge.

Or maybe I'm just looking for a reason, and if that's the case, I'm an even bigger piece of shit than I thought.

"Go check about the color scheme." Aria waves her away.

Jenny sucks on her teeth and nods, walking to the front of the shop where the counter is, then flagging down the florist and bending their heads close together so they can talk in a low whisper.

I smirk at Aria. "Give the girl a break, yeah?"

She rolls her eyes. "Jenny'll be fine."

"Yeah, but you didn't make it any easier on her."

Aria's foot starts methodically tap, tap, tapping against the black metal leg of the table. "Since when did you become Mr. Nice Guy?"

"I'm not nice." I sniff. "Besides, can you blame the girl? She can't help that her taste is clearly superior." I gesture to myself with a wide grin.

Aria's scowl melts from her features, and she throws her arms around my neck, pressing a soft kiss to my cheek before dragging her lips up to my ear. "Humble too. What a man you are."

"Now you're mad because I know what a catch I am?" I joke, pushing against her forearm to get some separation.

She laughs but leans in again, pressing her lips to mine.

They're sticky from gloss and probably leave a pinkish hue on my mouth, but I let her do what she needs to do because what kind of asshole would I be if I didn't?

A flash of Venesa's lips hits my mind, and I wonder how different kissing her would feel to this.

My cock jerks with the thought.

"I miss you," Aria breathes. "I feel like since we've been here, I've barely seen you at all."

Guilt, sharp and hot, worms its way through my chest.

It isn't Aria's fault I feel like I'm being slowly suffocated by how fucking *sweet* she always is to me.

Or that, for some reason, it's harder to pretend with her now that I've met her cousin.

"Me too," I reply, like I'm on autopilot.

Aria's hand presses against my cheek, and she kisses me again.

A bell dings as the front door opens, and a warm gust of wind whips through, hitting the side of my face. I turn toward the noise, and my heart stutters because there's Venesa, like I summoned her to life, and right beside her is that douchebag Fisher.

A bitterness grabs hold of me, squeezing green envy out of me from every pore. He's got an arm around her, and the way he's able to touch her so freely, with such purpose, makes me wonder where else he's touched and how often he may get to.

It also reminds me that I never will; it's like teasing me with the end of a rainbow but never letting me hold the pot of gold.

Damn. I had hoped the feeling Venesa has been inspiring in me was a fluke. I even halfway convinced myself it was all in my head. Something spawned by the cold feet of me being forced to agree to this sham marriage with a girl I owe my life to, instead of meeting someone who actually makes me *feel.*

But now, after less than a second in Venesa's presence, I know the only person I've been lying to is myself.

Everything else falls away when I look at her.

Everything.

She's glancing around the store and grinning at something Fisher's saying, that silvery hair piled high in a mess of a bun on top of her head. A few strands are loose around her face, and my hand twitches, wanting to push them out of the way, just so I don't miss seeing a single inch of her.

If you had asked me a couple of weeks ago, I'd say connections like this with people you've just met don't really exist. They're fairy tales. Delusory.

But I guess it's easy to pretend things are unrealistic if you've never experienced them yourself.

"What are *you* doing here?" Aria rubs at her temples like even seeing Venesa is a drain on her psyche.

Venesa's smile widens, and she looks over at Fisher with a smirk before both of them walk to where we're sitting.

"We're here to help." She pulls out a chair right next to me and slides into it, tucking a strand of that hair behind her ear and studiously avoiding my gaze.

Doesn't matter. The side of my body buzzes anyway, and I have to stop myself from peeking at her just to see if there's any sign she feels it too.

A flush of her cheek. A stuttered breath. A twitch of her fingers.

"Don't act so happy to see us here, Aria, baby." Fisher plops down next to Venesa, throwing his legs out wide and an arm behind her chair.

I grit my teeth, that new and unfamiliar burning swirling through my center as I watch them.

Aria's shoulders stiffen, a flush blooming under her cheekbones. "I'm not your baby, Fisher. You can't just go around calling people that."

Venesa's eyes narrow. "Have you ever met Fisher, Aria? He calls everyone 'baby.'"

Aria scoffs and crosses her arms.

"Then again, you should know that better than anyone." Venesa tilts her head.

"You're pathetic," Aria snips.

"I'm a lot of things." Venesa shrugs, amusement flickering like a candle in her gaze. She reaches out and picks up one of the white roses and then says, "You should do white daisies."

Aria frowns at her. "*Why* would I do that?"

Venesa twirls the stem in her fingers before bringing the rose up to her nose and inhaling. "They're good for wedding stuff. Happiness, love..." She glances at me. "Fertility."

My neck grows hot, and I shift in my seat.

Fisher opens his mouth, useless words flowing out yet again.

This whole thing is tiresome as fuck. It's like I'm watching them all be in high school, throwing low-grade barbs at each other just because they don't know how to deal with their hurt feelings and their petty jealousies.

"Enough," I demand. "All of you are giving me a fucking headache." I look at Aria. "They're here, whether or not you like it, so you might as well use them. I gotta go anyway."

Aria frowns, her eyes growing sad. "What? You're leaving?"

I nod. "Scotty and I gotta go do some things."

There's a question in her gaze, but like the dutiful wife she's about to become, she knows better than to ask.

Jenny waltzes back over with that clicky pen, and her footsteps stutter when she takes in the new duo sitting at the table.

"Hi," she says. "I'm Jenny."

She holds out a hand, and Venesa grins at her with that slow seductive smile I'm convinced she uses on people simply to disarm them.

"Jessica, you said?"

The planner shakes her head. "No, 'Jenny.' I said 'Jenny.'"

Venesa scrunches her nose and leans across the table. "Oh, good. Can I tell you a secret? I've never met a Jessica I've liked. I'm glad you aren't one."

She winks, and Jenny blushes, a pretty crimson color dusting across the bridge of her nose.

And fuck, now I'm turned on.

Is there anyone Venesa *doesn't* affect?

I glance at Fisher, wondering once again how many times she's fucked *him* and, even more so, why the hell I care.

"Remind me to never introduce you to my assistant," I pipe in.

Venesa ignores me.

"Jenny," Aria snaps, standing up and gripping her arm, pulling her to the side. "Do you have to flirt with *everyone*?"

Aria continues to berate the poor girl, and I take the opportunity to move my foot over and nudge Venesa's. "Hi."

"Hi yourself," she returns.

Fisher shifts in his chair, his beady eyes narrowing as they flick between the two of us.

"Jenny, baby." Fisher calls the planner back over. "Do you do birthday parties?"

Venesa's gaze swings to him. "No."

His brows rise. "You don't even know what I'm gonna ask."

"I *do* know what you're gonna ask, Gup. And the answer's no. I didn't even want you to come here with me, and I'm sure as hell not letting you take over a birthday I don't want to celebrate."

"You know, I don't really need your permission." He crosses his arms over his chest, a smirk lifting the right corner of his pierced lip.

"True." Venesa taps her pointer finger to her chin. "You won't need *anything* if you're dead."

Fisher snorts and tips his chair back until it's balancing on two legs. "Please, you could never kill me."

"Your birthday's coming up?" I ask, mainly because I want her attention back on me.

She sighs, chewing on her lip before she nods. "Yeah."

"Not just any birthday—her twenty-fifth birthday. It's a milestone. We gotta celebrate. Short Stack, come on, you're such a fucking downer."

"No. I don't wanna talk about it anymore."

Of course she wouldn't want to celebrate something like that, and I'm irritated that a guy who seems to be her boyfriend wouldn't be sensitive to her history.

Doesn't anyone actually *see* her? Do they even *care*?

I've only known her for a week, and I feel like I could school them.

My gaze swings back to Venesa and gets stuck again like glue, because I can't *not* look at her. She curls a strand of her hair behind her ear. Then picks at a cuticle. Teeth into her lip again. Nervous tics that seem so fluid, I can almost convince myself I imagined them, but they're there all the same. Little leaks of vulnerability, seeping out from boxes locked up too tight.

I can relate to that.

"When is it?" I ask, a little annoyed I don't already know.

"When's what?" Venesa retorts, looking anywhere but at me.

"Your birthday. When is it?"

"Doesn't matter."

"It's August eighteenth," Fisher cuts in.

"That's in three days," I note.

Jenny laughs uncomfortably, shifting on her feet as she looks over at them. "Well, I *do* birthdays but not ones on such short notice."

My phone chimes with a text from Scotty saying he's out front, and Aria sighs, turning her attention on me instead of whatever Jenny's saying. "Let me guess, you have to leave?"

Fuck yeah, I do.

Nodding, I try to adopt a sympathetic look as I stand, buttoning my suit jacket and brushing a hand down Aria's hair. "Ladies, it's been a pleasure, but my future father-in-law wants some attention."

Venesa tilts her head and gives me a curious expression, which immediately puts me on edge.

Is she here because of him?

Aria pouts. "You didn't tell me your stuff was with Daddy."

"You should be happy your dad and I are getting along." I lean down and press a kiss to the side of her head. "I'll see you later."

My chest burns when I meet Venesa's stare, and it takes everything in me to tear my gaze away.

Aria stands and wraps her arms around my neck, pressing her lips to mine, her tongue prying my mouth apart.

And again, I let her because *she's* the one I'm supposed to want.

CHAPTER 16

Venesa

I CAN'T DECIDE IF ENZO'S LEAVING BECAUSE he's doing something he doesn't want any of us to know or if he was lying just to get out of party planning.

But I highly doubt he's meeting with Uncle T.

Either way, his leaving really puts a wrench in my plans because the whole reason I'm here is to keep an eye on him. The way I've been told to. And now I'm stuck with Fisher and Aria, which is what I imagine the seventh circle of hell feels like.

When I look over at Fisher, I see him gazing after Aria as she walks to the front counter with a wistful look in his eyes.

I pick up a pen that's lying on the table and chuck it at him.

It hits him in the chest, and he jolts out of his daze, shooting me a glare. "Jesus. *What?*"

"You look like a lovesick puppy."

He scoffs. "I do not."

Leaning in, I lift a brow. "Do you need to not be part of this?"

His face drops, confusion screwing it up. "You usually like it when I go places with you."

"For moral support, not so you can torture yourself by being around someone who clearly still has you messed up in the head."

"I'm fine."

I laugh. "Yeah, okay. Sell it to someone who's buying it, Gup, because your feelings are plain as day."

"They are *not*," he hisses, but his eyes trail back to her. "Our past is just…complicated."

I stare at him for a few moments, but when he says nothing else, I decide to let it go.

Who am I to talk, honestly? All I can focus on is trying to keep myself off Enzo's dick.

"Whatever you say." I lift my hands in surrender. "Listen, this is boring, and clearly Aria doesn't need us. Want to do something fun instead?"

Fisher grins and nods, the front legs of his chair smacking on the linoleum flooring. "I'll go start the car. You can say bye to the wench."

He flicks his head toward Aria, making sure to not focus his attention on her.

It's a little too obvious how hard he's trying to seem unaffected now that he realizes I've noticed.

Aria's deep in what seems like a very important debate with Jenny, and I don't feel like talking to her anymore, so I shake my head and follow Fisher out instead.

He grins at me as we walk toward the door, but right before we leave, he glances back.

Protectiveness courses through me, because clearly Fisher can't control himself around her.

All these years later, and I still don't know *exactly* what went down between them. Not all of it anyway. Our friendship was always separate from whatever the two of them had going on, but I know they used to fuck around, and I know that when she left, he was never the same.

I think he loved her, even. Although I'm not sure how it's possible when she's so fucking awful.

But I'm not a prier, and if Fisher doesn't feel like it's something I should know, then I respect that about him. It's not like I'm sitting here sharing all my feelings about Enzo. I can barely admit them to myself. And they're ridiculous anyway. Who has feelings after a *week* of knowing someone? It's absurd.

Fisher grins at me as he opens the passenger door to his '72 Chevelle, and I pat his cheek before slipping into the bucket seat and putting on my seat belt as he slides in on his side and revs the engine.

"Where to, Short Stack?"

I strain my eyes, looking for the Maybach, and luckily I see it not too far ahead, about three stoplights up. "I want you to follow him."

Fisher's brows draw in. "Define 'him.'"

"Enzo, who else would I be talking about?"

Fisher nods and pulls onto the main street, letting enough cars stay in between us so they won't be able to tell they have a tail.

"So," he says, "it wasn't ever really about helping Aria, was it?"

I kick my legs up on the dash, grinning at Fisher when he glares at my feet. "What's wrong with checking up on someone you don't trust? Besides, it's on the boss's orders. You know how it is."

Fisher shakes his head. "Why's he got you chasing around after Aria's fiancé anyway?"

Irritation nags like a gnat, and I pick at my fingers, not wanting to admit out loud that I don't have a reason for a lot of things Uncle T is doing these days, because he isn't *telling* me. A melancholy sensation fills me at the thought that things are changing with us, and I'm not sure how to revert them. "Beats me."

Fisher taps his fingers on the steering wheel. "I just want you to be careful, Short Stack. You're good at what you do, but sometimes you get in over your head and don't pay attention to what's right in front of you."

I blink at him. "What's that supposed to mean?"

He runs a hand over his chin and then looks at me and winks. "What, a best friend can't look out for his number one girl?"

Enzo ends up at the boardwalk, which is an interesting turn of events.

I sent Fisher home because I don't want to be seen and two people are easier to spot than one, especially when one of those people has a bright blue mohawk and sticks out like a sore thumb.

Enzo and Scotty are walking down the pier, Enzo's hands in his pockets while they chat. My stomach clenches tight when he laughs at something, throwing his head back, his tattoos peeking out from his shirt collar.

Since he and Scotty seem to be taking their time out for a stroll, I definitely think he was just trying to get out of the party planning.

But why use my uncle as an excuse?

I hang back for a few more minutes, until Scotty pats Enzo on the shoulder and they split. Enzo ventures off on his own, down onto the beach and farther along, until he's at a hidden spot beneath a bridge and away from the tourists.

It's that time of day when the rays don't burn as bright and the ocean breeze cools, just before the sun sets. The sky is a beautiful orangey pink, and Enzo leans against one of the wooden posts, staring out at the water.

The urge to go interrupt him right away is strong, but I stay back and watch.

A small family plays down at the shore, and Enzo's focus is lasered onto them, watching as a little boy squeals when his mom chases after him and spins him around, the water splashing at their feet.

My gaze volleys between the family and Enzo.

He seems fascinated by them. And he has this look on his face, an innocence that makes me feel like it isn't E, the underboss and ultrahigh–net worth businessman watching the scene, but Enzo the boy.

There's a longing, one I can spot a mile away because it's the kind I feel in my soul. *Do I look like that too?*

It seems like a vulnerable moment, one I almost feel guilty about witnessing, but not guilty enough to keep myself from walking toward him. It's a tugging sensation right in the pit of my stomach, a hook reeling me into him like a fish on the line.

"Pretty," I say, walking up next to him and adopting a casual stance.

"Hmm," he murmurs, staring out at the ocean.

"You don't seem surprised to see me."

A small grin tilts his mouth. "I saw you the second you started tailing us."

I scoff and look over at him fully. "No, you didn't."

He finally takes his eyes away from the happy family to stare at me. "I always see you."

My chest draws tight, a heavy breath sticking in my throat, because what do I say to *that*?

His gaze tracks me slowly, starting at my toes and dragging up my legs, over my knees, tickling my inner thighs and sending a shot of arousal through my core, up my middle, over my collarbone, until it hits my face again.

He licks his lips. "In fact, I can't see anything *but* you, and it's fucking infuriating."

My hand shoots up to rub at my neck, and my teeth sink into my lower lip, trying to offset the sudden flare of heat sucking me in like a vacuum.

Pleasure from his words cascades down my shoulders and wraps around me like a blanket, and I grasp it because it *feels* good. Even if it's wrong. *Dangerous*, even.

"You can't say things like that," I force out.

His sleeves are rolled up just past his elbow and the muscles on his forearms flex, making the ink on his skin move like it's dancing. "There you go again, telling me what to do."

"I'm not—" I stop myself, because I am, actually. "You don't even know me."

"Yeah." He leans against the wooden beam. "Well, that's the problem, isn't it? I *want* to know you."

I swallow around the words stuck in my throat—*I want to know you too*—my thumb picking at my finger.

"That can't happen," I say with an undertone.

He purses his lips and nods. "I know."

We're quiet for a few moments, and I try to think about all the reasons *why* it can't happen. Uncle T would disown me or worse. Enzo's father would probably kill him. Or Aria. Or blame Uncle T. The possibilities are endless, and none of them are good.

Another hit of resentment slams into my chest at Uncle T for putting me in this situation to begin with: forcing me to spend time with a man I shouldn't be near for several reasons, including the secrets I can never speak out loud.

"And why are you following me?" Enzo's brow rises as he asks me.

I lift a shoulder. "Who said I'm following you? Maybe this was a coincidence."

He chuckles. "I know bullshit when I hear it. You following me because you don't trust me? Or because your uncle doesn't?"

"Should I? Trust you, I mean."

He looks out over the water, and again, I'm hit with the melancholy vibe as he watches the family pack up their belongings and leave.

"Does it matter?" he challenges. "Maybe I don't trust you either."

"That's probably smart. Trust should be earned, don't you think?"

He straightens and turns so fast that I stumble until it's *my* back pressing against the wooden post.

A sharp breath escapes me when he steps into my personal space. Again. Because that's all he ever does.

"I watched you torture a man and then cleaned you of his blood. I think that provides a certain level of intimacy, of *trust*, don't you?" he says.

I brush off the statement and turn my head to the side because I don't want him to see how much he's affecting me, because he can't affect me this way. Not when he's saying the things he is and standing so close. I can't *breathe* with him so close.

His hand moves toward me, and my eyes snap to the movement, anticipation making my heart kick against my ribs. He grips my chin between his forefinger and thumb, lifting my face until we lock eyes.

My stomach flips.

"I already told you," he utters. "I *see* you. Even when you look away."

My tongue sticks to the roof of my mouth, and I try to think of something—anything—to say. But my mind is blank. So I just continue to stare at him, my legs clenching together to stem the heat flaring between them.

"Your eyes are so familiar," he murmurs, releasing my chin and moving to ghost a gentle touch beneath my lashes. "Why is that?"

A flash of a memory hits me, his blood damp on my hands and his gaze locked on mine, the Hudson River lapping at his side.

Panic makes my lungs squeeze tight.

"What are you doing down here anyway?" I ask, turning away again and looking at the water. "I thought you were meeting Uncle T."

An exasperated chuckle escapes him, and he shakes his head, releasing me and stepping back. "Christ, you don't break, do you? Maybe I should just kill you and be done with it. One less person to drive me fucking mad."

"You could try."

He laughs again, his thumb chafing at the slight scruff on his chin.

"I didn't realize murder was on the table, if I'm honest." I lift my shoulders, trying to lighten the moment.

Because he's right. I *don't* break. I can't. Not for him. Not for anyone who makes me feel the way he makes me feel. My momma did that once, and look how it turned out for her.

I refuse to be my momma.

"It would certainly make things easier for me." He cocks his head. "Aria would probably be happy too."

Her name sends a sick type of envy swirling through my middle. "You could give my corpse to her as a wedding gift."

He gives me a look. "At least you can admit I'd succeed."

"A man's confidence is often his downfall. Maybe I'll kill you first."

He grins now, and the air shifts, some of the heaviness evaporating. "You could try," he says, repeating my earlier sentiment.

"And who could blame me? What with your threats of murder and all?"

"If I shouldn't kill you…" He looks at me from the corner of his eye before staring back out at the water. "Then what should I do with you?"

A warning siren blares in my head, screaming, *Danger! Danger! Do not answer!*

I ignore it.

"Whatever you want," I reply.

His gaze snaps to mine, and that light feeling in the air pulls taut, wrapping around my chest and squeezing. Heat blasts up my neck and into the apples of my cheeks, and

I place the back of my hand against them, attempting to cool off.

"Whatever I want," he repeats slowly, his eyes tracing along every single contour of my body, stripping me bare. "That's a dangerous thing to say to a man like me, piccola sirena."

A gust of wind blows by us, the smell of sea salt and sunscreen whipping across my senses, and a strand of my hair, loose from the bun, blows into my face.

He reaches out and tucks it behind my ear, the brush of his fingers lingering as it lazily drags down my jaw and then farther until his palm is resting at the front of my throat.

My breathing grows choppy, arousal winding through my center and dripping into my core. My hand moves up and covers his. "In a different life, I'd ask you to touch me."

His eyes blaze, his fingers twitching on my neck.

I close my eyes because I want to move him down my body until he dips under my clothes and makes me scream. But I pry his fingers off instead and move to the side so I can stand far away. "And in *this* life, I'm a lot of things, Enzo. But I'm not a cheat. And I don't think you are either."

He watches me for a minute, a storm waging war in his eyes, and then he nods. "You know, in my twenty-nine years, I've never *once* gotten to do whatever I want. Not really."

"Well..." I look around us. "What's something you want to do right now?"

His nostrils flare.

My stomach flips, and I put up a hand like I can stop

him from doing whatever it is that just crossed his mind. "*Not* that. Something…friendly."

His mouth pops open, and he licks his bottom lip. *God*, every time he does that, I want to feel his tongue everywhere.

"Friendly," he repeats.

I bob my head, even though my body is buzzing with how badly I want to take back what I just said.

If the situation were reversed and it were Aria standing here, I know she wouldn't give me the same regard. But this isn't about her. Not really.

It's about being no one's choice.

I could let him fuck me, and it would probably be incredible. But afterward, he'd go back to her. And based on the way he makes me feel, I know it would hurt. He'd flaunt her around, and I'd be stuck in the corner. An afterthought, left with nothing but pretty words and a quick one-night stand.

And if that didn't happen? If he decided he wanted more? Well…I can't give him that either. I'll never let myself fall prey to the whims of another person. Especially one who makes me *want* to please him.

I'm afraid I'll lose myself and never come back.

"Actually, there is something I want to do," he says.

I shake the longing off and paste a smile onto my face. "Oh? What's that?"

"Well, we're at the boardwalk." He looks around. "Let's make a memory."

CHAPTER 17

Enzo

FISHER'S CHEVELLE ISN'T REALLY THE KIND OF car that blends in, and I knew they were following me the second it pulled behind us on the interstate. I should have known better than to use Trent as an excuse in front of Venesa, but part of me wanted to see what she would do because I couldn't figure out whether she was there of her own volition or if she's been spending time around me for other reasons—orders passed down to her from Trent.

After our conversation just now, I'm confident it's not truly because she's desperate to be here.

I size her up again. *Is she lying to me? Hiding something?*

The thought of her trying to deceive me makes my chest pinch.

Truth is, I'm tired of being on edge all the goddamn time, and she's one of the few people whose company I actually enjoy. Though, apparently, I'm an idiot who spouts off things without thought because what the fuck was I thinking telling her all those things like they could ever happen?

She's right—I'm *not* a cheat.

It's just...when I'm around Venesa, it's hard to remember any of that. She makes me forget who I am, who I'm supposed to be, and makes me feel like all I *want* to be is hers.

I slip my hands in my pockets again and glance around the pier, the orangey hue of the setting sun a gorgeous backdrop as Venesa spins around and smiles at me. She's let down her hair, and the white-blond strands whip in the wind, as wild and untamable as her.

"I saw you watching that family earlier," she says.

My chest twinges.

I was watching them, green with envy over a fucking kid and the way his life seemed so simple and carefree. I hadn't realized I was being so obvious, though.

"You want to talk about it?" She stares up at me from under her lashes. "You know, friend to friend?"

Shrugging, I walk down to the shore, and she follows. "Just wondering what it would feel like, I guess."

"Having a kid?"

"Being one."

Venesa pins me with a heavy stare, her footsteps halting. "Take off your shoes," she demands.

I look at her incredulously and then to the water that's lapping dangerously close to our feet. "No."

She tilts her head, her eyes scanning me from head to

toe, like she's trying to strip away every single shield I've built up over the years to uncover the little boy underneath. The one who was smothered too soon because of the weight of expectation and the reality of what it means to be in a Mafia family.

She reaches into her cleavage, and my eyes follow the movement, wishing I could be those hands. Touch her skin. Cup her tits and feel the weight of them in my palm.

"It wasn't a request." She pulls out a knife, and my stomach somersaults.

"What else do you keep in there?" I peer down with a lascivious grin.

When she steps into me and puts the blade up to my jugular, a laugh pours out of my throat.

She's fucking wild. And I'm not 100 percent sure she won't actually kill me.

"Take off your shoes, or I'll slit your throat," she threatens in a joking tone.

I press into the metal, adrenaline suddenly pumping through me like a wildfire. "Do it."

Usually, I can anticipate people's actions, but with Venesa…I have no idea what she's capable of or what she's going to do, and it's attractive as fuck.

Her breasts brush my torso as she looks up at me, pushing the knife harder against my neck. Her gorgeous red lips part, and visions of me sucking the bottom one into my mouth fill my mind.

"Come on, Lover Boy. Live a little. I promise I won't tell."

I swallow harshly, because *fuck*—I want to kiss her so badly. But I know I can't. I've already made an ass of myself enough tonight, so I give a curt nod and playfully shove her back before leaning down and removing my shoes and then my socks. I roll up the bottom of my pants for good measure too.

"There, you happy now?" I throw my arms out to the sides.

I don't tell her how awful the sand feels on my bare feet. Or how I'm dreading the feel of the water against my skin. Or how I'm like a kid in a candy store just at the thought of spending more time with her.

She grins widely at me and slips off her shoes too.

A splash of icy water hits my toes and makes me suck in a sharp breath. I grit my teeth to keep from jumping. The water is shockingly cold for how warm it is outside.

Venesa must see my reaction because she throws her head back, a loud sultry laugh booming from her chest. The way her neck is elongated, her hair flowing down her back, and the sun setting behind her makes her look like an *actual* siren come to shore, tempting even the most loyal of men.

I'm fucking *gone* while I watch her.

The world could light itself on fire behind us, and I don't think I'd care.

Suddenly, she doubles over, her arm covering her stomach and her face contorting. Panic permeates through me, and I rush closer.

"Are you okay?"

Her hand drops into the water, and then she stands up and *throws* it at me.

The salty liquid hits my cheeks, and my lungs constrict. I run a hand down my face and point a finger at her. "Now you've fucked up."

"Oh, yeah?" She spins around like a twirling ballerina. "Story of my life."

I shake my head, droplets of water dripping from the strands of my hair. "You shouldn't want to fuck up with me."

"Well." She pauses. "That's okay because you're gonna have to catch me first."

She doesn't give me a chance to reply before she takes off, running down the shore like I'm chasing her.

There's a single moment where I consider how ridiculous this is, how juvenile, but it's gone in the next second, because if she's giving me a chance to grab her, to hold her in my arms for even a moment, I'm not going to let that opportunity pass me by.

So I do.

Chase her, I mean.

I reach her quickly, because she's not really a fast runner, or maybe she's going slow on purpose, and the thought of that—of her *wanting* me to catch her—pumps adrenaline through me faster. And then my hands are out and gripping her hips, my body buzzing like a thousand firecrackers are exploding beneath my skin.

My palms anchor her to me, and then I'm picking her up and throwing her over my shoulder, her screams making me laugh as I lock my arm around the backs of her thighs to hold her in place.

I march us down to the ocean, my chest feeling light and my mind feeling high as her fists bang against my back and her delectable body squirms against me.

"Let me down, you giant *asshole*!" she yells, but she's giggling in between each word, and it makes my chest feel fucking weird. Lighter, maybe.

"If you insist."

I toss her into the water, my cheeks aching from my smile splitting them in two.

When she emerges, my laughter fades.

She's a goddess, her wet clothes clinging to her curves, her shirt so thin that it's *almost* see-through. If I look hard enough, I swear I can see the shadows of her nipples through the drenched fabric. Pieces of her hair stick to her face, and her eyes are wild like a hurricane as she saunters toward me.

My mouth drops open, because *fuck*.

When she reaches me, she shoves me in the chest, and I fall back onto the sand, another chuckle breaking free. My stomach cramps like I just did a hundred sit-ups, and I can't remember the last time I've had this much fun or the last time I've felt so airy, I could float away.

I don't know if I've *ever* felt like this.

"You prick." She huffs, twisting different parts of her outfit and squeezing out the water.

I lean back and rest on my elbows, watching her.

She plops down next to me and lets out a sigh, peeking over at me with a grin and nudging my shoulder with hers.

This feels nice, this...*friendly* thing, and I think maybe we can do it. I just have to ignore the way she makes my body light up, the same way I ignore every other problem in my life I can't correct.

The sun drops completely beneath the horizon, and we sit in silence and watch the moon wake up, rising to take its place, thousands of stars dotting the inky sky.

"When I was little, before my momma died, I used to be so jealous of the other kids I went to school with," she says after a while. "When we were sitting in a classroom together, it was easy to pretend we were the same, you know? But as soon as we'd pile on the bus, it was harder to fake it. They were all friends, making spitballs and passing notes. And I was just...me."

"You didn't have friends?"

"Not really. I got invited to birthday parties sometimes, but my momma never really cared enough to take me, so why waste the paper? The invitations stopped showing up."

"That's fucked up," I say.

She picks up a small shell from the sand beside her, running her thumb over the ridges. "Yeah. It *is* fucked up, isn't it? She was usually too busy working or trying to keep my dad happy to care much about making sure I had an actual childhood worth remembering, though."

I don't really know what to say or if she even *wants* me to say anything, so I just sit still and listen.

This is what I wanted anyway.

To know her. And it feels like she's giving me a piece of her soul as she talks. It's selfish because I'm not giving much back, but like the greedy man I am, I take it anyway.

She sighs, throwing the shell toward the water. "I just…I get it. Why you watched that family, I mean."

Pressure builds in my throat, and I swallow around the ache. "I'm sorry you get it."

She gives me a sad smile. "Don't be."

Two people, older than both of us, walk by hand in hand, and I wait until they've passed us to reply. "It wasn't that I never got to be a kid. It's just…that boy earlier? He was so *happy*. So fucking *free*. I have no concept of what that feels like. All I can remember is how badly I wanted my pops's approval. How I wanted to be just like him. How I spent my formative years trying to act so grown, and then by the time I was and I realized what I had missed out on…it was too late. And this life, it's…" I shake my head, bending my legs and propping my elbows on my knees. "I love my life. I won't sit here and pretend I don't. But my ma didn't cope, started popping pills and chasing them down with vodka when I was fifteen, and the love of her life mistreated her." My chest throbs from the giant hole that's pulsing in the center: the space where my mother's love used to sit. "Your view on the world changes when you have to parent your parents."

She nods. "My dad was an alcoholic."

Relief washes over me that she's bringing it up, and maybe that makes me an asshole, but I just said the most vulnerable thing I've ever said to anyone, and she isn't judging me because she gets it, just like I thought she would. "That why you don't drink?"

She gives me a look. "Who says I don't?"

I shrug. "I'm observant."

Venesa nods. "He loved his aquavit, but it's hard to find in South Carolina, so he'd usually just pour anything he could get his hands on down his throat. His true love, though, was gambling. He'd go on benders and disappear for days at a time, and when he'd come home, broke and hungover, he'd never take the blame himself."

She scoffs and shakes her head, disgust clear on her face.

"Who'd he blame?" I ask, although I fear I already know the answer.

"Momma, usually. Sometimes me."

"Did he hurt you?" I try to keep my voice steady, but the thought of her being touched, of her being *injured*, makes fury pour through my body like lava.

She glances at me, and her hands twitch, her thumb moving to touch the nail of her ring finger as she fidgets. "Depends on your definition of the word, I guess."

"Aria said he killed your mom."

I hold my breath, waiting to see her reaction because *fuck*, maybe I shouldn't have said that.

She nods and stares up at the black sky and dark waters. "And got away with it. Can you believe that *bullshit*? Nobody even looked for him. No one seemed to care."

The urge to tell her I'll hunt him down is strong, but I don't say it because maybe she doesn't want that.

I would, though. Find him for her.

"My momma was a lot of things," Venesa goes on. "She worked all day and was lost in a man who didn't know how to love anyone but himself long before she ever had me. But she was still my momma, you know? And she did the best she could with the life she chose. I may not have ever been her first choice, but she was always mine."

"No offense to your mom, but that's really no excuse."

She breathes out a sardonic laugh. "Yeah, I guess it's not."

"Do you always let the people you love off the hook so easily for treating you like shit?"

It's really a rhetorical question, because even in the short time I've known her, I can tell she does. *Everyone* in her life treats her as an afterthought.

She shrugs and then leans back on her elbows, her hair dusting against the sand as she looks up at the stars. "Maybe I do."

I mimic her, lying back the same way. "Seems like it from where I'm standing."

"You know I can't cry?" she blurts.

"Like...you don't want to?"

"No, like I physically can't. Not for years now."

"No shit?" My brows shoot to my hairline because I've never heard of someone not being able to *cry* before.

"Another thing I can thank my sperm donor for." She chuckles softly again, but it's not a joyful noise. "He used to hate it when I'd cry. He'd leave the room and drag in Momma, and then he'd beat her in front of me until she was black and blue. He wouldn't let up until *I* stopped crying." She glances at me. "It's amazing how fast you learn to shutter emotions when you're protecting someone you love."

I feel fucking sick, but I don't know what to say. I have nothing I can tell her to take away the memories or to wipe away that haunted look on her face, but goddamn, I wish I did.

"Anyway." She sits back up and brushes the sand from her arms. "I don't know why I told you all that. I've never told *anyone* that, so if you open your mouth, I'll have to murder you for real."

She's trying to joke, to make some of the heaviness drop away, and I get it. Sometimes when you open up old wounds, the weight of them makes you feel you're sinking in quicksand. The humor is a way to drag yourself back out, to find a little hope when everything around you feels like it's pushing you down.

"Hey, thanks for this." I lean into her, bumping her shoulder with mine, the same way she did earlier. "It was fun being a kid, just for a bit."

She beams at me, and the sight steals the fucking breath straight from my lungs. "Anytime. Friends, right?"

My heart spasms at the word, wanting to reject it before it can even take root, but I know what I *want* isn't actually possible.

Not when I've already made commitments.

When I'm tethered to the will of my father and the debt of Aria saving my life.

It's either marry her like my pops demands or die. Plain and simple, no point in sugarcoating it.

"Right," I intone. "Friends." The word tastes wrong. "I've never really had many of those," I admit.

Venesa doesn't reply at first, just brings her knees up to her chest and wraps her arms around them, staring out at the water. "Me neither."

She jumps up and tries to brush the sand off her, but she's so wet from the ocean still, it clings to every crease and crevice of her clothes, sticking to her skin like glue.

I follow suit and then crack a grin. "You look like a drowned rat."

She narrows her eyes and stomps off, and she's so fucking cute, my stomach flips.

"At least let me buy you some dry clothes," I say, jogging after her.

She bends down when she reaches the spot we left our shoes, and my eyes memorize the curve of her hip, the arch of her back, the gleam of her skin.

"You bet your ass you're buying me new clothes. It's the least you can do."

I smile.

"Don't look at me like that." She wipes some sand from her shin and stands up straight after getting her shoes back on.

"Like what?"

"Like you don't care that I'm mad at you."

"Is this you mad?" My brows rise. "*Terrifying*."

"You're a real prick, you know?" she says. But she's grinning at me.

"I do care, piccola sirena. Forgive me, *please*." My hands come together in prayer. "I don't know how I'll go on if you don't."

She looks me in the eye like she's trying to gauge whether she can trust me.

And maybe, just this once, I'm lying to her.

Because the truth is, she could be mad at me for the rest of her life if it meant she'd stick around.

She makes me…*feel*. And maybe it's nonsensical, but it is what it is.

Friends.

CHAPTER 18

Enzo

VENESA IS WEARING AN OVERPRICED BRIGHT pink shirt that says "In My Mermaid Era" and a pair of men's board shorts with little seashells sprinkled all over that match the boardwalk's arch.

Her hair is thrown back up in that tangled, saltwater-style messy bun on top of her head, and her makeup, which had smeared from the ocean water, has been wiped completely clean off her face.

She looks different this way. More youthful.

Still just as beautiful, though.

I'm sitting on an uncomfortable picnic bench along a strip of the boardwalk that has oversize outdoor bulbs strung up on the railing, casting a yellow glow, and I watch as Venesa moves up in the line at a small food truck that says "Funnel Cakes & More."

She spins around after she orders, holding two giant

monstrosities of *something* in her hands, and her smile is so blinding, it makes my heart feel like it's careening off a cliff and deep diving into my stomach.

I run a hand through my hair, bouncing my knee beneath the picnic table.

When she makes it over, she holds up the greasy treats like they're trophies. "I got us funnel cakes."

I look at the fried monstrosity warily. "I've never had one."

She slides onto the bench across from me, her mouth dropping open in shock. "What do you mean, you've never had one?"

"Did I stutter?"

"Enzo," she admonishes. "That's unacceptable."

I shrug. "I don't know what you want me to say."

"Well…" She hands the funnel cake to me. "Prepare yourself to be a changed man."

I take it from her begrudgingly, looking down at the powdered pieces. I don't let the words fall from my lips—how I'm afraid I'm already a changed man just from knowing her.

She tears off a piece of her own snack and pops it into her mouth, her eyes closing, and then she fucking *moans*.

I clear my throat, my abs tightening and blood rushing to my dick from the noise.

Her gaze pops back open. "So good."

"This looks like it will ruin my shit." I gesture at my clothes.

"Don't be a messy eater, then," she retorts before popping another piece into her mouth and moaning again.

I stare at her instead of taking a bite, because watching her eat is like hearing your favorite symphony for the first time: a transcendent experience you never knew you were missing but somehow know you can't live without.

I've never heard someone make food sound so sexy.

Glancing around, I check to see if anyone else is paying attention, because the thought of someone else hearing her this way, even though it's innocent, makes me feel fucking crazy.

Those are *my* moans.

Except they're not.

"Enzo." She snaps her fingers in my face. "Try a piece. It's not that serious."

I lift a brow and look at the funnel cake. "You mean you didn't poison it?"

She grins. "Nah, just put a spell on it instead."

"I can't tell if you're serious or not."

Venesa laughs. "I'm kidding. That's not how witchcraft works. Besides, killing you by poisoning a funnel cake in the middle of a crowd isn't exactly high on my list of things to do, so go ahead." She reaches out and nudges the treat toward me again, her eyes wide and waiting. "Take a bite."

"Why are you staring at me like that?"

"I want to watch you enjoy it."

She's about to be disappointed. But I do it to make her happy, tearing off a small piece and popping it in my mouth.

It tastes like fried sugar.

I must make a face because her smile drops. "You don't like it."

"It's all right."

She scoffs. "God, you're a shit liar."

"I'm just not a sweets guy."

She stands, ripping the treat from my hand and taking it with hers to the trash can before throwing them both in.

Chuckling, I walk behind her, leaning down to whisper in her ear. "Don't worry, piccola sirena. You don't need sweet treats to impress me. You're impressive enough."

She spins around, her body brushing mine as she does, and my stomach jumps, my fingers curling into the palms of my hands to keep from grabbing hold of her by the waist.

"Well, you're the opposite of whatever *impressive* is," she says.

"Excuse me?" My brows lift, and I rock back on my heels.

"What kind of person doesn't like sugar?" she asks accusingly.

"Someone with superior taste, obviously."

"Now you're just being rude." She crosses her arms and starts walking down the pier toward the Ferris wheel.

I'm quick to follow her. "I'm not the one who tailed me here and won't tell me the reason. *That's* fucking rude."

If this were back in New York City and someone had been sent to spy on me, I'd have them in a basement somewhere, tied up and tortured until they told me what I wanted to know.

But not her.

I can't imagine ever hurting her.

She side-eyes me as we walk. "You're a smart guy. I'm sure you can figure it out."

I click my tongue and nod. *Her uncle.* That's what I thought.

If I *were* a smart man, I'd be navigating the possibilities of her playing me entirely, of having this night with me and then running back to Trent and giving him all the dirty details. Not that I'm worried about him, but it *would* be an issue if word got back to my pops.

But I don't think she will. Not after the time we've had here. It feels too genuine to be a ruse.

She beams up at me with a wicked grin.

Goddamn, she's beautiful.

Then she stops so suddenly, I almost run into her back.

"What are you doing?" I ask.

She points to a booth set up in between two shops. It's got a line of red, white, and blue bull's-eyes a few feet back from the front of the counter, and above them hang hundreds of stuffed animals of varying sizes. Live goldfish in small bags are lined up on a low shelf behind the guy running the place.

I lift a brow and look at her. "You're challenging me?"

She looks down at her nails. "What if I am? You scared?"

I undo my suit jacket, flashing the gun holstered to my side so she knows what she's getting into. "I just didn't realize you enjoy losing, is all."

"Ha!" she barks out. "Big words."

We walk over to the game, but before we get there, her footsteps stutter.

"You okay?" I ask, slowing down with her.

"Yeah," she replies. "I just went to high school with the guy working the counter."

"URCH!" he yells, his voice obnoxious.

Venesa's spine straightens. *Urch.* I hadn't realized it was a nickname used outside the family, and suddenly I'm wondering how she got it. The sinking feeling in my stomach tells me it's the woman I'm marrying who crowned her with the name.

"Hello, Rusty." Her tone is flat.

He grins at her, his beady eyes trailing up and down her body like she's a show at the carnival. "Damn, girl, you're a sight for sore eyes."

I bristle. I know she's not mine to get protective over, but he doesn't know that, and I'm standing *right fucking here*.

"Hey." I snap my fingers in front of his face and take out a bill, waving it at him. "Quit looking at her and do your fucking job."

His gaze moves to me, clearly sensing the dangerous position he's in, and then he clears his throat and pastes a customer-service grin on his face. "You got it, buddy."

He takes the money before handing us both neon-green water guns. His eyes land on Venesa again, and he licks his lips.

I stifle the urge to take out my real gun and shoot him.

"Heard your cousin's back in town," he says, instead of starting the game for us. "She was always a fun time." He glances at me for a second, and the motherfucker must have a death wish because then he steps closer to Venesa and leans in. "Maybe she can do me a favor like she did back in high school and make sure you and I have time to...*connect* again."

"Rusty," Venesa croons. "If you don't stop talking, I'm going to step over this booth and show you exactly what I think of how you treated me all those years ago. And trust me, you don't want that because I'm much better at standing up for myself now than I was back then."

What the fuck does she mean by that?

"Ah, come on, Urch. We had fun."

"You're right," she lilts. "Let's do it again, except this time we'll trade positions."

My eyes snap back to Rusty, and his face has drained of color, his eyes flashing with panic.

Rage taps against the edges of my calm. *What is she implying?*

"You two know the drill?" He doesn't make eye contact now. "The squid is going to pop up, and your job is to gun it down. The more you hit, the faster your own mermaid will rise to the top." He points to the red alarm that's perched up high. "When that goes off, game over."

I push the anger back down to deal with later and smirk over at Venesa. "Ready to be a loser?"

She smiles back and hip checks me. "You're *severely* underestimating my abilities."

The buzzer goes off and we start, and it's child's play, really, how quickly I get the little mermaid to the top. The alarm goes off, and I spin the water gun around in my hand and blow on the top like I'm hot shit, because let's face it, I am.

Venesa scoffs. "That was hardly fair."

"Don't be salty." Before I can stop myself, I brush a thumb across her cheek. "I won for you. Pick a prize, Venesa."

She sucks in a breath, and my heart skips in my fucking chest like I'm a schoolboy with a crush. Which I guess I sort of am.

Spinning toward the booth, she points to a giant plush squid that's hanging. "That one."

"A squid? After what we just did to all those metal ones? Brutal."

She makes a face. "I like the underdog—sue me."

Rusty's standing there staring at her, leaning against the counter with his arms crossed, and I snap my fingers.

"Hey, fuckface. Get us the prize, and stop looking at her before I teach you some manners."

He jolts to a stand and glares, but he listens, getting the stuffed animal down for us and passing it over.

It's gigantic, so I text Scotty to meet us by the Ferris wheel so I can hand it off to him to put in the car, and then I focus back on the douchebag who works the game. Reaching out, I grab the stuffed animal from him, but with my free hand, I grip his wrist and pull him in harshly. His stomach hits the edge of the counter, and he grunts.

Lowering my voice, I tell him, "I don't have to know the details to know you're a piece of shit, so let me make something crystal-clear: If you ever so much as even *breathe* in Venesa's direction, I'll know about it. And I'll come back here, and I'll find you, and I will take my time making sure *you* never breathe again. Do you get what I'm saying to you?"

He swallows, his body physically shaking as he nods. *Pussy.*

"Good. Glad we had this talk, sweetheart." I smile and release him, turning to Venesa and telling her we have to meet Scotty.

She eyes me curiously, and I'm confident she heard what I said, but she doesn't mention it. If anything, there's a bit of reverence in her gaze, like she's surprised someone would stand up for her.

It's a short walk to the Ferris wheel, and the entire time, I'm burning to have Venesa tell me what exactly that fucker Rusty did to her, but I hold back, because we've already hit the heavy topics once tonight, and I don't want to push her for more. Not when we're having a good time now. And if she wanted me to know, she'd tell me, same way she did with the story about her folks.

Still, I file away the information for later. Maybe I'll get it out of *him* instead.

Scotty's already waiting when we walk up, leaning against the small white metal fence, a giant goofy-ass grin on his face when he spots us walking up.

"Who's your new friend, E?" He points to the giant

"Fine." She frowns. "You don't have to be such a dick about it."

"And you don't have to be so goddamn bossy. Always telling me what to do."

Her smile grows, and she mimics my accent. "Big, bad gangsta afraid of a Ferris wheel. Who knew?"

My mouth twitches, and a little of the anxiety evaporates like water in the sun.

"Would you shut up?" I try to sound like I'm angry, but my words come out with a slight chuckle. "It's fine. I'm fine. Let's just get on the stupid thing."

I move to stand in line, my gaze flicking to the people in front of us slipping into the open death trap.

She follows me, watching carefully.

Reaching out, I grip her hand before I think twice, and immediately my chest loosens, a bit more of that anxiety shrinking. *So much for us not touching.*

Her eyes drop to where we're connected, but I'm too busy focusing on taking steps and keeping my breaths even to pay attention to anything else.

"Next," calls out the guy who's running the Ferris wheel.

His words lasso around my chest and squeeze like a constrictor until my breathing becomes choppy and my vision dims.

Fuck.

Venesa's grin drops from her face, the challenge replaced by a concerned look. Her fingers squeeze mine. "Listen, let's just forget about it."

"Nah. I'm good." I try to shake off the nerves, but my feet are locked in place like I'm wearing cement shoes.

"Enzo," she starts.

"Today, please," the Ferris wheel worker yells out.

Venesa's eyes flash dangerously, and she turns toward him and points a finger. "You can shut the hell up."

"Listen, lady—" he starts.

"I said you'll wait." Her tone is sharp, and there's an undercurrent of something sinister, something that sends a chill down my spine, and whatever it is she's infused in her pitch, the worker obviously feels it too because his entire body tenses and he curls his lips while he nods.

She turns back to me. "You don't have to prove anything to me, you know? It's really okay. This was dumb anyway. I actually don't even want to anymore."

I shake my head and lean in close, forcing a half grin even though my heart is pounding fast and my legs feel weak, my stomach churning from the panic. "I'll have you to keep me safe, right?"

She pins me with a look but then nods, those damn teeth of hers sinking into her lower lip like they're begging me to bend down and copy their imprint with my own.

"Yeah, Lover Boy. I promise I'll keep you safe."

CHAPTER 19

Venesa

YOU COULD HAVE BET ME A MILLION DOLLARS Enzo was afraid of heights, and I'm not sure I would have believed it. He seems like the type of man who doesn't have any fears, but I should've known better.

Everyone has a weakness. Some of us are just better at covering ours up with false bravado.

Admitting our own flaws is hard, but embracing them is even harder, so the fact he's willing to get on the Ferris wheel despite how afraid he is tells me a lot about him. Makes him more attractive, if I'm honest.

And him threatening Rusty, a douchebag from high school Aria locked me in a room with so he could rape me? That's just icing on the cake.

I glance down to where Enzo's still clasping my hand, his touch so electric that it makes my hair stand on end. He must take my stare as me being uncomfortable because he snatches it back and clears his throat, running those thick fingers through his hair.

I try to appease him. "Just think of this as your shadow work."

He looks at me curiously. "Shadow work?"

"Yeah. You know, the unconscious part of your personality that doesn't align with your ego."

"What the *fuck* are you talking about?"

We move onto the platform and sit down in the empty seats, bringing the bar down onto our laps.

"I just told you." I stare at him because what is he not getting? "You obviously have some type of trauma attached to your soul that makes you afraid of heights. Facing your fears is good for you."

"Okay?" He touches the metal across our laps like he's testing its strength.

"Have you ever considered wearing crystals?" I ask.

He looks at me funny. "No."

"Oh. Maybe you should. Could help, you know."

"Hey," he calls out to the worker, jiggling the bar. "Aren't you supposed to check this thing, make sure it's secure?"

Although his face looks calm and handsome as ever, I don't miss the way he's white-knuckling the bar he's referring to.

The worker grumbles as he makes his way over and tugs harshly on it. When it doesn't budge, he lifts his brows mockingly before he goes back to the control panel.

Enzo watches him blankly but says nothing else.

A wave of protectiveness washes over me, and I'm two seconds away from jumping up and throttling the guy for being such a dick.

The wheel jerks as it starts to move, and Enzo's hand flies from where it's gripping the bar to my thigh.

A whoosh of breath escapes me when he clamps down on my skin, his thick calloused fingers squeezing tightly, the veins pronounced, and even though it's hidden by his suit, I know they trail up his sinewy forearm and accentuate the ink that covers his flesh.

A deep, sharp stab of arousal hits me like lightning.

The ascent of the wheel is slow, stopping and starting every few seconds as more people are unloaded and reloaded, and I try to gauge how Enzo's hanging on.

He's watching me intently, almost like he's afraid of looking at anything else. He doesn't remove his touch, and I don't ask him to.

"It's okay to be scared of things," I remind him again.

He doesn't respond right away, his gaze moving down to where he's still holding on to my leg, and then back up. Finally, his jaw clenches and he nods.

"It's what makes us human. What makes us real," I continue.

"Some of us don't have that luxury."

"Because of who you are?" I press.

"Because of who I'm *supposed* to be."

I soak in his words because that makes sense to me.

Sometimes it's not safe to show your weaknesses because if people think you're human, then they'll realize how fallible and fragile you are. I suspect Enzo's world isn't so different from mine in that regard.

"Well." I hesitate, but then place my hand over his on my thigh. "How about when it's just us, we drop that expectation?"

"That's not real life," he argues.

"So let's pretend we're in a different one."

Something dark flashes in his eyes, and we jolt as we move again.

His gaze sneaks to the ground, the color draining from his face.

The guilt over making him come up here and, even worse, poking fun at what is obviously a serious phobia of his worms its way through me.

I grasp his cheek and turn his face toward mine.

"Don't look down," I demand. "Just look at me."

Surprisingly, he listens. Our eyes lock, our faces *way* too close to be anything other than inappropriate. But I don't really care right now because at least if he's focused on me, on whatever this *thing* between us is, then he isn't panicking.

Slowly, our breathing synchronizes, my fingers brushing against the edge of his sharp jaw and his still digging into the meat of my thigh.

I inhale; he exhales.

Neither of us looks away.

His body loosens, and before I can disengage from the moment, the energy changes, his eyes dropping to my lips.

I can tell he wants to kiss me. And I *want* him to, which is crazy because I've never kissed anyone.

It's too close. Too personal.

And I'm afraid I'll be bad at it.

"Better?" I choke out, clearing my throat when the word cracks.

The wheel jolts, and my body slides closer from the motion, practically falling into his. I try to move back, but his other hand shoots out and grips my waist, and he leans in, his nose brushing against mine.

My mouth pops open, and I can feel his breath on my tongue. My heart slams against my chest like a hammer.

"Are you gonna say something?" he murmurs quietly, his eyes flicking back and forth like he's trying to memorize the planes of my face.

I lick my lips, but I can't make any words appear.

His hand moves from my waist and settles right at the nape of my neck.

My eyes flutter closed at the feel.

I force them open because this *can't* happen.

No matter how much it feels like we're in our own little world up here, the reality is down below, and as soon as this ride is over, we'll be back on solid ground.

Back in the world where he's engaged to my cousin, and I'm nothing more than a distraction.

Even worse than that, really. I'm a lie. Not that he knows the truth.

"Say something." He demands it this time.

"Why?" I force out, my body so hot that I feel like I'm burning from the inside out.

"Because if you don't, I'll kiss the fuck out of you."

His words smash into me like a wrecking ball.

"I could stop you," I whisper, my stomach fluttering like it's spawned a thousand wings from how close our mouths are.

"You won't," he rasps.

I close my eyes and force images of Aria into my head, of *her* kissing Enzo, of her walking down the aisle and him smiling at her, looking at her the same way I swear sometimes he looks at me.

Of her finding out about this and running to Uncle T.

Of the fallout that would inevitably happen after.

Panic swims through my veins, warring with the *need* percolating in my chest like a poison.

I'll lose everything, and who knows what would happen to Enzo if he went against a marriage sanctioned by his father?

He could lose everything too.

Or worse.

So even though it hurts, even though it's against what I'm feeling in my body, my intuition, my goddamn soul, I reach out and push off his chest, separating us and ending the moment.

Because no matter how badly I might want him…

Enzo isn't mine to have.

And I'm not worth the fallout there would be if we gave in.

CHAPTER 20

Enzo

IT'S BEEN THREE DAYS SINCE THE BOARDWALK with Venesa, and I can't get her out of my head.

Plus, it's August 18.

Her birthday.

A day I know she'd rather forget.

Right now, I'm on the Kingstons' private beach, walking down the shoreline until I'm far enough away from the estate that I feel confident the cameras aren't picking me up and no one has followed me.

"So what's the problem?" Gio asks, his voice gruff in my ear.

I adjust my phone and glance around one last time before replying, "What makes you think there's a problem?"

He chuckles. "You just let me talk to you about bullshit for the past twenty minutes. When have you *ever* let me do that?"

"It's not my fault you talk so much."

"You love me. Don't deny it."

I find a spot on the sand and sit down, blowing out a deep breath so I can force the words I'm trying to find into the air. Once I say them, I won't be able to take them back, and even though they're just to Gio, they're still hard to get out.

Saying it out loud makes it real.

"What do you think the chances are that Pops lets me cancel this wedding?" I finally blurt.

Gio's silent.

I roll my eyes and lean my head back to stare up at the sky, squinting from the sun. "Yeah. That's what I thought."

"Listen, I'd love it if you could cut the bitch off, but we both know your dad is never gonna go for it. Not unless you can offer him something better. Something *more*."

I squeeze my eyes shut and rest my elbows on my knees. I feel like I can't breathe.

A tingle of awareness shoots up my spine, and my eyes pop open. I can't help this eerie feeling like I'm being watched. I glance around but don't see anyone.

I'm losing my fucking mind.

"Do you?" Gio presses. "Have something better to offer?"

Better? Yes. Something my pops will approve of? Fuck no.

Besides, I don't. Not really. It's not like I want to *marry* Venesa. That's crazy. I don't even know her. Only…it feels like I do. Feels like I always have, if I'm being honest.

Not that it matters. This entire conversation is ridiculous. *I'm* being ridiculous.

"I don't know, man. I just…things don't feel as cozy as I thought they would, if you know what I mean."

"Ah." Gio's quiet on the line for a few moments before he speaks, and when he does, there's an air of caution in his tone. "I'm gonna be straight with you, E: I don't know if your pops is gonna give a fuck about all that, especially since this was an arrangement made *with* Aria's dad, so if you want to get out of this—if you *really* want to—you better figure out your next steps."

"I couldn't give a fuck about Aria's dad."

"Yeah, but you *do* give a fuck about yours." He pauses. "Listen, E, I'm behind you one hundred percent, but shit won't be easy. You hear me?"

I swallow over the knot in my throat and nod even though he can't see me. "Yeah, I hear you."

"Okay. Good. *Cazzo*, you need to get back to New York, E. That Southern heat's fucking with your head."

Gio laughs, and I force myself to match his tone, but there's something stirring up inside me, and now that it's there, I don't think it can be tamed. A seed planted, even though he didn't say the words.

I can read between the lines: the only way out of this marriage is to make sure my pops isn't in charge.

The thought makes me sick to my stomach, but *would it really be so bad?*

"Any news on Frankie?" I shift the subject.

"Nothing."

My brows furrow. "What do you mean, 'nothing'?"

"I mean, the guy's a fucking ghost."

That's not normal. Having *no* paper trail is beyond the pale. It makes it feel intentional, like someone is trying to hide something. But what would be the reason to hide your involvement with a family as powerful and well-known as the Kingstons?

"Keep looking."

I'm still thinking about my conversation with Gio an hour later as I stare at Aria standing next to her bedroom dresser and putting on her jewelry.

"Maybe tonight we can do something just the two of us," she says, walking over to me and plopping into my lap, wrapping her arms around my neck.

I try not to grimace. "I thought tonight was dinner on your dad's yacht?"

Aria rolls her eyes. "Who cares? It's just some stupid thing for Venesa's birthday. Let's skip it."

"We should go," I argue.

"Has she said something to you?" Aria huffs, her body almost vibrating with sudden tension. "Don't fall for it. She's just like her momma, uncultured and unworthy. They're liars, all of them. *Liars!*"

I sit back in my seat, shock sitting heavy in my chest, and I blink at her. "Jesus, Aria, calm down."

She lets out a soft giggle and presses a hand to her upper body, closing her eyes for an elongated moment. When she reopens them, there's nothing behind her gaze. Just an innocent, doe-eyed look. "I'm perfectly calm, babe. As long as you remember that this is *your* ring on my finger, which means you're mine."

I stare at her because she's acting wildly different. I've never seen someone change personalities at the drop of a hat before, and I'm questioning which one of them is real.

She presses her palm to my cheek. "Sometimes when I look at you, it's easy to forget how close to death you were when I found you. Do you remember?"

Gritting my teeth against the sudden hit of guilt, I nod. "I remember what you told me."

"You were *so* broken." Her voice catches. "So vulnerable. But even then, I just knew you were meant for me."

Something stirs in the back of my brain. "You know, you never did tell me why you were there that night."

Her eyes flash. "Because fate took me there after a shitty date with someone else. To you. It brought us together, E—never forget that."

She's right. She did save me. I don't just owe her my loyalty; I owe her everything.

It's because of Aria I'm still around, and she loves me.

She isn't complicated.

She's no mess.

With her, things can stay exactly as they are, and I won't have to ruffle feathers. I won't have to make a judgment call about my own flesh and blood that makes nausea burn my throat.

"You should try to mend things with your cousin while you're here," I say.

She sighs and drops back from me, pursing her lips.

"Ask her to be a bridesmaid or whatever. Extend the olive branch."

"A bridesmaid?" She makes a displeased face, her eyes searching mine. "That would make you happy?"

I swallow because *no*, it wouldn't. And I know it won't make Venesa happy either, but a boundary needs to be set, and I need to remember who the fuck I am. I don't have the luxury of going after things I want, not unless I either want to upend an entire empire with it or wind up dead, and no matter what Venesa makes me feel, I can't act on impulses. Not like this.

"Yeah, that would make me happy," I fib.

The words taste like bile on my tongue, but now that they're out there, I can't take them back.

I don't want to take them back, I try to convince myself.

But even thinking it, I know it's a lie.

CHAPTER 21

Venesa

NOTHING GOOD EVER HAPPENS ON BIRTHDAYS.

It was my birthday when Momma would take me to the boardwalk and love bomb me, and it was my birthday when my dad beat her to death while I hid in a cupboard beneath the kitchen sink.

That's a truth I keep buried deep inside me, where I've torn it up into tiny little pieces and hidden it away. In fact, there's only one person on the entire planet who *knows* even part of that truth, and his fiancée is standing at the entrance to the Lair.

"Don't look so surprised to see me," Aria states.

"Well, don't just lurk in doorways," I reply. "It's creepy."

She walks in, running her finger along one of the saltwater tanks that line the entrance and then bends her knees until she can stare at the fish inside.

I *am* surprised to see her. It's not even noon on a Sunday morning, and the Lair is closed today.

Aria looks around, her bright red hair bouncing perfectly like she's a cartoon brought to life. "It's so dreary in here, Urch."

"Thanks for the notes. What do you want, Aria?"

She shrugs, the latest designer bag dangling from her arm. A hit of envy swirls deep in my gut because I've been on the waiting list for that bag for over a year, and even if I came off it, I'm not sure I have enough saved up to justify the cost. But *God*, it's gorgeous.

Aria slips it off her shoulder as she walks farther into the room and slings it onto the bar top like it's a crumpled-up napkin, not a three-thousand-dollar piece of art.

"I got curious," she says simply, perching herself on the barstool and crossing one of her long skinny legs over the other. "And I was bored."

A yawn escapes me, and I cover my mouth while walking behind the bar and starting the coffee machine that's nestled in the corner. "You want something to drink? Coffee?" I ask.

She taps her nails on the bar top and nods. "Of course I do. I don't suppose you have anything better than processed sludge?"

"Afraid not."

Smirking, I lean against the wall, the high-end liquor bottles on display above me, and I cross my arms as I watch her. She's not really focused on any one thing, but every so often, her eyes flick across the room like she's looking for something in particular.

Or someone.

A brief flash of panic hits me that maybe she's looking for Enzo and thinks he'd be here with me…but I brush it off because that's ridiculous.

"Fisher's not here," I say, testing the waters. "If that's who you're glancing around for."

Her eyes snap to mine, and she laughs, running a hand through her hair, snagging on the ends when she gets caught in a tangle. She frowns down at it and tries to pick it apart with her fingers, and when that doesn't work, she reaches out, grabs one of the silverware roll-ups, and undoes it, taking a fork and using it to comb through the ends.

Now I look at *her*. "I have a brush you can use."

She glances up from where she's running the fork through her hair, her brows hopping high on her forehead. "Why? This dingle thing works just fine."

"Because it's disgusting?" I phrase it like a question.

She scowls at me. "*You're* disgusting. Always have been. Stop projecting your self-loathing onto me. Momma used to use these all the time when I needed something to get out knots." She picks at her ends again.

"That's…strange."

"Says the girl who chants to the moon," she bites back.

A grin takes over my face. "Don't be mad because I know you're scanning the room for Fisher."

The fork gets stuck in her hair, and she jerks it free. "I am *not*."

"You are," I say, walking over to the coffee machine and grabbing two mugs. "You still take it black with two sugars?"

"Yeah," she replies.

I make the coffees and pass one to her before leaning on the bar, my elbows resting on the top while I bring the hot mug to my lips and take a long sip. "Why are you here, Aria?"

She takes her own sip before sighing and setting the mug down. "I told you, I was curious. I remember when we were kids, you used to talk about this place all the time, but Daddy wouldn't ever let me come see it for myself."

"He was right for that. This wasn't a place for any kid to be."

"You were here."

I grin. "And look how I turned out."

"How about now, you think it's okay for kids?"

"Now it's probably worse." I take another sip.

A ghost of a smile passes over her face, and this is weird.

It's been…years since we talked like this. In fact, the only time it happened was when I first moved into the estate, right after we met, when she bounced into my room and proclaimed me her new sister and that we'd be best friends.

Funny how short-lived that was.

Now there are too many years of hurt. Too many unforgivable things she's done that I can't look past.

"I saw Rusty last night," I tell her.

Her body stiffens, the mug poised at her bottom lip.

"Does that make you uncomfortable?" I cock my head. "Bring back memories of some of your worst traits?"

Aria sniffs and lifts her chin, placing the coffee cup down. "I don't know what you're talking about."

"You know *exactly* what I'm talking about."

It was her sixteenth birthday party, and she brought him to my room and barricaded the door so I couldn't get out.

Flashes of that night zoom through my mind, sending a ripping sensation down my middle, letting the hurt bleed out onto the floor.

Me screaming.

Him shoving a shirt in my mouth while he yanked down my sleep shorts and stuck his dirty dick inside me.

Fisher showing up after and forcing his way in, finding me sobbing in a corner.

Him telling Bastien.

Bastien calling the family doctor and not letting me leave my bed for a week while I healed.

A shiver rolls down my spine, nausea making my stomach churn, and I shake off the memories, smirking at Aria because if I don't, I might reach out and throttle her instead.

And Uncle T would probably kill me if I did, so like I always have, I rein the anger in.

"Why are you smiling like that?" she asks.

The grin drops from my face. "I'm not allowed to *smile* now?"

She scrunches her nose up, and a jolt of nostalgia hits me. She's always done that, made these innocent little gestures that sucked everyone in around her. Back in school, I used to watch Fisher stare across the cafeteria at her with this look on his face.

Longing.

Like she was the best thing in the world. And maybe she was to him.

Staring at her now, I try to see the appeal, although it isn't *Fisher* I'm imagining looking at her that way.

It's Enzo.

Jealousy weaves its way through my stomach and surges until it wraps around my chest.

"Listen, I need a favor," Aria says.

I can't help the laugh that escapes me. Her asking for a favor is beyond hilarious, if we're being honest. "The answer's no."

"You haven't even heard what it is."

I reach down to turn on the bar sink and toss out the bit of coffee left in my cup. "I don't need to hear about it to know I won't be helping you."

"Well, I want you to be a bridesmaid."

A cough pours from my throat from me choking on saliva, my eyes watering from the burn.

"I'm sorry," I get out after finally getting myself under control. "Why on *earth* would I do that?"

She won't meet my eyes. "Why wouldn't you? You're family. It's what Daddy would want."

"Since when have you cared what he'd want?"

She scoffs and taps her fingers on the bar top. "I've always cared."

"You've got a funny way of showing it."

"You have no idea what you're talking about," she retorts.

She twirls the fork she used in her hair before letting it drop with a *clink*. "He's just so suffocating; you know how he gets."

I don't. Not personally anyway. Uncle T has always given me so much space that I don't know what to do with it. And all I've ever wanted is to have him feel enough for me to be that suffocating.

Aria doesn't know how lucky she is, so I tell her as much.

She shakes her head. "You wouldn't understand."

"I guess I wouldn't. Listen, as much as I enjoy your impromptu visit, are you gonna be real with me? Because if not, you can leave. We both know you'd rather die than have me as a bridesmaid."

She sucks in a deep breath and looks around, twirling the ends of her hair through her perfectly manicured fingers. "Fine. The truth is that E told me to ask you, and I want to make him happy, so here we are."

Her words pierce through my chest and emotionally slam me into the wall.

Enzo asked for this?

I don't know why that stings, but it does.

And actually, it pisses me off, Mister "I can't see anything but you."

That anger swirls inside me until it fills every dark crease and corner of my soul, and I let it fuel me, reminding me of exactly who and what I am.

Fuck Enzo for thinking he can send her here and shove their marriage in my face.

Like I needed the reminder.

I'm the one who kept saying no, that fucking asshole.

"All right, I'll do it," I say with a smile.

She looks at me in surprise.

"But it's gonna cost you," I continue, looking down at my nails like I can't be bothered.

Aria groans. "I just *knew* you'd be difficult about it. I even told E this was a waste of time, but he insisted."

"That's life." I shrug.

"What do you want?"

I grin. "I'll be your bridesmaid, but I want you to get me the family painting."

She makes a face of disgust. "I've never understood your and Daddy's obsession with that thing. It's hideous."

"It has sentimental value." I reach out my hand. "Do we have a deal?"

"I don't think I'll be able to," she says, seeming nervous and unsure. "Daddy loves that stupid thing."

"I'm sure you can persuade him," I coo. I'm not lying. If anyone can convince Uncle T to give me the painting, it's her. He'd do anything for her: move mountains, kill people, fund an army just to wipe out her opposition.

"And if I can't?" She quirks a brow.

"Then you don't want to make your man as happy as I thought you would."

I'm not sure why my chest spasms when I call him her man, but I have to stop myself from rubbing at the unexpected ache.

Aria drops the piece of hair she was twirling around

her finger and then reaches out and grasps my hand in hers. "Deal," she replies.

A grin spreads across my face. "Excellent."

CHAPTER 22

Venesa

UNCLE T BOUGHT A YACHT WHEN I WAS THIRTEEN years old and named it the *Aquata,* and about once a month when I was growing up, he'd load the family into the back of his fancy cars and bring them out onto the open sea for dinner. It almost always involved others; usually it was about him showing off to someone he deemed important, parading his women around like rare jewels from a sunken treasure.

I never got the invitation, I guess because I've never been worthy of being shown off like a prized possession—a little too rough around the edges to sparkle the way Aria does—and I always accepted it as the way things were. Even though I primed, waxed, and sculpted myself into a perfect figure, hoping I was good enough to be shown off to the world, I never quite managed it.

And each time I was left behind, it would chip away a bit

more at my damaged spirit, proving it didn't matter whom I lived with or who called me family.

It was all just another version of the same thing.

I was always a burden. An obligation.

In fact, it wasn't until I was firmly under the umbrella of "employee," if not on paper then by actual trade, that I was invited on board, and in my twenty-five years on this earth, fifteen of those having been with my uncle, he's never *once* thrown me a birthday dinner.

So it's easy to imagine why I'm suspicious now.

And desperate to leave.

I'm sitting on the front deck of the yacht with Bastien, the cushioned back of the booth I'm lounged in supporting me like a cocoon. The South Carolina heat beats down on my pale skin like I'm baking in an oven, and I'm a little concerned about getting a burn even though I'm slathered with sunscreen from head to toe. Bastien is reading a novel across from me, a rectangular table between us, both of us waiting for Uncle T to actually show up.

He said to be here at three, but it's half past, and he's still nowhere to be found.

"You coming with me tomorrow to meet the Atlantis MC for the drop?" I ask.

"Mmm." He nods and flips a page in his novel. "Shouldn't be an issue."

"Good." I pause. "You think Johnston has any idea it was me?"

I don't elaborate because we both know I'm talking about

the fact I put his brother-in-law in the hospital. Last I heard, he's still alive, but barely.

Bastien glances at me. "If he did, I don't think your uncle would send you into the fire."

"True," I reply, even though it doesn't feel like it lately, which is a whole different can of worms. I chew my lip, wanting to spill everything to Bastien, just to see how he reacts, if maybe *he's* been feeling the difference with Uncle T too or if it's just me who's suddenly off-kilter like my world's been turned upside down.

"While we're waiting, why don't you tell me what you ended up doing with that Sean guy?" I ask instead.

Bas flips another page. "It's been handled."

I nod and tap my nails on the table. "You planning to elaborate?"

Now he does give me his attention, his amber eyes meeting mine over the lip of his book. "Don't worry about it."

"Don't you tell me not to worry about it, Bas." I point my finger at him. "I *am* worried about it. He came into my place and messed with my money."

I don't add in the fact he spilled he was here following Enzo, maybe because part of me is hoping Bastien knows and is going to admit it to *me* instead.

"Technically, it's your uncle's money," he deadpans.

My eyes narrow. "You know what I mean."

He sighs, glancing at me again. "And you know what *I* mean when I say it's been handled."

"I know it means you're being an asshole."

He smirks.

I stare at him for a few seconds, but he doesn't say anything else. "You're really not gonna tell me?"

His brow lifts. "He isn't important, V. He wasn't anyone worth a damn. Just some idiot who thought he could worm his way into our business because of hearing the rumor mill. I killed him; he's gone."

Something sour hits the back of my throat because I know he's lying. "What rumor mill?"

He opens his mouth to reply, but then his gaze slides past me, and my vision follows his.

Uncle T is making his way up the dock, and he's not alone, because of course he isn't.

Enzo and Aria are both with him, and don't they just look *so* cozy together, with Aria's hand wrapped around his so tightly, their arms look intertwined.

A heavy sensation drops in my gut, like thick green slime coating my insides and weighing me down. Enzo glances up, meeting my gaze from across the dock, and my stomach jumps into my throat, that envy whipping into anger.

I glare, and Aria turns toward him, whispering in his ear. His attention leaves me for her while he chuckles at something she says.

And why *wouldn't* he pay attention to her instead of me?

I'm nothing but a bridesmaid, after all.

I huff out an audible breath and cross my arms, earning me a curious look from Bastien.

"I thought this was supposed to just be the three of us," I murmur, keeping my eyes on them as they make their way up the steps and onto the yacht's deck.

Bas sighs, dog-earing the page in his book and closing it, setting it down on the table. "It was."

My eyes widen in horror.

"What?" He straightens like he needs to be on guard.

"What do you mean 'what?' How could you do that?"

He rubs at his jaw, his brows drawing down in confusion. "Do what?"

"That." I gesture at the book. "Get a bookmark, good lord. Were you raised in a barn?"

"Oh," he replies, picking the book back up and flipping it open. "You mean this?"

He takes another page and slowly, *torturously*, curls over the top part of the paper.

My skin crawls.

"You're disgusting," I spit out in horror.

He grins widely. "Feels good."

I grab a scrunchie from around my wrist and throw my hair into a loose messy braid just to get it out of my way, then sigh in relief when the ocean breeze ghosts across my exposed neck.

"You know Trent's never able to tell Aria no. She probably said she wanted to come along," Bastien notes. "She's been very into family things lately."

"It's *my* birthday, Bas. I should get to throw her overboard and never hear her voice again."

A haunted shadow comes over his features. "Don't let him hear you talk about her like that, you understand me? Actually, don't let *her* hear you talk like that."

"Please," I sneer. "She doesn't scare me. Maybe he's bringing dear ol' daughter into the family business."

I grin, and Bastien's amber eyes volley between me and everyone walking on board.

"There they are," Uncle T says, his tone light and jovial as the three of them make their way across the deck until they're standing in front of us.

"Uncle T." I smile and half stand to give him a hug. He presses a kiss to the top of my head and pats me on the back like I'm a pet. I don't make eye contact with anyone else because I'm really not in the mood to fake it today, and hell, it's *my* birthday. I can be icy if I want.

Not that anyone is actually wishing me a happy birthday right now.

I don't want them to anyway.

Still, them at least *trying* to pretend they care would be nice.

I sit down again and lean back in the booth, kicking my legs up on the seat in front of me like I can't be bothered to pay any more attention to them. It's an obvious snub, one I hope Enzo feels personally.

"Venesa." A smooth voice coasts over my skin like melted butter, and then a shadow covers my frame, Enzo's stupid face blocking the sun. "Happy birthday."

I swallow thickly and close my eyes, forcing out a stiff nod. "Is it?"

"Bas, my office," Uncle T snaps.

I wait for him to ask me to come along, but for every second of silence, I grow more disappointed. As usual lately, I'm left out here while Uncle T runs his business and tells me nothing.

My chest aches. *Is it me who's changing?*

I brush off the feeling. It's just because Aria's back in town, and she brought her douchebag fiancé, who keeps making me *feel* things. Once they're gone, things will go back to normal.

Sighing, I squeeze my eyes tighter, trying to block out the noise of Aria and Enzo talking. If I can't escape, then I might as well continue to pretend I'm oblivious to my surroundings.

Dainty footsteps get farther away, and the sliding door that leads to the living area inside opens and shuts. But even if I couldn't tell from the sound alone, I'd know it wasn't Enzo who left because I can *feel* his stare, the same way I always can.

There's a shift of weight on the cushions near me, jostling my legs, and then: "Hi."

I pop open one eye and look at Enzo, ignoring the way my stomach flips. I don't reply.

"How are you?" he tries again.

I adopt a lazy grin. "Swell. You?"

"Swell."

I bob my head a few times and then reach into the bag on the table next to me before grabbing my sunglasses and slipping them on so he can't see my eyes.

He throws his arm across the back of the booth and looks past me, toward the wall of sliding glass doors that separate both levels of the outside decks and the inside of the yacht. "Nice day."

"Mmm," I murmur, not really wanting to have a conversation.

"No business today?" he presses. "I thought for sure you'd be on the heels of your uncle and Bas."

I stiffen my jaw and tilt my head back against the cushion, ignoring the sting caused by thinking about them in there without me. "Well, darlin', you thought wrong."

He leans in, and the back of his hand barely brushes against the outside of my calf. I bite the inside of my cheek so hard, I can taste blood. "You doing okay today?"

Something heavy pummels me in the center of my chest, both because he's the *only* person to actually care and because he's acknowledging that today might be hard for me.

How dare he?

I drag my sunglasses down the bridge of my nose, just enough to glance at him over the top. "We're not doing this."

"Doing what?" He removes the slight touch and sits back.

"This." I wave between us. "This whole, 'I know more about you than anyone here and I care, so let's have a heart-to-heart' thing."

His brows draw down, confusion splashing across his features.

Anger swirls like a sea storm through my body. If he

doesn't realize what he's done, then I won't be the one to explain it to him.

The sliding door opens, and I twist to see who it is.

Aria walks outside, clad in a tan knitted cover-up and a large floppy hat that hides most of her face. Gold Cartier bangles line her arms, and when she lifts her hand to adjust the brim, the sparkle of her diamond engagement ring almost blinds me.

"Do me a favor. Worry about the people you're *supposed* to be worried about and leave me the hell alone, okay?" I snip.

He frowns but follows my gaze over to Aria. I hate that I can see what looks like adoration when he stares at her.

Even worse, I hate that I care.

"You should probably know you're fraternizing with the enemy by being over here and talking to me," I continue.

He looks back at me. "Is that what you think you are? My enemy?"

"Well, we're not friends."

"Ouch." He rubs at his chest and winces. "Why not?"

I laugh under my breath before leaning back and closing my eyes again because it really doesn't matter. "We both know why not."

A cheeky grin blooms on his face. "I thought we were becoming pretty good at the whole friends thing."

"Word on the street is you also think I'd make a good bridesmaid," I snark, my gaze snapping back open.

His grin fades, and I watch as the realization washes over him. "Venesa..."

I shake my head. "It doesn't matter."

"What's going on over here?" Aria's voice interrupts, and I bite back the loud sigh that wants to escape.

"Just getting to know my future cousin," I croon.

She saunters over to Enzo and sits down so close to him, I'm surprised she doesn't end up on his lap, and then she reaches up and runs her fingers through his silky dark hair.

He doesn't push her away. But then again, why would he?

"Hopefully not *too* well," she chastises lightly. "We all know what happens when you get too close to a man, Urch, no offense."

My stomach drops, but I wink at her. "Not just the men, honey."

"You're so crass," she sneers.

Confidence straightens my spine and makes a smile blossom on my face.

Aria's always been a jealous hag, but it's not like she has anything to seriously worry about with me anyway. I enjoy making her uncomfortable, but if I hurt her, if I did anything to truly piss her off, I'd be cast out by the Kingston family with a snap of Uncle T's fingers. I'm under no illusion that he'd pick me. He'd choose her a thousand times and in a thousand different ways before he'd ever place me above her.

She's his daughter, and I'm just an unfortunate byproduct of his family tree.

Clearly, Enzo feels the same.

Which, of course, he does. But why would I want him to place me above her anyway? I can't offer him anything.

Still, watching them together? It's making me sick.

Her fingers tangle one more time in his hair as my stomach twists, jealousy pouring through me.

Enzo's eyes snap to mine, and he grabs Aria's wrists, pushing her away.

She frowns at him and reaches back out, pulling both their hands until they're resting in her lap. He shifts like he's uncomfortable, like he's been caught with his hand in the cookie jar, and isn't that just the most ridiculous thing?

I track the movement because, despite my inner monologue screaming that I don't care, I can't help myself, and when I finally tear my vision away, worried that Enzo can see how much it's affecting me, I realize I had nothing to fear at all.

Because Enzo isn't even *looking* at me.

He's looking at her.

The same way everyone always does.

I turn my face, and when I do, my gaze clashes with a new set of eyes—dark brown—and my stomach drops to my feet.

CHAPTER 23

Enzo

I'M DOING EVERYTHING I CAN TO DISSUADE this feeling brewing between Venesa and me, but I just want to be next to her. To know her. To recreate the feeling of that day on the boardwalk, when I wasn't E "Lover Boy" Marino, wasn't a feared mafioso or a businessman.

I was just Enzo.

And I can't remember a time before her when that was the case. Even now, as I sit in the blue booth on this pretentious yacht, I'm putting on a show, and I can't help but wonder if Venesa is too.

She's pissed off at me, that much I can tell, but I had to put the barrier back up between us, and frankly, we both could use the reminder.

Because even though I may want her, it doesn't matter.

It isn't about what *I* want. I've made commitments, and if I don't follow through…

There aren't many options for me here.

My gaze keeps alternating between where Bastien and Trent disappeared inside, somewhere beyond the long row of glass doors that line the entrance into the living room, and back to Aria, who's moved her hands from my lap and is now lounging with her bright peach-colored toenails on my legs.

A sharp inhale of breath has me finally giving in and looking at Venesa. I partly expect her to be staring at me, and disappointment pings through me when she isn't.

Which...why would she be?

I follow her gaze to a new man who's standing on the edge of the yacht's deck, his blond hair slicked back, the ends hitting the top of his neck.

His eyes are *locked* on Venesa, and when I look back to her, all the color has drained from her face, almost as though she's seen a ghost. He's tall, possibly even more so than me, and there's a familiarity when I look at him that I can't quite place.

Maybe it's the aura of violence permeating the surrounding air.

Like attracts like, and this man? He's uncontrolled brutality. I can sense it in his posture. If I squint, I can almost see the waves of energy emanating from his pores. Vibrating, like barely restrained rage.

Him being here immediately puts me on edge.

Venesa's back is ramrod straight, and while she has a smile on her face, her eyes are sharp and narrowed and her lips are pulled tight at the corners.

The man rocks slightly on his heels and then takes a step forward.

Venesa bristles next to me before she slowly rises to her feet, and a spike of panic whirs inside me like a broken part rumbling in distress.

Does she know him?

It's a new feeling, this restlessness, and I'm not sure *why* I'm feeling it with her of all people when I know better than anyone that she can take care of herself.

But I guess things like emotion don't give a damn about logic.

Aria raises her hand, pushing the brim of her hat away from her face, and a surprised gasp leaves her. "He made it."

Venesa snaps her head to Aria, disbelief coating every feature. Her pouty red mouth pops open and then closes again, but no words come out.

I've never seen Venesa not have complete control over a situation.

She has a sharp tongue, always has something to say, so to see her speechless is...different. I don't think I like it.

The man walks over slowly, his eyes never leaving hers, until he's directly in front of us.

"Hi, Yrsa."

A flare of jealousy curdles my stomach at how easily he addresses her.

Who the fuck is this guy?

Venesa's looks stunned, like she has no clue how to use her limbs—yet another uncharacteristic thing for her—and then she stiffens her jaw and glares at the man. "Harald. What the *fuck* are you doing here?"

He gives a sad smile. "I was invited."

"By who?"

"By me," Aria interrupts, grinning. "I thought it'd be a nice surprise. Family together again at long last. Happy birthday, Urch!"

Venesa closes her eyes in a slow blink and then turns to face Aria. Her fingers curl into the palms of her hands, her knuckles blanching like she's afraid of what will happen if she doesn't keep them in fists.

"Does—" Venesa clears her throat. "Does Uncle T know he's here?"

Her voice is smaller now. Meek.

Harald glances at Aria with an unsure look.

"Of course he does." Aria scoffs. "Who do you think tracked him down and got him here?"

I see it, then. The moment betrayal cuts through Venesa's stunned exterior. It's subtle, and she covers it well, but when you're as obsessed with watching somebody as I am with Venesa, it's easy to spot the minute changes.

God, what I wouldn't give to take her away and place her somewhere no one can find her.

I don't know who this is, but I know she doesn't want him here, and if she were mine, I'd stand up, grip this sleazy fuck by the neck, and throw him overboard just to make her happy.

But she's *not* mine. And it's not my place.

Venesa inhales a heavy breath and then moves in slow, controlled steps like she's about to burst apart at the seams.

Harald follows her.

Aria's lips are twisted up as she watches her cousin and this stranger walk away, and my body is buzzing with the need to get up and follow them.

"Who's that?" I ask.

"That's Venesa's father."

Shock pins me in place, disbelief coating every inch of me like fresh paint. "Excuse me?"

Aria looks at me with a confused expression. "What's *your* deal?"

"And you invited him here?" I look back over at Venesa and that piece of absolute shit, violence thrumming like a car engine beneath my skin. I feel the desperate need to hurt him. To torture him. To make him feel even a second of what he made his daughter go through.

"I thought it would be a nice birthday surprise." Aria pouts, sticking her lips out like she didn't expect Venesa to *not* want to see the man who abandoned her all those years ago.

A disbelieving breath leaves me, and I blink at her, at this *stranger* who's wearing my ring. "You must be the most coldhearted bitch I've ever fucking met."

This is mean.

Cruel.

Unprecedented.

Aria's mouth drops. "Pardon? How *dare* you call me that? I'm your wife."

I shove her feet off my lap and shoot to a stand. "Not yet, you're not. Jesus *Christ*, Aria. How could you bring him here? Don't you know what he's fucking done?"

Suspicion fills her irises. "Do *you*?"

I grit my teeth, trying to calm down the hurricane of rage pummeling my insides. "You're the one who told me he killed her mom."

She watches me closely. "Like she's an angel? It's time for her to get some closure. I thought she'd be happy."

Her big, round eyes look at me like she's waving a white flag, only unlike every other time she's done it, I don't buy it for a second.

Honestly, I'm at a loss for words.

"We tried to get my uncle Frankie out here too," she adds, glancing at me from the corner of her gaze.

Now it's *me* who's suspicious, something uneasy fluttering its wings at the nape of my neck, urging me to pay attention.

Alarm bells start screaming in my head, but it doesn't make sense. There's absolutely no way anyone would have known I was digging for information on him, least of all Trent. And definitely not *Aria*.

The only person who knows is Gio, and it was only in text messages, and just his name and vague references to keeping an eye on Jersey.

I frown and look down at my pocket where my phone is. *Impossible*.

"Where's he at, then?" I look around, trying to remain nonchalant, but I'm very, *very* on edge right now.

She hums and watches me like she's the one who's trying to read *me*. "Couldn't make it."

"You said he's in Jersey, yeah? Maybe we can invite him to the wedding."

She smiles, her shoulders relaxing. "Yeah, maybe so."

My eyes shoot back to where Venesa disappeared, my body scorching with the need to check on her. To support her. To have her back because I'm pretty confident no one else on this boat will.

But even if I did follow her, I'm not sure she'd want me there. Not after what I did by having Aria ask her to be a bridesmaid.

Stupid, Enzo.

I hoped…

Well, I guess it doesn't matter what I hoped.

Venesa's never been one who needed saving.

And I'm not her knight in shining armor.

CHAPTER 24

Venesa

IN MY ENTIRE LIFE, I'VE NEVER FELT THE LEVEL of rage that I do right now. It's coursing through my body like hot black sludge so thick, my limbs are shaking from the weight.

There have been many times in my life when I've imagined hurting Aria.

When she kicked me while I was down on my first day of school.

When she instigated the rape that I still haven't fully processed emotionally.

The list goes on and on.

But none of that, *none* of it compares to how I feel right now, staring at my father—the man I still have nightmares about—while he stands across from me in the living room of the *Aquata*.

I need to go back outside and hurt her.

Beat her like my dad used to beat my mom, just so she can experience a *fraction* of hardship in her life.

She can play an innocent all she wants, but there's no way she doesn't realize how this affects me. She might not know the gritty details of my past, but she knows enough, and she did this on purpose. To be cruel, the same as she's always been.

But *I'm* not the same girl.

Staring at my father on my birthday is like being in a time vortex, snapped up and spun around until I'm thrown back into my past.

"Come out, come out wherever you are." My momma's voice is a singsong from the living room. I cover my mouth, stifling the giggle wanting to burst free.

I'm cramped in a cupboard to the right of the kitchen sink, and it's so hot and stuffy, the strands of my brown hair stick to the sides of my face.

"Er-sahhhh," Momma hums. "Where's my Yrsa, baby?"

My foot cramps and I jerk, my toes hitting the wooden siding.

Dang it, I just know that means she's gonna hear me.

Sure enough, a few seconds later, the door swings open, my momma's beautiful white grin spreading across her face as she leans back on her heels, her hands already shooting forward to tickle my sides. "Gotcha!"

"Momma!" I screech. "You're gonna make me hit my head!"

A car door slams out front, and suddenly the mood changes,

Momma's eyes growing wary as she looks to the side door off the long and narrow kitchen.

"Who's that?" I whisper, but the sinking in my heart gives me the answer before she does.

It's my daddy…at least, that's what I'm supposed *to call him. He's never really around enough to make it feel like the real thing. I barely recognize the man because of how often he's missing, and even when he is here, the way he likes to hurt Momma makes me not want to know him at all.*

I just wish she'd feel the same.

Momma pops up from where she was crouching in front of me and peers out of the small square window over the sink, a sharp inhale of breath following whatever she sees.

That sinking feeling in my chest drops to my feet.

If he's back, then that means I'm about to lose these moments with her. Again.

She never really loves me out loud for long, even though she promises each time will be different.

It never is.

If my daddy is a drug, then my momma is the addict, and she'll bleed for him until her veins run dry, even if it leaves me all alone.

Her lips thin, her face draining of color. That's a weird reaction. No matter how much he hurts her, she's always happy to see him.

"Is it Daddy?" I ask, unsure now.

She glances at me, chewing on her lip, and then she gives a sharp nod and crouches back down until she's looking me in the eye. "I want you to do something for me, okay? I want you to hide in here again, in this very spot, until I come and get you. No matter how long it takes. Can you do that?"

I scrunch my brows. "But you already know where I am."

"I do, but..." She leans in close. "Your daddy doesn't, and I just know he's gonna want to find you. It's your birthday, after all."

She's always doing things like that, trying to make him seem like a better person, a better parent, than he is. But just because I'm a kid doesn't mean that I'm dumb. I don't believe her for a second.

You can't erase memories from a brain by whispering sweet words, and even the heaviest of makeup washes away eventually, leaving nothing behind but the ugly truth.

I learned that the first time my daddy came home, then pulled me from my bed in the middle of the night while he beat my momma black and blue in front of me.

Punishment for her, he said. If she'd just behave more, then he wouldn't have to teach her lessons.

I cried and ran toward them, banging my little fists on his thick arm and begging him to leave her alone.

He stopped. For a second.

But only to throw me on our worn plaid couch and tell me to get myself together. That crying was for the weak, and Andersens were strong.

I learned quickly that if I didn't cry out, he'd stop sooner.

So I try to stay quiet when I hear them argue in the next room now. At least I think it's him.

He's drunk, I just know it. He's always drunk. Maybe that's why his voice sounds different.

I count backward in my head, trying to figure out the last time he actually came home instead of staying out all night gambling and drinking away Momma's tips, but it's been so long, I've lost track.

Fear for Momma makes my heart pound wildly in my chest. And fear for me because I don't want him to come grab me and make me watch the way he always does.

They scream for a few more minutes, and then I hear it.

The sound of flesh hitting flesh.

I squeeze my eyes shut, bringing my legs to my chest and wrapping my arms around them. I bury my head in my lap until my knees press against my ears, trying to muffle the noise.

He never found me.

And she never found me again either because that was the night she died.

When I finally crawled out of that cramped cupboard, I saw her on the living room floor, bled out, her eyes wide-open and lifeless. I remember trying to cry. Walking slowly to her bloody body and curling underneath her limp, lifeless arm, staring blankly at our blue wallpaper with white flowers that was stained yellow from years of cigarette smoke, willing the tears to fall and feeling guilty when they wouldn't.

I moved in with Uncle T three days later.

Everyone asked me what happened, but I never told a soul.

Hours in police rooms, them trying to ply me with sweets and ice-cold soda pop. But I didn't say a thing.

Except…I told Aria.

Not about everything, but that it was him who killed her.

And maybe over the years, despite what she's done to me, despite how cruel and awful she's been, I've held back and given her some grace.

Because at least she respected my boundaries for this one singular thing.

This dark thing she held for me like a personal secret keeper. As long as she did that, she was still family. *My* family.

But that's all dead and gone now.

And despite everything, I can't find it in me to hate Uncle T for arranging the trip and hunting him down because he *doesn't* know, and I have to believe he's only doing something he thinks will make me happy.

I *have* to believe it. Otherwise, what is there for me to believe in?

But even as I think the words, a dubious feeling slithers around me, latching on like tentacles, shaky and unsure.

I don't like it.

Being around Uncle T, being his sidekick—the one he turns to when he needs things done—has always grounded me. Given me purpose. I'm not sure what to do if that goes away.

It's all I've ever known, really.

Having Harald here, knowing Aria set this up even though it must have taken an elaborate amount of planning…it makes me feel like I've lost control.

But there is one thing I still have control over, and that's staying here with *him*.

I don't have to do it.

So I don't.

Without another word, I spin around, slide open the glass door, and leave.

CHAPTER 25

Enzo

I STAY FOR THE REST OF THE DINNER, EVEN though I'm beyond ready to leave.

I'm disgusted with any of them calling themselves Venesa's "family" when they don't show up for her in any way that matters, and I'm even more disgusted with the fact I have to sit here and pretend I still want *anything* to do with the woman next to me, but I don't know how to get out of this wedding unless I kill my father, and I don't know if I'm ready to accept that or anything that comes with it.

I promised Ma to never go against him, and now…

Today has made my indecision waver because now I don't know if I can *make* myself marry her.

Dinner is stilted. Or maybe it's just in my imagination. Bastien and I seem to be the only two people at the table who give a fuck that Venesa, the person whose birthday we're supposed to celebrate, isn't here.

Aria, Trent, and Harald—the motherfucker—are jovial. Laughing and drinking wine like this is the best night of their lives, as if they've been friends for years.

I thought they didn't even know each other and that Venesa's mom had been cut off for choosing him. Yet here they are, one big happy family.

And again, Venesa is missing.

Anger is so potent in my bloodstream, it makes my skin itch. It's literally as though none of them even notice she's gone.

"I'm sorry." Bastien interrupts the conversation, throwing his fork on the plate and sitting back. "Are we all going to just sit around here and pretend like it's okay that this motherfucker is at the table?"

My acceptance of Bastien blossoms into respect.

"Not me," I reply, cutting a look to Harald.

He shrinks under my gaze, clearing his throat and draining his wineglass.

There are so many things I want to say to him, but if I *do*, I'll have to answer to Trent and Aria as to how I know them. And I'm not an ignorant man. I know when to play my cards and when to keep them close.

"Bas, a little decorum," Trent chastises.

Bastien laughs and scoots back from the table before standing up. "Not this time, Trent. I do a lot of things for you, and I hold my tongue on a lot of others. But this is fucked, even for you."

Trent's lips thin.

"That girl loves you more than she loves herself, and all she's ever wanted is for you to treat her like family," Bastien continues.

I nod along with him.

"And this is what you do?"

"You wouldn't understand," Trent says.

Bastien's knuckles press against the table as he leans in. "Then explain it to me, boss."

Trent's eyes flare, and his shoulders broaden like he's trying to make himself look as large as possible. "Peacocking" is what we call it back home. Posturing because you need to show off something you don't really have.

"I don't need to explain anything to you," Trent says, "and I'll tell you right now to change your tone and remember your place before I remind you of what it is."

Bastien sighs, throwing down his napkin and walking out of the room.

I desperately wish I could follow, but I can't.

Maybe I'm a coward. Feels like it.

"I'm sorry about that, Harald." Trent takes a sip of his wine.

The bastard shakes his head and chuckles. "It's fine. I've got a lot to explain to my daughter. A lot to make up for. It isn't his fault he thinks I'm a piece of shit when I've been one."

My brows shoot to my hairline because is *this* what he's going with? This is the story he's telling?

I bite my cheek to keep from speaking or from launching

myself over the table and beating the fuck out of him, the same way I used to when I'd fight in the underground cage matches back home. Back when I could partake in such activities. Now they're considered beneath me.

"Well, Venesa's never been someone who has the decorum to be around people anyway, if you ask me," Aria throws in. "Ungrateful, honestly."

I breathe deeply, flexing my fingers to keep my calm, but it's no use. I have to get out of here, or else I'm going to explode.

"Excuse me," I say, shoving out my chair to stand and leaving without another word. The same way Bastien did.

The urge to disappear completely and force Aria to find her own way back to her house is strong, but I resist, because until I can figure out a plan, I can't afford to piss everyone off.

But I was a fool. I thought I could put this thing aside, that I could marry Aria and make my pops happy and settle for whatever life everyone else has laid out for me, but if it means this? If it means being tied to a woman this cruel and not being able to speak up for someone who deserves it? I don't know if I can do that.

A deep realization settles inside me, right in my solar plexus, my anxiety whistling through my bones like leaves in the breeze.

Things have to change.

I step outside onto the deck and stare up at the stars, trying to decide what the hell I'm going to do. Whatever it is, it will have to wait until I'm back in New York. I don't trust that my phone isn't tapped after Aria mentioned Frankie to me, and I'm also not convinced she is as innocent as she tries to play.

There are a lot of things going on here that make no sense, actually, and it makes my hackles rise, because is there anyone I *can* trust?

Venesa.

Her name pops into my head so quickly, it almost doesn't even register as a thought. I've only known her for a short time in the grand scheme of things, but there's a connection there, one I've never felt with another person, and I know she's real with me, maybe one of the only people who ever is.

She's one of the few people I can trust.

I sit down in the same spot Venesa was when we first arrived and close my eyes, trying to feel her energy or… something. I don't know what I'm doing exactly, but the thought of her having been here just a few hours before is like a balm to my anger, and I don't want to fight the feeling. She's into that vibrational shit, so maybe I'm hoping it will rub off on me.

I'm not sure how long I sit here, my eyes closed, picturing Venesa's face in my mind, but it's long enough for Harald to walk outside by himself, stumbling over his feet and clearly intoxicated as he makes his way off the boat. If I were thinking straight, I would go back inside and make up an excuse to Aria about why I have to leave because the last thing I need is one more fucking headache to deal with while I figure everything out. It's important my pops stay clueless to any thoughts I have swirling around in my head. But I don't want to lose sight of Harald for a second.

Because I just thought of the perfect birthday gift.

CHAPTER 26

Venesa

I'D LIKE TO SAY I'M SLEEPING WHEN THERE'S A knock on my apartment door in the middle of the night, but the truth is I've been pacing back and forth in my silk shorts and spaghetti strap pj's, visualizing all the ways I can murder Aria and get away with it without losing everything.

So far, I haven't come up with any solutions.

I also haven't come up with any way to get rid of this rage that feels like a flood being held back by a crumbling dam.

All it's going to take is one minor quake for the entire thing to blow.

So whoever is knocking on my door at—I look over at the clock—three in the morning better have a good reason for being here.

If it's Fisher, I'm going to strangle him.

I tried to text him earlier, but my hands were too shaky, and telling anyone about why I'm so viscerally upset would mean actually talking about it, which is definitely something I don't want to do.

Fisher knows nothing about my childhood.

He's my best friend, but our friendship is more of the "sit in silence and respect boundaries" type, and avoidance of our pasts has always been a major player in why we enjoy being around each other. We both have daddy issues, and we both have unresolved trauma we handle in less-than-healthy ways. That's why we connect. *Talking* about things would only make them worse, and we gravitated toward each other because we didn't push the way others did. Didn't judge.

And now, even after all these years, there's a silent boundary in place, urging us to never break it open *too* far, or else we'll ruin the years of silent acknowledgment that we've built.

Grumbling to myself, I throw off my blankets and make my way to the door, throwing it open.

Enzo.

Of course it's him.

He's looking at the ground, his forearm resting on the top part of the door. His hair is mussed, bits falling just over his eyebrow like he was in a fight and didn't have time to fix himself up.

He's dressed down compared to his usual suits, wearing just his button-up shirt rolled past his elbows, tattoos on full display.

Butterflies explode in my stomach at the sight of him, and like usual, I hate myself for it.

"What are you doing here?" I sigh. "I'm not in the mood."

He looks up, his blue eyes piercing as they gaze into mine. "I have a surprise for you."

"Well, I don't want it," I say firmly.

He frowns, and I try to close the door on him, but he kicks his foot out, wedging it into the frame. And I might be pissed, but I don't want to *hurt* him.

"It's rude not to accept gifts." He clicks his tongue.

"Fuck off." I smile sweetly. "How's that for rude?"

"I'm sorry," he says.

Shrugging, I lean my head against the edge of the door, ignoring the way my chest pulls tight. "For what?"

He licks his lips. "For having Aria ask you to be a bridesmaid. That was fucked up of me."

"She's your fiancée. You don't owe me anything."

"Will you let me explain why?"

I cock my head. "Will it make a difference?"

He stares at me like he thinks maybe it will, but in the end, he shakes his head, his arm still resting on the frame as he leans in farther. "Come with me? Please?"

My teeth sink into my bottom lip while I think about it. I want to, mainly because I wonder what he has for me. "I don't like gifts; that's more your *fiancée*'s thing. Why don't you give it to her?" Anger vibrates up my spine at the thought.

Enzo gives a half grin. "This is more of a you-specific surprise."

My brows rise, curiosity spinning its web and trying to snare me. "I hate it, thanks."

"You don't even know what it is."

"So?"

He groans, rubbing his hands over his face, and then he straightens, determination lighting his features. He steps fully into the room, his hand forcing the door open and making me stumble back.

I stiffen my spine, because who the hell does he think he is?

"It will make you feel better," he promises.

"Is it Aria's head on a stick?" I grin wickedly at him.

He cuts me a look. "Close, but no."

Well, now I'm really curious.

I purse my lips and weigh my options. "Still, no. Thanks for asking, though."

Spinning around, I intend to head for my bed, but Enzo grasps my arm and stops me in my tracks. He twirls me back easily.

Everything he does with me seems to be effortless.

He runs his fingers up my arm, goose bumps sprouting in their wake, and then grasps my chin. "I wasn't *asking*, piccola sirena."

His deep voice vibrates through me like static electricity.

"I'm not going anywhere with you," I argue. "And to be completely honest, I think it's really presumptuous and *such* a man thing to tell me what to do and then, on top of that fact, to even—"

I screech when Enzo lifts me by the hips, throwing my

body over his shoulder and locking my legs in place before whirling around and carrying me out the door to my apartment and down the spiral staircase.

Blood rushes to my head as I bang my fists against his back, and I cannot stand the way his muscles ripple with every step, my body jostling as he makes his way across the hall and then opens the wood panel to the basement.

My surprise is down here?

"Stop fidgeting." He smacks my upper thigh, and the breath whooshes from my lungs at the sting, arousal flaring deep in my core.

I do, but not because I'm listening to his direction; it's only because I'm afraid if he smacks me again, he'll be able to feel wetness dripping down the inside of my thighs from how turned on this whole thing is making me. I may be pissed off at him, but I'm not *dead.*

By the time we make it all the way to the basement, I'm resting my elbow on Enzo's shoulder, propping my chin on my palm.

Scotty's by the door to my aquarium room, and I beam at him. "Hey, cutie."

He chuckles, straightening and opening the door, and Enzo marches us right in.

It isn't until we're in the room that he finally sets me down, and he does it torturously slowly, the front of my body sliding along the front of his, every inch connected with just a thin layer of fabric separating our skin.

The air thickens, and heat flares through every single

part of me. My eyes meet his, and my insides flutter from the way he's staring.

I don't say anything because I'm afraid of what will happen if I do, especially since I'm supposed to be mad at him, so instead I turn away—and there's my gift, front and center and absolutely perfect.

Enzo hovers behind my back, his body heat wrapping around me like a cocoon, and suddenly, I'm not so angry at him anymore.

"Surprise," he whispers.

My father is bound to the torture table, gagged, bruised, and bloody.

"You really did bring me a gift," I murmur, taking a stride forward.

"Happy birthday."

I grin.

"Hey, Dad," I say, a sudden pep in my step. "Let me introduce you to my babies, Jack and Flora."

I take my time getting things ready because I've dreamed of this moment many times over the years. I never thought it would really happen. I assumed my father had run off or was dead in a ditch somewhere, and although I'm sure it's unhealthy and won't give me any peace, I can't help but wonder why he actually came back.

Adrenaline pumps through my limbs as I take a knife and drag it across his forearm, the skin splitting like butter, a thin red line of blood bubbling on the surface.

He grunts, and satisfaction rips through me when tears escape the corners of his eyes and drip down his face.

"Are you *crying*?" I tsk-tsk, excitement fluttering like bird wings in my stomach. "*Daddy*. Andersens don't cry. Andersens are *strong.*" Leaning down, I place the blade at his leg and whisper in his ear. "Crying is for the weak, remember? You taught me that."

Screams from my father sound so sweet when they're at my hand, and I slam the knife into his upper thigh, reveling in the muffled noise that pours out around the gag. Sighing in satisfaction, I stand and walk over to where my stonefish venom is, then make my way back to the torture table.

I'm hyperaware of Enzo standing against the far wall, the same way he did the last time he was down here with me. And maybe this makes me a freak, but having him here *still* feels erotic.

Vulnerable.

It makes my skin tingle and my senses spark.

And this gift? It's the best birthday present I've ever received. I've never had anyone who just *gets* me before, and Enzo Marino? He understands me in a way that transcends the physical.

Focusing back on my piece-of-shit father, I stand at the head of the table and lean over him until my face is upside down to his view.

His face is busted. Bruised and blackened with giant contusions on both sides. Judging by his dilated pupils, I'd be surprised if he doesn't have a concussion. I glance at Enzo, noticing his knuckles are red and puffy.

He did this for me.

Nobody has ever shown up for me this way, and it makes my body warm.

Shaking off the emotions, I focus back on my father. "I'll make you a deal, Harald."

I smile at him sweetly when I notice his Adam's apple bob from a heavy swallow.

"I'll undo the gag for you, let you have your last words. But you need to tell me why you came back here. Otherwise, I'll keep you alive for days, sending this poison here"—I hold up the needle—"through your veins repeatedly, until you beg me to kill you." My eyes narrow, hatred bleeding into the moment like a thick black cloud. "Similar to how my mother begged right before she died."

Reaching down with my free hand, I rip the tape off his mouth and pull out the balled-up shirt, damp with blood-tinged saliva.

To his credit, he doesn't scream or cry out; he just moves his jaw like it's sore.

"Speak." I place the needle at his knuckle.

"I came back because Trent Kingston told me to."

"That's not good enough." I shake my head. "Not when you killed Momma. How *dare* you show your face here like everything is gone and forgotten after all these years." Leaning forward, I press the needle into his skin and release the venom. "I'll never forget what you did to us. To me. And I'll *never* forgive you."

Harald's brown eyes widen, and his head shakes slightly

back and forth. "Yrsa, I…I'm not a good man. I can admit that. But I didn't kill your mother. I wasn't even there that night."

"Liar!" I backhand him, making his face hit the metal and a tooth fly out of his mouth before skittering onto the floor. "Don't you lie to me."

He whimpers, blood pooling beneath his lips, but he focuses on me again. "I'm not lying. I had run away. My gambling was—it was out of control, Yrsa."

"Don't call me that," I say through gritted teeth, anger making my vision blur.

"I'm telling you the truth."

"I don't believe you."

Sweat beads at the temples of his blond hair, and his body jerks. The venom is settling in nicely, but I want answers before he loses consciousness or I lose control and kill him.

"I hadn't been home in a couple of months at that point, don't you remember? There were gambling debts I couldn't pay and people after me I knew would kill me before I could get them the money. I *wasn't* there."

Standing up straight, I digest his words and try to separate fact from fiction.

"Momma said it was you when I asked who was home." I step back, dropping the needle onto my rolling table. "She *told* me."

But a flash of her thinned lips and scared expression floats through my memory.

He coughs and grunts, his left arm swelling and growing pink. "She was lying."

I scoff. "Convenient. If it wasn't you, who was it?" After grabbing the knife I placed down earlier, I hold it at the side of his neck. "And don't pretend like you don't know. Tell me the truth and I'll make your death fast, even though you don't deserve it."

"If I had to guess?" He coughs again, blood seeping from the corners of his mouth. "The people I owed money to."

I press the blade harder into his neck. "And who was that, Harald?"

"Your uncle. Trent Kingston."

CHAPTER 27

Enzo

HARALD ANDERSEN IS DEAD.

Good fucking riddance.

I'm back at the front door of Venesa's studio, standing behind her, my mind reeling from what Harald said before he died.

She hesitates before walking inside, spinning around to face me. There's a haunted look to her expression, like her entire world was obliterated and she can't figure out which way is up.

"Do you think he was telling the truth?" She doesn't even look me in the eye, her focus on her bare feet.

I lift her chin, leaving my finger beneath it so she can't turn away, wishing I could wipe away her confusion, her sadness, and take the brunt of it on my own shoulders just to bring her peace.

"I don't know," I reply honestly. "You never do with guys

like that." I hesitate before adding, "I don't know why he'd lie, though."

She swallows and nods, her hand coming up to cover my wrist, and when her fingers wrap around my skin, I swear it burns wherever she touches.

"I should have made him suffer."

"This wasn't about him," I say. "This was about closure… for you."

She gives me a sad smile, squeezing where we're connected. "Thank you. I don't know how I…well, nobody has ever done something like this for me before."

My gaze drops to her perfect mouth that I've imagined a thousand different times in a hundred different ways. My thumb brushes against her bottom lip, and I wish I could replace it with my tongue.

She exhales, and the air grows charged—thick and heavy—pushing us closer together, until her body heat warms my skin.

"Enzo…"

My heart pounds in a staccato rhythm.

"In a different life"—I cut her off, pressing even closer until her neck cranes—"I'd kiss you."

My gaze locks on hers, my thumb still skimming back and forth against her lip. "I'd drag you inside, and I'd spend all night taking away the pain he caused."

"Don't say that," she starts, but I press hard against her mouth to keep her from continuing, because if I don't get this out now, I don't think I'll be able to breathe.

And even if we can never act on it, she deserves to know. I *want* her to know.

"I'd tell you I only had Aria ask you to be a bridesmaid because I was trying like hell to do something—*anything*—to keep you in the box you're supposed to be in for me, instead of letting you fill every goddamn space in my head."

She inhales shakily, her breath hot against my fingertips, but she doesn't reply.

"In a different life"—I bend until my mouth is centimeters from hers—"I would do anything to make you mine, and I'd bring you any person who's wronged you and make them beg for death at your feet. All you'd have to do is say the word."

"Enzo." Her voice is deep and raspy. Like she's seconds away from giving in and letting me have her in all the ways I dream about.

"Shh." I stop her from speaking. "I know what you're about to say, and I know we can't…but I just needed you to hear it, out loud, at least once."

I let go of her face and reach into my pocket, then pull out her *actual* gift and pass it over. Leaning down, I brush a kiss to her cheek, but her face moves at the same time, and instead I ghost across the corner of her lip. My body lights up with flames, my heart slamming against my rib cage like it's trying to break from my chest and fall into her hands.

"Good night, piccola sirena. Happy birthday."

Aria sighs loudly next to me as Scotty drives us back from a date she insisted upon.

I ignore her, because I don't really have it in me right now to give a fuck, not when my head is filled with images of Venesa last night, of how she doled out retribution so flawlessly and how I couldn't take away her pain.

"You okay, babe?" Aria asks, brushing her hand down my arm.

I shift away from her.

She scoffs. "You're a real drag since last night on the yacht, you know?"

"So call it off, then," I bite back.

Her body physically recoils and slams into her seat. "I…I don't even know what to say to that."

I run a hand through my hair, tugging on the roots.

"Why are you mad at me?" Her voice is meek now, and for the first time, I can hear the manipulation in its tone.

Christ, is this how I'm supposed to live the rest of my life?

"How could you have done that?" I spit out.

She gives me a confused look. "Done what?"

"Brought Harald Andersen here."

A dark look covers her features, and the innocent, gorgeous girl I proposed to washes away like sea-foam being taken out by the tide. "This is all because of *her*?"

I roll my eyes. "You have *got* to get over whatever shit you have going on with your cousin. That's not how you treat family."

"How many times do I have to tell you? She's not family."

I chuckle. "You're being delusional."

"And you're being a prick."

My tenuous control snaps, and I lean forward, gripping her face in my hand harshly. "I'd remind you to remember just who the fuck it is you're talking to. I may be your fiancé, but I'm not your bitch, and I'm getting real tired of this spoiled-princess routine your dad helps flourish. You may get away with mouthing off to him, but you won't disrespect me again."

Tears line her lower lid, and a bit of guilt whips through my middle.

I loosen my grip. "You get me?"

She swallows and nods, a few tears creeping out of the corners of her eyes and trailing over my fingers. I pat her cheek before releasing her and sitting back in my seat.

We don't speak another word until we get to the estate, and even then, she simply opens and slams the car door before disappearing inside. It's funny, because for the longest time, I was *wishing* for the fire she just showed me, but now it feels like a square peg in a round hole or a shoe on the wrong foot. Uncomfortable and out of place.

And I'm wondering if I ever really knew who Aria was at all or if she's been putting on an act this entire time—similar to how I am, I suppose. Though it's not like she knows the marriage is a business arrangement.

At least I didn't used to think she knew. Now I don't know *who* I can trust.

I send Scotty away with the car right after because I'm not in the mood for chitchat, and I go on a walk around the estate instead of heading straight inside. I need to clear my head before I see Aria again. Unfortunately, in this life, games have to be played carefully, and I can't piss her off too much until I figure out what the fuck I'm doing.

I need to get back to New York.

After about an hour, my head no clearer than it was before, I make my way to the front of the mansion, preparing to head inside, but my footsteps stutter to a stop right before I turn the corner when I hear voices.

"What do you mean, you're not coming?"

My heart skips a beat. *Venesa.* Moving forward slightly, I see her standing on the front steps, talking with Bastien.

"Babysitting duty, on orders of His Majesty," he replies, crossing his arms and leaning against one of the white pillars that line the front porch.

Venesa sighs, and I don't have to see her up close to imagine the way those teeth are sinking into the pillowy-soft bottom lip of hers. "*Babysitting* duty?"

He nods. "Yeah, Aria's…out of sorts, I guess? Came running into his office with tears, screaming about how she was losing Enzo."

A brief stab of panic hits me because the last thing I need is for gossip to get back to Pops, especially when I haven't spoken to him in days while I try to figure out what the De Luca family wants with me.

Venesa laughs, but the sound is hollow. "Of course, he

has you watching her instead of going with me." She glances at the front door and then back. "I should go ask him why. In fact, there are *several* things I need to speak with him about."

Bastien grips her arm tightly, rooting her in place. "We don't ask questions, V. You know that. That's not how this works, never *been* how this works."

"Well, what the hell am I supposed to do, go to meet these pricks alone? You know how they get. Especially if Johnston knows I took out his brother-in-law."

My ears perk up with interest, and I take a step out from where I'm hiding behind the building so I can take in Bastien's face. *What does she mean "go alone"?*

His brows are drawn down, concern etched plainly on his features. "You've got your gun?"

Venesa scoffs. "Please, give it up. You know I hate that thing."

"I don't enjoy thinking about you dead."

"They won't kill me."

He shrugs. "They might."

"Then come with me, Bas."

He shakes his head, seemingly frustrated. "I can't, V."

I take a step forward, my foot crunching on rock. Venesa doesn't turn around, but Bastien's eyes flick to mine for a single moment before he lifts his chin, his nostrils flaring.

"I wish *someone* would, though."

CHAPTER 28

Venesa

I STILL CAN'T BELIEVE BAS DIDN'T COME WITH me to the gun drop.

My chest aches from the realization that my uncle might not be who I thought he was. My father's words ring in my ears, but I brush them off, because believing the words of my dad means upending everything I thought I knew about my uncle.

And what would be the reason? To collect on a debt? He'd kill his own *sister* to send a message?

I can't just barge into his office and ask, because that won't get me anywhere, and if it's not based in any truth, then it will only damage our relationship more than it already is. He used to brush off my outbursts or when I'd do things my own way instead of how he wanted, but things are different now, and I don't know *why* that feels like the straw that would break the camel's back, but it does.

I'm at the southern docks, where the MC always meets us to do the drop. The Atlantis MC and the Kingstons have had a mutually beneficial relationship for decades, one hand washing the other. We supply the guns to them, and they sell them at a markup, giving us 60 percent. It's been the deal with them since years before Johnston took over as president, when his dad was in charge.

But we all know who really runs the show here, and it isn't them.

The Southside docks are owned by Uncle T, but they're in a bad part of town and off the beaten path, which makes them the perfect place to meet. Other than some empty warehouses and my uncle's freights, there's nothing and nobody here at this time of night, and it's far enough away from civilization that Johnston can test the guns with no one calling the cops when they hear the shots.

But I wish they'd hurry and get here. It's thirty minutes *past* the time we're supposed to meet, and every second makes me grow antsier, my brain running a mile a minute, my nerves making me feel like bugs are crawling underneath my skin.

Finally, there's the distinct rumble of motorcycle engines, and my spine bristles at the sound, my hackles rising like a shield.

Showtime.

Five motorcycles pull up, and their engines go silent one by one, the men standing from their bikes. Their leather cuts are faded, and I've always wondered if that's from their rides in the sun or if they're made that way on purpose.

The guns themselves are already packaged into crates, and Johnston walks over with a scowl on his face, barely visible through the long, wiry black beard covering it.

Anxiety pricks at my back like needles.

"You," he states, his voice a deep growl.

I cross my arms as I lean against one of the wooden crates. "Me."

"Where're the men?"

"Oh, I'm sure they're out somewhere being a disappointment."

His scowl deepens. "Trent sent you here unprotected?"

I bring my hand up, curling my fingers and looking at my nails like I'm unbothered. Even though my heart is pumping trepidation through every single piece of me.

"He seems to think it's *you* who needs the protection." I grin widely.

But seriously, fuck Uncle T for letting me come here alone.

He cocks his head to the side. "You do a lot of the grunt work for your uncle, don't you?"

I know what he's really asking: *Was it you who fucked with my family?*

"Sometimes," I reply.

He watches me closely for a few seconds, taking out a cigarette and lighting the end before he blows the smoke in my face.

My eyes water, but I ignore it.

He smiles. "You've got fire, girl. I like that in a woman."

I laugh, because *what?* "Honey, no offense, but you couldn't handle a woman like me."

His eyes look me up and down, and it feels sleazy, like he's stripping me bare and leaving me exposed. It's an odd moment to realize how much I like when Enzo does it, and how the feeling changes when the intent is different.

"You let me worry about what I can handle," he says.

I tap the top of the crate. "All you need to handle is right here, Johnston."

His smile widens, and it makes my stomach churn. Ugh, he's so disgusting.

There's a system to how these drops go down. They look in the crates, they can take them out and fire them if they wish, and then they load them up, and I leave.

Easy as pie in theory.

"Most of them are around back." I gesture to the warehouse we're standing in front of, and he puts his arm out like he wants me to lead the way.

So I do, hyperaware of him following me the entire time.

When we get to the bulk of the guns, Johnston walks up behind me, pulls out his own gun, and gestures toward the crate. "Open it," he demands.

My palms are clammy, and the urge to wipe them down the front of my outfit is strong, but I resist because I don't want to show any weakness.

"You need a lady to do your heavy lifting, John?" I ask. "What would the others think?"

He flicks his cigarette to the ground and moves quickly, pressing in close to my body, violence mingling with the stale scent of tobacco and whiskey. It smells like broken dreams and a man who isn't actually man enough to deal with his issues.

He reaches down and brushes his hand against my ass, his sticky breath ghosting across the side of my neck, and I go on full alert.

"Give me some space," I say, "or I'll call up your ol' lady and let her know you don't know how to behave."

He grips my ass harder and grunts. "She knows her place."

A click of a gun sounds, and my body stiffens, thinking it's him, but then *Johnston* goes ramrod straight, and a voice says, "I'd love to show you yours."

Enzo.

"Take your hands off her. Now."

Johnston does immediately, his hands in the air, palms facing outward, and his gun dangling from his thumb. I spin around and see Enzo holding his 9mm to the back of Johnston's head, a fiery expression on his face.

What the hell is he doing here?

I'm equal parts annoyed to see him and relieved I'm not alone.

Johnston cuts me an accusing glare before looking at him. "Who the fuck are you?"

"I'm the guy who's about to kill you if you touch her again." Enzo's voice is low and lethal, and it's inappropriate timing, but heat flares between my legs. "In fact, don't even *look* at her."

Johnston chuckles but keeps his hands raised. "Buddy, I've got four of my guys right around the corner, and they're not gonna like seeing this. I don't think you know who you're fucking with right now."

Enzo's face is all dark lines and menace, and he's dangerous in a way I've never seen before. All traces of the fun and easygoing *friend* I've spent time with are gone, and in his place is E: the man the rumors are all about.

I'm not sure which version of him I'm more attracted to.

He grins, and a shiver races up my spine.

"Ask me if I give a fuck who you are." He leans in. "Go on, ask me."

Johnston stiffens his jaw, and Enzo brings back his gun and pistol-whips him in the head. The biker flies to the ground, his gun skittering across the gravel and into the grass a few feet away.

My eyes widen because *what the hell is he doing*? But before I can even blink, Enzo's shoe is on Johnston's hand, and he's grinding down with his body weight until Johnston yells out in pain.

There's a thrill working its way through me, pumping adrenaline through my body like a drug at the violent display. One that's happening because of me. Even better: *for* me.

"Oh, I'm sorry," Enzo says. "Does that hurt, sweetheart?"

"Fuck…you." Johnston grunts and spits out a blood clot.

Enzo laughs. "Nah, fuck *you*."

He releases Johnston's hand from under his foot and then crouches, running the gun down the side of his face. "I want to make something crystal-clear: killing you right now would cause problems for *her*, and that's the only reason I'm being generous and letting you live." He pushes the gun into Johnston's temple again. "But if I find out you tucked tail like a bitch and ran to anyone about what happened here, I'll hunt you down like the dog you are, and I will strip every piece of skin from your body before I kill you. I'll make it last all night long, professing my love for your death. That's a promise."

The way he's speaking, it's soft and low, like sex and candy mixed with a tinge of violence, and I wonder if this is why they call him Lover Boy. Because he whispers sweet nothings into their ears while he hurts them.

"You don't know who you're fucking with," Johnston spits, his words muffled.

"I don't need to know who you are," Enzo continues. "I'm a Marino. If I want you dead, that's the way it will be."

Even in Johnston's precarious position, his eyes widen with recognition.

"Now quit being a pussy, stand up like a man, and apologize."

Johnston follows the direction, bringing his mangled hand to his chest immediately, his eyes whirling with anger and blood dripping down the side of his face.

And I feel…thankful. Nobody has ever stood up for me the way Enzo does. Repeatedly, he's proven he cares. And I know Uncle T will be upset this happened, but when I'm with Enzo, it's becoming difficult to care about what my uncle thinks.

Let this be a lesson to him. This is what happens when he doesn't take care of his "best assets" properly.

Enzo presses the gun to Johnston's head. "Did you not hear me? Apologize."

Johnson clears his throat. "Sorry."

I smile, cupping my ear like I'm trying to hear him better. "I couldn't quite hear you, Johnston. Better speak up."

"I said I'm sorry."

"For?" I quirk a brow and cross my arms.

Enzo smirks.

"Say it." Enzo pushes the barrel against the back of his dome. "Say, 'I'm sorry, Venesa, for being a *cunt*.'"

Johnston grits his teeth and nods. "I'm sorry." He wipes the blood dripping into his eye from where he was pistol-whipped. "For being a…"

I walk up close to him, fire dancing in my eyes, no longer afraid. "A *cunt*, Johnston."

Johnston's nostrils flare and his chin lifts, retribution burning in his gaze.

Enzo prods him with the barrel of his gun.

"I'm sorry for being a cunt, Venesa."

Nodding, I place a hand over my heart. "Thank you, sugar. That really means a lot."

Enzo chuckles and puts his gun down, like he's not concerned in the slightest about retaliation. Like even though we're surrounded by weapons and Johnston has four of his guys standing on the other side of the building, he knows he won't be touched.

And most likely, he's right. It would be a death sentence to touch the prince of the Italian Mafia.

Enzo looks at me. "You got everything you need? We're leaving."

Normally, I'd want to argue. But I'm so ready to get out of here that I nod and follow his direction, letting him lead me around the corner and to the front of the docks, past Johnson's men.

Again, Enzo acts like he's not concerned in the slightest.

And the way they're all staring at him with disquiet makes me think something happened before he got to me.

It isn't until we're in the car, one *without Scotty* driving this time, and all the way back to the Lair, that he speaks.

"You good?" He jerks his chin at me.

I lick my lips and bob my head, and his gaze drops to follow the motion of my tongue.

"I can take care of myself," I say, the same way I always do.

He reaches out to grip my chin, tilting my face up to meet his. "I know. But just because you *can* doesn't mean you should have to."

And those words, something about the way he says

them, or maybe because he's even saying them at all…they unlock something inside me, a sensation I've never felt but is so overwhelming, I can barely stand it.

I've always prided myself on being independent. On not needing anyone other than my uncle, whom until now I've trusted with the world. And I don't know how Enzo knew where I was, why he was there, or why he came out and jumped to my defense, but right now, I'm so thankful, I could cry.

Hypothetically. The tears don't ever actually come.

All I can do is look him in the eyes and say, "Okay."

He releases my chin and skates his touch down my neck before resting his fingers loosely at the base of my throat. "Have you opened your present?" he asks softly.

Biting my lip, I shake my head. "Not yet."

He nods and drops his hand, and I feel empty at the loss of his touch.

I lean over the console to brush my lips across his cheek. He turns at the last second, and I pull back quickly, but not before our mouths graze. Just like last night.

Just barely.

Just a hint.

A whisper.

But it tilts my world on its axis anyway.

He sucks in a sharp breath, his hands gripping his steering wheel so tightly, it might break.

"Thank you," I murmur.

Then I open the car door and walk away, because if I

don't…I'm not sure I'll survive the engagement party tomorrow night.

When I have to watch him with another woman, even though it feels like he should be mine.

CHAPTER 29

Venesa

THE ENGAGEMENT PARTY IS AT UNCLE T'S estate, and I'm taking Athena with me.

There's no way in hell I'm going alone, and Fisher said he'd meet me there, which is a little out of character for him, so I was stuck between a rock and a hard place.

Athena is at least nice arm candy and can serve as a distraction.

It's what I need. A shield. Something to get me through this night until Enzo and Aria disappear and I can go back to pretending like they don't exist.

Good riddance, honestly.

And if that doesn't work, then I have an unbinding spell ready to go at home, just to make sure and cut any ties to Enzo that might be left over.

I'm a big believer that time is an illusion and doesn't mean much in the grand scheme of things, but that doesn't mean

I'm comfortable with knowing someone for a couple of weeks and letting them have such a big impact on my life. And Enzo has *impacted* me in ways I'm not sure I'll recover from.

And for the first time, I empathize a little with my momma, because maybe this is how she felt with my father. An overwhelming type of attraction she didn't have the discipline to control. Maybe that's why she always let him back, every single time, with a smile on her just-healed face.

Maybe that's why she always picked him above me.

Above everyone.

Above herself.

The engagement party itself is absolutely beautiful. Fit for a queen, or in this case, the princess of Atlantic Cove, and Uncle T has ensured that the who's who is here to rain their gifts and praise down on the happy couple.

Gag me.

The theme of the party itself is the Lost City of Atlantis, which I know was more Uncle T's idea than it was Aria's because she's never been too into the Kingston lore—at least not the way Uncle T is.

The party is being held in the ballroom that sits in the estate's basement, and it's bathed in beautiful moody blue lighting, giving it the impression of being underwater. Thick white pillars surround everything, and there's a sense of ethereal beauty, an ancient feeling I'm sure took an ostentatious amount of money to achieve.

A waiter passes by with a tray of champagne, and Athena grabs one and hands it to me.

I shake my head and set it down on the bar behind me. "I don't drink."

She looks at me funny. "Oh. Sorry, I…I didn't know that."

And why would she have known? Athena isn't someone I share my life with. She's just someone who's good at making me come.

"This is gorgeous," a random woman says, standing at the bar next to me.

Athena locks her arm around my waist, leaning in and brushing her nose along my ear. "Almost as gorgeous as you."

I appreciate the sentiment, but I'm really not in the mood for her brand of flirting.

Still, talking to her is better than the alternative of having to face this night alone.

Especially when I see Johnston Miller walking over with Uncle T, Enzo, and Aria in tow.

My eyes widen with shock as I look at Enzo, and he gives me a quick nod. Maybe to tell me there's nothing to worry about, but…

Why the hell is Johnston even here?

They're clearly heading toward me, and my heart skips a beat. There goes hoping I can get away with hiding in the corner all night.

"Who's that?" Athena asks, her fingers tightening around my waist.

"Nobody important, darlin'. You just stand there and look pretty." I smile back at her.

Enzo's eyes are fiery when they land on mine, dropping to where Athena has her hand on my hip. Like *I'm* doing something wrong.

I have to physically hold back the scoff at his audacity, because I'm sorry, but is this not *his* engagement party?

"Venesa," Johnston says when he reaches us. "How *fortunate* to see you again so soon."

Something isn't right here.

"Johnston. You look a little banged up." I gesture to his black eye. "Hope that doesn't hurt too bad."

I don't acknowledge Aria, because fuck her. And fuck Uncle T too, honestly. He hasn't even checked in on me since everything went down on my birthday.

Aria smirks like she knows something that I don't, and Uncle T leans in, pressing a kiss to my cheek.

Enzo just stares at me like he wants to either fuck me or kill me.

Aria looks around and then lifts a brow as she focuses on me. "No Fisher tonight?"

My protective nature swings forward, and I bristle. "Fisher isn't your concern, Aria. Worry about your man."

She narrows her eyes at me.

"And who's this?" Enzo pipes in, nodding toward Athena.

"This is my date." I grin widely. "Athena."

"So you finally admit it," Aria says. "You're a lesbian."

"Well, I'll tell you a secret, sweet Cousin." I cup my hand around my mouth and incline my body toward her. "The women make me come harder, but the men are easier to train. So I like them both but for very different reasons."

Uncle T stiffens because he's a bigot and prefers to pretend like my bisexuality doesn't exist. Aria chokes on her champagne.

Enzo has a practiced grin on his face as he rubs her back and presses a kiss to the side of her head. "Careful, princess."

A hit of jealousy sears through me when his lips touch her skin.

"Well," I snap. "As fun as this is, don't you all have some schmoozing to do?"

I wave my arm to the few hundred people pretending to give a damn about their nuptials, but I see the spark in Aria's eyes when I bring it up.

This is her moment. She loves the spotlight, always has. It's the reason she's here with Enzo right now, the reason *all* this is even happening.

"That's a fantastic idea," Uncle T says. "Aria, why don't you go say hi to the mayor? I just saw him and his wife walk in." He looks at me. "I need to speak with you." Then he turns to Enzo. "Both of you."

"Daddy, does that have to happen right *now*?" Aria protests. "This is my party!"

"I'm sorry, baby girl. Unfortunately, it can't wait." He smiles at her and then turns to Johnston, clapping him on the back. "I'll have Bas take you to my office, and I'll be there shortly."

Uncle T looks over the crowd and waves, and Bastien

appears out of thin air, maneuvering his way through the room and taking Johnston away. He barely meets my eyes as he does.

Why is he acting so weird?

Aria rises on her tiptoes to press a kiss to Enzo's mouth, and my stomach churns, envy slithering up my spine and wrapping around my chest like a constrictor until I can't breathe.

This is ridiculous.

Sighing, I turn to Athena. "You don't mind, sugar, do you? I'm sure you can entertain yourself until I get back."

She grins and kisses my cheek before moving her mouth to my ear. "Don't leave me for too long with these people. I'd rather get you home and on your back."

My eyes flick to Enzo and see his jaw clenched tight, his eyes narrowed dangerously on her.

We follow Uncle T out of the main ballroom until we're in a hallway off to the side. Enzo's trying to get my attention, but I studiously ignore him because having us both back here with Uncle T is either because he can tell we've been less than appropriate with each other or, more likely, Johnston ratted us out about last night.

Why else would he be here?

The tinkling of champagne glasses and inaudible murmurs of people from the ballroom just beyond us filter through the air, and I cross my arms and lean against the wall, waiting for Uncle T to speak.

Finally, he clears his throat. "Either of you care to tell me what went on last night with Johnston Miller?"

"You didn't let Bas go with me," I state.

Uncle T looks at me incredulously. "And that's your excuse for having E go with you instead?"

"Excuse me? I didn't *have* E go with me. I don't even know why he was there. I was handling things just fine."

Enzo snorts from beside me.

I glare over at him. "What?"

He shakes his head. "Nothing."

Uncle T's fiery gaze turns on him, and he points a finger. "It's starting to feel like you're fucking with my business."

"I was saving your niece from being assaulted," he says icily and takes a step forward, seeming to grow in height with every move he makes. "Something you should thank me for instead of trying to reprimand me like I'm some asshole you picked up off the street."

The tension ramps up.

Uncle T hits back. "She can handle herself."

"I was uncomfortable," I admit. The words feel foreign on my tongue, but I don't take them back.

Uncle T's brows rise, and he crosses his arms like he's waiting for elaboration.

"Every time I've gone for a gun drop, you've sent Bas with me, but this time you didn't. And I told you how worried I was about Johnston wanting to retaliate for his brother-in-law, so sending me there without backup felt like...it felt like you didn't give a damn."

Uncle T huffs, but he doesn't disagree with me.

It stings. Like salt water in an open wound.

"Why didn't you?" I press.

"Bas had more important things to deal with."

I bite back the sharp inhale of breath his words cause.

More important.

Uncle T steps in close. "You're lucky I have a good relationship with the MC, or else I'd be having you fix what you interfered with. You should know how important their relationship is to our bottom line. *Decades* of work that you could have fucked up last night if it weren't for me smoothing things over."

"She didn't interfere," Enzo interrupts. "I did."

Enzo moves until he's standing directly in front of me, like he's protecting me. Standing up against the one man I've never been able to find the backbone to stand up to myself—not with anything that matters anyway.

"And you're out of your fucking mind if you think I'm gonna stand here and let you berate her when all this woman does is bend over backward to do whatever you want, even when you continually treat her like shit."

My chest pulls taut, hurt swelling in the cavity like I've been sucker punched.

Uncle T stiffens, standing straighter, but it doesn't matter, because even if Enzo weren't taller than him, his aura would tower over my uncle anyway.

Enzo eclipses everything around him.

"I think in these past few weeks, you've forgotten who it is you're dealing with," Enzo says, his voice dark, the same way it was last night.

Uncle T's jaw locks. "I deal with your father, boy. Not you."

Enzo chuckles. "Maybe. But I've always learned that sometimes it's better to ask forgiveness than permission."

A flash of fear coasts across Uncle T's eyes, and it sends my emotions into a tailspin. I've never seen him afraid before, and part of me still feels loyalty, like I'm betraying him by letting a man who has no business standing up for me do so, even when he doesn't have to.

But the other part of me feels vindicated.

Enzo places a hand on Uncle T's shoulder and squeezes. "You're lucky I don't walk into your office where that little shit is waiting and make him regret running to tell you about last night in the first place."

"When your father—"

"How about you let me worry about that? I'm going to suggest you make your way back to the guests you've so lovingly invited to this...*celebration*. Now's not the time, and it's not the place."

"You're getting into business that has nothing to do with you, son."

Enzo chuckles, and a dark look crosses over his face. "I'm not your son, Trent. And I promise you don't want to make me your enemy."

Uncle T lifts his chin and looks between us before leveling *me* with a glare.

I'm surprised when he actually turns around and walks away, but I'm not an idiot. He will not take this insult from

Enzo lightly; he's just smart enough to realize he can't openly attack the underboss of the Marino family without severe repercussions, ones even he can't beat.

I'm so lost in my thoughts that it takes me a minute to realize that now it's just Enzo and me, alone again, in a dark, empty hallway.

I turn to leave.

"No words for me, piccola sirena?"

His voice stops me in my tracks, and I close my eyes. "I can't do this with you."

He walks up behind me, and his body heat envelops me like a cloak, sending pinpricks of pleasure skittering along my arms and down my legs. "Do what?"

"You *know* what," I reply.

He presses in even closer until I'm suffocating from the feel of him. Still, though, we aren't touching. I turn until I'm facing the wall, trying to get some space.

Enzo follows.

"You came here with someone else," he accuses.

"You're *engaged*," I exclaim. "You have no right. Absolutely no right to do this."

His hands come out and cage me in, pressing against the wall, and my fingers curl into fists.

"Don't touch me," I plead.

He's silent for a moment, and then says, "I won't."

But he moves in closer, his front brushing against my back.

There are sounds coming from just inside the main

ballroom, and my heart pitches into my throat, my anxiety going haywire. Anyone could walk out at any moment, and I'm trying *so* hard to keep myself from making a mistake.

If we give in…

It's wrong. Even if I can't *stand* Aria. Even if it feels like he's the only person on earth who has ever understood me.

Even if he's the only one who cares.

He's not *mine*, and he won't ever be.

His forehead drops against the back of my head, rolling back and forth, and I stiffen like a board to keep myself frozen in place.

"I won't," he repeats. "But I want to, so fucking bad that it feels like I can't breathe."

"Well, sometimes what we want doesn't matter." I try to make my voice sound stern, but I don't think it works based on the way it wobbles as it hits the air.

His face lowers until it's next to my ear. "Sometimes…it feels like you're the only thing that does."

CHAPTER 30

Venesa

"YOU OKAY?" ATHENA ASKS, STANDING NEXT to me in the back of the ballroom.

"Yeah," I reply distractedly.

I'm not okay. Not by a long shot, but she doesn't need to know that.

"Just a lot on my mind." I look at her, but I don't think she buys it because she narrows her eyes and then leans in until she's close enough to whisper dirty words in my ear, and while normally I'm all for the sexual appetite she brings—it's the only reason I keep her around—I can't help but notice the difference in the way my body feels when I'm with Athena as opposed to Enzo.

Maybe that's why I don't hear what she said. I'm too focused on someone else.

"She's fine." Fisher's voice cuts through the tense moment as he saunters over and knocks back a glass of the overpriced champagne in one gulp. He sets the empty glass down on the bar and then winks at us. "Aren't you, Short Stack?"

Relief douses me, and my shoulders relax. "There you are. I was thinking you wouldn't show up."

He gives me a goofy grin and sways slightly before righting himself.

"You drunk, Gup?" I hide my smile.

He doesn't drink often, but when he does, he's either the life of the party or the mood ruiner. I've tried to tell him he needs to find better control, but there are demons Fisher's been dealing with for a long time that we don't talk about, so instead, I just make sure I'm here to weather the storm with him.

"I am *perfect.*" He places a hand to his chest.

He's decked out in a bow tie and suit, and while I appreciate the effort, he still sticks out like a sore thumb.

"You look good, Fisher." I reach out and straighten his bow tie. "And here you thought you couldn't pull off dressing formal."

He grins at me, his eyes swimming with *something*. "Yeah, well…"

A high-pitched whine from a microphone being too close to a speaker cuts through whatever he replies with, making my ears ache. The people around me wince, but then Uncle T takes the stage with a bright, beaming smile, and the room goes silent, everyone paying rapt attention to the King of the Sea, waiting with bated breath.

Or maybe none of us really care, but we're all forced to pretend like he's the most important thing in the room.

My bitterness has clearly started to supersede my love for him.

"Here comes our lord and savior," Fisher mumbles into his fresh glass of champagne. "Everyone shut up and listen, or else he'll ruin your life."

I give him a sarcastic smile and face the front again.

Uncle T drones on for a long time about how much Aria means to him and how long he's waited for this moment, and I try real hard not to roll my eyes at the sentiment, because *we get it.*

She's his sparkling jewel.

A lot of occlusions if you ask me, but maybe I have a keener eye than everyone else.

It isn't until he calls Aria and Enzo up on the stage that I actually pay attention.

I shift on my feet and notice Fisher doing the same. I give him a weird look, letting his awkwardness distract me from the fact that I've done the one thing I promised myself I never would do.

Fall for a man.

How...*disappointing.*

"You know," Uncle T continues, "there's a long-standing tradition in the Kingston family, one that's been passed down for generations."

His words make me perk up, my gaze snapping to the front like a magnet.

"My great-great-great-great...and probably a few more greats in there"—he pauses with a sparkling grin, and right on cue, everyone chuckles—"kept a journal. And in that journal, he talked about the long line of royalty that's in our blood. One he traced back to Atlantis."

More chuckles filter through the room but not from me. My eyes narrow on him instead.

"Doesn't even make sense," Fisher mumbles into Athena's ear. "How can you find a bloodline in a city that's been lost?"

"I know it sounds like a child's tale." Uncle T waves his hand like he can't be bothered. "And maybe it is. But it's become an important tradition. One that means, well…" He runs his hand over his beard. "It means everything to me."

He nods, and Bastien moves onto the stage, his eyes meeting mine across the room.

I stand up straight as a board, blood whooshing so fast through my body, I can hear it in my ears.

"There's a family painting that's been in our family for over a century." Uncle T pauses, his gaze searing into mine.

An icy chill runs down my spine because I *know*. I just know he's doing this to punish me.

I watch with a sinking dread as Bastien presents the painting to Aria.

"Today, friends, is a momentous occasion," Uncle T declares. "Because today is the day I pass it on to my pride and joy, the *only* one who's deserving of such a sentimental and momentous item of our history: Aria." He calls her over.

She leaves Enzo's side and walks to her father, and my insides drop to the floor as she gives him a hug and then turns to the crowd, taking the microphone.

"Thank you, Daddy, for all your support in everything." Her eyes scan the room and don't stop moving until they find mine. And then she grins, victorious. "I know there are many people who claim to be 'family' who have had their eye on something so precious. But they don't deserve it. It's *tradition*, after all."

She turns to her father and grasps his hand before speaking into the microphone again. "It belongs with a *real* Kingston. Even if I won't technically carry the name for long."

Laughter filters through the crowd, and she continues to speak, but I can't hear her anymore, because the world has become muffled.

My vision blurs, and I reach out, grasping Athena's shoulder to steady myself.

Uncle T watches me from the stage, knowingly, and I can feel the moment the last little strings of my loyalty shrivel and wither away until nothing but betrayal and hate sit in their place, heavy and dark.

"V, you okay? You look like you've seen a ghost." Athena reaches out to rest her hand on my arm, but I can barely feel her touch.

"Oh, shit," Fisher says, his panicked eyes looking at me and then up at Aria.

I don't know what to do.

My entire life has been focused on one thing. Making my uncle happy. But that trident painting, as silly as it may be, was my last connection to my momma, and while she may not have been a great one, she was still *mine*.

If there's one thing a man will do, it's disappoint you.

And I shouldn't have thought my uncle would be the exception.

Enzo excuses himself from being onstage and walks away. I track his movements, my heartbeat pounding in my ears, watching as he leaves the ballroom entirely. And after all these weeks, all these hours of torment holding myself back and trying like hell to be a good person, to not disappoint Uncle T by betraying Aria…I can't find a single solitary fuck to give now.

So I follow him out of the room.

Because maybe it's time I truly put myself first and go after the things that *I* want.

Starting with my cousin's fiancé.

CHAPTER 31

Enzo

I LEFT BECAUSE I COULDN'T STAND UP THERE for another second while Trent waxed poetic about his daughter and lauded us both.

And what was that whole thing with them being descendants of the Lost City of Atlantis and then presenting Aria with that family painting like it was a gift straight from God?

I don't mind the painting. I *do* mind the way Venesa looked after Aria made those bullshit comments about being a *true* Kingston. But that's probably because I'm hyperaware of Venesa in a way I've never been with anyone else.

And I can't physically go through with this sham of a wedding, which means I have to either convince my father it isn't the right choice, or I have to kill him and take over, which I'm not sure is even possible logistically…or what I want.

Regardless, after tonight, I'm going to be thrown back into the fire.

Back to reality. Back to the droll life that was mapped out for Peppino yet is being fulfilled by me.

Splashing water on my face in the bathroom, I chuckle.

God, I'm fucking pathetic.

I wash my hands and then exit, but right when I swing the door open, I'm slammed into, my body physically being pushed until it's inside the small room.

Venesa's standing there, determination in her gaze. She smirks at me and saunters forward like I'm her prey.

"You okay?" I ask.

"Shut up," she demands.

I close my mouth, throwing my hands in the air and miming that I'm zipping my lips. I'll never say another word again if it means she'll keep looking at me the way she is right now.

She looks ethereal. Cheeks flushed, a gorgeous floor-length black gown lined with purple, hair a beautiful swirl of a mess on her head, and I'm…

Fucking lost in her. The way I always am.

She hesitates when she reaches me, her fingers running up the front of my chest and slipping beneath the lapels of my suit. Her tongue peeks out and licks her bottom lip, and my gaze follows, my own mouth watering from the thought of what it must taste like.

"I want to pretend…just for one night, that it *is* a different life."

It takes a second for her words to register, but when they do, embers flare to life.

If this is the only chance I'm ever going to have to be with her, I'm going to take it.

I don't care that it's my engagement party to another woman. I don't care that it technically makes me a cheater. I'll live with the guilt for the rest of my life if it means I can have Venesa for even a fucking second.

"What do you need?" I ask, keeping my voice low because I'm afraid to ruin the moment.

"You."

That single word stokes the flames and makes them erupt into a wildfire. I lean down and try to grab her lips with mine, but at the last second, she turns her head. My chest pinches, but I brush it off and keep moving forward. My hands fling out and wrap around her body, her soft curves melding into my hard planes like we're two long-lost pieces to a puzzle *finally* clicking into place, and I groan at the feel of her fully pressed against me.

She's just as soft and perfect as I imagined.

And she's clearly out of sorts, so if she needs me to keep her anchored, then I'll be that for her, and if it gets out, if there are any repercussions after, I'll deal with them as they come.

Her fingers dig into my suit. "Just...make me forget for a little bit, okay? *Please.*"

My brow furrows. I can taste the desperation in the air, and it's so out of character for her, I almost stop completely and ask if she wants to talk instead, but I know that will only send her running.

"Okay," I tell her.

And for as strong of a woman as she is, for *everything* she is that no one else sees,she's asking for me to take control. To relieve her from being someone who always has to take care of everything on her own, because if she doesn't, then no one will.

I grip her tightly by the hips and flip her around until her ass is pressed against me. My cock jerks at the feel.

"Put your hands on the wall," I command in a low tone.

She sucks in a breath and hesitates for a moment, but she doesn't disobey, slowly sliding her fingers up the wall until her bloodred manicure is at my eye level and her palms are flat against the surface.

My heart flutters—fucking *flutters*—and I take my time touching her, relishing in the feel of her curves as I skim up her sides and glide my hands to the front of her body, teasing the undersides of her breasts.

"I need—" she starts.

"I know what you need," I interrupt, then put my lips next to her ear. "Let me take care of you."

And I mean it, even if I shouldn't.

Because the only thing that matters is *her*.

She blows out a heavy breath and then nods, and I can feel when she surrenders, her body turning to putty against me.

"That's my girl." My hands wrap around her fully, cupping her breasts, my cock twitching again from the weight of them.

"I've dreamed about touching you," I murmur.

She moans, pressing against me further. Blood rushes to my dick, and it pulses against her, and fuck, I wish I could just slip her dress up to her thighs and sink so deep inside her that I forget the world, but I won't.

Not like this.

This isn't about me; this is about what *she* needs, and I don't know what pushed her to this point, but I know that if this is my only chance to be with Venesa, then I'm going to make her remember it.

I want her to feel cherished. Taken care of.

Even if it's just this once.

And if I ever get the chance to be with her fully? I don't want it to be in her uncle's bathroom at my engagement party to another woman. Besides, if I give in and give her a quick fuck here, I know she'll compartmentalize our entire encounter, making it seem like less than what it actually is.

Because what it *is* is fucking everything.

I groan as I manipulate her flesh, digging into her breasts and ghosting over where I know her nipples are hiding beneath her dress.

"I'm not going to fuck you," I whisper in her ear.

Her body stiffens, but I slip my hand over the top of her cleavage and finger the neckline of her dress, dipping below the fabric until I slip underneath completely and I'm groping nothing but flesh.

My eyes roll back at the feel of her, skin to skin, and when she makes a mewling noise and moves on me like I'm not giving her enough, I thrust my hips forward, starting a slow, torturous friction against the curve of her ass.

She's plastered to the wall, and I reach one of my hands up and intertwine our fingers, putting them on her chest and then moving us down her body together. Slowly, torturously.

My other hand leaves her tit and slides her dress up her thigh until the material is bunched around her waist, and I'm so fucking turned on, I might explode without her even *touching* me.

And I'm not touching her either.

Not really. Not the way I want.

"I'm not going to fuck you," I repeat. "Because when I do, I'm going to take my time, cherishing every single inch of you, drinking up your cries and drowning in your moans. Tell me you understand."

She sucks in a breath and nods, her face turning until her cheek is pressed against the wall. "I understand."

"Such a perfect girl," I murmur against her skin.

Our entwined hands move beneath the bunched-up fabric, and arousal makes precum drip from the tip of my dick when I feel the heat of her cunt through our fingers. She's not wearing any underwear.

"Show me how you make yourself come," I demand, biting my cheek so I don't fuck this up and make this end too soon.

"Enzo," she pleads.

The way she says my name makes me fucking crazy, and I groan, my left hand fisting the fabric at her hip.

"Show me," I tell her. "So when I'm alone, late at night, I can close my eyes and picture it. Knowing you're lying somewhere, touching yourself and thinking of me."

"I need you to fuck me."

"You need me to take care of you," I correct. "To put you first. I won't let you turn this into a one-night stand. Not when it's more, and you know it. Now, take your hand, play with that pretty little pussy, and make yourself come."

My breath hitches when she starts a slow motion with her palm, my hand moving on top of hers from the way we're intertwined, and I swear to God it's the most erotic thing I've ever experienced in my life.

She moans when she moves us farther down, wetness dripping as she teases her entrance with our fingers.

"That's it, baby. Give it to me," I urge.

Her head flies back and lands on my shoulder, and I plaster myself to her, my forearm locking across her stomach, my fingers twitching with the need to take over completely. To show her what it feels like when I draw out her orgasm on my own.

"Enzo," she mewls, and then she slips us inside her, just a little, just the tips of our fingers.

Goddamn.

"In a different life," I start, my voice shaky from the restraint of holding myself back, "I would be on my knees, feasting on you every day for the rest of our lives."

She groans, her head lolling and her breathing becoming choppy. She pushes us in farther, her tight channel gripping our fingers as she slowly slides back and forth, her palm moving in circular motions against her clit.

"In a different life, it would be *you* on my arm, and *you* I'd get to marry. And I'd take you home and fuck you in *our* bed, sinking my cock so deep inside you that you'd never get me out."

Her hand moves faster; her pussy is drenching both our palms.

Drops of my cum drip down my length, making me a mess. I push against her ass, and it shoves our bodies closer to the wall, applying more pressure to her clit from the added weight.

"In a different life..." I pause, emotion suddenly clogging my throat. "I'd love you out loud."

Something shifts and changes when the words drop off my tongue unbidden. I didn't mean to say them, and part of me is worried that I ruined the moment, but her cunt contracts and pulses, and she explodes, her moan so loud, I'm worried everyone in the ballroom can hear. My free hand that was holding her by the stomach shoots up and presses against her mouth to stifle the noise, her cheek plastering my fingers to the wall as she comes undone.

She's a vision.

She's everything.

But she's still not fucking mine.

We stay like this, pressed against each other even after she comes back down, because I know that once I move, this will be over. The spell will be broken. I can already feel the whispers of Ma creeping up my spine and into my psyche, but I push them back down, not wanting to destroy things.

And I have this sinking feeling this is all we'll ever get. A stolen moment, hidden away in a locked bathroom, and it makes me sick because she deserves so much more.

She twists her head and gives me a small smile, those damn dimples making my heart a fucking mess.

And then there's a click, and the door bursts open behind us, and the moment is smashed into a thousand different pieces.

Because her uncle just walked into the room.

CHAPTER 32

Enzo

WELL...THIS IS FUCKED.

Luckily, neither of us is in any state of undress, so it's easy enough to step back and let her dress fall, but I'll be damned if I'm going to let Trent see any part of her, so when I turn around, I stand in front of her to offer her protection because I already know this won't go down well.

Was it the smartest choice to do this here, right across the hall from everyone, at my *engagement* party to another woman?

No.

Do I feel like a piece of shit?

Yes.

But I don't regret it. This isn't the same thing as Ma and Pops. I've never loved Aria, and we're *not* married yet.

My fingers are dripping, and my only regret is that I didn't get to taste them before Trent walked in and demolished the moment.

Well, that and not kissing her.

Which Venesa avoided, and I'm not sure why.

A shot of panic hits my stomach when I imagine this little rendezvous being found out by my pops, but I push it to the side because my immediate concern is right here and now with Venesa.

She's strong, she's *so* fucking strong, but her uncle is her weak spot, even if she can't see it, and familial ties are hard to break, even the dysfunctional ones.

I would know.

And even though she was the one who instigated this moment, I can't help but feel like this is my fault.

The door slams behind Trent, and he flicks the lock, his eyes as stormy as a hurricane.

"You ungrateful little bitch," he spits.

"Uncle T…" Venesa murmurs from behind me.

"I'd think carefully about the next words that come out of your mouth, Trent," I cut in, because I don't really feel like hearing her try to explain this away. Part of me is terrified she's going to minimize what just happened. I don't know if I can take it if she says something to make this seem like it didn't matter. Like it didn't just change everything.

Or worse—that it was a mistake.

Trent slides his eyes to me, his chest heaving like he's a fire-breathing dragon. "You little piece of shit. Just wait until your father hears about this. I suggest you take your leave, go out there, get yourself together, and find your *fiancée*. You know, the one who's wearing your ring and has been looking for you for the past thirty minutes?"

I swallow, guilt weaving its way through me, not because I have feelings for Aria but because I'm not that guy. I'm not a cheater.

Although, technically, I guess now I am.

But it doesn't matter. I'm not leaving Venesa until she tells me to.

I shake my head. "How many times do I have to tell you, Trent? You don't get to tell me how high to jump and expect me to submit." I take a step closer to him because surely he's out of his fucking mind. Or else he has no clue what I'm capable of.

"I suggest you don't push me." I lower my voice until it's a dark rumble. "Or I promise you won't like the outcome."

"Son, when your father finds out what you've done, I'll be the least of your concerns. You better hope you make it back to New York tomorrow before he hears from me."

"Enzo." Venesa's voice is powerful behind me, deep and sultry, with a pleading note.

She moves until she's in front of me, facing me, and I take a second to soak her in, because there's a sinking feeling in the pit of my stomach from the tone of her voice that tells me this might be the last chance I get.

She's going to push me away.

My heart cracks at the thought.

She's so fucking beautiful. Her hair is mussed, her cheeks are flushed, and her eyes have a glaze that only a spectacular orgasm can provide.

"It's okay." She gives me a soft smile and squeezes my arm before spinning to face her uncle, who is standing across from us, fuming.

"I'm not leaving you here alone with him," I say through gritted teeth.

She looks back at me. "I can take care of myself, remember?"

I step into her, not giving a single fuck if Trent is watching, and I lean down until I'm next to her ear. "And still… you shouldn't have to."

The words taste bittersweet on my tongue. I mean them, more than I've ever meant anything in my life. But Trent isn't wrong. I'm suffocated by the will of my father, at least for now.

I've never hated being part of the family, of promising Ma I would stay loyal, until this very moment.

Venesa sighs and turns to face me again, her chest brushing against mine as she gazes up at me.

"Venesa…" Trent starts.

I cut him a glare, and he clenches his jaw. But at least he shuts up.

"We both knew what this was, right?" she murmurs.

"I'm not leaving you," I repeat.

Her gaze softens, and she stares up at me from underneath her long black lashes, her hand cupping my cheek. My eyes close and I press against her, my chest feeling like it's physically cracking in half.

Fuck this.

"In a different life, right?" she whispers.

My lids snap open.

And then she rises, her hand wrapping around the nape of my neck and dragging me down, and she presses a soft, chaste kiss to my lips.

My heart stalls out, and I free-fall because it wasn't supposed to be like this.

She lingers for a few moments before pulling back, a sad look in her eyes.

I swallow around the knot in my throat, hating myself for what I'm about to let her do. But at the end of the day, I need to control the narrative with my father before Trent gets ahold of him. And the only way to do that…is to walk away.

For now.

My nostrils flare with my inhale, and I grit my teeth so tightly, my jaw aches.

She takes a step backward, and she looks every bit the calm, collected woman I know.

In a different life…

But in this one?

I'm bound by the Mafia and a woman I'll never love.

CHAPTER 33

Venesa

THE SECOND ENZO LEAVES THE ROOM, I BLOW out a deep breath, ignoring the way my chest is aching. I'll focus on that later. Right now, it's time for my uncle and me to have a chat.

I didn't want Enzo to leave; I would have done anything to let him stand next to me as a pillar of strength. The one he's been for me since the moment we met. The one I don't deserve for many reasons.

But I know that even more dangerous than the wrath of my uncle is Enzo's situation. He's tied to a life that has chains and rules I can't even begin to understand. And I know him being the underboss, and his father's son, only gets him so far.

If his father wants this marriage to Aria, then it will happen, whether or not Enzo agrees, so there's no point in him taking hits for me that will only hurt him. And truthfully, no matter what just happened here, there's no future for us.

It still doesn't make it hurt any less for him to walk away.

He told me in a different life, he'd love me out loud.

Letting him walk away is my way of loving *him*. Because I know what would happen if he went against this marriage to Aria.

The marriage his father arranged.

The one that my uncle approved.

Nothing but death and destruction would await us, and at least right now, I can try to minimize the damage. Besides, there are things Enzo doesn't know. Things he can *never* know.

Not really.

He thinks he'd love me out loud, but the truth is, he'd never be able to love me at all.

So his departure is a weight off my shoulders. A breath exhaled because I should be the only one bearing the burden of what just happened. After all, it was me who instigated it.

I blink twice, letting my eyes unfocus and then refocus, and I move my gaze from where Enzo disappeared to my uncle. I meet his stare, lifting my chin and hiding the tremble in my hands.

"After all I've done for you," Uncle T hisses. "I don't even know who the hell you are."

That's fair. Some days lately, I don't even think I really know myself.

"You know who I am," I reply, my voice low. "I'm just like my momma…right?"

I won't lie, this hurts. Having Uncle T stare at me like I'm a stranger. Like I'm the biggest disappointment he's ever seen. It sears into me like a serrated knife, jagged and cold, but I don't know this version of him, this untrustworthy, secretive man who keeps me locked out and lies to my face.

A twinge of grief taps against my chest.

"Don't look like that. Don't you *dare* make that face," he spits at me again, taking a step closer. "Do you have any idea what you've done?"

"What I've done?" I laugh incredulously. "All I've *ever* done is what you've asked of me. I bend over backward for your approval, to try to get even a smidgen of what you reserve for your precious daughter."

"So you fuck her husband instead?" he asks.

"They're not married, and I didn't fuck him."

"Semantics."

"But I should have," I say, taking a step closer.

He stands up straight, towering over me even though we're almost the same height, his eyes narrowed and icy.

My uncle is an intimidating man, but this is the first time he's directed it at me in full force.

Doesn't matter. I'm too angry to be afraid.

"Watch your mouth," he snaps.

"You don't get to tell me what to do anymore."

"I can't even fucking *look* at you," Uncle T says. "I knew there was something going on. Saw you two on the cameras that first day. I should have known you wouldn't be able to keep your legs closed long enough to actually accomplish something useful." He pauses and lifts his chin. "You're right. You *are* just like your momma."

I point my finger in his face, my teeth clenched, trying like hell to maintain composure. "You keep her name out of your mouth."

He throws his head back and laughs. "Keep her name out of my mouth? Little one, you have no idea, do you? You stupid, insignificant, motherless child."

Each word is a stab to my already-broken world. But my illusion of him has shattered, and I see this for what it is. See *him* for what he is.

The devil.

My enemy.

"She was a useless slut when she was younger, and she was a useless slut when she died," he goes on.

My insides ice over. "Was it you?"

"I don't know what you mean."

"You know exactly what I mean." I step forward until there's barely any space between us. "Was. It. You who killed her? I deserve to know that much, at least."

"No." He leans in, his eyes angry. "But I wish it had been."

"Was it my father?"

He scoffs. "How would I know that?"

I reach out and grab a glass vase filled with flowers, then slam it on the ground at his feet. "Don't lie to me!" My voice comes out shrill and high.

His eyes widen slightly, and he backs up a space now.

"Tell me the truth, for once in your fucking life."

"The truth," he says slowly. "The truth…okay, Venesa. You want the truth? Your father was a no-good drunk who owed me money and didn't pay, and I saw an opportunity. My sister was worthless, but our daddy loved her like the moon loves the tides, and even after she cut us all off, he *still* wanted to give her everything, like a fool."

I shake my head. "You are really just a pathetic, jealous old man, aren't you?"

He reaches out and backhands me, his gold rings cutting into the side of my lip.

Fury burns through me, but shock keeps me in place, my palm coming up to clutch at the spot he hit.

"Don't speak on things you know nothing about, little one." He steps on top of the shattered glass, the crunch of it loud in the otherwise quiet room. "I didn't kill your momma. But I sure as hell made sure she was dead."

"Who was it?" I whisper, still clutching my cheek.

"The Atlantis MC, of course. The men you've been working with for the past few years." He laughs, one of his brows rising—challenging me to do something. But I stumble back instead, my body hitting the wall. My hand moves from my face and clutches at my chest now because I can't breathe, I can't *breathe*, and he's slowly suffocating me with his truths.

"Did you ever actually love me?" I force out, although it's hard from the knot that's lodged in the center of my throat.

He's silent.

I huff out a laugh and shake my head. "All these years, and you've just been using me."

"I gave you a *home,* you ungrateful little bitch," he calls me again. "You are who you are *because* of me." He slams his fist against his chest. "Get out of my house. Get out of my state."

My eyes grow wide. "What?"

"You're finished here. Do you understand?"

"Uncle T, I…"

He levels me with his stony stare. "You don't deserve the Kingston name, and you're no family of mine."

I let out a sarcastic laugh, anger quickly replacing my heartache, and I grasp it, letting it fill me like gasoline and set ablaze the raging inferno inside.

God, I've been so blind. So ignorant.

"You said I am who I am because of you," I whisper, pressing my nails into the insides of my hands until red drips down my fingers.

I step forward, my heart pulsing with rage and vengeance until its inky poison pumps through my veins like blood.

"Just wait until you see who I become in spite of you."

Pushing past him, I walk out the door.

I walk out of his life.

For good.

CHAPTER 34

Venesa

"SO, YOU'RE SKIPPING TOWN?" FISHER ASKS, leaning against the corner of my vanity and flicking a Zippo lighter open and closed.

"On orders of the king," I joke, although the sentiment falls flat.

I move the two candles off my altar, the rope between them singed and burned from where I just finished a cord-cutting ceremony for my relationship with my uncle.

I'm tired, it's late, and I'm really not in the mood for company. But I called Fisher over because I'm leaving tonight. I don't know where I'm going, and I don't have very much money, but I know I need to get out of here until I figure out my next steps.

My duffel bag is half-packed with my favorite pieces of clothing, my makeup, and a few odds and ends I can't leave behind. Mainly, my crystals and a few basic herbs.

I don't let myself think about my babies in the basement because, as much as I wish I could bring them with me, it's not realistic. They need their environment to thrive, and it's not like I can take a saltwater aquarium wherever I'm going.

I move to my rack of clothes and grab a lace shirt, then toss it harder than necessary; it hits the edge of my bag and drops to the floor.

Fisher leans down to pick it up, folds it, and places it gingerly in the bag, then sits on the corner of my bed, his leg bouncing rhythmically.

"What's up with you?" I ask. "You're fidgety."

"So?"

I lift a brow. "You're never fidgety."

He shrugs and doesn't meet my eye. "Sorry, my best friend is leaving. Am I supposed to be calm?"

Guilt sits heavy in my middle because I haven't exactly told Fisher the whole story. I want to, but…there's just something whispering in my head, telling me to keep Enzo close to my chest for now.

And I've never been one to ignore my intuition.

Plus, once I put the full truth out into the world, then it doesn't really feel like *mine* anymore, and tonight is something I want to keep forever.

"Daddy T didn't tell you why?" he asks.

I chew on my bottom lip and debate how much to say. "All I know is he went from being everything I depended on to the person I think I hate most in the world."

"Well, this is fucked, Short Stack."

"I don't know, Fisher, it's just…it is what it is." I blow out a breath and sit next to him, giving up on packing for the moment.

He gives me a look. "I'm just having a hard time wrapping my head around it. Your uncle *needs* you, more than anyone else. You're his right hand."

"Don't let Bas hear you say that." Another pang to the chest. *Was Bas ever really on my side?*

"I don't give a fuck about Bas." He huffs. "So what's gonna happen with the Lair? You're coming back, right?"

Melancholy filters through every part of me, because I don't *know* what's going to happen with the Lair. His guess is as good as mine. It's never been in my name. I've been a glorified manager this entire time, deluding myself into believing something different.

The more my eyes are opened to reality, the more rage builds inside me, because why should my uncle get to have everything? He may be the *King of the Sea,* but a king is nothing without his loyal subjects.

And he just threw me away like trash.

He doesn't *deserve* it.

Fisher sighs, his leg still bouncing. "Where will you go?"

My stomach churns with anxiety. "I have no clue."

He glances at me and then looks back down at his lap, taking that Zippo and flicking it open and closed again. "You can just stay with me, you know."

"No. I need to get away entirely. At least for now. It's

just…Uncle T has used me for a long time, Gup. And he owns this state. I'm not safe as long as I'm here."

He nods, sadness covering his features. "You could always forgive him. Apologize or…I don't know, something."

"I'm tired of being someone's burden and not someone's choice."

He wraps his arm around me, resting his head on my shoulder. "You've never been a burden to me."

Pressure clogs my throat and builds behind my eyes, and I will something to come out. But like always, nothing does.

"Look out for things here while I'm gone, yeah? You'll take care of my babies?"

He makes a face. "You know I will."

Fisher stands and I follow suit, wrapping my arms around him and sinking into his hold. I close my eyes, cherishing the moment and committing it to memory, because who knows when I'll get the chance again?

"Love you, Short Stack. Don't be a stranger." Fisher's voice cracks.

"Yeah," I murmur. "Love you too, Gup."

I walk him to the door and close it behind him, resting my back against it and squeezing my eyes shut.

Come on, cry, Venesa.

Nothing. Just an ever-growing ache in the center of my chest.

Sighing, I head to my vanity and open the drawers, making sure I didn't forget anything important. I suck in a breath, my heart skipping when I see something in the bottom one.

A small black box with silver wrapping paper and a purple bow.

Slowly, I reach down and pick up Enzo's present, my hand shaking and my chest feeling like it might burst open. I slide my nail beneath the taped paper and unwrap the gift, and when I open the box, there's a necklace there.

A coral seashell on a black rope.

The one I wouldn't let him buy me.

The throbbing in my chest expands until it squeezes my lungs and steals my breath.

A folded note falls out when I move the necklace, and I set the black box down, picking up the paper with my free hand.

It shakes as I hold it open.

To making memories… Happy birthday.—Enzo

Pressure builds behind my eyes and scorches up my throat, and it feels like I'm about to crack in two.

Glancing down at the note again, I run my thumb over the writing and then walk to my bed and slip it inside my duffel bag.

I place the seashell around my neck. It's cold against my skin, and heavy, and every time I take a step, I feel it pressing on my chest, reminding me that at least once, there was someone who made me feel loved out loud.

And I'll accept nothing less again.

Suddenly, the answer to Fisher's question becomes

so clear. I *am* coming back. And I'm going to take everything from my uncle the same way he's taken everything from me.

But first, I'm going to tell Enzo the truth about everything.

CHAPTER 35

Enzo

THERE'S A CRICK IN MY NECK FROM SLEEPING on the worst bed known to man, but I'm ignoring it. Actually, I'm using the pain to ground me because my mind has been a whirlwind since the engagement party last night, and today, I'm not sure what the fuck I'm going to do.

I didn't go find Aria like Trent asked me to because I couldn't in good conscience go to her when Venesa's cum was still coating my hand and her moans were reverberating in my memory.

I'm a dick, and I've done some fucked-up things in my life, but that's a little too much even for me. So, instead, I stayed at the bed-and-breakfast with Scotty, and I slept on an old, creaky pullout couch. "Slept" being a generous term. Betty refused to let me rent a room, the old hag.

Really, I stayed up all night trying to figure out how the hell to come to terms with the man I want to be and the man I'm *forced* to be. And the one person I really need to speak with, the only person I'd trust to help me, is Gio, who's obviously in New York. It was always in the plans to head back there today, but I've moved up my itinerary, my plane ready to leave as soon as I'm done talking with Aria, who's the only reason I'm back at the Kingston Estate.

I expected there to be hustle and bustle, recovery and cleanup from last night's party, but it's as silent as ever in the mansion. Nobody except quiet housekeepers and empty rooms.

Aria's not in her bedroom, and she isn't out back by the pool or the private beach, so I'm making my way through the house, room by room, trying to find her. I don't know what I'm going to say or what I'll do, but I know I'm leaving, and I'm not taking her with me.

I can't marry her. I won't.

Voices filter through a crack in Trent's office door when I hit the hallway, and I head that way. I'm about to knock, even though it isn't fully closed, but I pause when I hear Aria's voice, pushing it open just a smidge more instead.

"I don't want to hear it, Aria." Trent's voice is stern. "He doesn't deserve you, and that's the end of it."

"I think I know what I deserve."

"He's fucking around on you. That's the life you want for yourself? The life you expect to have?"

She knows. I can't believe he told her.

"We needed you to *control* him," he continues. "Not be a pretty accessory on his arm."

My stomach twists, Trent's words weaving a neural lamp that's lighting up new pathways.

Aria stomps her foot and slams her hands on his desk, her face growing ruddy. "I don't care! I don't care, Daddy. He's what I want, and he's *mine*. I won't let that bitch take him from me. I deserve to have him.

"I did exactly what you asked me to," she continues. "*Everything* I've done since coming back here was at your beck and call. Because you promised me if I did, you'd make sure I got what I wanted..."

My blood turns to ice.

"Sweetheart," Trent starts.

"Don't you 'sweetheart' me!" she yells, swiping her hand across his desk and sending his belongings to the floor with a crash.

My heart picks up speed, banging against my chest.

"You want to talk about control? *You're* the one who didn't hold up their end of the deal. You were supposed to get him to put a hotel down here, make it easier for us to keep him under our thumb, but instead, you handed him to Venesa on a silver platter, and just like I warned you, she had to be a dumb bitch about it."

What the fuck?

"I even put that stupid tracker on his phone, which was a reckless idea, by the way."

"Aria—"

"I did all of it without question!" she screeches. "I've been your puppet for years without any recognition for it,

Daddy. *Years*. And now you're here telling me E and I can't be together? That you're 'calling it off'? What about what I want?"

"You don't know what you want!" he yells back.

My hand is frozen on the door, and my stomach is a lead weight on the floor.

"I do know. I've always known. I want *him*."

Trent sighs. "He won't treat you right, baby girl. You deserve better."

"But, Daddy…" She sniffles.

"It's not up for discussion."

"I love him."

"Oh, sweetheart." He sighs. "Stop using words you don't understand."

"Don't you tell me what I understand," she hisses. "He owes me. He can't just…walk away."

"Spare me the dramatics, Aria, please. Like you've always said, you weren't even the one who *saved* him."

His words hit me in the solar plexus like a sucker punch, and I take several large steps back.

What the fuck do they mean she didn't save me? If she didn't…then who did?

My mind flits through every situation—every moment—of my relationship with Aria. Waking up to her on the Hudson, then again in the hospital. Every time she's reminded me of how fate brought us together and how scared she was when she thought I was dead.

It was all a fucking ruse. She was *lying*.

I feel betrayal for sure, but more than that, I feel… relieved. I can finally let go of the tether tying me to her. The debt I owed her is fake. It doesn't exist.

I exhale my obligation, and I turn around and walk away.

Let them wonder where I am and what I'm doing.

I'm going home. It's time to make some changes.

CHAPTER 36

Enzo

MY DAD'S HOUSE DOESN'T FEEL LIKE HOME.

Not that it should. He's only lived here for the past ten years, and I've been out on my own since I was seventeen, long before our small two-bedroom apartment turned into sprawling landscaped lawns and bathrooms with heated marble floors.

This house feels like an acquaintance. There's no nostalgia, no memories of bologna sandwiches and quarter waters from the corner store.

Maybe that's for the best.

Now that I've been to South Carolina, it's easy to see the resemblance between where my pops lives and the Kingston estate. Both are flashy with wealth and tucked away from civilization, and just like with Trent, for the first time, I wonder how out of touch Pops is with the streets he runs, since he doesn't live and breathe them.

I've only spent a few years as part of the administration instead of being out there with my crew, but already even I feel the heartbeat of everything dulling. It used to pound feverishly in my ears, pump through my blood like the city's soul was flooding my veins, and now it's just a whisper.

Nothing is like it was.

I know Pops is here today, although when I walk in the front door, the emptiness echoes through the white marble foyer and resonates in my chest.

I bypass the kitchen and head to his office in the back hallway of the right wing. I'm surprised when I peek my head in and he isn't there, and I wander around, trying to find him.

Every minute since I've left Atlantic Cove, my mind has been whirring, uncovering red flags from the people in my life like an archaeologist digging up fossils.

I have questions. Lots of them. And I'm not sure if my father had any part of creating the mystery or if he's just as in the dark, but this is a game of chess, not checkers.

There's noise filtering from the den, and I make my way there, surprised when I hear voices.

No fucking way he's got people here.

Something smacks me in the chest and jump-starts my heart, making it twitch in anticipation, and I follow the noise.

The den itself is dark when I walk in, shades drawn and nothing but a small lamp with low yellow lighting casting across the burgundy leather sofa and shining on Pops's face. He's staring at the TV and absent-mindedly swirling a tumbler of whiskey in his hand. He moves the glass around and around, his eyes fixated on the television. I follow his gaze, and that vise clutching my middle squeezes tighter.

He's watching home videos.

Most of which he wasn't ever home to actually *be* in, but I guess that's why we record things: so we can experience memories we were never truly part of.

"Pops," I say to him as I walk into the room.

He doesn't reply, just keeps his eyes steady on the television, the crystal glass in his hand still swirling. The fireplace heats the side of my body when I walk by it, the crackling sending small sparks off the brick walls of the hearth, but there's an odd tension in the air that keeps my skin chilled. I move around the mahogany coffee table and sit on the other side of the couch, sighing when I lean back to take in what he's watching.

It's a tape of Peppino from after high school graduation, in the driveway of our old house, loading up the last of his suitcases on his way to Yale. Ma is standing off to the side, and the sight of her makes my throat swell. Her arms are wrapped around her small frame while she tries to hold back her tears, but she isn't successful. She never was good at hiding her emotions, especially when it came to us.

I remember this day.

"Pops," I try again.

Finally, I get his attention, his hazy, bloodshot gaze swinging from the screen over to me. There's a heavy feeling in the air, a melancholy look covering his face, and I know without having to ask what's going through his head. Right now, Pops is an open book while he mourns his murdered child, the one who was supposed to raise us to new heights in a way I never could.

I blow out a heavy breath, run a hand through my hair, and look over at him. "How long have you been in here watching these?"

He grunts but doesn't respond. Instead, he reaches beside him, places his drink down, and picks up an empty glass and his crystal decanter. He pours before passing it to me without a word.

And that's how we spend the next few minutes, sitting in silence, swirling our drinks, me pretending the burn in my chest is from the whiskey and not from the sound and sights of my dead family on the screen.

Or the woman I met and left behind in South Carolina.

Just as I've gotten used to the silence, the alcohol pumping through my veins and dulling the sharp edges, Pops speaks.

He takes a sip and then swallows. "You're back."

I nod and take another drink, suddenly grateful for the balm to this talk.

He glances around. "And did you bring your pretty fiancée?"

I lick my lips and place my glass down on the table, my heart pounding from the conversation I'm about to have. "No."

Now he looks at me fully. "So explain to me why you're here."

"That's a long story."

His bushy brow, tinged with gray, rises in question. "That's funny. Trent Kingston was able to tell it in mere minutes."

My father's jaw clenches, a brief flash of mistrust on his face. It's the same look he's been getting increasingly over the past five years, since he murdered half the commission and demanded subservience from the rest.

Corruption. Greed. Power.

I tried to warn Peppino that Pops was losing his mind, but he never listened, and he ended up clipped.

I'm not out here about to make the same mistakes that he made.

"Trent's version of events is skewed," I say.

"Ah, again, similar to what he said. Coincidence, no?"

I shake my head. "I don't believe in coincidence."

He smirks then. "*Bene.*" He takes another sip of his drink before setting it down. "So you got caught dipping your dick in the wrong *puttana* and then ran away instead of being a man. A *Marino*."

I strongly disagree. "You shouldn't trust anything Trent Kingston says. He's a fucking snake, and so is his daughter. You believe him, and you're giving him control he doesn't deserve. Control over *me*."

"You don't know what control *is*, *figlio mio*." He chuckles in an empty, menacing way that sends a chill up my spine. "Control is quiet. It's masterful. It doesn't need to make a show or take up space because it *is* the space, and it allows everyone to exist within it. If you think Trent fucking Kingston can take control from you, then you never had it to begin with."

I swallow and lick my lips one more time, trying to figure out what exactly it is he wants me to do.

"The wedding is off," he finishes calmly. "Congratulations."

He looks at me with disappointment shining in his gaze, but all I can feel is relief.

Maybe I don't have to do what I feared. Maybe things can go back to the way they were before.

Maybe…

"And Aria?" I ask.

"Aria Kingston is no longer your concern." He points a finger at me. "Your brother never would have failed the family this way."

Nodding in agreement, I pick up my drink and take another sip, respite rushing through me like a waterfall.

Suddenly a glass crashes as Pops throws his crystal tumbler across the room, the shards smacking against the fireplace and skittering on the floor.

My body jolts from the sudden noise, the hairs on my arms standing on end.

"You have nothing to say?" he hisses. "You should be on your knees *begging* for my forgiveness."

Swallowing around the sudden dryness in my throat, I gingerly set down my own glass, making sure to keep it on my side of the table.

"You, Enzo Marino, are the worst kind of failure. I gave

you *one* job. I ask this of you, to marry that stupid girl and make me proud. An easy task, no? Yet here you are, coming to me like a bitch with your tail tucked between your legs."

"I'm sorry."

"Sorry," he repeats, the word rolling off his tongue like he's savoring the taste. His body shoots forward suddenly, his gun appearing like it came from thin air. He shoves it against my temple.

My heart kicks against my ribs, but I keep a blank face. Reacting to his outburst will only make it worse. Briefly, my mind flits to Venesa and all the years she spent learning to *not* react. For some reason, thinking of her gives me strength in this moment.

"Maybe I should kill you," he whispers. "Are you trying to fuck with me on purpose? Working with someone else?"

Blood pounds through my ears. "I would never do that, Papá."

The gun clicks as he unlatches the safety, the metal cold against my temple. "How do I know I can trust you, *figlio mio*? After all, a simple pussy can sway you from your duties."

My chin stiffens. "If you want to kill me to make sure I don't betray you, then do it. I won't resist," I lie. "But if I'm gone, *no one* else will have your back."

It's a risk, stoking the flames of his paranoia this way, but I'd rather he focus on how he needs me versus all the reasons he doesn't.

Pops's hand is trembling. It's slight, but it's there, and I wonder if it's a constant tremor or if maybe he's not as unruffled as he's trying to appear. If maybe...he *does* actually care whether I live or die.

"Put the gun down, Papá," I say with a soothing tone. "I'm sorry I fucked up. It won't happen again."

A second goes by.

A minute.

Two.

Finally, he drops the weapon, placing it on the table in front of us and leaning back on the couch, his eyes going to the TV as though nothing happened at all.

Peppino's smiling face is mocking me from the screen.

I sit back, my lungs aching for a deep breath and my heart crashing against my sternum.

"What do you want me to do?" I ask, clearing my throat.

"Now you forget the Kingstons ever existed, go back to work, and I try to forget the way you brought shame to our name."

His voice is monotonous, and his words are meant to cut, but they don't hit like they used to.

I don't believe he's over this for a second.

And I may have disappointed my father, but he's out of his fucking mind if he thinks I'm going to just forget everything I overheard Trent and Aria talk about.

Starting with figuring out what happened the night someone tried to kill me.

Because if Aria wasn't the one who saved me, then who the fuck was?

CHAPTER 37

Venesa

I'M NO STRANGER TO NEW YORK, BUT IT'S NOT like I'm a frequent traveler.

Still, I've been here enough over the last few years of my life that it doesn't feel foreign. It never has, even when I was visiting for the first time. The hustle and bustle of the city is comforting in a way that can't be replicated anywhere else.

Back in Atlantic Cove, things are slower paced. And everyone knows everyone who knows something about someone else. Here I meld with the crowds, and there's a sense of peace in the anonymity that provides.

This *is* my first time tracking down Enzo while I'm here, though, and if I thought he was bigger than the world when he was visiting South Carolina, I had no idea how big he really is here in New York.

Everyone knows his name, which works out in my favor, because I wasn't 100 percent certain he'd be back home already.

I always thought the Mafia would live a simple life, hidden in the shadows and away from the public eye, but I guess John Gotti really changed the landscape with his flashy suits and paparazzi-perfect smile.

I'm thankful for it, though, because it was incredibly easy to figure out that he was back home already and get some tips on where he might be.

When I first arrived, I took a couple of days to gather myself. I scraped together all the money I had, which amounted to about three thousand bucks. Not a lot when you're traveling to a different state and have nowhere to stay.

I've been at a cheap motel in Yorkville, saving every penny until I can figure out what I'm planning to do. The only part I've got so far is to find Enzo, tell him the truth about *everything*, and ask him to help me take down my uncle for good.

It's a risk, and it's not one I'm taking lightly.

There's a really high probability he won't say yes and an even higher one he'll kick me out on my ass, or worse, kill me when he finds out what I've been keeping from him.

But every time I rethink my decision of coming out here and finding him, I reach up and grasp my seashell necklace, and a sense of belonging overcomes me.

I have to take the chance.

Then I'll let him marry Aria, and I'll walk away, never asking for another thing, which is why I'm at one of Enzo's clubs, the Royale.

It's nice. Busy. Easy to blend in, which is what I'm hoping for. At least right now.

I slip onto the only open barstool at the bar and order a club soda with lime, just to give me something to do while I figure out how to find Enzo. I don't even know if this is where he is; I just know this is one place he frequents.

"You're not from around here, are you?" the bartender says to me with a smirk, throwing a white towel over his shoulder.

I smile back at him and take a sip of my club soda, leaning my elbows on the bar top and looking out over the small round tables and stages with gorgeous women dancing half-nude. It's a beautiful sight.

"What gave it away?" I ask.

He laughs and wipes down a spot beside me before picking up a pint glass and filling it from the tap. "Where are you from? Tennessee?"

I purse my lips. "Mmm."

His grin grows when I don't reply with an affirmative or negative.

"Come on, pretty. Don't play so hard to get." He leans in closer, and I can tell he's flirting. It feels nice, so I don't dissuade him.

My eyes slide past him to the edge of the bar, where I *do* see someone I know.

Scotty.

A spark of warmth hits my chest, and it catches me by such surprise that my hand flies up to cover the feeling.

I glance at the bartender. "Who says I can be 'gotten'?"

Scotty's eyes skim over the room, widening when they

land on me. Immediately, he heads over, his gaze flicking back and forth between the bartender and me.

When he reaches us, he grips me harshly by the upper arm. "What the hell are you doing here?" he asks, sounding almost panicked.

I pat his hand and remove his fingers. "Hi to you too, cutie."

"Scotty, you know anything about this one?" the bartender asks. "She's a steel trap." He laughs, but it dies off quickly when Scotty reaches over the bar and punches him in the shoulder.

"You don't talk to her." Scotty points his finger. "You don't even *look* at her."

"Oh, it's like that?" He backs up from the bar and puts his hands in the air.

I scoff and roll my eyes. "It's *not* like that."

"You don't worry about what it is neither," Scotty demands. The guy nods and listens, barely giving me another glance before he's off and down to the other end, talking to another patron.

I click my tongue. *Coward.*

"Wow, you're a powerful man around here, huh?" I ask Scotty.

"Does E know you're here?" He reaches for me again, but I slide from the barstool and stand just out of his reach.

"Quit trying to manhandle me. And no, actually. I'm trying to find him. Do you know where he is?"

He shakes his head and taps his fingers on the bar. "You

shouldn't be here, Venesa. This ain't no game. New York's no place for you right now."

I reach out and cup his cheek, giving him a wide grin. "Scotty, quit treating me like I'm some damsel in distress and tell me where to find Enzo. I need to talk to him. It's important."

He purses his lips and tilts his head, like he can't quite decide what to do with me. "Listen, he's not here, but I'll tell him you're in town, okay? You got a number for me?"

I nod, disappointment settling heavy in my chest as I tell him where Enzo can reach me, and then I sip from my drink as I watch Scotty disappear into the crowd.

Something feels off, so I slip a ten out of the pocket in my bra and leave it on the bar top before following Scotty across the main floor and into a back hallway.

The layout here is actually pretty similar to the Lair, except on a larger scale. But it's the same hallway and then stairs into a basement where things are *not* what they seem.

The underground of the Royale is a different world. I can smell the sweat and testosterone in the air, and bodies are packed together like sardines, hovering close to a cage with a platform in the center.

Two men are there, bloody and bruised, whit tape on their hands as they fight. If the club upstairs is nice, then this place is primitive.

I find Enzo immediately.

Scotty, that little liar.

Enzo is standing off in a corner, dressed to perfection as

usual, with his hands in his pockets. His brows are scrunched, and his head is tilted while he listens to something a large man with dark brown hair and a gun strapped to his shoulder is saying in his ear.

I push my way through the bodies, attempting to get closer to Enzo, but I don't walk all the way over yet. I hang back, watching him in his element.

He's more at ease, maybe. More in control. There's a sophistication to his posture, and it's clear everyone defers to him, leaving space like they know better than to get too close.

Suddenly, his head snaps in my direction, and his eyes glance around.

Is it silly to think that maybe he can *feel* me here?

Men are surrounding him—real bodyguards, I can tell immediately. And this version of Enzo Marino is *much* different from the vacation version I saw of him in South Carolina.

A petty part of me—the envious part—wonders if Aria has ever seen him like this, and if she has…did he like it when she saw?

But of course, who am I kidding? He probably parades her throughout New York, the shining beauty at his side.

A hand grips my upper arm tightly, and I bite back a hiss, coming face-to-face with Scotty's panicked eyes.

"Hey, cutie." I grin. "Miss me?"

"Did you follow me?" he asks, glancing around.

"No offense, Scotty, but you're not so great at being inconspicuous, you know?"

He blinks at me.

"Take it as a lesson." I reach out and pat his cheek. "Something to work on for later."

I pull away from his hold, but he tightens his hand on me again. "Come on, I gotta get you outta here before E sees."

My grin drops, and I scowl at him because I *don't* appreciate being manhandled. "Take your hands off me. I won't ask again."

He freezes, probably because I've never spoken to him this way, but he doesn't remove his grip.

"You lied to me, Scotty. And I don't appreciate liars, so let me tell you a truth. If you don't take your hands off me, everyone in here will get to see what a *real* show looks like."

Scotty's jaw clenches like he can't decide if my threat is genuine, and then his eyes widen and look behind me.

Goose bumps sprout along my body from the presence suddenly at my back.

"No free shows, baby," says a dark voice.

CHAPTER 38

Enzo

I'M A LITTLE DRUNK.

Believe it or not, that's unusual for me. I usually cap myself off before I feel more than a slight buzz, never wanting to lose control of a situation or be caught off guard. And maybe it's because I'm drunk that I swear I can *feel* Venesa here.

I brush it off because that's ridiculous. Nobody can actually feel a specific other person. That's shit you see in the movies. Not real life.

"E, man, you hear me?"

I turn my head to look at Gio, realizing it feels so much heavier than it normally does.

A lazy grin spreads across my face. "Yeah, man. I'm always hearing you."

My eyes scan the room again when a trickle of awareness drips through me.

Seriously, what the fuck?

Gio leans in closer, but since he's a few inches shorter than me—something I never let him forget—I have to tilt my head down to hear him.

"You gotta get a new phone, man," he says. "And the De Lucas are trying to reach out."

"Ah, fuck," I complain, running a hand over my chin. "I knew it."

Yells erupt from in front of us, and my attention goes to the fighters in the ring, my knuckles itching to reach out and taste blood for myself. Back before I became Peppino 2.0, I was in this ring a lot. It was the perfect outlet, letting me execute the violence I feel inside without it overtaking every other aspect of my life. Pops would probably be pissed off if he knew I was showing my face here. This is Gio's spot to run now, although technically it's still mine in name.

A flash of silver white screams at me from the corner of the room. My eyes slam over to it, but it's dark and I can't see shit. Plus, my vision is just the *tiniest* bit blurred.

"I don't want to talk about this right now." I pat Gio on the back.

A wicked look glints in his eyes. "You're fucked up."

I scoff and roll my neck. "Please. Just feeling good, like you suggested."

Gio throws up his hands, that stupid smirk high on his face. "Yeah, yeah. Hey, sweetheart," he hollers to a girl who walks over in booty shorts and a bedazzled bra top. I think she's worked in our underground ring for a while, but I never get to know their names. It's better if I keep separation.

"What's up, Gio?" she replies.

"Grab my boy some water and some black coffee, would ya?"

She nods and winks at him. He smacks her ass before she walks away.

"You hitting that?" I ask.

He smirks. "Nah, I don't like to mix business and pleasure, you know that."

"Speaking of idiots who can't separate business from pleasure, where the fuck is Scotty? Have you seen him?"

"I don't know, man. He's running around somewhere, probably talking shit."

"Scotty 'The Gossip' Andretti. That's gotta be his nickname when he gets made, because the kid's always running his fucking mouth. We'll have to get a handle on that if he ever wants to be on the books," I say.

"Ain't that the truth?" Gio straightens and looks around. "Speaking of…there he is."

My eyes follow where he's nodding to, and I see Scotty. His back is tense, and he's gripping somebody, although it's hard to tell who with the way they're angled.

Interesting.

And then suddenly it's as though the clouds part, the sun shines, and the birds fucking chirp, because he moves, and Venesa's perfect face appears. I *knew* I wasn't losing it.

Gio's talking in my ear still, but I move off the wall and make my way toward them, leaving him hanging midsentence.

I'm over to them in a flash, and the closer I get, the more excitement I feel, because she's here, and so am I, and I'm not engaged, and she's fucking *here*.

She whispers something into Scotty's ear, and he's gripping her arm like he's trying to hold her in place. Something foreign and hot rips through me at the sight, similar to how it felt when that woman was groping all over Venesa at the engagement party.

I've never been the jealous type, but I can't *stand* watching other people touch her.

When I get close, I glance around, noticing lingering eyes trying to eat her up. I shoot them dark looks, and their gazes skitter away like ants.

She's saying something to Scotty about giving everyone a show when I step up behind her. Scotty's eyes catch mine and widen like he's in trouble.

I lean down and whisper in her ear. "No free shows, baby."

Goose bumps sprout along her skin, and I want to lick them. I hold myself back, but only just.

"Scotty, I'd listen to her if I were you," I say. "I've seen firsthand what she's capable of, and I'd hate for her to embarrass you in front of your boys."

He snatches his hand back in a heartbeat.

Venesa spins around and smiles at me, those damn dimples highlighting the apples of her cheeks. "Enzo."

I grin back at her like an idiot. "Fuck, I love the way you say my name."

Rowdy screams and catcalls break out behind us, then a

loud thud as one fighter gets knocked out and slams into the metal cage.

"I need to talk to you," she says loudly, trying to speak over the raucous noise of the space.

My eyes drop to her lips.

"You can do whatever you want with me," I reply, but I don't know if she hears me.

I place my hand on the small of her back, anticipation flooding my body at the simple touch, and push her forward, leading her toward the small office we have down here.

We pass by Gio, who's still where I left him with his back leaned against the wall, his arms crossed. His eyebrow quirks as he watches me walk Venesa by him.

But he doesn't stop me. He knows better.

All I'm concerned about is how good it feels to have her here.

We reach the office, and I swing the door open, then push her inside before closing it behind us. I lean against the wall, slipping my hands into my pockets for no other reason than I'm not sure I can control what I'll do if I let them free.

She walks through the room, scrunching up her nose and turning to face me as she leans that delectable ass against the edge of the small desk.

Then Venesa's body relaxes like she's dropping a shield. "I pictured you in a skyscraper with a fancy office and secretaries at your beck and call."

"I can show you that tomorrow morning if you'd like."

She playfully rolls her eyes. "Of course you can."

I stare at her with what I'm sure is a goofy-ass grin on my face.

"Why are you looking at me like that?" she asks.

My smile widens. "Like what?"

"Like you're happy to see me."

Moving forward, I slip my hands around her waist, dragging her into me. She gasps, her palms coming up to rest on my chest.

"I am happy to see you," I say.

"Enzo, I…"

"I want to kiss you," I blurt. I don't know why I say it, other than it's all I can think about now that she's here. It's all I thought about even when she wasn't.

"Enzo." She laughs.

"I'm serious. Why won't you let me kiss you?"

"Are you *drunk*?"

She tries to push off me, but I pull her in closer, flipping us around until her body is nestled between my legs as I lean back against the lip of the desk.

"Drunk on you," I murmur, running my nose along her neck. "Fuck, you smell good."

She giggles and tries to push me again. "You're *handsy* when you drink, huh?"

"Can't help it." I grunt, digging my fingers into her hips. "I knew you were here."

She lifts a brow and pulls back slightly. "I'm surprised you saw me at all, to be honest."

"Baby, you walk into a room and every head turns. You think you can be *anywhere* I am and I won't notice?"

Her eyes widen a bit as she stares up at me, her hands still gripping my chest—maybe to keep me away—I'm not sure. If that's why she's doing it, then it doesn't have the intended effect. It does nothing but heighten the desire coursing through me like a goddamn inferno.

"Don't say things like that," she murmurs. "You *can't*."

I lean in, ghosting my lips across the side of her face, my free hand coming up to cup her chin. "I can do whatever I want."

She sucks in a breath, and her fingers clench in my shirt.

I try to press my mouth to hers, but she turns her cheek. "This isn't why I came here."

Sighing, I drop my forehead against hers, rolling it back and forth. "You're driving me fucking crazy." I grip her face in my hands and pull her back to me. "Why won't you kiss me?"

Venesa inhales, her eyes dipping down.

"Don't do that," I murmur. "Just tell me."

"Well, you're engaged to my cousin, for one."

I shake my head. "No, I'm not."

She gasps, her gaze shooting back to mine. "What?"

I slide my hand through her hair, tangling my fingers in the strands and cupping the back of her neck. "I'm all yours, piccola sirena, if you'll have me."

"Enzo, I have to tell you something."

"Tell me why you won't let me kiss you."

She hesitates, her teeth sinking into her bottom lip. "I'm afraid I'll be bad at it."

I scoff, my fingers tightening in her hair. "Impossible."

"I've never done it before. I…"

Energy flares in my chest at her words, something carnal and possessive rushing through me and making me feel like a king among men.

"Don't be scared," I tell her.

Kiss the girl.

I brush my nose against hers again. "I'm going to kiss you. And I promise it will be the best one of my life."

"How do you know?"

My thumb slips along her lower lip, my eyes following the movement. "Because it's with you."

And then I capture her lips with mine.

Fireworks explode in my chest, sparks floating down and settling deep in my abdomen. Everything around me dims, paling compared to this moment.

I'm finally kissing the woman I'm in love with.

The realization hits me like a ball against a baseball bat.

Goddamn. I love her.

She doesn't move her mouth at first, and my hand on her chin softens as I slide it to her jaw, trying to coax her gently to respond. She does, and I groan when she kisses me back. My other hand tightens in her strands, tugging the smallest amount. My tongue sneaks out and licks along the seam of her lips.

She moans, and my cock jerks to attention at the sound.

I'm immersed in everything Venesa, and I could live here forever.

She breaks away from me, panting, and I try to dive back down to recapture her lips again, because now that I've had them, I don't know how I'll ever go without.

"Enzo, I really need to—"

"Later," I say. "It doesn't matter what you have to tell me. There's nothing you could say that will change how I feel. Just…let me have you. Finally. *Please.*"

It's not like me to beg, but the alcohol loosened my grasp on my morals and my control just enough for me to be vulnerable and honest.

I have to know what she feels like. It's been torturing me for weeks remembering the feel of her pinned to the wall beneath me, so close to touching yet so far from being intertwined. I want to slip down her body, put my mouth on her cunt and suck until she creams, and then I want to slip my cock inside her until I feel like she'll never be able to get me out.

The thought of coming inside her, of making her moan my name while I claim her in the most primal way, shooting deep into her channel, makes my balls tighten, and my tongue swirls with hers again, my mouth pressing against her harder.

The air turns frantic, and she becomes an active participant in the kiss, her hands sliding up my chest and wrapping around my neck until she tangles her fingers in the strands of my hair and tugs so she can press against me more firmly.

Another moan escapes her, and then I'm moving, my touch gliding from her face and behind her head, skimming down her sides, sliding up her dress until my hands drift beneath it and I'm touching hot, slick skin.

Our lips never separate, and it's messy and she's unsure, but it doesn't matter because it's with her, so it's perfect.

It's like she's been starved for so long and now that she's given in, she can't get enough. I don't know why she's never kissed anyone before, but I'm not going to question it. Knowing I'm the only one to get that from her? It's a gift. One that fills me up and makes me want to fall and worship at her feet.

Which I do.

I push her back slightly, finally breaking away, and I spin us around again, my hands going to her hips and lifting her until she's perched on the edge of the desk. I drop to my knees, slipping her dress up her body. When I glance at her, my stomach clenches and flips.

She's breathtaking.

Her chest is heaving, cheeks a rosy pink, and her eyes are half-lidded and dreamy, sexual in a way that makes it hard to think. To breathe.

"Enzo, *please*," she begs, her hands finding purchase on the top of my head.

"Shhh, baby. I want to take my time. Memorize this moment so I can think about it whenever I want."

Leaning in, I press soft kisses to her ankle, her calf, her inner thigh. Her legs part wider, and I'm fucking thrilled when I realize she, once again, isn't wearing any underwear, her cunt on display, pink, swollen, and fucking perfect.

My mouth waters, my hands gripping her outer thighs and pulling her into me roughly until her ass scoots to the very edge of the desk.

She gasps, and then her eyes flare and she tightens her grip on my hair, pushing my face into her pussy.

Heaven.

This must be what it feels like.

"Tell me what you want," I demand, blowing soft puffs of air on her clit.

"I want you to lick me."

My tongue sneaks out and gives a tentative swipe, barely there, just ghosting along her lips and around her clit. She pushes on the back of my head harder, and I sink in willingly, her taste exploding on my taste buds and making my eyes roll back. She's tangy, like pineapple and woman, and my cock is pressing against my zipper so hard, I think it might break through, precum dripping down my length and making a mess on my skin.

She moans and releases my head, falling back on her elbows, her breasts moving up and down with her heavy breaths. "Oh, *God*, Enzo, that feels…."

Her words urge me on, and I can tell from how open she is to this experience that although she may have been a virgin with kissing, in other areas, she's definitely not.

My tongue circles her clit and dips down to her entrance, lapping up her wetness and then heading back to where I know she needs me most. One of my hands moves to grip her inner thigh, forcing her legs open more, and my other goes to her dripping hole, my fingers slipping inside her and moving back and forth, curling upward with my motion.

She moans again, and I watch her from where I'm settled between her legs, my cock pulsing with need when she throws her head back, her hair brushing against the desk as she pants out her pleasure.

Goddamn, she's fucking perfect this way.

"Don't stop," she begs. "Just like that."

Her hips rotate on my mouth, and I move the hand that was gripping her inner thigh up to her side, helping her move against me.

When I look up again, I almost come on the spot because she's gotten her breasts out of the top of her dress, the fabric bunched underneath them, and she's playing with her perfect rosy nipples, twisting them between her fingers until they're stiff, firm points. And even more than that, she's wearing the necklace.

A pretty pink seashell rests in the valley between her tits, and it sends a rush through me because it feels like it's a mark, one claiming that she's mine and I'm hers.

I break away from working on her clit, and she looks down at me, her hands leaving her perfect tits and gripping my head again, shoving me back into her hot cunt. "I said don't stop," she repeats.

She isn't afraid to take what she needs, and I work her harder, loving the way it feels when she practically rides my fingers and moves her swollen, puffy clit back and forth along the tip of my tongue.

Her breathing grows even choppier, and her legs snap closed on the sides of my face, her limbs trembling against me.

"Oh *God*..." And then she comes apart, her body vibrating and her pussy flooding my mouth with her incredible taste. I drink it up like I'm starved, continuing to work her with my fingers and tongue until she comes down fully, and only then do I let her go, sitting back on my heels, her wetness smeared across my face and her scent covering me.

"*Christ*, you're sexy when you come," I tell her.

She sits up, her eyes flaring, and reaches out, gripping me by the shirt and dragging me into her, smashing our mouths together.

Her tongue tangles with mine, and I'm so fucking turned on, I can't even breathe properly because the thought of her tasting herself on *me* is the hottest thing I've ever experienced.

I break away from her lips so I can tell her that, but she slips her fingers through the hairs at the nape of my neck and pulls me back in, her mouth circling my bottom lip and biting like she can't get enough of her own taste. She tangles our tongues again, and I groan into her when she *sucks* on mine, and fuck, I was wrong before because *that* is the hottest thing I've ever experienced.

My dick is aching to be released, and her hands move down the front of my shirt to my belt buckle, undoing it without even having to look, and then she's pushing my pants down just enough.

I help her, moving her back on the desk as I stand

up straight, the air pulling taut with tension and frantic desperation.

It may have only been a few weeks, but it feels like I've been waiting for this moment forever, and I don't want to wait anymore. My cock pops out, sticking straight up, cum bubbling on the top and dripping down like a faucet from how turned on I am.

Her eyes flare, and she leans forward, gripping me in her hand and physically pulling me toward her mouth.

When her hot tongue laps at the head of my dick, my entire body lights up like fireworks, and my hands move to the back of *her* head, my gaze snapping down so I don't miss a second.

She's a vision with her mouth on my cock.

It jerks, and my balls tighten again, and *goddamn*, I'm about to come already from how worked up she has me, and that's unacceptable, so I push her back.

"Lie on the desk," I demand.

She pouts. "I wanted to—"

I shake my head, my hand resting on her chest right above her cleavage and pushing her lightly, encouraging her. "What did I say?"

"You said to lie back," she replies as she does so.

I follow her backward until I'm leaning over her, my dick rigid and throbbing, ready to slide into her until I can't tell us apart.

My stomach tenses in anticipation.

"That's my good girl," I coo, dipping my face down until

my mouth is next to her ear. "I know you're used to taking control, to having everything at your beck and call, but when it's us, I want you to relax and let go. Let *me* take care of *you*. Can you do that for me, baby?"

I pull back slightly, my right hand gripping the base of my cock and tugging up to the head, my fingers slipping in the precum and spreading it around to lubricate my shaft. I don't take my eyes off her for a second.

Fuck, I need to be inside her.

She bites her lip, her face flushed with arousal as she nods. "I can do that."

My dick is at her entrance now, and I prod her tight hole before sliding up and pressing the head against her clit, smacking it lightly.

She's hot and wet and so hot, I can barely believe I'm about to sink inside her.

"That's my girl."

Venesa shivers.

I grab her hand and move it to my cock, forcing her to sit up slightly, her soft palm a contrast to my rough one as we both grip my length and put it back at her entrance. "I want you to feel me going into you."

She doesn't reply, just bites that lower lip again, but her hold tightens, her fingers overlapping mine so we circle my base completely.

And then I'm there, and I'm pushing in, and I swear to God I nearly black out from the pleasure of finally—*finally*—being inside her.

She exhales on a gasp, and I try to focus, to slot every second of what she feels like into my memory as I inch my way deep into her, burying myself to the hilt.

When I'm all the way in, my groin against hers, I pause, my eyes scouring her like a starving man, which I guess I am.

I'm desperate for her.

To memorize the way she looks right now—right this second—when we're so connected, it feels like the world could burn down around us and nothing but this moment would matter.

"Fuck," I breathe out.

"Enzo, *move*."

My hand moves up and slips behind her head, cradling it because I'm about to fuck her rough and I don't want her to get hurt but also so I can tangle her hair in my fist and pull.

Which I do.

Hard.

"Tell me what to do again," I threaten, the same way I always do when she gets bossy.

She lets out a loud groan when I pull her hair harder, and then I'm moving, sliding my length in and out of her at a fast pace, my cock hitting her so deep with every thrust that her breasts jiggle and her body moves up the desk.

She feels fucking incredible, so I tell her that.

Her eyes roll back in her head, sweat beading at her temples and making strands of her hair stick to the side of her face.

"Fu—I..."

Leaning over her, I press my mouth to hers, wanting to suffocate myself with everything that is *Venesa* until I drown.

"Enzo," she cries out.

My name on her lips sends possessiveness swirling through me like a tornado, and my hips jerk out of rhythm; I'm perilously close to coming.

My free hand moves to slip underneath her, and I pull her until I'm standing straight and she's sitting up; the front of her body is plastered against mine and her ass rests on the edge of the desk. My cock never stops dipping into her, and this new angle creates a friction that's massaging my length and pumping me closer to release with each second.

I pull her hair again with my fist, and it brings her head back, elongating her pretty pale neck.

Leaning down, I press sloppy kisses to her throat. "Tell me you're mine."

I can feel her swallow, and I bite her skin until it leaves a mark, my hips slamming roughly into hers.

There's a brief moment where I think maybe she won't say it, and it sends a sharp stab of fear through my chest, but before I can focus on the feeling, she's crying out.

"Yours," she exclaims. "I'm yours."

Heat spreads down my spine, her words causing a euphoria that not even a drug could touch.

"I'm yours too," I say, giving her one more nip on the neck.

She groans, her eyes rolling back and legs shaking around my hips.

My grip on her hair tightens, and I pull, moving my mouth to her ear. "I'm going to come inside you."

Her pussy walls flutter around me.

"Would you like that, baby? For me to own you that way? To claim you?"

"Ye—yes," she stutters.

"I'll pump you so full, it leaks down your legs, and then parade you in front of the world, just to make sure everyone knows you're mine."

Her gaze sharpens, the cloud of lust clearing for just a moment, and her nails dig into my shoulders. "As long as they know it goes both ways."

"Give it to me, then," I demand, my hand on her lower back urging her hips to meet my thrusts. She does, and *fuck*, the added rotation is sending me flying.

Our bodies are slick with sweat, and they're hot and sticky as we come together over and over, the smell of sex strong in the air.

I move my hand from her lower back and press my thumb against her clit, rubbing it in a circular motion while I fuck into her with my cock.

Her body starts to spasm around me, and I know she's close because her cunt is contracting, her slick walls massaging my length and urging me to come.

"*Fuck*, that's it, baby. You're doing so well. Such a perfect girl for me."

She screams, *loud*, and her pussy clamps down on me like a vise, and that's it for me; I explode, my cock jerking wildly as I thrust one more time and then hold myself as deep as I can inside her.

My orgasm is so strong, my vision goes black and stars dot the edges, and I throw my head back, groaning as I empty myself.

Panting hard, I open my eyes, trying to regulate my breathing. When my vision returns, I look down, noticing how out of sorts she is on the desk.

She looks fucked hard and put away wet, and she's so perfect, I have an urge to grab my phone and snap a picture, just so I can jerk off later to the sight of her this way.

"That was…" she starts.

I collapse on top of her, my breathing shaky and my body coated in a thin sheen of sweat.

"Perfect," I finish for her. "That was fucking perfect. Just like you."

I rest my forehead against hers while I will my heart to calm down.

"Now what?" she murmurs against my face.

I pull back and flash her a grin. I feel sober now, but I'm flying higher than I've ever been.

"Now we get you cleaned up, I take you back out there, and I show you how good we can be in *this* life, not a different one."

CHAPTER 39

Venesa

I LIE BACK ON MY HOTEL BED, MY HAIR FLUFFing when I hit the cushy down pillow.

This is definitely a step up from the motel I was staying at in Yorkville. Enzo offered to put me in his hotel, and I accepted with open arms.

I shouldn't have slept with him, though. Not without talking to him first.

He was drunk, and I was—am—scared of what he'll say when he finds out the truth.

But I won't lie and say I'm not enjoying being in a suite at the Marino. The lap of luxury is nice.

Is this how he lives all the time? Is this how Aria lived?

Uncle T and the Kingston name get her far in life, but it's nothing to this level. This is…outrageous. Enzo's name makes him seem like a god in this city, and if people know you're one of his guests?

I've never been treated so well.

My stomach growls and caves in on itself, nausea creeping through my esophagus; the type that comes on fast and only hits when you've waited too long to eat and hunger isn't an option anymore. It's just straight to feeling ill.

Glancing around, I walk to my duffel bag and dig inside, pulling out the few hundred dollars I have left to my name.

It's pathetic. Not the "having no money" part—that I'm an expert in. Money defines nothing other than it's nice to have it. Makes life easier.

But it's pathetic because after all these years, after everything I've done for my family, this is all I'm left with. I was brainwashed, clearly. Too blinded by my loyalty to Uncle T to see that he wasn't even paying me my worth, and I'm worth a hell of a lot because I'm fucking fantastic. He won't ever find someone better than me.

Still, the realization that our relationship differed from the way it was in my head makes me feel like garbage. Like everything I did means nothing.

Like my *life* means nothing.

Like *I'm* nothing.

The dichotomy of both emotions battling for supremacy in my head is tiring.

Suddenly, there's a knock at the door.

"Room service!" A muffled voice hits my ears.

That's weird. I didn't order anything.

I didn't pack my gun because I hate it, and to be honest, I didn't even *think* about grabbing it before I left. Regret hits me at that decision now, though, because I don't trust anyone who knocks on a stranger's door. I can just imagine Bastien yelling at me over the years about situations exactly like this. It's why he forced me to get the gun.

My chest aches when I think about Bastien. I didn't even get to say goodbye, and even though I've written out a text a hundred times, I'm wary to send it. What if he's loyal to my uncle, and they track me down somehow? What if he was part of everything and never really on my side at all?

The thought of it makes me sick.

Another knock and I consider grabbing my knife instead, but it's all the way in the bedroom, so I take a chance and move toward the door instead.

"Room service!" the person yells out again.

I strain my ears, trying to hear if I recognize who it is, if there's anything I can read from the tonality, but this is a nice hotel and the walls are thick...or maybe my heart is just beating in my ears and muffling the sound. I flex my hands, shaking out the sudden anxiety. There's a globe on the side of the entryway table, all in gold, and I pick it up to test the weight.

Heavy and solid. Not my ideal weapon, but it will do in a pinch if I need it. I look through the peephole, my brows scrunching together when I see a man in an actual hotel outfit, white chef coat with stitching on the name and an honest-to-God delivery cart.

My fingers tighten on the doorknob until my knuckles turn white, and I don't know why I feel so untrusting other than being here again after so many years has me on edge.

After all, this isn't my first time here. I murdered Joey three years ago at this very hotel, in a suite just like this.

The guy looks young and bored, and he sighs, tapping again. "Room service!"

I swing the door open, hiding the globe as best as I can behind my back.

"Miss." He tips his hat.

"What do you want?" I ask harshly.

"Uh..." He reaches up and scratches behind his ear before jerking his chin toward the cart. "Room service?"

Why does he seem unsure?

I swallow around my dry mouth, shaking my head and pressing my free hand to my temple with a silly grin. "I'm sorry, darlin', you're right. Where are my manners? Bring it on in."

His shoulders relax, and he smiles at me. "Cute accent. Where are you from?"

"You sure you're supposed to be asking questions like that?" I lift a brow.

His face flushes with embarrassment.

"You know, I don't remember ordering any room service." I bring the globe in front of me now, tossing it between my hands until my forearms burn.

He turns to me, his eyes shooting into circles when he sees me bouncing what's basically a solid gold statue in my hands. "I'm just following orders, ma'am."

I walk past him and pick up one of the metal tops covering plates of food. Pancakes. Looks like chocolate chips too. Side of fruit. Bacon. Eggs. Toast.

In fact, the more lids I peek under, the more I'm surprised, because it looks like someone ordered me the entire breakfast menu.

My stomach growls on cue.

And the coffee smells nice.

"I don't have money to tip you," I tell him.

He tracks the globe in my hand. "I was told not to accept anything."

"Who'd you say sent it again?" I cock my head, placing down the heavy weight, amused at the way his nervous eyes follow it.

He swallows and shifts again on his feet. "Uh, Mr. Marino, ma'am."

Surprise flitters through me, although I'm not sure why. I should have assumed it was from him. I'm just…tainted from my life. I don't trust anyone, but when the guy freaking salutes me and walks out the door, I believe him.

Gratitude flows through me like a waterfall, and I close my eyes and let myself really sink into the moment, giving thanks that despite everything, this right here is something to be happy about. To immerse myself in.

A smile breaks over my face, and I sit down to eat without a second thought, because I'm hungry and I'm not too proud to accept a meal. Or ten meals, which is what it looks like on the giant rolling tray.

I'm only a few bites into my meal when *another* knock rings out. "Room service!"

The voice sounds different this time, but I grin, wondering what else Enzo sent me. I stand up and walk to the door again.

Sighing, I press my hand to my forehead and then swing it open. "Honestly, this is getting…"

My words cut off midsentence, getting stuck in my throat when Bastien stands on the other side, a look of disbelief on his face.

"You didn't even check to see who I was," he reprimands.

My heart skips, hope filling me like helium. "What are you doing here?"

He scoffs and pushes past me, stomping to the living room like *he* has any right to be mad at *me*.

The audacity.

Placing his hands on his hips, he twists around, whistling. "Damn, E put you up in this suite?"

I glance into the hallway and then close the door before walking over to where Bastien is.

He plops down on the couch so hard, he bounces, and then he grins at me. "Plush."

I can't really blame him. It *is* a soft couch.

"You didn't answer my question." I go to the dining area and push the rolling tray over to the living room, sitting down next to him and putting the plate of pancakes on my lap.

"What are you eating?" He reaches out like he's grabbing a piece, and I smack his hand away.

"Mine."

"Are those *blueberry*?"

I shovel a bite into my mouth and grin. "Chocolate chip."

He groans, rubbing his stomach. "I'm starving."

Shrugging, I take another bite. "Tell me what you're doing here, and maybe I'll share."

He sighs and runs a hand over his chin, leaning back on the couch. "I'm here because I can't *not* be here. I won't just sit by and watch your uncle fuck everything up. He shouldn't have kicked you out, and considering I could have been here to kill you and you just opened the door without a second thought, it's a good thing I came."

"My uncle shouldn't have done a lot of things." I grab my coffee from the tray and take a sip. "Does he know you're here?"

Bastien's dark eyes grow serious. "He knows I'm tracking you down. I don't want him to think I'm not on his side. Figure it can be useful if needed in the future."

I tilt my head. "So you're what, like a double agent?"

He shrugs. "Call it whatever you want."

My heart pumping with affection, I push my plate of pancakes over to him and hand him the fork. "For you."

He beams at me and takes it, stabbing a giant cut piece and eating it.

"I'm glad you're here," I admit. "Thank you for coming."

He quirks a brow. "You're not going to tell me I should go back home and save myself?"

I shake my head. "You don't need saving. And you won't

lose anything, Bas. You're gonna get more when I take it all from him."

He sits back and nods. "You sure you're up for it?"

"Of course I am," I retort. "But first, I have some questions."

"Like what?"

"Like...did you know Uncle T had Momma killed?"

Bastien blows out a heavy breath and falls against the couch like he's got the weight of the world on his shoulders.

The hesitation in his answer confirms what I've been worried about all along. That he *knew* about it, and he didn't tell me.

A pinch of betrayal twinges in my chest.

But can I really blame him? None of us are perfect. None of us are the good guys here, and there are things I haven't told people, things I haven't told *Enzo*, so am I a hypocrite if I can't forgive Bastien for the same transgressions I've committed against others?

I'm no better than him. Not really.

Like I've always said, we've all got our things.

"Venesa..." He pauses, and I brace myself for his answer. "He didn't just kill your momma. He stole the Kingston empire out from under her entirely."

I give him a confused look, my brain muddling. "What? Momma wanted nothing to do with the family's legacy or with any money. She made that pretty clear when she chose my father and cut off everyone else for years. I never even *met* my granddaddy."

Bastien shakes his head. "Your momma left on purpose, but Percius Kingston never got rid of her trust, and it's irrevocable. On his death, she was supposed to get *everything*."

My stomach flips, my mind racing a mile a minute. "I don't understand. If it's legal and binding, how did it all go to Uncle T?"

Bastien smiles sadly at me. "Come on, you know better than that. Your uncle owns Atlantic Cove. You think he can't pay off a judge and a few lawyers?" He side-eyes me. "You think he can't burn down a house and everything in it?"

My heart pitches forward, because I think he's telling me Uncle T killed his own father. My brows furrow as I try to piece together the information. "So then he had Momma killed, and there was no trust to be found..."

"Can't find something that's turned to ash," Bas confirms. "But I'll tell you a secret, Venesa Andersen. That painting you all love so much? I found some things while I was preparing it for the engagement party."

I sit forward, my heart pounding against my ribs.

Bastien locks his gaze on me. "Trent shouldn't be running the Kingston empire, Venesa. It's supposed to belong to *you*."

CHAPTER 40

Enzo

I'VE GOT A HEADACHE.

It's pulsing to the beat of my heart while I sit behind my *fancy* desk in my skyscraper, with my assistant, Jessica, outside the door.

Just knowing Venesa is in my city has me walking around with pep in my step. Despite the situation I'm facing in every other aspect of my life, I'm in a great mood and nothing can bring it down. She's mine.

I've had her, she's here, and I'm never letting her go again.

My head pulses and I groan, rubbing my temples. *This* is why I don't drink much anymore. Not only because my body doesn't recover the same way it did when I was twenty-one, but because things grow fuzzy. Memories become hazy, and part of me is worried I'm misremembering last night, forgetting things, when I want to have our first time together branded on my fucking skin and in my soul for eternity.

Not to have to struggle to remember each breath and every moan.

My office door opens, a pair of heels clicking softly on the carpeted floor.

Jessica's holding out a bottle of Tylenol and a black coffee. One of her blond eyebrows is arched, and she gives me a knowing grin.

Behind her, Gio slips through the door, maneuvering around her, taking both items from her hands and haphazardly placing them on my desk before dropping into one of the seats.

Jessica frowns and glares at him before looking back at me. "Anything else, Mr. Marino?"

I wave her off, smirking at Gio instead as she leaves the room. "What, no water?"

Gio smirks, his long legs stretching out in front of him. He pulls out a phone and tosses that on the desk, too.

Right.

"It's tomorrow," he says as a reply. "Your phone got fucked with by your bitch ex, so here's a new one."

Sighing, I scrub a hand down my face. With everything else that happened, I had forgotten about this. Picking up the new phone, I give him a questioning look. "This one's good to go?"

"Same number, contacts all transferred over and everything."

I nod and rub my fingers beneath my chin, placing it back down.

Did Venesa know about Aria tapping my phone and working with her uncle? About her not saving me?

My stomach knots up from the possibility.

"What are you thinking about?" Gio asks.

"About how I should kill Trent Kingston before he tries to come for me."

"You could always hire out."

I snap forward in my seat, a light bulb going off in my brain. "What did you just say?"

Gio runs his fingers over his scruff and then picks a piece of lint off his pant leg. "I said you could contract it out. Pain in the ass, but I'm with you if you think it's the right call."

My brain is going a mile a minute, jumping from Peppino's death to my attempted one and back again, trying to piece together a puzzle I don't have a full version of.

"I actually asked Pops once if he thought someone was contracted to take out Peppino and me. He said it wasn't worth looking into, brushed it off almost entirely." I pause, giving Gio a pointed look. "Don't you find that weird?"

"What, like *he* contracted out to kill his own sons?" Gio shrugs. "Your pops has gotten increasingly overconfident and sloppy as hell, so it wouldn't surprise me. You really think he'd try to take out his own flesh and blood like that though?"

"Who knows with him these days." I nod again, rubbing my hand underneath my chin. He's probably right. "And you still can't find anything on Jersey or the Frankie Bianchi and Trent connection?"

Gio's brows draw in. "I can find you Frankie, E…but there ain't no paper trail that ties him to the Kingstons. And you always know the De Lucas in Jersey are willing to sit down and talk. You want me to set up a meeting?"

I shake my head. "Not yet. But if you can find Frankie, then we don't need a paper trail. Bring him to me."

Gio shoots finger guns at me, making *pew-pew* sounds like a douchebag, and stands up. "You got it, Lover Boy. Hey, who was that chick last night at the fight?"

My heart pounds with impatience, knowing I've got Scotty on his way to pick up Venesa from the Marino and bring her to me as we speak, and I can't help the smile that breaks across my face.

"I don't know who you mean." I play nonchalant.

Gio laughs and slaps his leg. "Oh! You've got jokes. Tits like *Madonn'* and that sparkly white hair you just know looks good wrapped around a fist—"

He makes a thrusting motion with his hips, and I'm out of my seat faster than lightning, my hand wrapped around his throat in the next second. "Watch your fucking mouth."

Gio's eyes widen as I release him, and he reaches up to rub at the red marks on his neck, chuckling. "Oh, fuck. It's like that, huh?"

I drop into the chair next to him, annoyed at my lack of control. "Yeah, it's like that."

A grin spreads across his face.

Before I can respond, my office door swings open wide.

"Christ, does *anyone* work out there?" I yell to Jessica. "What the hell do I pay you for?"

I see a flash of her through the opening, and she gives me a wide-eyed look that screams, *What do you want me to do?*

It's a second later I realize why. My father waltzes into my office as though he owns it, a small black cane in his left hand that he doesn't need and doesn't use, just brings along to have an extra weapon at his side.

"Pops," I say, clearing my throat.

The hammer inside my head smashes against my skull, and I wince.

He takes a seat *behind* my desk.

"You look like shit," he says.

"I'm fine." I brush off his comment.

"Leave us," he commands Gio.

Gio hesitates, his brows shooting to his hairline as he looks at me. I give him a subtle nod.

My father leans forward in the chair after he's gone. "Can we speak freely?"

I know he's asking if there's a chance the office is bugged, but it gets swept every morning before I come in. "Yeah, everything's good."

"Good," he repeats.

I hesitate. "But it *wasn't* in South Carolina."

Despite Pops's old age, he has an air of power around him that can't be mistaken. His is the one I first learned to emulate.

"Someone tapped my phone." I pinch the bridge of my nose. "Not someone. *Aria.*"

Pops leans back, and an affable grin crawls over his face. "How is that possible, *figlio mio*?" He cocks his head to the side.

"Because I trusted her." I run a hand through my hair. "I never thought…I know *you* never thought about it either." My eyes track his reaction, watching. Testing. Seeing if he shows any sign of knowing more than he should.

There's something in my gut telling me I need to be careful around my father. That I don't have the full picture of what's been going down for the past three years. Maybe even before that.

"Tell me what happened," he says.

"I texted Gio to check out Frankie Bianchi, that little creep from New Jersey who used to make waves when he got picked up for loan sharking and spent five years in the pen. You know him?"

My father waves me off. "I know who Frankie is. He's worthless. Nothing. Inconsequential. Looking for him is a waste of time."

"Did you know he's Aria's uncle?" Again, I watch him closely.

His nostrils flare, but he's otherwise calm. Steady.

Almost *too* steady. Too practiced.

"I did not." His words are simple and to the point.

And just like that, my entire world tilts like tectonic plates shifting.

My heart kicks against my chest cavity, and I'm anxious about making sure *I* give nothing away now. "Well, fuck. I was kind of hoping you would have known."

"Why would *I* have known that?"

"Because you're you," I say. "I thought you knew everything."

Pops takes his cane off the top of my desk, placing it in his lap. "I'm disappointed to hear about this turn of events with Aria. Seems like your fiancée isn't who we thought she was at all. Tapping phones, keeping familial ties from you. It's good we're done with her and her family, no?"

"Yeah."

My stomach is rolling, trying to see where he's taking this. I don't know much about my father's state of mind, but I know when he's lying.

And he's been lying straight to my face this entire time.

CHAPTER 41

Enzo

MY FATHER DOESN'T STAY FOR MUCH LONGER, and I've never been so grateful for his absence. He *lied* to me. And I don't know if I've been a fool this whole time when it comes to him or if there's been an actual shift here.

I have to assume the problem is with me, and I've just been blind, believing his loyalty ran as deep as he preached. If he's lying to me now, what else has he lied to me about?

Is anything he tells me true?

Throughout my entire life, with all its difficulties, there's been one constant: The foundation on which I was raised was sturdy. Strong. Never made me stumble or shake, and I could always come back to that in the face of adversity.

But today there was a goddamn earthquake.

I've just finished a meeting with one of New York City's largest commercial builders. He uses *our* construction workers, *our* concrete, *our* men for everything. The setup is beneficial for our legitimate businesses but also for the racketeering where we skim money off the top and add bullshit charges to clean the cash we otherwise can't explain.

One hand washes the other…kind of. Obviously, we come out better at the end of the deal, not that the builder needs to know that. Even if he did…it's not like he could stay in business long if he didn't agree to our terms.

Marino Inc. owns New York.

My door is closed, and my headache has dulled to a throb instead of an automatic drill and hammer blasting against my skull, but when I hear muffled voices from outside the door, that ache taps dangerously, threatening to come back in full force.

I'm *definitely* considering firing Jessica, even though she's been with me since I took over and my pops brought her in. She's decent at her job, but she flirts, and over the years, the skirts have gotten shorter and the buttons have gotten more undone, no matter how many times I tell her I don't dip my dick into the company ink. She's persistent. But she's also good at her job, except that she's apparently incapable of not letting people in my goddamn office today.

No matter, though. Jessica's not my type, and maybe she's just having an off day.

The thought of who *is* my type sends blood rushing through my veins. My mouth on her. Me feeling her come around my fingers and then my dick.

My heart skips a beat when I realize Scotty will have her here soon.

I'm excited. More than that, actually. I'm downright antsy to see her again, and it's not even about the sex, although I do plan to strip her down and fuck her in my office. Something I've never done with *anyone*. But mainly, I just love her company.

I love *her*.

It's fast, but I don't give a fuck. In this life especially, you never know when your time is up, and I'm not willing to waste another second without her. Sometimes things happen beyond explanation, beyond what we believe to be realistic. The universe doesn't give a fuck about any of that.

Laughing, I press my palms to my eyes. *I sound like Venesa with her woo-woo shit.*

Fuck, is she ever going to get here?

More voices from outside my door, and then it swings open, Venesa waltzing in with an annoyed look on her face. She marches across the room, her hips swaying from side to side and drawing my attention, hypnotizing me with the motion.

Arousal flares low in my abdomen, and I know she can tell as my eyes meet hers, because her steps stutter for just a second before she makes her way to my desk.

Jessica runs in after her, yelling something at her back, but I don't even hear it. Every sense of mine is attuned to Venesa, and she drowns out the rest of the world.

Venesa leans over my desk, her hands in fists and her knuckles resting on the wood until half her body is hovering over it and her face is close to mine. She grips the lapel of my suit's vest, then pulls me toward her and lands a harsh kiss on my lips.

I groan, grasping the back of her head and driving my tongue into her mouth, desperate to taste her again.

She makes it last a few seconds, clearly proving a point, and I let her, because frankly, I'll do whatever she wants me to do.

Finally, she releases me, and I fall back against my chair with a *whack*. She stands up straight, her knuckles going back to the desk as she levels me with a look.

I glance around the room and realize Scotty and Bastien—the latter of which surprises the hell out of me—are standing inside the office now, both of them looking more than amused. I quirk a brow as I look between all of them and then back to my woman.

"Hello, piccola sirena," I coo, trying to hold back a grin but being completely unsuccessful.

She runs her red nails down my cheek. "Call off your bitch before I put her down."

I smirk. "Handle it yourself."

Jessica's face transforms, like she thinks I'm siding with *her*, and she crosses her arms with a new confidence, tapping her toe on the floor. "I'm sorry, Enzo, she just barged in."

Venesa stiffens when she hears Jessica say my name, and the amusement that was flowing through me evaporates because who told her she could *ever* call me that?

"It's Mr. Marino to you," Venesa hisses, turning toward her with a glare.

"*You* don't tell me what to do. I've been working with him for years, and that's a type of relationship you could only dream of."

Venesa throws back her head and laughs, and I become distracted by the milky expanse of her throat. I want to hold it under my palm. Feel it beneath my teeth. Lick it with my tongue.

Christ.

I stand up and walk around to the front of my desk and reach out, grabbing Venesa's hips and dragging her into me. She comes willingly, but her eyes stay on Jessica. Leaning down, I press my lips to her neck because I can't help it, nibbling on the side of her throat.

Venesa lets out a soft laugh, and then her glare is on me, her hand pressing against my chest and pushing me away. "Do you mind, Enzo? I'm *dealing* with something here."

"My bad." I grin at her and lift my palms.

Jessica interrupts. "Sir, she just barged in like she owned the place, and I know you've made it very clear I'm not supposed to let anyone else in today."

I slip my hands in my pockets, rocking back slightly on my heels. "*She* can come in whenever she wants, Jessica. In fact, anytime you see her face, assume I need the rest of the day to myself. I expect you to clear my schedule, treat her like she owns you, and get her *anything* her heart desires. Do you understand?"

Jessica's cheeks flame red, and her stature crumples, losing the ill-placed confidence she had before. "I thought you were with—"

"It doesn't matter what you thought, sugar," Venesa pipes in. "What matters is that you learn how to listen to your boss before I take him up on that *generous* offer of owning you."

Jessica's eyes narrow. "You're a bitch."

"And you're fired," I return.

Her eyes grow into circles, a gasp escaping her when she looks at me. "What? No, Mr. Marino, you can't fire me. Your father..."

I step forward and lower my voice. "Did I stutter? Go out there, pack your shit, and leave. I never want to see you in this office again."

Jessica lifts her chin, tears rimming her eyes, shock ghosting across her face. "Your father hired me, not you."

More reason to fire her, if I'm being honest.

The thought hits me that her having access to Pops after seeing me with Venesa isn't the smartest thing for me to allow, but I'm so amped up from her disrespecting Venesa in the first place, I can't find it in me to take back what I said.

"Then I suggest you go take it up with him." My eyes fall behind her to where Scotty and Bastien still are, and I jerk my chin. "You two mind escorting her off the property?"

Scotty tips an imaginary hat. "Sure thing, E. You really know how to put on a show, you know? The ladies, they love you, although I don't know why. We should sit down and smoke one of those fancy pipes while you teach me your ways."

"I don't smoke pipes." I laugh. "That's Pops's thing."

"Eh, no matter," he replies. "Always feel like I'm trying

to play the sax or something when I use those thingamabobs anyway. We can go straight up with a cigar instead, where I can snarf up the tobacco and enjoy it. I'm not picky."

Bastien scowls at Scotty. "What the fuck are you talking about? Are you *ever* serious?"

They both move forward, each of them grabbing an arm, and Scotty looks at Bastien over Jessica's head. "Do you ever lighten up?"

"You're an idiot."

Scotty's face drops. "Stop being a hater, Bas. The ladies at Suzy's Salon say it gives you wrinkles."

Bastien's lip twitches, and then he looks down at Jessica. "Let's go, lady. You heard the man."

Scotty and Bastien drag her out, and she's sticking her heels in the carpet muttering something about my pops, but I'm not paying attention to what she says because I'm turning to Venesa with a soft grin, drinking her in.

"Hi, baby."

"I'm going to kill her," she states plainly.

I wrap my hands around her waist, dragging her into me. "Okay. You want to do it right now, or can I have some time with you first?"

She huffs and presses her hands against my chest, shaking her head. "I hope you know I'm not kidding. How long did she work with you anyway? And you let her call you 'Enzo'?" Her fingers pick at my shirt. "I thought only I called you that."

Her possessiveness turns me on. I grab her hand and put

it on my cock to show her as much. "You're hot when you're jealous."

She scoffs, but her fingers wrap around me and give me a slight tug, a smirk gracing the sides of her mouth. "I don't get jealous."

"Clearly," I mutter, maneuvering us around until she's pressed against the edge of the desk. "I think I have a fetish for you on desks."

"Enzo, please, can we talk?" She laughs when I nip her neck, and she must be ticklish there, so I do it again. The noise of her happiness is cute and so different from her normal tone, but I like them equally, and I make a mental note to ensure she gives me both her joy and her neutrality every single day.

Because I plan to have her with me now, *every single day*, and I want to have every part of her.

"Enzo, I'm serious," she tries again.

"So talk." I bury my face in the crook of her neck, picking her up, putting her on the edge of my desk, and settling in between her legs. "But if I don't have you right now, I'll go insane."

She laughs like I'm joking. "Can you be serious?"

"I *am* serious." My hands move to her hips, and I lean into her, whispering in her ear. "Now be a good girl and let me eat."

I drop to my knees, and I make quick work of pushing up her skirt until it reveals her glistening, puffy pussy to my eyes.

Sending up a quick prayer of thanks that she both almost always wears a dress of some sort and that she seems averse to underwear, I spread her legs apart, my palms pushing the insides of her thighs until my head can fit between them.

And then I dive in, not wasting any time, because I'm *starving* for her, and ever since my first taste, I haven't been able to get the memory of it out of my mind.

My mouth suctions around her clit immediately, sucking in a rhythmic motion while my tongue swirls the bud like it's ice cream.

Better than, if I'm being honest, but again, I've never been a sweets kind of guy. I much prefer the salty, tangy taste of a woman.

She moans and collapses against the desk, the same way she did last night, and I make quick work of her pussy, paying attention to where she needs me most. I reach down with one of my hands and undo my belt and zipper while I keep my tongue on her cunt, freeing my cock, tugging from the base to the root and back again.

She sits up slightly on her elbows, her mouth half-open as she watches me eat her out. Her gaze moves to my arm. "Are you stroking yourself?" She pants. "I want to see."

I almost tell her no, that I'm not letting her move until she comes all over my face, but she sits up fully and forces me off her. My hand keeps moving on my dick, and her eyes flare before she's off the desk and shoving me back until I'm lying on the floor, my cock sticking straight up.

My eyes widen, surprised by how quickly she took

control, and I'm about to say something, but then she's there and her mouth is sliding down my length, and instead of being able to speak, I find she steals every ounce of breath from my lungs.

It's hot. Wet. Fucking incredible.

She keeps going, working her way until she's at the base of my shaft, the flat of her tongue slipping out of her mouth and licking the top part of my balls while I'm inside her throat from root to tip.

Goddamn.

I don't think I've ever had anyone take me this deep.

She breathes through her nose, and my hands shoot to the back of her head, holding her in place. I expect her to complain about it, but her eyes flick up to mine, and she stares devilishly at me from beneath her lashes; it sends a spark of arousal arcing through my body like a meteor. My hips lift from the ground without thought, and my dick moves farther down her throat.

She moans—she fucking *moans*—and the vibration massages my cock and makes my hips thrust harder, my fingers tangling in her strands just to keep me grounded.

I won't last long if she keeps this up. My hands move to grip more of her hair, holding it back so I can see her pretty face as she works my dick from base to tip, her tongue swirling around the shaft as she does.

My abs tense, every muscle tightening as I fly higher and higher. "Goddamn, baby, you look so fucking good taking my cock."

She hums around me, and my eyes roll back in my head, my movements growing jerky.

Saliva drips from the corners of her lips and down onto my lap, and it's messy and fucking amazing, and I'm so close to exploding in her sweet, hot mouth, but I don't want to come this way.

I tell her as much, trying to pull her face off me, and she follows, releasing me with a pop, a string of saliva connecting from my tip to her lip, her red lipstick smeared.

My dick slaps against my stomach, and I'm so on edge, I reach down and grip myself at the base, gritting my teeth and trying to think about fucking *anything* other than how sexy every single experience with her is.

I count to ten and get myself together, and when I open my eyes, she's staring out my floor-to-ceiling windows that line the far wall.

She looks back to me and smirks. "Interesting choice of office for someone with a fear of heights."

That does it. I am no longer close to coming. "It would be if I was afraid of heights. Which I'm not."

"Oh yeah?" She arches a brow. "Prove it."

Anxiety pumps through me, but I'll be damned if I let her think I'm a coward about it, so I accept her challenge and lean back, stripping off my clothes entirely until I'm naked.

She watches me with a gleam in her eyes, and it doesn't miss me how the power balance has shifted since she threw me on the ground and drank up my cock like it was dessert. And now I'm here on full display, and she's fully clothed.

But I don't need her naked to fuck her, so I move quickly, diving forward and scooping her up before standing and walking us both over to the windows.

My heart ratchets in speed, but I ignore it, pushing her against the glass and sliding my hands down her arms until my fingers slip between hers.

"Hands on the window, baby. Don't you fucking move."

I avoid looking down, because we're thirty-five stories up, and I'm trying to stay hard, not have a panic attack. I release her fingers and move back down her body, slipping her skirt off her hips and dragging it along her legs until it's pooled at her feet. She steps out of it and tosses it somewhere to the side, and I pull her until her spine arches beautifully. I drag one of my hands down it, then lean forward, my dick brushing against her, slipping between her legs. My mouth follows the trail of my touch along her back, pressing kisses to every inch until I reach the dimples that dot just above her full, round, *delicious* ass.

"Enzo, *please* fuck me."

I groan, my cock jerking against her cunt. "I love the way you say my name."

And then I'm gripping myself and slipping between her folds, thrusting back and forth, teasing, torturing us both with how close I get to her entrance before I move back up until I skim across her pulsing clit.

Her thighs tighten, adding to the friction against my length.

"You want me to fuck you?" I ask, hovering over her and

moving one hand to grip her hip tightly, the other wrapping her hair in my fist.

I've decided that's my favorite thing to do.

"Tell me how you want it," I whisper. "Hard or fast."

"I want you to shut up and just *do* it," she snarks back.

My hand flies out and smacks her ass. She moans, just like I knew she would.

"You and that fucking mouth."

My fingers tighten in her hair, and I pull hard, her head dragged toward me by the tension, making her back arch even more, her ass pushing into me and forcing the tip of my cock to spread her open as I slip inside.

Fuck, she feels so damn good.

I thrust forward until my hips slap against her ass, and I'm transfixed by the way she sucks me in like she was made for me, her body immediately moving to try to get me in deeper.

She moans, and I grip her hair tight as I start a punishing pace. I'm already so ramped up, I could come any second, but I'm determined to feel her quiver and explode around my cock again.

It's my new drug.

My eyes skim over her body, focused first on the way it looks as I disappear between her thick thighs and into her tight pussy, and then to the way her ass cheeks ripple and shake with every thrust. They continue up her beautiful hips that flare out from her waist. My hand leaves her hair and wraps around her to cup one of her heavy breasts, molding it into my palm and squeezing, leaning over until my chest is almost touching her back.

My eyes flick to the window, a shot of panic rushing through me when I see how far away from the ground we are, but then Venesa moans, taking one of her hands off the glass and moving it down to rub her clit, and I focus on that instead, my fear dissipating.

"That's right, baby. I need to feel you come all over me," I say. "Show me how good it feels."

She does, her fingers slipping down even farther until she makes a V with her first two digits around my shaft, right where I'm sinking inside her, and the added sensation makes my body tense and sparks of arousal shoot off inside me like flares in the sky.

My grip tightens on her tit, my other hand squeezing her hip as my movements become out of rhythm. I'm barely hanging on here, and I need her to come for me.

And then she does.

Her cunt clamps around my cock, massaging it as she shakes, and her body tenses and then melts into my hold until it feels like my grip on her is the only thing keeping her upright.

She lets out a loud groan, and her head flies back, her body straightening until she's plastered to my chest, and I tighten my hold to keep her pressed against me.

My balls tense up, and my cock lengthens.

"Fuck, I'm about to come."

She flies off me, and the sudden shift in temperature, losing her body heat, puts me in a tailspin.

But then she flips around, sinks to her knees, and tells me to come on her face.

And I fucking explode without another touch, my cock jerking wildly in the air. One of my hands slams against the glass, and I grip my length quickly with the other, aiming it as I spray, painting her gorgeous features with my cum.

It's a beautiful sight.

She's dirty and depraved, and so fucking mine.

It takes minutes for me to catch my breath after, my chest heaving and my cock still twitching as I come back down.

Venesa grins at me, takes a finger, dips it into the mess on her cheek, and then slips it inside her mouth, her eyes fluttering closed as she moans at the taste.

My heart pitches off a cliff.

I lean down, wrap my hand around the base of her neck, and pull her to me so I can kiss the fuck out of her.

"You are the sexiest thing I've ever seen in my life," I say. "I'm so happy you're here."

She grins against my lips. "I'm happy too."

I help her stand after and tell her to go get cleaned up in the en suite.

It's about thirty minutes later when we're all put back together, clothes on, satiated, and well fucked.

She's sitting on the couch near the entrance to my office, and I plop down next to her, reaching out to twirl a strand of her hair.

"Okay, now we can talk." I grin. "How long are you in

town for?" I grab her fingers with my other hand and press a kiss to her knuckles.

She hesitates before responding. "Well...that depends."

"Does Trent know you're here?" I ask. "How did things play out with him?"

She shakes her head. "No, and he can't find out."

"Why not?" I know he was probably pissed at her for what happened between us and for the dissolution of my engagement with Aria, but Venesa's his right hand. His family. That's what I kept telling myself because that's what I *had* to make myself believe, or I never would have been able to walk away, even knowing it was temporary.

Thinking about that possibly *not* being the case makes me rage.

"He kicked me out," she says.

I sit up straight, dropping the strand of her hair. "What do you mean, he *kicked* you out?"

She shrugs, and betrayal sits heavy in her eyes. "He said he had Momma killed, and then he kicked me out, told me to leave and never come back to South Carolina. He took *everything* from me."

"Whoa, whoa, back up a minute. I thought your piece-of-shit dad killed your mom." She's dropping some bombs here, and I'm having trouble wrapping my head around them.

"He was telling the truth in the end, I guess. I never actually saw my dad that night. It was all based on what Momma told me before she made me promise to stay hidden. It was Uncle T the whole time. Well..." She chews on the corner of her mouth. "He hired out to the Atlantis MC." She spits out the name like they're dirt beneath her shoe.

But I'm stuck on her other words. *He hired out.*

"Enzo." She reaches out and grips my forearm. I move until my hand tangles with hers, our fingers intertwined, and then I bring it up to my mouth and press soft, chaste kisses to the back.

"I need your help," she says.

"Anything you want, piccola sirena, and it's yours." I press another kiss to her hand. "Want me to burn his kingdom to the ground?"

"No," she whispers, her eyes flicking up to lock on mine. "I want to burn *him* to the ground and take his kingdom for myself."

Anticipation lights up my insides, and I cup her cheek, ghosting my thumb across the planes of her face. "Then let's make you queen of the ashes."

CHAPTER 42

Venesa

I FEEL BETTER AFTER TALKING TO ENZO, BUT there's still so much weight sitting on my chest with all the things I *haven't* told him. But I don't know how to make myself say the words, and the longer I take to get them out, the harder it is.

I'm a coward, allowing myself to settle into this new feeling of being in his arms, of being shown just what it's like when Enzo Marino looks at you like you hung the moon. I've never been someone's choice before, not like this, and the feeling is intoxicating, but it also makes me terrified of it slipping away, and I know after I tell him what I need to…I'll lose it. Lose him.

The thought makes my stomach drop.

We've been in the back of his car for an hour; traffic in New York City is no joke, and I glance out the window, realizing we've finally made it out of downtown and are clearly in another area.

The buildings are older, the signs worn and faded, the streets filled with people hanging outside at round tables and kids playing on the sidewalks. Suddenly, I'm interested. I hadn't expected to come to a place like this, and the familiarity of a community that feels *lived* in, cared for, reminds me of the Southside of Atlantic Cove.

It's comfortable here.

Scotty and Bastien are both up front, bickering like brothers. I can't tell if they enjoy the back-and-forth or if they genuinely hate each other, but either way, it's amusing to see someone else giving Bastien shit.

"I thought you were taking me out on the town," I say.

Enzo lifts a brow. "Does this not look like a town to you?"

"You know what I mean, smart-ass."

He grins. "We're meeting my guy here, Gio. And I wanted to show you where I grew up."

The car slows down before halting when we hit a stoplight, and there's an elderly woman on the corner of the street, struggling with paper grocery bags in her arms as she tries to open her trunk.

Enzo notices. "Scotty, pull over."

"You got it, E."

The sound of a blinker comes on, and then Scotty's parking right along the sidewalk, and before I can say a word, Enzo's popping out of the car.

There are a few stagnant moments where I think about staying in and watching from afar, but when Bastien messes with the radio and Scotty smacks his hand, I get out, not wanting to listen to them argue like a married couple.

This is a whole new world for me. It's like when I got to New York, I stopped being the girl everyone looked at as an obligation and started being more.

I still miss Fisher, though. I glance down at my phone, seeing that he still hasn't texted me back, even though I've messaged and called several times.

When I catch up to Enzo, he's already at the elderly woman's side. "Mrs. Coppola, it's been a long time."

She's beaming at him like he's the best thing since sliced bread, and he smiles back, grabbing the groceries from her hands and putting them into the trunk of her car before closing it.

"You're such a good boy, Enzo," she croons, patting his cheek like he's a child.

"You shouldn't be grocery shopping on your own, Mrs. Coppola."

She scoffs. "Oh, I'll be fine."

"Do you need a ride home?"

She laughs and waves him off. "No, no, but it's good to have you back here. It's been a while since we've seen you around."

He runs a hand through his hair and grimaces the slightest bit. "Been busy."

"Hmm," she hums, looking at him, then glances at me for the first time. "I can see that. Is this your new girl?"

He smirks, and I expect him to say no, because how bad

would it look for him to be seen with me when he and Aria were the it couple, and very media friendly, for the past year? But he surprises me by wrapping his arm around my waist and tugging me into his side, pressing a kiss to my temple. "She's the *only* girl."

"She's much better looking than that last one you had." She winks at me. "Enzo's a good boy. He's the whole reason my Donny could go to trade school and make something of himself. This community doesn't know what we'd do without him."

Mrs. Coppola reaches up and pats his cheek again, then moves to get in her car. Enzo lets me go only to help her in and close the door behind her. She speeds off into the street, a bit haphazardly, and I turn to him. "Should she be driving?"

"Probably not."

"And *you*," I say, wrapping my arms around his middle. "You're such a *good boy*."

He grins. "Yeah? You gonna reward me for it later?"

"Play your cards right, you never know what can happen."

I expect him to push me back toward the car, but he leads me down the street instead, taking my hand and strolling along the sidewalk like we have all the time in the world.

"I thought you lived in the city," I note as we walk.

He looks at me. "I do. You'll see it later, when I move you from the hotel into my place."

"Oh, you don't have to do that." I shake my head.

He stops walking and grips my upper arms like he's worried I'll run away.

I'm not going to. I'm his for as long as he'll have me.

"One day, you'll stop telling me what to do," he says, his hand sliding up until he's playing with my seashell necklace. "I want you in my bed. Every night and every morning."

"Yeah?" I grin

He kisses me again. "Yeah."

I make a face, an unwelcome thought hitting me. "I'll be honest, the thought of being in your bed where you've had my cousin is not high on my list of priorities."

He settles back, his eyes searching mine, and then he tips up my chin, gives me another peck, and nods. "I'll take care of it."

I don't argue, because honestly, I believe him.

And right now, before things get heavy again, before I focus on how I'm going to take down my uncle and take back what's rightfully mine…I'm going to enjoy this light moment.

This is everything I never thought existed, and no matter what happens when I finally work up the courage to tell Enzo the truth, I know one thing: I'll forever be grateful for the time we've had here. For him showing me that not all men are absolute trash.

Not all of them are horrible.

I don't know if he'll ever realize how deeply he's changed my life and my outlook on it. It breaks my heart knowing things won't stay this way forever.

"So," I say, looking around because I don't want to focus on the emotion swelling in my chest. "What's the story around here?"

He grabs my hand, linking ours together and letting them swing between us. And it's such a normal thing to do, but for me, it's monumental. I never thought I'd be able to have something so...simple but have it mean so much.

"This is Trillia, Brooklyn," he replies. "I grew up here."

We keep walking down the street, and I'm taking it all in.

"That butcher shop right there?" I look at where he's pointing, a bright white sign with blue writing that says "Max's Meats." "My ma used to send me out here every single Monday to grab beef for the week, but I was a little asshole. I used to start fights out front and then use my pops's name to keep me out of trouble."

I can picture what he's saying perfectly, and it makes me smile thinking of a young Enzo with a chip on his shoulder and a whole lot to prove. "I can see it. Who's Max?"

"The butcher. He was a good guy, tried to do his best for me and keep me on the up and up, but it never really worked out."

"That's sweet you had someone looking out for you, though."

He shrugs. "I was tied to this life the moment I was born, despite Max's best efforts. He's gone now, though. Left the place to me, if you can believe it."

I glance at the sign again. "You own the butcher shop?"

"On paper. I give everything to his wife and kids. Take care of 'em, you know?"

My heart swells. "You know, you're actually a really sweet guy."

He looks at me like I've offended him. "I'm *incredibly* sweet, and it's offensive you thought I wasn't."

I snort. "Please."

We continue to make our way down the street. Eventually, I ask, "So how come you don't live here now?"

"Makes more sense to be in the city. Can't control the streets if you aren't there yourself to see them. And can you imagine the drive? Forget about it."

Suddenly, he stops walking and pulls out his phone, his brows drawing down when he swipes his screen. "My guy Gio's here. Come on, we've gotta head back to the car."

It only takes a few minutes to get there, but in the time we've been gone, Scotty and Bastien both have made their way out of the vehicle, Bastien leaning against the passenger door while Scotty talks to a tall, broad man I've never seen before.

They all turn to us when we walk up.

"Who's this?" the guy asks, his brows wiggling at Enzo.

Enzo drops a heavy arm around my shoulder and drags me into his side. "This is Venesa." He points at Gio. "You'll treat her with respect, or I'll fuck you up."

Gio smirks and reaches out his hand. "Ah, Venesa. Heard a lot about you."

I place my palm in his, and he brings it up to his mouth. He lingers, and I have a sneaking suspicion it's on purpose.

Enzo smacks the back of his head. "That's enough."

I smile and take my hand away. "Nice to meet you, Gio."

Enzo groans and squeezes my hip. "I'm gonna go chat with Gio real quick. You good?"

I suck on my teeth and nod.

Enzo tells Scotty to start the car, and the second they're both gone, Bastien levels me with a look. "You tell him yet?"

His question startles me because how does he know I need to? Ashamed, I shake my head. "It's not that easy."

"Fuck that, V. You've gotta tell him. Get it over with."

Something lodges in my throat. "He'll hate me."

"You let him decide that. But you can't keep it from him. You need to be honest."

"I'm going to," I snap at him. "Don't push me. It's none of your business anyway."

Bastien chuckles and shakes his head, stepping toward me. "*You* are my business, V. I'm here for you, playing both sides and keeping your uncle none the wiser. I'm with you here, but you've gotta handle your shit. Tell him."

It's irritating to have Bas on my back, but that irritation is because deep down, I know he's right.

Enzo walks over, a serious look on his face. "Change of plans. Gio found someone I had him looking for." He glances at me. "You ever heard of Frankie Bianchi?"

My brows shoot to my hairline. "No, but Bianchi is my dead aunt's maiden name."

He nods. "Frankie is apparently Aria's uncle, and someone I'm dying to talk to. You want to come with? Or else I can have Scotty drop you at the hotel."

I nod, because *of course* I want to go with him.

Laughing, I cover my mouth, and Enzo quirks a brow. "What's so funny?"

"Nothing, this is just…our thing, I guess. Touristy outings followed by a round of torture."

He chuckles, brushing the back of his hand down my cheek. "A perfect night, in my opinion."

He grabs my hand again.

"He's *here*?" I ask.

Enzo gives me a half grin. "In the basement of Max's Meats."

CHAPTER 43

Venesa

I NEVER KNEW FRANKIE BIANCHI EXISTED, BUT I know I want him dead the moment I see him.

He looks *just* like my aunt Antonella, and I've always hated her.

She was the Wicked Witch to my Dorothy, the evil stepmother to my Cinderella. She truly embodied everything that I despised about spoiled, rich, entitled people, and frankly, I blame her for the way her daughter turned out. I see a lot of her in Aria, and now that the puzzle pieces of my life are all coming together instead of having someone there obstructing the view, it makes perfect sense why I've never truly felt like part of the Kingston Family.

It's because they never *let* me be.

We're in an actual meat locker, and I'm quickly realizing that moving through hanging body parts of different animals is not my idea of a good time. There are even pigs' heads lined up against the wall.

I'm not normally one who gets the ick easily, but being in here definitely does it for me.

Scotty stayed outside with the car. He's not a made man, so Enzo said he wasn't allowed to come inside, but he did let Gio tag along, and Bastien—mainly because I pushed for him to be in here—and the two of them waltz in silently behind us like bodyguards.

I guess, in a way, they are.

In the middle of the room, Frankie's strung up just like the animals that surround us.

The only difference is he's still alive.

A shiver races through me because it's *cold* in here, and Enzo notices immediately, undoing his suit jacket and placing it over my shoulders.

I've never been in a relationship before, and to be honest, I'm not entirely sure that's what we are now, but I like how he cares for me in a way nobody else ever has.

I stand back to let Enzo work, gripping the lapels of his jacket and bringing them up to my nose so I can be surrounded by his scent. My stomach flutters, a cozy feeling lighting me up from the inside out.

Enzo doesn't speak, and neither does anyone else. Between the silence and the cold of the room, the tension is palpable, a foreboding tingle firing like synapses against my skin. Enzo sighs heavily, tilting his head and watching the way Frankie hangs limply by his wrists, tied together by a chain and hooked to the ceiling. Blood drips from cuts on his face onto the linoleum floor, down a drain that's directly beneath him.

That's smart. Why didn't I ever think of doing that?

I look behind me at Bastien and raise my brows as if to say, *Can you believe this room?* and notice how tensely he's holding his body.

Bastien loves his torture. I bet it's painful for him that he's forced to be a spectator and isn't able to take part.

Enzo rolls up one sleeve of the black button-down beneath his suit vest, slowly revealing sinewy forearms and tattooed muscle. First the left and then the right, taking his time with each. Like there's no need to rush. And I guess there isn't.

It's not like Frankie's going anywhere.

It's almost erotic watching him prepare himself for this, and I squeeze my thighs together to stem the ache. Now that I know what it's like to have him inside me, it's like my body is on overdrive, telling me I need to stop being such a prude and allow him to make up for lost time.

Orgasms and torture. They really go hand in hand.

Also, kissing him is…different from what I imagined kissing would be, and I don't know if it's because it's kissing with *him* or if I've been missing out this whole time.

Probably a bit of both.

There are a few of what look like large orange paint buckets lined up against the wall next to Enzo and a sink that's just beyond that, and he walks to the buckets and picks one up. It looks heavy, and when he gets closer, I realize it's filled with ice and water.

What is he gonna do with that?

I don't have to wait long for my answer because he takes the bucket and throws the water on Frankie, who jolts out of his woozy state with a start and a sharp yell.

"Wake up, sweetheart." Enzo's voice is low and controlled.

It's the same type of tone he gets when he's fucking me, but lacking the warmth. Doesn't matter—I find it turns me on terribly anyway.

He drops the bucket next to him and stands directly in front of Frankie, his arms crossed. I can only see Enzo's back from here, but I wish I could walk up behind him and press a kiss to his shoulders.

Frankie groans, his head lolling to the side a bit before he shakes himself out of the stupor.

"The more you pass out, the longer this will take." Enzo smacks his cheek lightly with his hand. A double tap, tap, but it's enough to make Frankie open his eyes more.

Sighing, Enzo cracks his neck and turns to me. "Your turn."

My brows lift, and I look behind me before pointing to myself. "Me?"

Enzo grins and nods, gesturing to the long metal table he was just at, and that's when I realize what's on top of it. Before now, I had just been focused on Frankie and trying to ignore the dead animals and the smell of blood and death lingering in the air.

Do they actually kill the animals down here? Gross, if yes.

"I thought you'd want to play," Enzo says.

I walk over to the table, realizing there are different things here I *could* actually play with. My fingers dust over the needles and syringes, then to vials labeled and filled with powders and liquids.

"How did you get all this here?" I ask, glancing back at him.

"I own this city, baby. If I want it, I get it." He reaches across his chest and grabs his gun from the holster, holding it sideways and flipping it back and forth like he's inspecting it. "Plus, Gio's resourceful."

My heart warms at the touching gesture. "And you did all this…for me?"

He glances up from his weapon and smiles widely. "I'd do anything for you."

Looking back at the table, I pick up a white powder labeled *dextroamphetamine* and tilt my head. "You want me to wake him up?"

"It'd be helpful," he replies.

I take my time with the powder, mixing it in with a bit of water before filling the syringe and spinning around to grin at Enzo. "This is really thoughtful of you, you know? I would have been fine just watching."

I walk over to Frankie, sinking my teeth into my lower lip while I stare at him.

God, he looks just like my aunt Ella. Fury marinates in my bones.

I jab the needle harshly into his thigh and press the syringe, watching the amphetamine go into his system. I didn't weigh it out, but I know from eyeballing it that it should be enough to get him going: heart racing, feeling euphoria, and my favorite—the chatty-Kathy syndrome.

It might also backfire and cause him to panic since he's hanging from a ceiling with blood dripping from his wrists. It looks like his right shoulder might be dislocated, and there's *definitely* something wrong with his foot based on the angle it's bent.

He jolts awake with a start, inhaling a heavy gasp, his eyes flinging around the room.

Recognition flares in his irises, his body flailing even though the movement is only hurting him.

I spin around and beam at Enzo, and his eyes soften. His arms are crossed over his broad chest, the gun in his hand resting on top of his right bicep.

"Frankie, you know why you're here?" he asks.

Frankie grunts but doesn't respond. He stops trying to fight his chains, though.

"Do you know who I am, Frankie?" Enzo asks again.

A shiver runs down my spine.

Frankie licks his cracked lips. "Yes."

Enzo nods. "Good. Then you know it's in your best interest to be one hundred percent real with me right now, correct?"

Again, Frankie creaks out a faint "yes."

He isn't arguing, which is a little disappointing because

I wanted to see Enzo in his full glory, but it's great he isn't being difficult, especially because it seems like Enzo thinks Frankie is going to be the missing link to everything.

A shot of anxiety rushes through me.

"Tell me how you're related to Aria Kingston, and don't lie to me, Frankie, because that's only gonna piss me off."

Frankie grits his teeth, his jaw stiffening, and I can see the vulnerability shining through before he even says anything.

"Hey." Enzo snaps his fingers in Frankie's face. "I'm talking to you."

Frankie rasps, "I'll tell you everything you want to know. Just let me die with a little dignity."

Enzo tilts his head, the hand holding his gun reaching up and scratching at his temple. "You tell me what I need to know without argument, and I'll let you die with honor," he confirms. "I can respect that."

Frankie sniffs, droplets of blood dripping onto the floor from his swollen and broken nose. "I'm Aria's uncle."

I truly didn't know she had a living uncle, and it just drives that knife deeper into my chest—yet another thing proving I never really was part of the family at all.

"And tell me, Frankie, are you *close* with your niece?" Enzo asks.

Frankie shakes his head and spits out a clot of blood. "No."

"How about her father?"

There's a tense silence, and Frankie's jaw twitches. "Yeah, okay? I've been doing business with Trent for going on two decades now. He's the one who sent me out here in the first place."

I tilt my head, watching him, letting the betrayal of my uncle stream through me like static, filling every fissure in my heart that *he* caused. I thought we worked together, and now I know we never did—I was always just a puppet on invisible marionette strings.

The anticipation in the air heightens. "And what business do you have with Trent Kingston lately?" Enzo continues.

Frankie lifts his head and looks at Enzo, spitting more blood from his mouth. "The same business I have with your father."

Enzo physically stumbles back but recovers quickly.

Shock filters through my system, and I step forward, unable to bite my tongue. "Are you telling me Trent and Carlos Marino are working together?"

Frankie turns his focus on me, recognition flaring in their depths. "You're Venesa."

His eyes volley from me to Enzo in confusion. A jolt of panic hits me dead in the chest, and I move quickly, walking to Frankie and bringing my hand back, then connecting with his face to keep him from saying something he might regret—or more likely something I'd have to *make* him regret.

Enzo laughs like he's happy I stepped in and bitch-slapped his hostage.

I lean in close to Frankie and murmur, "I'd watch your mouth if you know what's good for you. Enzo might be scary, but I promise I can be worse."

Frankie swallows, but I know he got the message.

I hope.

Enzo stares at me in awe as I spin around and move away. "Fuck, you're sexy."

I grin and wink at him, trying to hide the tremble in my hands. "Focus, Lover Boy."

He looks back at Frankie. "I'm tired of this game. I have a woman to keep happy, and every second I spend here with you is a second longer I'm not alone with her, so tell me what I need to know."

Frankie shifts, the chain clanking, and he grimaces. "Your dad came to me a few years back, worried…panicked, even. Like he was losing his mind."

Enzo's chin lifts, the barrel of his gun tapping against his thigh.

"There were whispers in the ranks, he thought," Frankie continues. "He needed someone who was connected enough that he could trust but not anyone *in* his circles."

"And that was you," Enzo confirms.

"Yeah, that was me."

"And?"

"Your dad, he's…you know he's not right in the head anymore, don't you?"

Enzo's jaw clenches. "You let me worry about what I know."

"He's crazy, man. Paranoid. Thinks everyone's out to get him. He told me he needed to make connections. Wanted to know more about my sister's husband, and I'm just ecstatic because I figure, if I can be useful, maybe he'll remember it when it comes time for the books to open, you know? So I hooked him up with Trent. Told him my brother-in-law was a powerful man in the South. Had secret weapons." His eyes flick to mine. "Things could get taken care of easily without ever tracing back to Carlos."

A sick sense starts to crawl its way through my middle, anxiety pumping through my blood.

"What things?" Enzo presses.

"Things like being able to do whatever you needed—kill anyone you wished—without all the bullshit tape and blowback. Things that won't get traced to you."

Enzo moves forward and pistol-whips him across the face.

Frankie lets out a curse, blood pouring from a large gash on his cheek caused from the sight on the gun. "Fuck, man, I'm *telling* you!"

"Quit being cryptic and spit it the fuck out, or I swear to God I'll make sure you rot with no honor," Enzo spits.

Frankie inhales a quick breath and then looks Enzo in the eyes. "Your dad is the one who tried to kill you, and he used Trent Kingston to do it."

CHAPTER 44

Enzo

BETRAYAL IS A DISEASE.

A slow-moving bitch of a thing that goes down like cheap liquor, burning your throat and sitting sour in your belly.

I like to think of myself as a forgiving person, but knowing my father was the one behind my attempted murder? That *I* threatened him so much he tried to take me out and lied about it for the past year?

That's something I can't forgive.

And it's definitely something I won't forget.

I held up my end of the bargain with Frankie. Obviously, I couldn't just let him go, but I unchained him, took him out to a deserted area, and made his death quick with a pop to the head.

He didn't fight it. Just stood there and waited like a man. And it felt good doing something on my own again, thrilling to make a kill not sanctioned by my pops.

Afterward, we came back to Venesa's hotel suite, because I know she isn't comfortable being at my penthouse, and it's not fair of me to ask her to stay there when she's made it clear where she stands. A problem I'll be rectifying tomorrow.

Venesa scooches behind me on her hotel bed, rising on her knees and running her hands over my shoulders. I lean back into her, letting my head fall onto her chest, near her collarbone, where her necklace rests, wishing that her presence were enough to drown out the noise in my head. I don't know if there *is* anything that can quiet the noise. Too many moving pieces, particles of dust I have to somehow find and make a tangible thing.

"I need to talk to Gio," I tell her.

She presses a kiss on the inside of my neck. "Everything can wait until the morning."

I shake my head. "I knew my pops wasn't well, that he'd been growing more unhinged, but I never thought he'd actually be the one trying to take me out."

"Family's fucked," Venesa replies. "He wasn't successful, that's what matters." She slips her hand down to my chest, pressing her palm against my heart. "You're here. Your heart's beating. You have a woman at your service, ready and willing to do *anything* you need."

I give her a look and then spin around until I'm facing her on the bed, my fingers sliding up her thighs and gripping the soft curves of her waist. "Oh yeah? And what do I *need*, piccola sirena?"

She moves forward, sliding her legs around me until

the heat of her cunt is pressed against my hardening cock, and she wraps her arms around my neck, leaning in to press a kiss to my lips. "You need to take it out on me. All that frustration…" She glides her hips back and forth, creating a delicious friction that has a fever spiraling through me. "That anger, that hurt…you can use me, Lover Boy."

She moves her lips, ghosting them across my cheek and along my jaw until she slides farther down, nibbling on my neck. Goose bumps spring up everywhere she touches, and I grip her tighter as I thrust upward, rubbing against her fabric-covered pussy.

"Don't say things you don't mean, Venesa. I don't want to hurt you."

"You won't," she replies. "I trust you."

I push her back slowly until she's lying on the bed, her hair splayed around her like she's a goddess, and I'm so fucking hard, dripping with the need to sink inside her, to lose myself in her so I don't have to face the reality of my world.

Of how everything is upending. Changing.

"Hurting you doesn't interest me," I murmur, my fingers moving up her body and slipping beneath her shirt until it slips over her head. "I don't want to bring you pain, only pleasure. But we should have a safe word just in case anything we do becomes too much."

Her breasts pop free, and my mouth is there instantly, sucking and biting, the taste of her flesh like ambrosia in my mouth.

“Seashell,” she says.

“Perfect.”

She pauses, reaching down and pulling my face up until I can look her in the eyes. “You won’t hurt me; I can take whatever you want to give, whenever you want to give it.”

My eyes volley between her gaze and her mouth, and I’m so overcome with how much I need her that I dive down, tangling our tongues together, kissing the fuck out of her like I’m afraid I won’t ever get the chance again.

Hazy brown eyes. A murmuring voice. “What did they do to you?”

“Don’t die. Don’t let them win.”

I wake with a start, that deep sultry voice echoing in my ears and sending chills down my spine. I look over at Venesa, but she’s not there, and I hear the distinct sound of a shower running.

I’m tempted to go in, find her, and spread her out in front of me to feast before I start my day, but my dream has me frozen in place, pieces of a fucked-up puzzle finally clicking together in my head.

Because I remember now, when I didn’t before.

I don’t know how I got on that shoreline or what saved me, but I could swear I dreamed I saw *Venesa* leaning over me, pressing something against me that caused pain to shoot up my side.

The shower turns off, and I sit up in bed, running a hand through my hair.

Venesa walks out a few minutes later in a small white towel, steam billowing around her, and goddamn, she's a fucking vision. But it's tainted right now because I'm wondering if she was part of my attempted murder and just how much she knows that she *isn't* telling me.

Was anything real?

I don't want to think the worst, and my body refuses to let my mind even go there fully, convincing me that I'm just on edge because of the revelation of my pops's betrayal and how fucked up everyone is in both our worlds.

"Morning." She smiles at me, rubbing a towel on her hair.

"I can't get this dream out of my head," I start, the words spilling out of me because I can't hold them back. "Of the night I almost died."

She freezes in place, her movements slowing as she walks to the edge of the bed and sits down. "Enzo," she says, sucking on her lips.

I crawl over to her, gripping her face until she *has* to look me in the eye. "It was you, wasn't it?"

Something flashes across her features—trepidation maybe.

"*You* were there. *You* saved me." I laugh and shake my head.

"Enzo..." she says again, warily.

My heart feels like it might burst out of my chest, but I

have to ask her. "I need you to be really honest with me. Did you know about your uncle and my pops?"

I don't know what I'll do if she was part of it.

Disquiet fills the air. "No. I was sent to New York that night to check up on Aria. Uncle T used to have me do it all the time. She was there…just walking along the Hudson with a broken heel and a tale about a date gone wrong. And then we heard you groaning, and I didn't know who the hell you were, but I knew you were probably *someone*. To be honest, if I knew the truth, I probably wouldn't have tried to save you. I was scared to be seen there with you anyway, so I gave Aria what she needed to wake you up, knowing she'd want to be a news story, and I ran away."

"Did *Aria* know?" I ask, even though I'm sure she won't have the answer.

Venesa purses her lips. "I doubt it. She didn't really want to save you; honestly, she was kind of freaked out by the whole thing."

I let out a disbelieving chuckle. "So this whole time I felt chained to a life with a woman who saved me, and it was… you? I should have been chaining myself to *you*."

She breathes out a small laugh, her eyes fluttering. "You shouldn't chain yourself to anybody, least of all me."

"Fuck *that*. I lived a lie for an entire year, and that bitch manipulated me every step of the way." I sit back on my heels and stare at Venesa. "But of course it was you. It's *always* been you, hasn't it?"

I literally owe her my *life*.

"There are a lot of things you don't—"

Leaning forward, I cut her off with a kiss. "I don't care. I don't care about any of that." My thumb brushes along her jaw. "All I care about is that you're here now, with me. You're *mine*, and I am so fucking yours, Venesa Andersen. Tell me you know that."

She swallows heavily and leans into my palm, closing her eyes. Then she nods like it's painful for her to admit. "I know."

I wish I could stay here all day, blow off my responsibilities, and sink inside her while I prove just how true my words are, but I won't be able to relax until I make moves. The quicker I take care of things on my end, the faster I can help Venesa take care of hers.

And then there will be *nothing* standing in our way.

"I need to go meet up with Gio and figure out what the hell to do."

I kiss her again and drag her into my lap. Her thick thighs wrap around me, as she grinds down, just a quick movement back and forth. My hands shoot out and grip her hips, thrusting up into her. "Don't start something we don't have time to finish, piccola sirena."

She grins. "What's the matter, Lover Boy, can't take a little tease?"

I smack her ass, and she bites her lip and moans, and *fuck*, she's doing this on purpose.

"Be good. Let me take care of this so I can come back and take care of you."

She sighs and stops her hips, ending the torture.

"I'm gonna have Scotty come by and pick you up in a little bit, okay? Don't go around the city without him. I should have kept Jessica in my sights just to make sure she doesn't run to tell Pops that you're here."

She scoffs.

I brush the back of my hand against her cheek and shake my head. "It's not a leash. I'm not trying to control you. I just want to keep you safe."

"Okay. But I have Bas too, don't forget."

"Yeah, well, I don't know enough about Bas to trust him with your life." I pat her ass, then move her off me and head to take a shower.

An hour later, I'm in the passenger side of Gio's car, and we're sitting in the parking lot of a secret spot just on the outskirts of Brooklyn. Turns out, while I was busy trying to figure out what to do, Gio had reached out to the De Lucas, who agreed to meet with us.

I glance over at Gio, bouncing my leg. "You think this is a trick?"

Gio shrugs, puffing on a cigarette with one hand and resting his other on the steering wheel. "Could be."

"They could be too afraid of Pops to take the chance."

He side-eyes me. "But you're gonna take the risk anyway."

"I'm gonna take the risk anyway," I confirm.

He puffs on his smoke again before flicking it through the open window, then reaches over to squeeze my shoulder. "You're my guy, you know that, right? To the ends of the fucking world, I'd ride for you. So when we walk into that warehouse in a few minutes, and we meet with these guys? I'm with you. And they'll be with you too. You should run this shit, not your pops. Everybody knows it; they're all just afraid of what will happen if they say it out loud."

"I never *wanted* to run this shit."

Gio nods. "Yeah, well…maybe that's the reason you should."

I let his words settle over me like a blanket of calm, and then I nod, staring at the warehouse in front of us before glancing to Gio. "You ready?"

He grins like a schoolboy. "Always."

I'm not sure what to expect when we walk into the warehouse. Even though Gio called the meeting with the De Luca family, it could easily be an ambush, and I'd be lying if I said I didn't feel the nerves scattering through my body like fire ants, stinging every spot they touch. But the important thing is I don't let it show on my face.

The warehouse itself doesn't have much in it, its soaring metal roof creating an echo chamber that makes our voices ricochet off the walls, and when we walk in, there are two men standing in the center, with perfectly pressed suits and slicked-back hair, their dark brown eyes already on me.

Matteo De Luca and his consigliere Leo.

I walk forward, gritting my teeth and reaching out a hand. "Matteo, thanks for coming."

We shake, and something curious gleams across his

irises, his head tilting to the side. "The great Enzo Marino calls for a meeting? How could I say no?"

I smile. "I'll get to the point, then. Things have recently come to light that changed my perspective on a few things."

Matteo tilts his head. "This is my problem because...?"

"Because my father forced you out of the decisions, out of power, and I thought you might be interested in getting some of it back."

Leo laughs and spits on the ground at my feet. "You mocking us? Fuck you."

Gio steps forward and opens his mouth, but I cut him off before he can say anything with a hand on his shoulder and a shake of my head. "It's all right, Gio. They have no reason to trust me." I look back to Matteo. "But I have a feeling it was *you* who sent that little spy to South Carolina to follow me. Wasn't it?"

Matteo's chin lifts but he doesn't reply.

"How's he doing by the way?" I chuckle, my thumb brushing against my scruff. "Listen, Matteo, I don't have time for games. I'm offering you something here, a way to bring back the round table, but you're gonna need to work with me. Don't forget who actually has the power in these parts right now. This is a gift I'm willing to give you."

"We were protecting our interests," Matteo replies finally. "If you Marinos can use guys from Jersey to do work you don't want coming back to nobody, then so can we. It's still *our* town."

My brows lift. "You talking about Frankie?"

He nods and continues. "We sent someone to follow you because nobody around here trusts a Marino, especially not your crazy-as-fuck father. Once that little rat Frankie squealed about working with Carlos and…others to try and take you out, I thought maybe you oughta know." He shrugs. "But I had to make sure you weren't part of the fucked-up system your family's created, that Frankie wasn't spouting bullshit as some type of game or trap. Sean was sent to watch you and report back."

"Well…sorry he never got the chance to say his goodbyes."

I watch his reaction, and when he gives a short chin jerk in confirmation, I know at least now that Sean really did end up dead after Venesa had her way with him.

"I just recently found out about Frankie and my pops," I confirm. "You could say it's changed my outlook on a lot of things. Redefined what loyalty is."

Matteo's eyes flash. "Your father wouldn't know loyalty if it smacked him in the face."

"Yeah," I agree, although admitting it is like a knife in my solar plexus. Blowing out a breath and cracking my neck, I meet his gaze. "Well, my father and I differ in a lot of ways. I don't want unlimited power, have no use for it. I find that working *with* others is a lot better in the long run… So I'd like to bring back the commission."

Matteo narrows his eyes. "And you want our help?"

"I don't need your help to do what needs to be done. I just want to know you've got my back with the other families when the time comes, the same way I'll have yours."

There are a few tense, silent moments when all of us are standing in the in-between, waiting for a decision to be made that will outline our futures. And then Matteo smirks, puts out his hand and nods.

"You have my word. You take out the trash, and we'll support your seat at the head of the table."

CHAPTER 45

Venesa

SCOTTY BROUGHT ME TO ENZO'S PENTHOUSE, which…I'm not thrilled about, since I thought I made myself clear on where I stood on staying here when Aria's tainted every piece of furniture.

Still, objectively, I can admire how badass the place itself is.

It's immaculate, really. Again, very high up in the sky with a lot of windows, but maybe he just likes to torture himself.

Clearly, we've figured out a way to get him to conquer those fears, and as soon as this apartment doesn't feel like Aria's space anymore, I'll let him fuck me up against these windows too.

Scotty didn't stay, just brought me here and then said he had errands to run, taking Bastien with him and letting me know they'd be back later to keep me company.

I'm thankful for the alone time, honestly. Gives me a chance to walk around and get a sense of Enzo. It quickly becomes obvious that although he was engaged to Aria, she didn't live here because it screams *sophisticated single man*.

The lines are very straight and narrow, with lots of monochromatic schemes. Black couches and white tables.

Expensive artwork on the walls and expressionist sculptures.

There's no personal touch. No pictures of family or friends.

Not that I had any either. I just always assumed *he* would.

I studiously avoid the bedroom, not ready to face it, and I make my way back to the living room and sit on the couch. I take out my phone and send another text to Fisher.

Me: Are you okay? I'm getting worried. Call me!! I have so much to tell you! Miss you, Gup.

Surprisingly, three dots pop up before I can put my phone down.

Fisher: Hey, I'm good. Just missing you. Wanna chat?
Me: Call me!

He sends a video request, and I answer immediately.

"God, I was thinking you'd been abducted," I say.

He laughs and leans back in the driver's seat of his car.

"What are you up to?" I ask.

"Just trying to take a few minutes. Things have been wild since you've been gone."

My brows draw in. "How so?"

He shrugs. "Just running the Lair, which your uncle is still letting me do, if you can believe it. It's like he's trying to replace you with me." He runs a hand down his face. "I don't know how you did it."

I'm not surprised. He wouldn't get rid of the Lair because of the money it brings in, and Fisher's the only one who knows that place like the back of his hand. Uncle T might hate me now, but he's not someone to miss taking advantage of simple situations if they present themselves.

"But I don't want to talk about me," Fisher goes on. "Where are you? What's up? I miss you, Short Stack."

"I miss you too. I'm in New York…with Enzo."

"Yeah…I heard about you and him."

I'm speechless. He heard, and he didn't immediately call and yell at me for not telling him myself?

"Is that why you've been avoiding me?" I ask, trying to make sense of things.

He clears his throat. "You mean, does it hurt to know my best friend is having this whole-ass *Romeo and Juliet* affair and didn't even bother to tell me? I had to find out from your cousin, who, by the way, is not handling it well."

"Aria's still there?"

"Yep."

I wasn't sure if she'd come back to New York or bide her

time. It's good if she stays, since it makes it easier to kill her and my uncle at the same time. Two birds, one stone, and all that.

"I'm sorry I didn't tell you. I just…this was something I wanted to keep close to my chest, you know? It felt too new or something."

His mouth twitches. "I'll forgive you if you tell me one thing."

"Anything," I reply.

"Does he have a big dick?"

A grin spreads across my face. "Almost *too* big."

He scoffs. "No such thing."

"There is!" I argue, laughing. "Anything over nine inches is pushing it, and sometimes that's too much. It will shove into your cervix, and it's *painful.*"

"Ugh, whatever. So, what, you and him are together now, or…?"

"I don't know what we are. He makes me feel…I think I—" My heart skips because of what I almost just said out loud. "Look, I can't say much, but just hang on, okay?"

His brow arches. "What's that mean?"

I chew on my lip, trying to figure out what I can tell him over the phone. "It means things are about to change… things *are* changing, and when they do, I won't just forget about you."

"Changing where, exactly? Here? Or in New York?"

"Both," I admit. "You just have to trust me. Can you do that?"

He runs a hand over his mouth and sighs. "I worry about you, Short Stack. But yeah… you know I've always got your back."

"Good." Relief flows through me. "And hey, stay away from my cousin, okay? There's no good that comes from it."

"Yeah, yeah." He waves me off, and then his eyes flick beyond the camera, and he frowns. "Hey, I've gotta go. I'll talk to you later, Short Stack. Love you."

Click.

I stare at my phone for a few seconds, because what the hell? He hung up on me.

Tossing the cell on the table, I lean back and close my eyes, calming my mind and trying to center myself. I haven't been able to meditate properly in weeks, ever since Enzo came into my life, and I feel like I'm losing my grasp on the delicate balance of my spirituality and reality.

Even now, I can't get it together, the conversation with Fisher sending prickles of unease sprinkling along my skin like microneedles.

The elevator that opens directly into the foyer of the penthouse dings, the doors sliding wide.

I shoot up straight, everything in me going immediately on guard because I didn't think anyone else could get in here without the elevator key to unlock this floor.

Again, I'm alone and without a weapon. Bastien would murder me himself if he knew.

A beautiful woman with curved eyes and golden skin walks inside, her outfit screaming class, and her face warm and welcoming. She smiles, a giant three-ring binder tucked into her side. "You must be Venesa."

I raise a brow at her. "Depends on who you are, I suppose."

Again, the elevator dings behind her and opens, men pouring out of the small space and walking into the room, filtering through the penthouse.

"What the hell is going on?"

"I'm Vivian, Mr. Marino's interior designer." She walks in farther, places her binder down on the coffee table, and claps her hands once. "Gentlemen, we need every piece of furniture taken out, immediately. Thank you!" she says in a singsong.

I blink at her.

Her smile drops. "Did he not tell you to expect me?"

"He did not, I'm afraid."

"Well, maybe he wanted it to be a surprise. It's not every day you get to go on a shopping spree and furnish a ten-thousand-square-foot penthouse."

I squint at her, still unsure, and then I pick up my phone and dial his number.

"Piccola sirena."

"I think you're being robbed."

I'm being serious, but all he does is laugh. "I sent her. Pick out whatever you like, make the place your own. Erase your cousin and everything she's ever touched."

I lift my brows, shocked he's willing to get rid of what must be an exorbitantly expensive amount of furniture just to make sure I'm comfortable.

But you won't hear me complaining.

After a lifetime of not being anyone's first choice, it's nice to be spoiled like this, and with the way he continues to *keep* spoiling me, it's something I could get used to. Quickly.

Honestly, I deserve it. I'm done with not putting myself first. And I know this thing with Enzo won't last forever, but I'm sure as hell going to enjoy it while it *does* last. Besides, I've never really lived in the lap of luxury, even though I've been a prisoner, forced to watch it from the inside.

"You're sure?" I ask.

"Yes, baby. I'm sure. I gotta go, but I'll be home tonight, and we'll break in the new stuff."

"You're getting furniture I choose here today? How is that possible?"

He chuckles over the line. "How many times do I have to tell you I own this city before you believe me?"

I don't know why that sentence turns me on, but it does. "That's…incredibly attractive to me."

"Oh?" His voice lowers. "What are you wearing?"

"Do you want the truth or want me to lie?"

He sighs. "The truth. I don't have time to handle you the way I want right now."

Emotion overwhelms me as I watch the movers take out furniture piece by piece. "Thank you for this. It's…it means a lot. I'm not sure how to thank you properly."

"You're welcome, baby. You can thank me by spending as much as you can."

I smile, and three words almost trip off the end of my tongue, but I bite them back at the last second.

When I hang up, Vivian is back in my face with a beaming grin and that thick binder. "Ready to spend his money?"

Enzo wasn't lying when he said the furniture would be here today, because as soon as I pick items, Vivian is on her phone, and then they're here within hours, showing up like magic.

By the end of the day, right after sunset, she's gone, and the apartment is filled with new things. Nice things. And most importantly, things *I* picked and that I know Aria never would.

Scotty and Bastien are back, having gone to the grocery store and bought enough food to feed an army, and we're all in the open kitchen right off the living room.

Scotty's cooking dinner—his homemade meatballs—and Bastien is sitting at the island next to me.

It's comfortable, and for the first time in forever, it feels like I have a place. A family. Like I'm *home*. It doesn't have to do with blood—not really—and maybe that's where I've always gotten it wrong. I've been searching for things in the wrong places. But there's a part of me just waiting for the other shoe to drop, and that makes it impossible to grasp the comfort fully.

It's rare that good things last, and people are great at being their own downfalls, myself included.

Scotty's droning on about some new people who moved

in a few floors down, but I'm not paying close enough attention to care about what he's saying.

"Let me ask you something, kid." Bas finally cuts him off. "How the hell do you know so much random shit?"

"I pay attention, Bastien. Something you should try every once in a while, you know? It's good to listen to your surroundings. Women love a listener."

"You're an idiot."

Scotty stops forming his meatballs and turns to Bastien with a frown. "You know I don't like it when you call me that. We've talked about this a hundred times already."

"Yeah, Bas. Be nice to Scotty." I reach over and smack him on the arm.

He gives me a wide-eyed look and then sits back in his chair, tapping his fingers on the countertop.

"What did you two all day anyway?" I ask.

Scotty shrugs. "Just burned daylight."

"*Burning daylight?*" I ask, because what the hell does that mean.

"You know...shooting the shit. Wasting the day away until night falls and the real fun can begin." He waggles his brows and then asks, "So what's up? You all moved in now, or what?"

"Like I'd tell you, the world's biggest gossip," I joke. But I don't feel the amusement.

What am I going to do, move to New York and become a mob wife?

He pats the meatball he's forming and grins. "That hurts,

V. Honest. You're killing me. I gotta deal with this knucklehead all day"—he gestures to Bastien—"and now I deal with you too? How's a guy supposed to feel the love with all this animosity?"

"I'm not focusing on things I can't control, Scotty. I'm only focusing on the right here and now."

He purses his lips and bobs his head. "E know you feel that way?"

I studiously avoid Bastien's gaze. "You let me worry about Enzo."

Bastien snorts.

I glare. "Cut it out. Focus on your make-believe stories, not on me."

He rolls his eyes and throws his hands up in a surrendering gesture.

Faintly, I hear an elevator ding, and Scotty looks into the hallway, then jerks his chin at me. "Better go see who it is. You're the queen of the castle, babe."

"What if it's somebody here to kill us?" I'm only half joking. I don't really like that an elevator opens directly into the penthouse, despite it only being accessible by a key.

Scotty laughs. "Then I guess you'll die and give us time to either escape or be prepared."

"That's not funny," Bastien says.

"Babe, it's a penthouse apartment for one of the most powerful men in New York. You think they let just anyone waltz up here?"

Before I can stand, Enzo saunters into the room and

heads straight to me, then scoops me up and takes me straight to the bedroom, not even sparing anyone else a glance.

I let him, because honestly, when he carries me like this or throws me over his shoulder, it's hot as hell. Even if I wanted to complain, I don't think my vagina would let me.

When we get to the bedroom, he kicks open the door and closes it behind him before throwing me on the new bed.

I toss a hand out. "Wait! Tell me you like the furniture."

He ignores me and strips off his suit jacket, then his vest, and then his shirt underneath. And I watch him because I'm never one to turn down a free show, and I've been dying to really soak him in topless—to get a better look at his ink—since the moment I saw him at my uncle's estate. He takes his pants off next, leaving him in black boxers, and then he's on me, pushing me back on the bed and kissing down my neck, his hand already heading toward my breasts.

"I'm serious," I tell him. "I want your approval. I'll just be thinking about it the whole time if you don't, and then I won't be able to come."

Sighing, he sits back, scanning the room. "It's nice."

I quirk a brow. "Nice? That's all I get?"

He grins lasciviously at me. "I'm more interested in *this* view." He brushes his hand along my front and dips beneath my jeans, but they're tight, and he can't get very far.

He frowns. "I like you in dresses. I need easy access."

I reach down and undo my button, and he pulls my pants off slowly, leaning over and giving small bites and kisses to my pussy.

"I love that you don't wear underwear."

He's right, I rarely do. It's constricting, and I hate the way it feels. My girl needs to breathe.

"I'll never wear them again," I moan, my eyes going half-lidded as he gets me naked from the waist down and then tongues my clit.

He gives me a few more licks before he crawls up my frame, pressing his mouth to mine.

I can taste myself on him, tangy and a little salty, but it's incredibly erotic. I swirl my tongue around his and drag it into my mouth so I can suck myself off him, which I've realized quickly is one of my favorite things to do. It turns me on, bad.

He groans, gripping my hips, and then he flips us over until he's on his back and I'm on top of him.

"Ride my face," he demands, digging his fingers into my thighs and pushing me forward.

And well, who am I to argue?

So I let him move me until my pussy is hovering above his mouth, his hot breath cascading over my center.

He grips my ass in his hands and then smacks one side hard enough to sting.

A sharp jab of arousal slices me in half before settling between my legs.

"Sit on my face, baby. Suffocate me."

And then he uses his hold on my cheeks to force me down.

I suck in a sharp breath because his tongue is going to *work*, and it feels incredible. I move my hips back and forth, grinding against his mouth, my eyes locked on where he's licking me, and I know I won't last long like this. He's easily the most skilled man who has ever eaten my pussy, and I'm glad he seems to enjoy the job.

My hands shoot out and grip the headboard so I can ride his tongue better, and his fingers come up and slip through the crack of my ass, then go lower. Teasing. *Testing.*

It's enough to make me shatter.

I come so hard, stars dot my vision, and he groans when I flood his mouth, keeping me locked against him while he laps me up like I'm fine wine.

I've never felt more attractive to someone than I do at this moment. And it's…powerful. I move off him after my orgasm ends and try to catch my breath.

"That was amazing," I sigh, my head lolling to the side. "You really like eating pussy, don't you? Wear me out with it, honestly."

After rolling over, I tuck myself into his side, my chest heaving as my lungs try to catch up with my heart. My fingers trace the designs of his ink, ghosting across the letters of his last name tattooed on his neck.

"Do all your tattoos mean something?"

He hums, the vibration deep as it reverberates through his chest and into my body from where I'm lying against him. "Not really. I just like the feel. It's addicting, getting them."

He lifts his arm and turns it, nodding toward two different sets of numbers. "These do though."

I reach out and touch where he's referencing. "What are they?"

"Dates. One for my Ma's death, and one for my brother's."

His words slam into me like a wrecking ball, and I bite my cheek so I don't inhale an audible gasp. My stomach rolls and heaves anyway, though. "That's nice," I force out.

He quirks a brow at me. "I don't want to talk about depressing shit."

I grin at him then, relief washing away the bad feeling that was brewing in my center. "We can talk about how exhausted I am from riding your face instead."

He chuckles and then rolls on top of me. "It's adorable that you think we're done."

And then he stands, grabs my hand, and moves me in front of the new floor-length mirror I set up in the corner of his room.

CHAPTER 46

Enzo

COMING HOME TO VENESA IS AN *EXPERIENCE*.

She may not realize it yet, judging by how surprised she was when I had her refurbish the entire apartment, but she's it for me. And I don't care what anyone else has to say about it.

Maybe it's the honeymoon phase, and maybe it will wear off in the future, but whenever I look at her, whenever I *think* about her, I feel the same way I did when I was a kid, wishing I had true love.

I'm scared to tell her that, though. She's wary of men, of relationships, and…I don't want her to run away. I want to know that she's in this too.

And Gio, the smart motherfucker that he is, suggested we sit down and *talk*.

So that's my plan.

After I fuck her again, obviously. I'm riding high from my meeting with De Luca.

Turns out, when someone forcibly takes power the way my pops did, they make more enemies than friends. And those enemies have been biding their time, waiting for the right moment.

I'll kill my father, take over his seat, and reinstate the commission, letting the don of each family have a place at the table.

Grabbing Venesa's hand, I pull her up from the bed and move her to the mirror, because I want her to see us together, want her to watch what she looks like to me, and I want to see it on her face as she realizes how fucking perfect we are.

And maybe she already knows, but it doesn't matter if she does because I'll tell her every day anyway.

I slide my hands down her arms as I stand behind her, staring at our reflection.

She already looks freshly fucked, her makeup smeared, her red lipstick rubbed off almost entirely and smudged around her lips.

"Hands on the mirror, baby."

Venesa does what I ask without complaint, and it sends a rush through me to have such a powerful woman surrender so completely. To *trust* me the way she does.

It's fucking sexy.

I grip the base of my cock and line up behind her, my head prodding at her tight wet hole. My free hand glides along her back, glistening with a sheen of sweat, most likely from how hard she just came all over my face. I lick my lips to get another taste.

My palm keeps moving until I reach her shoulder, where I give a slight squeeze before continuing until I wrap around the front of her neck, cupping her throat, keeping pressure off her windpipe.

I watch her reaction in the mirror.

Her eyes flare, and she bites the corner of her bottom lip.

She likes it.

It's torture when I push into her slowly, holding back even though she's wrapping me up so tightly.

"Do you see how good you look, under my hands, taking my cock?" I ask her. Our eyes lock on each other in the reflection.

"Yes," she murmurs, pushing herself onto me, trying to take more.

Tsk-tsking at her, I pull back out and tighten my grip on her throat. "Greedy girl, aren't you?"

"Enzo, fuck me."

I lean over her, my stomach flipping and cock jerking with the need to obey *her* command. "Don't tell me what to do."

And then I slam into her, doing what she wants anyway.

She lets out a guttural moan, her eyes rolling up in her head at the feel, and I squeeze her neck again, my palm resting on the necklace I bought her. It fills me with so much joy when I see her wearing it. Especially when it's the *only* thing she's wearing.

"Do you like this?"

"Mmm." She nods.

I pull out and slowly slide back in, and she's so wet, my dick glides in easily.

My heart spasms in my chest, and I thrust harshly again, slipping my cock in from root to tip, then rotating my hips once I'm all the way inside her. My fingers tighten more on her neck, slowing her breathing down, but I'm watching carefully to make sure she isn't in pain.

Her mouth parts and her eyes widen, but she never drops my gaze. And her cunt is *drenching* me.

I'm fucking up into her now at a steady pace, her tits jiggling with the motion, hanging down from how she's bent over while I take her from behind.

My free hand reaches up and holds her breast because I can't resist when they're right there, so juicy and full and begging me to hold them.

I watch her face turn red and feel her pussy quivering around me. "That's my girl."

Releasing her breast, I move down and pull my cock almost entirely out of her, my fingers dipping into the wet, sloppy mess and dragging it up until I circle the sweet round bud of her asshole, making it well lubricated.

She tries to suck in air, but it's restricted, and the sight of her at my mercy, so trusting, has me almost losing it before she does.

Fuck.

My eyes meet hers in the mirror, and I thrust my hips forward, my cock slipping back into her tight channel inch by inch. At the same time, my finger brushes against her other entrance, pushing through the resistance and sliding in and out slowly. Softly, because I know it takes preparation and a slow stretch to really feel good.

Her pouty mouth parts, and her eyes roll up in her head, her body growing lax beneath my ministrations. My hand tightens on her neck, anchoring myself to her while I fill both her holes with me, and her palms smack against the mirror, leaving smudged handprints on the glass.

Her pussy contracts around my length, squeezing and releasing, and the sight of her this way, so open and vulnerable, has heat spreading through my lower abdomen and wrapping around the base of my spine like wildfire.

I peer down at where I disappear inside her, my cock jumping at the sight. "Look at you, greedy girl, sucking me in like you can't get enough."

"Enzo," she groans. Sweat beads at her temples, making her hair stick to the sides of her face, and her cheeks are flushed the perfect rosy pink.

She's close.

"That's it, baby. Give it to me. I'm so proud of you," I whisper, because I know praise gets her off.

She explodes around me, and I'm right there with her, sinking all the way inside and unloading deep in her pussy, imagining my cum filling her up and tying her to me in another way, a way that means she could never leave, making my orgasm last for what feels like ages.

Out of breath, I collapse onto her back and release her

throat, pressing lazy kisses to her spine, my face sticking to her skin from the perspiration.

I wonder if she realizes she holds all the power here, that I would crawl on my knees to be wherever she is.

I'm still wondering the same thing an hour later when I'm standing behind Venesa and pulling her into me while she heats two plates of food Scotty covered and left in the oven for us with a note.

Now Scotty and Bastien are both gone, obviously leaving when they realized I was making Venesa scream.

The elevator dings, and my brows furrow as I look over toward the entryway.

Who the fuck now?

Venesa stiffens slightly and looks back at me. "You really just let anyone walk into your apartment like this? Honestly, Enzo, it's ridiculous."

"Not usually, no," I reply.

The doormen know I'm not supposed to have any more visitors. I don't know who the fuck that could be.

I debate going for my gun, but it's in the other room, and even though Venesa can take care of herself, I don't want to leave her alone. Still, I turn around and keep her behind me when I hear footsteps walking down the hall and into the living area.

My body tenses further when Pops walks into the space, then turns until he sees us in the kitchen.

"Well, isn't this cozy?"

Fear grips me. *Damn it.* I didn't want him to know about her.

Ever.

And his being here right now? It makes me nervous because I can count on one hand the number of times Pops has stepped foot in my apartment, and it's never been for a friendly visit, and the fact it's happening directly after a meeting with Matteo De Luca has me on edge.

He smiles at me, and I fake one back, grabbing Venesa's hand and bringing her to my side.

I'm incredibly uncomfortable, but I don't want him to suspect anything's up. To him? We should be copacetic.

"Well, aren't you going to introduce us?" He nods toward Venesa and moves into the kitchen until he's standing directly across from us.

I smile and clear my throat, hoping the panic doesn't show on my face. "What are you doing here?" I ask.

He gives a smarmy look. "Am I not allowed to visit my son?"

"You are," I say slowly. "You just usually don't. But it's a nice surprise." Swallowing, I introduce them. "This is Venesa."

I expect her to cower, the same way I think anyone else would. Carlos Marino has a reputation, and meeting him has to be especially hard for Venesa because she knows he favored her cousin. I wouldn't blame her for being nervous.

"Ah," he says. "The woman who ruined my son's marriage."

She forces a grin, those dimples popping out, and releases my hand to walk forward and shake his. "It's a pleasure, Mr. Marino. I've heard a lot about you."

If I wasn't sure before this moment that she was my queen, then this would confirm it.

She's poise and grace in the face of adversity. Polished on the outside. And it gives me a thrill to know she's capable of being so bad at the flip of a switch.

He takes her hand and brings it to his lips.

My hands clench to temper the urge to rip her away from him.

"I'm sorry I can't say the same," he replies, clucking his tongue. "Not from my son anyway."

What's that supposed to mean? My spine stiffens. He's implying he heard about her from someone, and I flip through who even knew about her to say something.

A rat.

"I *know* you, though," he continues. "I'm very surprised to see you in my son's kitchen. You're a much more forgiving man than me, Enzo."

Venesa takes a step back from him, ripping her hand from his grip.

My brows furrow in confusion, and I can't help the laugh that escapes me. "Why's that?"

I move next to her, giving her a funny look.

"Nervous?" Pops smiles at her.

Her chin stiffens.

"Oh, I see." He tsk-tsks. "You didn't tell him, did you? You stupid little girl."

"Don't talk to her like that," I snap. "What the *fuck*?"

He chuckles and shakes his head. "You've always been

so naive. So blind to what's right in front of you, *figlio mio*."

"This isn't the time, Pops. You're in *my* house. You'll respect the people in it, including me *and* her."

"I think this is the perfect time," he parries, his voice like a thunderclap that strikes across the room. "Don't you, *Venesa*?"

He elongates her name, almost making it sound like a song.

Again, I look at her, expecting for her to look just as confused as I am.

But she doesn't. She looks scared.

And that terrifies me.

"Somebody better tell me what the fuck is going on right now."

Pops's eyes twinkle with mirth, and he keeps staring at Venesa. "I've waited a long time to look into the eyes of the woman who tore this family apart."

I laugh, thinking it's a joke, but the way Venesa stiffens sends red flags waving and sirens blaring in my psyche.

"What the fuck are you talking about?" I demand.

Now Pops looks at me. "I'm talking about the fact the woman you're fucking is the one who killed your brother."

CHAPTER 47

Venesa

I'M FROZEN IN PLACE.

Enzo laughs again, disbelieving. But then he looks at me, the humor slowly dropping from his face until all that's left is dawning realization.

I don't have the will to keep watching because I know what will come next.

Betrayal.

Hatred.

My heart heaves and quivers, fissures cracking down every part like spiderwebs that bleed.

His father grins even wider, a sinister type of smile, when he sees what's happening. "You and your uncle called him 'Joey,' though. Right? Very American, but that's how he did business, thought it made him more *appealing*."

I shake my head, but I'm not sure what for. He's not lying. And as much as I want to hate him for bringing it to light, I can't, because I've had plenty of opportunities, and I've been too weak. Too lost in the moment.

Too afraid to lose something I've been aching for my entire life.

Enzo looks from me to his father and then back again, and now he's shaking *his* head, stepping away from both of us, his perfect hands tugging on the roots of his inky hair.

Bastien warned me this would happen, and deep down I knew it would too, but as much as I wanted to, I just couldn't make the words come out, because I didn't want to see him looking at me the way he is right now.

"Well." His father claps his hands together once, reaching out to pick up the cane he stashed against the island. "What a pleasure it was to be the one to break the news. If your uncle and I weren't on good terms when it happened, you'd be at the bottom of the Hudson, your body nothing more than fish food. But we made a deal instead. We work together and I let you live."

His words hit their mark, but I don't take my eyes off Enzo.

"My uncle was hired by someone," I say, suspicion winding its way through my gut. "It was an order, not an attack by him."

"Like that makes a difference," Carlos hisses.

He takes a step toward me, and when Enzo doesn't move to stop him, those fissures in my heart gape wider.

"You're a plague on this city, and your uncle is a dumb American idiot who was useful for a time but now ceases to matter," he continues and then looks to Enzo. "You told me you had my back, *figlio mio*. That you were the *only* one I could trust. So prove it."

Enzo's jaw stiffens.

"Kill her. Or I'll come back and do the job myself."

My stomach bottoms out, but I don't try to move away.

I expect Carlos to stay, to make sure the job is done, but he surprises me, spinning on his heel and leaving as quickly as he came.

The air is so tense and silent, I almost wish he had stayed.

"Enzo," I whisper brokenly, taking a step forward, reaching out to touch him.

"Don't," he snaps, jerking his arm out of my hold before I can get a good grasp.

Swallowing over the lump in my throat, I lick my lips and try again. "I never meant to hurt you. I didn't…I didn't know you back then."

"What the fuck, Venesa? What the *fuck*?" His voice cracks, and hearing that vulnerability, that slight break in his stature, well…it feels like it's breaking *me*. I stand still and let the hurt come because I know I deserve it.

A weird pressure builds behind my nose and eyes, and I force it back down.

He finally looks up at me, his eyes burning with anger and hurt. "Tell me it's not true."

I shake my head, my mouth opening and closing because it's still hard to find the words.

"Say it," he hisses, taking a step closer. "You had all the

time in the world until now, and you were silent. You fucking owe me this. *Say it.*"

Everything inside me wants to deny it, to take a metaphorical piece of duct tape and slap it over my mouth so the words won't come out. He's right. I *do* owe it to him, even if it ends up being at my own expense.

"It's true," I admit.

I should have told him when I had the chance.

"I swear to God, Enzo, if I knew I was gonna fall for you…if I knew that I'd fall in—"

He storms forward, pressing his hand to my mouth and backing me against the wall. It's gentle, the way he does it, and the fact he still isn't hurting me is almost more painful than if he had.

"Don't you *dare* say those words to me," he snarls.

The first real crack in my chest happens now. It aches like I'm bleeding out, a pulsing, throbbing monster that's roaring inside my body and demolishing everything in its path, and it's so overwhelming, I wonder if it's possible to actually die of a broken heart. If the pain will be too much and I'll just collapse and wither into nothing.

I deserve it, if so.

"I can't even stand to touch you." He drops his hand from my mouth, but he doesn't back away.

"I had never met him before," I force out. "But Joey—"

"Giuseppe," he corrects.

"Giuseppe…he worked with my uncle, like he told you. They were planning to expand. And then I guess something went wrong? I don't know the details. Uncle T just told me what to do, and I did it. The same way I always did."

He huffs out a broken laugh. "And that makes it okay?"

I throw my hands up, desperation filling my bones and leaking out through my pores because I can tell I'm losing him. The way I knew I would.

These past weeks of finally feeling like I mattered, like I was someone's choice and I…well, I guess I never chose him. Not really anyway. Not enough.

"What did you want me to say? What's the appropriate way to tell someone you care about that you murdered their brother?"

That pressure's back now, building in my throat and behind my eyes, and then suddenly, a sob breaks from my mouth, and it catches me so off guard, my hands fly up to cover the noise.

Enzo gets in my face, his nose almost brushing mine.

It's the first time I don't feel the attraction between us, because it's stifled—muted—transformed into this ugly, vile thing that digs its teeth into breaking organs and shatters them until they're jagged and bleeding.

"How did you do it?" he asks.

I shake my head. "It doesn't matter."

His hand flies into the wall next to me, punching it so hard, a crack forms. My heart jumps into my throat, but I don't flinch, because I know that no matter how angry he gets, he wouldn't hurt me. Not like this. Not with punches and kicks.

He might kill me for what I've done, but I don't fear it.

"Your brother liked his escorts," I admit.

Enzo's face pales even further than normal, and he stumbles back a step. "Did you sleep with my brother?"

"What?" My brows furrow, a dawning horror sweeping over me. "God, no. I just posed as one to get into his room. I drugged his drink and did what the contract said to do."

This gives him pause. "You were told *how* to kill him?"

I shrug, forcing the words out but unable to meet his eyes because there's this giant ball of tension forming in my chest, and if I look at him right now, it feels like it will explode. "Yeah, sometimes Uncle T has stipulations on how it goes down. Does that not happen in your world?"

I risk a peek at his face, and he swallows, lifting his chin. "It does."

My brows draw in, my mind piecing together a puzzle. "You don't think your father…"

He shakes his head, looking at me with disgust, and that look, *that's* what I was trying to avoid. Enzo's the first person to stare at me like I'm the only thing he can see, like I'm the most important person in the universe and he'd choose me a thousand times over.

Now he just looks cold, and his hatred pours over me like ice water.

But I'll wait to let it consume me until I'm alone because I've already done enough damage. The least I can do is not fall apart right in front of him.

"You should have told me." His voice cracks. "Why didn't you fucking tell me?"

"If I had told you back in South Carolina, I would have been betraying my uncle. My *family*."

"Well, congratulations, Venesa." He grips my wrists, and his touch burns like an iron brand. "Now you can live with knowing you've betrayed *me*."

I try to move in closer to him, but he firmly holds me away.

"If I had known you back then..." I drop my gaze to the floor because suddenly it's too hard to speak.

"I should kill you," he says in a broken whisper, his grasp tightening until blood stops flowing to my fingers.

"So kill me." I force the words out. "Do it. I won't stop you."

I won't fight him off if that's what he chooses. If it's something that will bring him some closure—some peace.

The only problem is some wounds can't ever heal.

Betrayal by a person you trusted.

The death of someone you loved.

Whether or not Enzo wants to admit it to me, I know what we have was real, even if it was for a short time. And he has a soft heart, gentler than mine. One that torments itself. And a part of me just knows that as angry as he is, as much as he might hate me...if he kills me, he'll never forgive himself.

His eyes latch on to mine, and even though it hurts, even though it feels like pieces of my heart are being chipped away and falling into dust at his feet, I don't look away.

His hands tremble against my skin, and water lines his lower lids.

Nausea crawls up my throat.

He drops my wrists, backing up several steps. "You're not worth it."

Then he turns around and walks away.

I'm frozen in place, a strange feeling mounting from the base of my stomach, up into my chest, and surging through my pores. This…pressure.

The elevator dings, and he's leaving.

He's leaving.

Even though I have no right to stay.

Slowly, I slide to the floor, my back against the side of the island, and I stare blankly at the oven, where our dinners sit, half plated and growing cold. My hand absent-mindedly reaches up and grips my seashell necklace like it's a lifeline.

In a different life…

That pressure's back, churning and building, and then something wet escapes the corner of my left eye, trailing over my lashes, down my cheek, and dripping off my chin.

I watch as it forms a small dot on the fabric of my shirt.

And then another.

And another.

I press my fingers to my flushed skin, my heart pounding faster and faster until it ruptures, like a dam breaking, water rushing over a dry landscape and engulfing everything in its wrath.

"See ya later, Lover Boy." I hiccup softly.

And for the first time since I was a child, I'm crying.

It took me a while to get myself together and leave Enzo's house, but I knew it was what had to happen.

He won't want me there when he gets back, and despite everything—regardless of how my soul feels broken and bruised—I respect him enough to not stay and beg for forgiveness on something that's unforgivable. I always knew this would be the outcome.

And honestly, I'm not sorry I killed his brother. It was my job. It's what I've done a hundred other times, without question, and it happened long before Enzo and I even knew of each other. But I regret how it's hurting him, and I *definitely* regret with every single part of me that I was too much of a disaster to find the courage to tell him about it when I had the chance. I don't know that the outcome would have been any different, but at least he would have heard it from me, instead of feeling like I've been lying to him.

Technically, it was just an omission, but an omission is sometimes worse than a lie.

I'm back at the hotel room in the Marino, and I'm throwing my few belongings in my duffel bag, phone up to my ear as I try to call Fisher and tell him I'm coming back and need him to help me stay under the radar until I'm ready to do what I need to do.

Kill my uncle. Even if I have to do it with a broken heart.

It's a risk going back there to plan, but it's the best option I have.

Of course…it would help if Fisher would actually answer his phone.

It clicks over to his voicemail *again*, and I throw it down, tapping my foot and debating what to do.

I'll just go to Bastien's hotel room.

The only thing I know for sure is that I can't stay *here*. Even if I wanted to, this is Enzo's hotel, and I don't deserve it. Besides, he didn't kill me the way his father demanded, and if I stay, I'll only be putting his own safety in jeopardy.

I pick up my phone and shoot off a quick text to Bastien.

Me: Hey, he found out, and it didn't go well. You're right, I should have told him. Come by my room or I'll be by yours in 20.

My chest aches when I type out the words, and I reach up to grab the seashell around my neck for comfort, but just hit blank skin, then remember I took it off back at Enzo's and left it on his kitchen island. I don't deserve to have it because that necklace represented our romantic relationship but also our friendship, both of which I ground into dust carelessly when I withheld something so monumental even after I knew I had feelings for him.

There's a knock on the door right when I finish zipping up my duffel bag.

My mind is speeding in a thousand different directions,

and it's hard to think straight anyway with how badly my soul hurts, so maybe that's why there's a moment where I've convinced myself it's Enzo.

That maybe he's forgiven me even though I don't deserve it.

My chest cramps at the thought.

Ridiculous, Venesa. He wouldn't be here.

But Bastien would.

I don't even look in the peephole. I'm going on autopilot and assuming it's Bastien.

"I don't want to talk about it," I say when I open the door, turning before I see him.

Because I know what I'll find, and I don't want to deal with an "I told you so" look right now.

"Good. I don't want to hear it anyway."

My entire body freezes, and I spin around, coming face-to-face with that *bitch* of Enzo's assistant, Jessica.

"What the hell are you doing here?" I ask, confused.

She grins. "Just following the boss's orders."

My brows furrow. "Enzo sent you?" *Wow. Talk about hitting me when I'm down.*

She smiles, throws back her head, and cackles. "Enzo's not the man in charge, honey. Carlos is."

Then she pulls out what looks like a tranquilizer gun and pulls the trigger.

I look down, shocked, and feeling like the stupidest person on the planet, I see a tranq dart sticking out of my leg. I try to move forward, but my head is already woozy, and I stumble back instead, my hand flying to the small bookshelf against the wall and knocking against that damn globe. It falls to the ground and breaks, but my hearing must be fuzzy because the sound is muted and dull.

So is my vision.

I drop to the floor, my knees cracking against the marble, and then Jessica moves over me with a grin on her face. "Oh, I'm *so* going to enjoy this."

Then she shoots me with another dart, and I see nothing but black.

CHAPTER 48

Enzo

I HAVEN'T BEEN TO PEPPINO'S GRAVE SINCE his funeral three years ago, but right now, it feels fitting that this is where I head first after walking out and leaving Venesa in my kitchen.

I'm angry.

Frustrated.

Blindsided.

Like there's nothing I know anymore, twists and turns continually being thrown in my face and showing me that things I knew as fact—as *truth*, things I felt soul deep to the marrow of my bones and beyond—are all bullshit.

I searched for my brother's murderer for years. Always assumed it was one of the other families. I *killed* people for information.

And this whole time it was her.

The fact Peppino and I were never close, never saw eye

to eye, doesn't diminish the fact he was still *my* brother, and the woman I opened my life to, my heart to, my *home* to, is the person I've been searching for during these three years. How can I believe anything she says now?

Steps sound behind me, the freshly cut grass of the cemetery crunching underneath their feet.

I should turn around and see who it is, but I don't because I already know without looking that it's Gio. I called him in a panic, my words not flowing and my chest feeling like it was physically ripping apart into a thousand broken pieces. *He's the only one I can trust.*

He says nothing at first, just comes to stand at my side, his hands in his pockets and a look of consternation on his face as he stares down at Peppino's tombstone.

"You remember when we were kids and used to fuck around on the corner outside Max's shop?" he asks.

I don't reply beyond a quick jerk of the head because I don't think I physically can push words out right now. My chest aches so badly, it's taking everything in me to not reach up and try to rub away the pain.

"We were so stupid back then, yeah?" He chuckles. "Always making dumb mistakes. I don't know if I ever told you this, but one time, I was fucking around out there, on a brand-new bike I saved up all summer to get. You remember the one, with the—"

"Cherry-red frame and black accents. Yeah, I remember."

Gio loved that bike, had been talking about it for months

and doing odds and ends like mowing lawns and getting groceries for the ol' biddies around town.

"That's right. And one day, I was picking up groceries for that Mrs. Greenfield lady who lived three apartments down from you, and your brother stopped me and told me if I wanted to keep the groceries, I had to hand over the bike."

"No shit?"

"No shit," he confirms.

"What'd you do?"

He shrugs. "What was I *supposed* to do? I was a kid being paid to deliver the goods, and your brother was older. The son of Carlos Marino. I gave him the bike."

I shake my head. "Peppino was always a fucking prick."

Silence for a few minutes, and then Gio speaks again. "He *was* a fucking prick, and he never deserved your loyalty. He never loved you the way you loved him. The way you've honored him." Another pause, and then: "There's only been one person I've ever seen love you the way you deserve."

My mouth goes dry, but somehow I manage to unstick my tongue from the roof of it to speak. "She lied to me, Gio. She *killed* him."

"Yeah, I know." He rocks back slightly on his heels. "But she also *saved* you."

My stomach feels like an overturned ship in a storm. "I'm done feeling like I owe people for that."

He moves then and steps in front of me, gripping my shoulder with his hand and squeezing. "You know I've got your back in anything. You tell me we're gonna put a bullet in her head for what she did? I'm behind you a hundred percent, but I gotta tell you…I think it's a mistake. And I think you'll regret it for the rest of your life."

The thought of Venesa with a bullet anywhere near her makes bile collect at the back of my throat and my mouth go sour. I have to keep myself from lashing out at Gio for even suggesting it.

And maybe that makes me a pussy.

But I can't kill her, even if I wish I could. It sure as hell would be easier.

"Man." Gio whistles, looking at Peppino's grave. "A lot of blood's been spilled because of him and your father, you know?"

I nod. "Part of the life."

He rocks back on his heels. "It is…and it is for her too."

My jaw clenches. "So, what, I'm supposed to just forget about it?"

Gio shrugs. "That's up to you, E. But we both know if the shoe were on the other foot, if it had been your father who ordered you to kill *her* brother, you would have done the same damn thing. And back then? She didn't owe you her loyalty."

"She didn't tell me once she did."

He quirks a brow. "That's true. But what would you have done?"

I blow out a heavy breath, because fuck if I know. But I *do* know it would be the hardest thing to tell her, even if it was right.

"So are you hurt because she killed him or because she didn't tell you?" he continues.

I'm not sure. "Does it matter?"

Gio shrugs. "Only you can say if it matters. If you can forgive her."

Bricks settle in my chest like heavy weights. "Would you?"

"Those are two very different transgressions, so I don't know. But I know life's too short to hold grudges and hate in our hearts for the people we love. There's no—"

He stops talking suddenly, a choking sound coming from him instead.

I turn to look at him in confusion.

His eyes widen, his mouth opens, and his hand clutches at his chest, red seeping from between his fingers.

"Fuck, Gio." I rush forward, catching him as he falls. Ice fills my veins when a thick and sticky wetness covers my palms. I lay him down on the ground, wishing I could give him the attention he needs, but if he just got shot, that means I need to think quickly.

I stand, pulling out my gun from my holster and spinning around.

The grim reality of my situation settles in quickly when I see my father holding a weapon with a silencer attached.

His eyes look calm and collected, which means he's anything but.

Gio's trying to move, but I can't afford to lose focus, so I keep my stare on Pops, even though everything in me wants to turn around and make sure the only friend I've ever had doesn't bleed out in front of my piece-of-shit brother's grave.

"You followed me," I state. It's not a question; it's the only way he would know that I'm here.

My heartbeat pumps erratically, but on the outside, I maintain a calm composure, matching my father's stance. Even if Gio dies, I can't break.

My gun has never felt so heavy in my hand, but my soul feels light knowing that however this turns out, this is going to end once and for all.

Either I die, or my father does.

This wasn't what I had planned, but I'm nothing if I'm not adaptable.

He takes a step toward me, clucking his tongue. "*Figlio mio*, you never learn."

I grit my teeth and don't reply.

He looks beyond me to Peppino's gravestone, the one that's now covered in Gio's blood spatter, and then back to me. "Poetic—you'll end up dead right here next to your brother. It saddens me to have to take things this far, but alas, what else is there to do?"

"Have you considered not murdering everyone who has your back?"

Pops laughs. A deep, head-thrown-back belly laugh. "Has *my* back? I asked you to prove your worth, and you *failed*. Like usual, I had to send in someone else to clean up the mess you left behind."

My heart stalls, panic flooding my veins at the thought of something happening to Venesa.

"You really are the biggest kind of disappointment," he goes on. "Don't insult me, thinking you can spin those lies, telling me you have my back. You and your brother were a risk I couldn't afford."

My breathing stutters, because is he admitting what I *think* he's admitting?

Realization settles heavy into my bones. "You took out the hit on Peppino. Of fucking course you did, Jesus *Christ*."

"I *had* him taken care of," he snaps. "He was going to do it to me, so I beat him to the punch. You fools think I don't know you want my empire? You want what's mine?"

I shake my head. "I've never wanted what's yours *or* his. I was just fine being your loyal lapdog." I don't raise my gun, because I know if I do, then he'll get tipped off that I'm about to kill him, and I'd rather he stay on his soapbox. The thing about men like my father is they become so headstrong, so inflated by their own ego, it becomes almost impossible for them to take someone out without waxing poetic beforehand. And my pops has always been someone who loves to hear himself speak.

His overconfidence has made him deluded enough to think that he's unbreakable, impenetrable.

So even when he moves forward, backing me into a tree with his gun at my forehead…I let him. And when he wrenches the weapon from my hand with his free one, I don't resist. And maybe I'll die right here. Hell, it's been feeling like I'm on the edge of death all day anyway, so perhaps this is the way my story ends, but fuck going without a fight.

I just have to wait him out and find the right moment.

My eyes flicker behind Pops to where Gio's splayed out on the ground, not moving. I squint, trying to see if his chest is rising, but he's too far and my focus is too split.

"This ends here," Pops says, the barrel of his gun cool against my skin. "You've always been weak. But I never expected it to be a whore who took you down, the same way she took down your brother. I won't let you make *changes* around here. Be grateful you're my son, because it's the only reason I'll show you any mercy."

Suddenly, with those words, everything in my life snaps into focus, and the only thing I can think of—the only thing that matters—is Venesa. And the only person who deserves any mercy is *her*. The hurt of her omission is there, and it won't go away overnight, but the anger dissipates, clarity replacing every fractal of my thoughts, and I'm overcome with…sadness.

"Thinking about your little slut?" Pops asks.

The disrespect makes me want to lash out, but I still don't make my move. Let him think he has the upper hand.

He leans in close, something flaring in his eyes. "I'll be sure to test out what makes her so special before I kill her."

My insides are churning. I won't let him near her.

I react as fast as possible, rage blinding my vision, mixing with the need to protect Venesa. To get the chance to forgive her. To let her right her wrongs the same way I'd want her to let me try if the situation were reversed. I grip my father's wrist, twisting it quickly until it cracks, flipping the gun out of his grasp and into my hands until the barrel is pointed at *his* head. "You stupid motherfucker," I spit. "If you had taken one goddamn second to learn anything about me—your *son*—you would know that I know how to disarm someone."

Panic flashes in his eyes now. "If you kill me, you'll never find her."

I pause, for just a second, wondering if he's telling me the truth. But I'm not stupid enough to fall for his tricks, and even if he is being honest…I can't take the risk of keeping him alive.

Shaking my head, I lean in close, spitting out the words. "I'll *always* find her. But at least if you're dead, I'll be able to sleep at night while I do."

And then I pull the trigger, closing my eyes when warm blood sprays across my face.

There's immediate silence following his death, and I expect to feel relief. Instead, a deep longing fills me, an ache to hunt down Venesa as quickly as possible and tell her I love her, because a few seconds ago, I wasn't sure I'd ever get the chance.

It may take a while for me to forget about what she did, but I think I can forgive her. Her being dishonest doesn't wash away the fingerprints she's ingrained in my soul.

Because life's too short to not hold the ones you love close.

So I'm going to find her, and then I'm going to spend the rest of my life loving her out loud, just like she deserves.

CHAPTER 49

Venesa

I'VE NEVER HAD SUCH A SEVERE HEADACHE IN my entire life, and as I come to, blinking to clear the blur, I try to press my hand to my face to stem the pain, but my arms won't move.

Clank.

My brain feels slow, like I'm swimming through sludge, and I'm having trouble getting my bearings to figure out where exactly I am.

Closing my eyes, I feel like I'm spinning, so I reopen them because the last thing I need is to throw up right now.

I'm lying down on something hard and cold. Definitely metal. I try to move my arms again, and this time a sound registers. Like nails on a chalkboard.

Clank. Clank. Clank.

I know that noise.

The longer I'm awake, the more I remember what

happened and why I'm feeling so out of sorts, and I blink rapidly, trying to clear my vision.

That bitch Jessica shot me with a tranq gun. *God, Bas is going to murder me if I make it out of this alive.*

I don't bother moving again because I know it's no use, as surely as I start to suspect exactly where I am.

My legs twitch, and the noise happens again. Metal hitting metal.

Clank.

I have to remember to ask Bas to change the material on these.

I will my eyesight to clear, but it's still blurry, and *God*, my head.

Closing my eyes and breathing through the nausea, I focus on my other senses.

If I listen closely, I can hear the faint sound of a running motor, the same timbre and pitch of my pookies' saltwater aquarium.

My heart sinks.

I open my eyes again, willing them one more time to un-blur, and finally they do, at least a little, and my suspicions are confirmed.

I'm at the Lair. Chained to the table I've used so many times on others.

The irony is not lost on me.

My spirit guides have a sick sense of humor, doling out retribution this way.

Pulling at my restraints would be nothing more than a waste of energy, so I stay still instead. I know better than anyone there is no escape from here. Not unless someone frees you.

Who has me down here? Bastien? Uncle T?

Are they working with Carlos? They have to be.

Jessica said he was the real boss, and there's no reason I'd be back here unless Bastien brought me. Uncle T's only been here once or twice since he bought it, and he's never been the kind of guy to get his actual hands dirty; he just loves doling out that responsibility to everyone else.

My heart hurts thinking Bastien may have come out to New York to trick me into trusting him, but right now, it's the only option I can make sense of.

He knew I was leaving. I texted him.

I brought him along on almost every single outing with Enzo while we were in New York. He became friends with Scotty: the biggest gossip ever and definitely someone you'd want to sidle up to if you needed some information to slip.

Besides, when I really think about it, beyond my being the equivalent of his annoying little sister, Bastien has no reason to stay loyal to me.

Nobody does.

The nausea increases at the thought of yet another person I put my trust in betraying me, and I swear if I puke all over myself when I'm chained down and unable to get away from it, I will be mortified.

Please don't let me die covered in vomit.

The sound of a door opening sharpens my senses, but I

don't bother trying to lift my head. I'd rather save my energy in case an opportunity to escape this place presents itself.

Shoes click on the hard floor, and they sound like heels, and then Aria's looking down at me, a wide grin spreading across her face. "Oh good, you're awake."

Surprise flickers through my middle. I didn't expect to see her here.

"Hello, sweet Cousin," I drawl, acting bored.

Damn. It's embarrassing I'm going out this way.

Even in my perilous position, the need for vengeance booms like a drum with every beat of my heart, and I'm not giving up hope that somehow, someway, I'll be able to get myself out of this. Seeing her face only solidifies the anger fueling me. I have a lot of years to make up for with her and her daddy.

"Where's Bas?" I ask, keeping my tone neutral.

A look of confusion screws up her face. "Why would he be here?"

Relief drapes over me like a blanket. It may be surprising that Uncle T has her down here and working with him, clearly another thing he kept from me on purpose, but I'm not surprised she snatched up the opportunity when it came her way.

It wasn't Bastien.

But if it wasn't him, then who the hell got me down here?

I home in on Aria's hands and realize she's holding a knife from the collection Bastien keeps in the room. But her hand is shaky.

Amateur.

"That's always been your problem, hasn't it?" she says. "You think I'm stupid, that I'm not useful to Daddy the same way you are. Well, *surprise*, Urch. Guess who's been his real sidekick for the past year?"

I laugh, because she's wrong. I actually think the *only* person she's useful to is her daddy, but I don't tell her that.

Her free hand reaches out and smacks my cheek. "Quit laughing at me!"

I open and close my jaw, trying to stem the burn, because who knew Aria had it in her to hit like that? Honestly, if she were anyone else, I'd be mildly impressed.

"I'm not laughing at you," I reply. "I'm laughing at your delusion. Do you really think bringing me here is the smartest choice? I know this place better than anyone."

"Better than *almost* anyone," she corrects.

The words falter and die on my tongue when she says that, an eerie tingle working its way through my limbs.

"I can see you're confused." She leans in close, her nose almost touching mine. "Let me help you figure it out. You took something from me, so I took something from you."

My bruised heart misses a beat, aching.

She straightens, her hand still trembling with the knife. "Although I guess Fisher was technically mine first too, wasn't he?" She looks at me, and her face screws up in disgust. "God, what is it with you and my sloppy seconds?"

I won't believe it. He wouldn't. "You're lying."

She tilts her head. "You sure about that?"

Panic infuses my breaths, and it's difficult to get it under control, but I try like hell anyway. And I almost have it, but nothing, and I mean nothing, prepares me for the betrayal that slices through me when Fisher walks out from the shadows and into my line of vision.

The remnants of my fractured heart shatter from what feels like a Judas kiss.

He won't look me in the eye, though.

That fucking bastard.

I swallow around the painful lump in my throat, well-versed now in the feeling of when tears are going to come. Now that I've started crying, it's like a faucet, and I'm trying to figure out how to shut it at will.

I keep them at bay, barely. Neither of them deserves my tears.

"Still a sucker for a pussy, huh, Gup?" I let out a sardonic laugh.

He shakes his head and scuffs the floor with the toe of his worn shoe.

"Can't even look at me? Coward."

Aria smacks me across the face again, which is getting incredibly annoying, and my head slaps against the metal table.

"That's for fucking my fiancé," she snarls.

"Ex," I correct, turning my face back to her and grinning.

Her brows rise, her hand on the knife growing more agitated. "What did you say?"

"I think you heard me."

"E and I are just in a fight. It happens to every couple. But he's still mine, and we both know it."

"Huh," I reply.

She stops. "What's that mean?"

I glance down at the knife again, and it's really not in my best interest to rile her up right now, but sometimes, I just can't help myself.

"Nothing." I shrug, but since my wrists are chained over my head, it doesn't do much other than bring back that ugly clanking. "Just that he must have forgotten while he was fucking me all over New York."

"He can have his fun. Everybody knows we belong together." Her eye twitches, and she smiles at me. "Besides, if he wanted you so much, where the hell is he now, Urch?"

My heart spasms, the broken pieces throbbing like salt poured in open wounds. "Probably staying as far away from your psycho ass as possible."

She scoffs. "He loves me. I saved him. We're meant to be together."

I stare at her, my eyes widening because she has truly lost the plot. "You didn't save him, you lunatic. I have half a mind to believe you were the one there trying to kill him in the first place."

She lunges toward me, the knife nicking the skin on my arm and making me suck in a sharp hiss. "And then *you* came along and fucked everything up, and plans changed. You just couldn't leave well enough alone."

Her admission is a concrete boulder crashing into me,

but I should have seen it coming. After all, I've been truly blind to what's been going on for years; it was just an illusion that I was part of the bigger picture.

"Sorry, but you did a shit job, Aria. He was still alive because *you* fucked everything up." A sharp laugh escapes me at the sudden realization. "It's no wonder Uncle T sent me out to check on you that night. He *knew* you'd fail and need my help—he just didn't want to tell me why."

Aria scoffs, her nostrils flaring. "Well, I didn't need it."

"Clearly," I deadpan.

"The backup plan worked out better anyway, and we have you to thank for it. Marrying E was a much better option, and once we convinced his father that we'd keep him under control and report back everything we found, it was easy to get that ring on my finger."

"This whole time, you've been a shady bitch. I should have known." I adjust my wrists, the metal chafing against the skin.

Aria's staring down at the blood slowly dripping from my arm onto the table. It's a shallow cut, but she seems to be weirdly affected by it.

She snaps out of her daze and meets my eyes. "Doesn't matter. I love him, and he's mine. Fate always works out. You of all people should know that. What is it you say? The universe always provides?"

"I also say karma's a bitch."

My eyes flick to Fisher, expecting him to have some type of reaction to the delusional things Aria's saying, but he doesn't seem surprised by her statements, and I have to wonder why.

Why doesn't it bother him to see her so out of sorts? Why isn't it bothering him to hear her speak about Enzo like they're soul mates? Why doesn't he care at all that I'm here, chained to a table and bleeding, most likely about to die. Is he that far gone?

I should have paid closer attention to how much he was fixating on her when she came back to town, but I got distracted. Messy. Let my shit take precedence over his. I guess Uncle T was right: I am sloppy.

My mind races, trying to think of a way out of this. I can't use my body. I can't do anything except lie here at their mercy, so I have to use the only other weapon I have available.

My voice.

And Aria's always been a girl who can't resist a good manipulation tactic. With her, it's all about the angle.

"Look at you, being the picture-perfect Kingston daughter. Who would have thought after all these years of trying to get away, you would end up right back where you started?"

Her eyes flare, and she points the edge of the knife at me. "I am not."

I raise my brows. "Could have fooled me."

Aria crosses her arms, tapping the blade against the inner part of her elbow. "What do you mean?"

"Well, I imagine he's promised you things."

She lifts her chin. "So?"

"Here's the thing, Aria. You may know him as your

father, the doting, overprotective, wealthy man who will stop at nothing to make sure his baby girl is safe. But me? I know him as the King of the Sea. Ruthless, self-centered, willing to lie to get his way. And I'll admit that despite all those things, I know he loves you more than almost anything in the world."

She huffs. "What do you mean, 'almost'?"

"Well, I can't be sure." I look away from her. "Never mind, it's ridiculous. You're probably right that he's just around the corner waiting to say how proud he is of you for all this."

Her jaw clenches. "You don't know what you're talking about."

I give her a pitying look. "I do. I know it better than anyone, unfortunately. And we *both* know there's one thing he loves more than any of us."

She lifts her chin. "And what's that?"

"Power, of course."

She drops the knife. "Well, you're wrong. And he's not here."

I laugh, and the chains rattle. "You think I don't know that? Do you know how many people I've chained to this exact table and done exactly what you're about to do, just so he'd look at me with pride when I went back home and told him?"

She scoffs. "Stop trying to compare us."

"Oh, but we're so very comparable, sweet Cousin. You see, Trent Kingston didn't get to where he is by being a dummy. He knows every single move you're gonna make before you make it, because when you're working with him, it's all an illusion. It's him pulling strings and making you think you're getting your way. It's his specialty."

She turns away from me, but I know she's listening. My words are a hook thrown out to sea. I just have to reel her in slowly.

"He doesn't treat me the same way he treated you," she proclaims. "He *loves* me."

"Now that we already agreed on. But the boss is clearly on a roll, bringing you in to do the dirty work he used to have me for. Replacing me with someone he knows he can kick when she's down and she'll just roll over and ask to be kicked again." I click my tongue and sigh. "Before you know it, you'll be just…like…me."

"I will never be like you." She spins around, her eyes blazing. "Daddy promised I'd get to leave after this, go back home with E."

My brow lifts. "And you believe him?"

"Yes," she says, but I can sense the uncertainty in the air.

"Fair enough. But if you kill me…" I continue. "He'll have something to hang over your head. Something that ties you to him, and to this place, forever."

"I'm not staying in Atlantic Cove."

"I'm sure you believe that," I agree.

"He wouldn't."

"The only constant in life is change," I say. "Heraclitus said that."

Aria's face screws up. "Okay, and?"

"And the one thing I know is your father would move heaven and earth to keep you here, locked to his side. That is a constant in this life. So, what's the part that's changed?" My eyes flick to the knife. "Once your hands are dirty, Aria, there's no amount of washing that can clean the stains. He'll always know how to make them show."

She lets out a frustrated groan. "I'm supposed to kill you. I *want* to kill you."

"Kill me, then." I say lackadaisically. "Or…"

She leans in slightly.

"We could make a deal."

CHAPTER 50

Venesa

FISHER IS STILL STANDING SILENTLY NEXT TO my pookies' aquarium with his head hanging, his hands in his pockets.

He really is nothing but a pathetic guppy.

Hurts to admit, but here we are.

"Why would I make a deal with you? You don't have any power," Aria says, drawing my attention back.

My fingers twitch, and the chains rattle against the metal table. "Power's in the eye of the beholder. The only reason you think I'm powerless is because you've got me chained down. Aria…you don't know the things I'm capable of."

"Like what?"

"Like getting you out of Atlantic Cove without tying yourself to Uncle T."

She rolls her eyes. "You're just trying to trick me."

"Believe what you want."

Aria looks at me from her periphery. "And why would you help me anyway?"

"Self-preservation, obviously. I don't want to die, and if that means we have to work together, then so be it."

Her gaze narrows. "What are you planning to do, kill Daddy?"

A smile spreads across my face. "Now, I can't tell you everything. Where's the fun in that?"

Aria looks to Fisher. He's stone silent, still staring at the ground, and a small part of me, beyond the hurt and anger at his betrayal, wonders if he's letting me try to talk myself out of this because he cares. Maybe. Just a little.

"With me, you'll be free." I purse my lips, going in for the kill. "And I can get you back to Enzo. Back in his good graces."

She lifts the knife again. "How?"

I laugh. "Sweet Cousin, that's what I do. Getting things done? I live for it."

She narrows her eyes before glancing over her shoulder at Fisher. "Is she telling the truth?"

He finally glances up, meeting Aria's gaze head-on, and I ignore the way my stomach feels like it's turning itself inside out.

At least he doesn't have a problem looking at her. But then again, I guess that was his problem.

He was *always* looking at her.

"Venesa's a lot of things, but a liar isn't one of them." Fisher clears his throat. "If she makes you a deal, then she's good for her word."

Aria gives me her attention again. "I don't want you to hurt Daddy."

"Life's full of hard choices," I reply.

Her brows draw down, but so does the knife in her hand, and my heart levels out, just a little.

She cocks her head. "I want you to promise me you'll stay away from E. Forever."

My heart cracks, his name sending a mix of heat and angst through my system.

Well, he hates me and will never forgive me, so that's the easiest deal I've ever made.

"I'll stay away from Enzo. Forever," I confirm, my voice catching on the final word. "As long as you hold up your end of the bargain."

I can feel it in the air that she's about to agree, her mouth popping open, and then…

The door slams open, the sound of it crashing on the wall grating against my eardrums.

"Bastien," Aria gasps.

Hope flickers to life like a burning candle inside me. Bastien's here. By Aria's surprised voice, I'm assuming he *isn't* part of their plan, although I hope he is still playing Uncle T to gain information. I assume so, since he apparently knew I was down here.

I hear his footsteps as he moves farther into the room, but it isn't until he's standing next to Fisher that I can see him fully.

"Hey, Bas." I grin at him.

I'm not really in a smiley mood, but everything at this point is a tactic to throw off Aria. She's an amateur, and it's honestly a little insulting Uncle T sent her and Fisher to do his dirty work, especially after waxing poetic for years about how he wanted to keep her away from this side of the business. But maybe all that was a ploy to make sure I never knew he was using her to begin with.

To the average person, Bastien looks calm and collected. But I can see the tense shoulders and the way his jaw muscles are twitching. He's on edge. Nervous.

"You got my text, I take it?"

He gives a chin jerk, confirming he followed me home.

"How fortuitous of you to show up right on time," I continue. "Aria and I were about to make a deal."

Bastien lifts a brow and looks at Aria, then at Fisher, and then back to me. "What deal?"

"She's going to switch sides. A good ol' coup d'état, if you will, against my uncle."

"What's a coup d'état?" Aria asks.

I grin. "Overthrowing of the power, darlin'. Don't worry your pretty little head about the specifics. All you need to know is if you side with me, you gain your freedom. You can take those long legs of yours and run away forever with your man."

She sneers. "You have no power without Daddy."

Bastien steps forward now. "Technically, she has all the power."

Aria points the knife at Bastien now, which is laughable. He doesn't even flinch. "Explain," she demands.

"The back of that family painting? There's an irrevocable trust inside. One even your daddy doesn't know exists. One he thought he got rid of. And it leaves everything to Venesa's mother, Adrina Andersen. And in the event of Adrina's death, everything goes to her." He nods toward me.

Aria's mouth drops open as she glances back and forth between us. "Is that why you tried to get me to hand that ugly thing off to you?"

I smile. "Guess you'll never know, will you?"

But inside, I'm reeling, the same way I was when Bastien told me the truth back in New York. I didn't even know there could be something hiding inside the painting. I just wanted it because I promised Momma.

Bastien steps forward. "I can prove it to you. You have the painting, don't you? Take me there; I'll show you."

Aria's face is conflicted.

"You've got your loyal little fish boy here to keep watch over me," I say, my eyes cutting to Fisher with a glare. "You don't even need to unchain me until you get back."

"Better hurry and decide, though, princess," Bastien warns. "I have it on good authority E is on his way, and I know you like to play up that innocent act around him."

My heart skips at the thought of Enzo showing up.

"Pass," she snips. "I can just get them out and destroy them myself."

"You could," Bastien says. "But I've already made copies. Several of them. You sure you want to take that chance?"

Aria's silent for a few moments, and the room is quiet

beyond the pounding of my heart, hoping she's naive enough to fall for our simple parlor tricks and twisted words.

She points the knife at Bastien again. "You come with me, and she stays here."

"Of course."

She spins to Fisher. "Don't let her out of your sight until I'm back. Do you understand? And if Daddy calls, you stall him."

He nods, and I scoff out loud, because if I don't, then I might have to focus on the gaping wound he's caused in the center of my chest.

Pathetic.

Aria softens her features and walks over to Fisher before pressing her palm to his cheek. "Remember what's at stake, Fisher. If you fuck this up, there's no chance for her."

Now that piques my interest.

While she's talking to him, Bastien takes the opportunity, catching my eye and mouthing one word.

Cabin.

Aria turns and lets Bastien lead her out of the room. And as they leave, Bastien's shoulders relax, and he looks back at me one more time with a pointed look.

There's no need. I know what he's telling me.

He'll take care of Aria, and it's my job to take care of Fisher.

Somehow.

If only I could get out of these goddamn chains.

After they're gone, neither Fisher nor I speak, and the silence is so overwhelming, it makes me want to scream.

I have a thousand questions running through my mind, a broken soul and a shattered heart and the burning need to ask him *why*, even though he probably won't have the guts to tell me.

Fisher sighs heavily, the toe of his shoe going back to work scuffing against the linoleum floor.

"Is it because you love her?" I ask.

Now his head finally snaps up, and his gaze meets mine.

There's that fire. Pity I'll have to snuff it out.

The thought makes my chest ache, so I shove the words from my brain, centering myself so I can stay in the moment.

"Have you been working for Uncle T this whole time and just pretending to be my friend?" I continue my rapid-fire questions, but my voice cracks on the word "friend," and I hate that I just showed him a vulnerability. I want to go back to the Venesa who felt nothing, who couldn't shed a tear even if she prayed for one. It was easier that way.

"You don't understand," he says lowly.

"So why don't you try to explain it to me?"

"I didn't have a choice. When Aria came back..." He pauses and shakes his head. "Before she left, we were—"

"Can you unchain me?" I interrupt. "It really is uncomfortable."

He looks from my wrists to my locked-up ankles. "I don't trust you won't kill me."

"I'm the only one who's ever understood you, so don't come at me with that condescending bullshit," I spit back at him. "I was loyal to you for years. I've been nothing but your friend, and this is how you repay me?"

I jerk my limbs, making that god-awful clanking sound again. "I know you two had your thing in school. But God, Fisher. Is she really worth all this?"

"Did you know Aria was pregnant?" he blurts. "When she left town…she was pregnant with my fucking kid, Short Stack. She didn't run away because she hated it here. She ran away to save our baby. Aria's not the devil you make her out to be."

I suck in a breath, trying to fit together new square pieces into round holes. "She's lying."

He shakes his head sadly. "We found out together, and she promised things would be different. She said she loved me, and I…"

A bit of understanding flows through me. "And you loved her."

He lifts a shoulder, shoving his hands in his jeans pockets. "She's the only one I ever have."

Ouch.

"So you were only my friend to what…try to stay close to her?"

"No, nothing about our relationship was fake or forced."

"Except at the end, apparently."

Pain flashes across his face, and he swallows audibly. "It was a few days before Aria came back. You were… somewhere, doing something for your uncle, I'm guessing, since he showed up to the Lair knowing you wouldn't be there. He took me aside, told me I needed to give him information."

My mouth runs dry. "What kind of information?"

Fisher shrugs. "About you. What you were doing, whether he could trust you."

I scoff. Was everybody backstabbing me this entire time, and I was just a blind fool?

Fisher takes a step forward. "I refused. I swear to God, I told him to get fucked."

"Clearly," I drawl.

"He pulled out pictures. Pictures of a kid, and I… She has this bright blond hair and freckles just like Aria's. He said if I didn't, then he'd kill her, and I…I may never get to know my daughter, but I'll be damned if I live in a world where she doesn't exist."

Now it's pity that fills my chest, and I relax my shoulders, trying to keep my arms still because the metal chains around my wrists chafe like a bitch. "He's lying to you, Gup. They're lying."

"No," he says vehemently. "I saw the pictures, Short Stack."

"Don't call me that," I bite out. "You don't get to call me that anymore."

Fisher takes a giant step toward me. "If I didn't give him what he wanted, they were going to kill my kid. That's my kid!" He smacks his chest.

"Well, you've always been pretty fucking gullible," I snap back. "There is no kid, Fisher. *God*. Don't you think they could find a random girl? Or manipulate a photo?"

I scoff and turn my head to the other side of the table. Because of course it was him. I told him so much on that phone call when I was in New York, and it wasn't even a day later that Enzo's father showed up to tear us apart.

It was Fisher who told them I was there. Where I was staying. Everything…was all Fisher.

"They're lying to you," I say sadly. "I know you want to believe them, but, Fisher…they're using your vulnerability to manipulate you."

"Oh, and you're not?" he spits, moving until he's right next to the table. "You don't tell me shit. You have me here running things for you, but you never tell me the whole story. Just bits and pieces that suit you, that cater to you, that make you look good."

"I was protecting you, you moron!"

"I don't need your protection."

"Clearly." I shake my head again. "I'm telling you right now, Fisher, if Aria was pregnant, if she was truly pregnant, your kid isn't out there. There's no pot of gold at the end of the rainbow. And Uncle T didn't send her away."

"You don't know that."

"I do, actually. I was there when he lost his mind over her being gone, and I was sent to check in on her all the goddamn time. I saw Aria just a few months after she left, and for the record, she was very much not pregnant and very much there on her own accord."

He grits his teeth, nostrils flaring. "How do I know you're telling the truth?"

I exhale heavily, hurt piercing through my chest, because how can he ask that? "Maybe I've left some things out for your protection, but I've never lied to you. They're playing you, and you know what hurts the most about it? You just took them at face value, threw away years of our friendship, threw away my life, without even making sure it was worth it."

His eyes well up, tears lining his lower lids. "I didn't have a choice."

"There's always a choice, Gup." A sudden thought hits me. "How long?"

"What?" he asks.

"How long were you feeding information to my uncle? Since Aria came back like you said or longer?"

"Since Aria came back. Daddy T had you…" He swallows and looks down. "He was setting you up. Having you spend time with E in case things went south. They could still kill him and pin everything on you."

My mouth pops open, a short burst of air escaping. *Of course*. That's why he had me on babysitting duty. Insurance.

And Fisher knew the whole time. Was *betraying* me the whole time.

"So you had plenty of time to verify things, to come clean to me…and you didn't."

A tear escapes his eye, and he wipes it away. "I wanted to, so many times, but I…I just couldn't take the chance. They put me in an impossible situation."

I hate that I understand, because as soon as he says that,

I'm filled with regret over all the things I didn't tell Enzo when I had the chance. If Fisher's a coward, then so am I. Doesn't make it hurt any less, though.

"You told Uncle T about New York," I confirm.

He nods and looks down at the floor again.

"And he told Carlos Marino."

Another nod.

I think back, trying to remember everything I told him on the phone. I kept it vague, but one thought keeps repeating in my mind. A single line.

There are going to be some changes.

Panic for Enzo whips through me like a storm, because if they have me here, who knows what his father's doing to him there?

"Fisher, listen to me. If you ever cared about me at all, even a little bit, you'll let me go. Unchain me."

He lifts his chin, trepidation in his stare. "How do I know you won't kill me?"

I give him a sad smile. "I guess you'll just have to learn to trust the right people, Gup."

CHAPTER 51

Enzo

GIO'S LAID UP ON HIS FOUR-POSTER BED WITH a sling around his arm and a dopey grin on his face, thanks to the painkillers our on-call doctor loaded him up with after removing the bullet from his shoulder.

I smirk at him. "You feeling good, buddy?"

His head lolls. "I should get shot more often."

"Don't joke about that shit."

He smiles wider at me. "You love me."

I move my legs out farther from the chair I'm sitting in. "Don't get sappy, Gio. I'm just saying. You're not allowed to die on me, you understand?"

He sighs. "You love me."

"Yeah, man," I admit, not caring if it makes me sound like a pushover. "I do."

"Stop it." He wipes an imaginary tear from under his eye. "You're making me verklempt."

My lips twitch. "You're an idiot."

"But I'm an idiot you *love*." He grins. "What an honor, honestly. Being loved by a Mafia don."

I huff and cross my arms. "Don't call me that. I'm just E still."

He laughs. "Nah, you're the big boss man now, Lover Boy. Better get used to it."

I lean forward, resting my elbows on my legs. "And that means you're my consigliere."

He nods, his face growing serious. "You tell the families yet?"

I shake my head. "They'll know. I left Pops's body in front of Peppino's grave. Paid off the cops to find him and run the news story in the morning."

"Bold move."

Shrugging, I run a hand through my hair. "Let them rot together."

A twinge of pain hits my chest when I say the words, because even though I mean them...they were still family, and that type of bond doesn't go away, even when it's marred and twisted up from years of abuse and neglect.

But this is the way it has to be.

My leg bounces, and I pull out my phone, bringing up Venesa's number and debating on pressing Send.

I need to make sure she's okay. That Pops was just bluffing to save his ass. Unfortunately, because of Gio's immediate need, I sent Scotty to the Marino to check on her and get ahold of Bastien.

Before I can even pull up his number to call, my phone buzzes with pictures.

My heart stalls when I see them, panic rushing through me like a storm surge, annihilating every other emotion in its path.

Venesa's hotel room.

Her duffel bag on the ground near the door.

A broken decoration next to it.

A bit of blood spatter on the marble entryway.

Fuck. Fuck. Fuck.

Me: Find Bastien. Now.

Scotty: He's not in his room, but I've got his number. I've been trying to call him.

Me: Send it to me

Gio's watching me with dazed eyes, and I shoot to a stand, walking over to him. Even fucked up, he can tell something's off. "What's up, E?"

I smile at him, not wanting to add anything to his plate when he should be focused on healing.

My phone vibrates with Bastien's contact information coming through. "I think Venesa might be in trouble."

His brow quirks. "And you care?"

My heart pounds in my chest, because even though I'm still pissed off at her, even though I'm so fucking angry, I still love her.

I nod.

Gio blows out a relieved breath. "Good for you, man. I just…you deserve love, you know? I love love. Love is… it's good. It's great even. Wish I had it. I mean, besides you loving me…which I know you do."

Laughing, I pat his good shoulder. "Enjoy the high, buddy. I'll be back soon. You need anything, you call Scotty."

"You trust him enough?"

I nod. "He's about to be a made man when I open the books."

I'm dialing Bastien's number before I walk out the door.

I really hate South Carolina now, and it's not because of the actual place itself. It's because every time I come here, it's for things I'd much rather not be happening.

I finally got ahold of Bastien, although he never answered my call. Instead, he texted me.

Bastien: Can't answer. Aria's off the deep end. Venesa's in trouble at the Lair. Basement.

And then another one.

Bastien: Don't trust Fisher.

My heart is in my throat, and I lean forward, tapping the back of the cab driver's seat, because although I got my private plane fueled up, arranging a driver to fetch me at the airport on such short notice was a no go, so here I am in a fucking cab.

"Hey, can you go faster?"

"I'm already going twenty over, guy. Calm down."

Irritated, I reach into my pocket, pull out my money clip, and throw a few hundreds in the passenger seat. "Drive faster. Now."

The driver glances over at the seat, and his brows shoot up. "Bro, I can't just break laws because of money."

Sighing, I pinch the bridge of my nose and then pull my gun from my holster, pressing it to the side of his head. "How about now? You feel like breaking a few laws yet, sweetheart?"

His body stiffens, but he steps on the gas.

I move the weapon back and pat his shoulder. "Good man."

Anger leaches from my bones and into my bloodstream when I think about why I'm here, and I swear to God, if they touched one hair on Venesa's head, I will make them all wish for death.

I need her to be alive, but even beyond that, I need her to be unharmed. There are so many things we left unsaid, so much we have to do to heal, and if there's anything the past couple of days taught me, it's that life can be taken from you in the blink of an eye. Things can mold, and maneuver, and change, and we either learn to adapt, or we go down without a fight.

I don't want to go down without fighting for her. For us.

The cabbie pulls into the Lair's parking lot, and I'm out the door before he even slows to a stop, bursting through the back entrance and racing down the stairs, then pulling my gun out when I hit the bottom.

I walk to the room where I know she'll be and swing it open.

My heart's pounding in my ears, the ever-steady whoosh of blood pumping through veins, and my adrenaline is sending me on a high that has my vision turning red before I can even think logically about what I'm seeing.

That motherfucker Fisher is hovering over her, and everything blanks.

I don't think. I react, pulling the trigger as fast as possible, panic spreading through me at the thought of what he could be doing, what he could have already done.

Tortured her, hurt her, cut her, injected her with her own poisons.

He drops to the floor like a bag of potatoes, and Venesa shoots to an upright position, rubbing at her raw wrists and looking back and forth from me to Fisher with wide eyes and an open mouth.

I rush over to her, my gun hanging limp in my hand and my eyes traversing every single inch of her body to look for marks.

But other than a stream of blood down her arm and raw wrists, she looks fine.

Sighing, she looks at me. "Like usual, I had it handled."

She swings her legs off the side of the table but continues

to sit, her gaze going to the pool of red seeping from Fisher's body and then flicking away like she can't stand to look.

"Yeah, really seemed like it," I reply, my hands coming up to cup her face. The gun makes a clicking sound when it touches her cheek, but we both ignore it, my eyes locking on hers, relief swimming through me. She's okay.

She's here.

I'm holding her, and she's trembling, her jaw clenched and her thumb working hard at the cuticle on her ring finger. I slip the hand not holding my 9mm over her cheek and behind her until I'm grasping the nape of her neck. "Fuck, it's good to see you. Are you hurt?"

She sucks in a breath, her eyes coming up to meet mine, confusion lingering in their depths. "Would you care if I were?"

"I'm here, aren't I?"

Venesa swallows and bobs her head before glancing again at Fisher's body, a frown marring her face. "He didn't have to die."

"I beg to differ."

"He was letting me go."

"After putting you down here in the first place?" I raise a brow.

I'm not 100 percent sure that's what happened, but the fact Bastien said not to trust him and then him being down here with her all alone is enough for me to make logical deductions.

She lifts a shoulder. "We all make mistakes, and

Fisher was…troubled. He did what he thought he needed to do."

"No offense, baby, but I don't give a fuck about him. I only care about you."

Her bottom lip quivers, but she bites down on it in the next second. "He was still my best friend."

My chest aches when I see her obvious sorrow. "You're telling me you wouldn't have done the same in my position?"

"No, I would have. I just…I'm sad is all." She looks up at me again, her hands gripping my forearms. "I'm so happy you're here, though. I didn't think you'd—" Her voice catches on the words.

My eyes flick to where she has red marks, chafed and rubbed raw around her delicate wrists, and I lean in, pressing soft kisses to each of them. "Don't you ever, ever get yourself in a position like this again. Do you understand me? Scared me half to fucking death, thinking I lost you forever."

"Like I did it on purpose?" she scoffs. "Besides, I thought you hated me."

Is she about to cry?

"I don't blame you if you do," she continues.

My breathing is shaky as I press my forehead to hers, my fingers grasping her head so tightly, she might bruise, but I can't make myself let go because I'm too afraid that if I do, I might lose her again. I just need to know that she's real. Tangible.

"I'm pissed at you. I'm so fucking angry I can feel it with

every breath. But…I don't think I could ever hate you. Not when I love you so goddamn much."

She sucks in a sharp gasp, tears welling in her eyes and dripping down her face. My thumbs catch every single one like they're precious water from an untapped source.

"You're crying," I murmur.

"Seems you bring it out in me." She sniffs. "I don't deserve your love, Enzo. I should have told you, and I…"

"Baby. I just killed your best friend. Maybe we can call it even for now. We'll deal with working through the rest later. Day by day, okay?"

She swipes at the tears rolling down her cheeks and nods. "Yeah?"

"Yeah."

She gives me a small grin. "We'll do the adult thing and talk or whatever."

I smirk at her, leaning down and pressing my lips to hers, solace filling me because even though we're far from perfect right now, we're still here, together.

And there's hope on the horizon.

"Enzo?" she murmurs against my lips. "I'm in love with you too, you know?"

My heart skips. "You are?"

She presses her lips to mine again, and I take the opportunity, tangling our tongues and groaning into her mouth, moving one hand to the small of her back and pulling her into me.

I know she's grieving, and so am I, honestly, but right now, I just need to feel her here with me.

There's nothing like death to make you want to live.

"I'm not sorry for killing your friend," I whisper, dragging my fingers down her face, then reaching in my pocket and pulling out her necklace. Slowly, I place it back around her neck, latching it and then pressing a kiss to the seashell. "But I'm sorry that it hurts you."

She swallows, glancing at his body and then back at me. "Yeah. Me too."

Venesa slips off the metal table and walks over to her saltwater aquarium, squatting until she finds what she's looking for. She taps the glass and mumbles words too low for me to hear.

It's oddly endearing to watch her in her element, speaking to her pets.

"So now what?" I ask after giving her time with them.

She spins around and looks at me, fierce determination flashing through her beautiful dark gaze.

"Now we clean up the mess here and then take back what's mine."

CHAPTER 52

Venesa

"WHAT WOULD YOU DO IF I EVER GOT *kidnapped?"*

It's a question I don't ask Bastien lightly, but it's something I'm curious about, because Aria's been gone for less than fourteen hours, and although Uncle T can tell where she is from all the GPS trackers he installed in everything she owns, he's convinced someone took her in order to get to him.

It's…very annoying.

The way Uncle T is acting completely unhinged at the thought of someone touching his precious daughter has me realizing even the greatest of men have their weaknesses.

And it's usually a woman behind their downfall.

Also, it stings seeing him get so emotional over her when I can't imagine anyone ever being that way for me.

But that's the way life deals my cards, I guess.

Bastien shrugs. "I'd pray you had finally learned how to

be more aware of your surroundings and that you had your gun."

I snort, because he's always going on about that. I hate guns. They're so…pedestrian.

"He needs to get it together, or else everyone will realize they can use Aria against him," I mutter.

Bas gives me an exasperated look while Uncle T stomps back and forth in his office, flinging random things around like he's a child having a tantrum.

"Where would you take someone if you were going to kidnap them?" I continue my line of questioning, mainly because I'm curious but also because I'm bored with watching Uncle T lose it.

We all know Aria ran away. She's been desperate to leave since forever, and the fact she's in New York, the place she had plastered all over her walls for years? Speaks for itself.

But Uncle T isn't big on logic right now, apparently.

Whatever. I'm in a great mood because ding, dong, the bitch is gone. Fisher seems sad, though.

"I don't know," Bastien replies.

I loll my head back and give him a smirk. "Now, I don't believe that for a second. You've always got a plan for everything. Come on, Bas, it's me."

He sighs, crossing his arms and looking over at me. "I have a cabin I'd probably take them to."

"You have a cabin?" My mouth drops open.

"Yeah, so?"

"Rude. I can't believe you haven't taken me there."

"You should be happy I haven't, since that's where I'd take my victims."

"I guess." I sink back in my seat. "Well, I want to see it anyway. Where is it?"

"I'll take you." He looks at Uncle T again, who isn't paying us any mind because he's currently screaming in a housekeeper's face. "But you have to promise it stays between us."

I reach out my little finger. "Pinky swear."

It's funny how moments that seem inconsequential turn out to be the things that save you in the end.

It's *because* of that seemingly inconsequential moment and Bastien's mouthed word earlier that I know exactly where he went with Aria.

Three hours inland and in the middle of a forest sits an unsuspecting cabin registered to a John Doe. It has no neighbors for miles, and it's so densely covered with trees that cell signals don't even get picked up.

"This is fucked," Enzo states, Fisher's car, which we jacked, bumping this way and that as we wind up a narrow, unpaved drive.

"Yeah, well, what about our situation isn't fucked right now?"

He grins over at me. "When we're done with this, I'm going to fuck *you*."

A laugh breaks out of me. "You're so romantic."

"We haven't had our makeup sex." He pouts. "I'm still pissed. I plan to take it out on every part of your body."

Arousal shoots through me at the thought. "Promise?"

"Guaranteed." He side-eyes me, then looks back out at the road. "So what's the plan when we get there?"

I look over at him with an arched brow. "You mean you don't have one?"

"This is your show, baby. I'm just along for the ride."

I frown. "What about your father?"

The lighthearted moment dissipates at my question, and his face drops into a scowl. "He's been handled. It's over."

"I'm sorry." I'm not. Not really, but I am sorry he had to be the one to do it.

"He had to die anyway. It was the only way."

"Fisher told him I was with you. He only knew because of me, because I said things to Fisher I shouldn't have."

His brows lift, and he nods. "Then I'm really not sorry I killed him because it's his fault you were in danger."

A pang of hurt punches my chest. Even though Fisher betrayed me, even though he chose Aria over me, I'm still sad he's gone.

"Also," I say, "you should know it was your bitch assistant, Jessica, who actually kidnapped me, so if you haven't killed her yet, I'd appreciate you letting me have the honor."

His fingers tighten on the steering wheel. "Jessica?"

I shrug. "Yeah. Your dad had her under his thumb, I guess."

"Noted." His jaw clenches.

And then he laughs at me.

I cut him a glare. "What's so funny?"

He lifts a shoulder. "I'm just…*Jessica* bested you? Baby, you've gotta get better at paying attention to your surroundings."

Irritation slithers up my spine and wraps around my middle. I am going to kill her extra hard just for that.

Enzo puts the car in Park when we pull up to the cabin, turning the engine off and letting the world go quiet. We sit for a few minutes, and he reaches over, grabbing my hand in his and squeezing. "You ready?"

"As ready as I'll ever be."

We get out of the car and make our way to the door. It's unlocked, so we walk inside, and even though I've only been here once after begging Bastien to bring me, I vaguely remember the layout. Not that it matters because even if I didn't, Bastien's easy to find.

He's in the kitchen by himself, demolishing a sandwich, the Kingston family painting propped up in front of him on the square table. He gives us both a chin jerk when we walk into the room. "Oh good, you're alive," he says after he chews.

"Was there ever any doubt?" I grin at him.

"And Fisher?"

Another shot to the heart. I shake my head, my fingers aching to pick at each other.

He grunts and gives me a knowing look. "He would have let you die, V. You don't have to feel bad for how things went down."

"Doesn't change what he was to me for years. He was a good friend."

"Until he wasn't," Bas replies.

"Yeah, I guess." I brush off the heavy feeling, looking around. "Where's Aria?"

He points to the hallway, a piece of turkey falling from his sandwich. "In the back room, locked in."

"Is she hurt?" I ask, peering down the dimly lit hall.

He shakes his head. "Nah, I didn't know what you wanted to do with her."

"I want to use her to lure out my uncle, of course."

Enzo looks between us. "You think that will work?"

"I know it will."

The words come out confident, but honestly, I'm not sure. I'm basing it entirely off the fact my uncle has always gone batshit if anything threatens Aria's safety, and I'm hoping that still rings true.

The only thing I'm not as sure about is what he'll give up in order to save her.

What's more important to a man like my uncle: his daughter or his power?

The atmosphere in the cabin is heavy, and I walk up to the painting, chewing on my lip when I stand in front of it. I flick my gaze to Bas. "Were you serious? About the documents being here?"

He nods and gestures toward it. "See for yourself."

After walking forward, I pick up the painting and flip it around, noticing there's already a thin line splitting open the backing paper. I reach in and pull out two thick envelopes.

I snap my head up to Bastien. "Why are there two?"

"The first is your momma's will—not anything fancy, just a scribbled piece of paper, but still. And then, your grandpa's. Where he states emphatically everything belongs to his daughter and then is to be passed down to you."

"I don't understand," Enzo chimes in. "Why would Trent keep those instead of destroying them?"

Bastien takes another bite of his sandwich, a knowing smile gracing his face. "Trent never knew. He used the MC to bribe everyone who knew of their existence and thought he burned all the copies, starting with the ones in the house when he killed his dad." His eyes flick to me. "But when he gave me the painting to prepare for the engagement party, I found these hidden in the back. Figured it was best to just let them be. Trent doesn't need to know everything."

I nod, pulling out the papers and reading over the fine print, my hands shaking when I realize Bastien isn't lying. He never was.

Uncle T stole the Kingston empire out from under my momma.

That's why he killed her.

And that's why I'm going to kill him.

I place down the documents and then spin around to look at Enzo, hating what I'm about to tell him. "I need you to do something for me."

He quirks a brow but walks toward me, wrapping his hands around my waist. "Anything, piccola sirena."

"I need you to pretend that you love Aria."

He jerks back, shaking his head. "Fuck that."

My arms come up to rest on his biceps. "She's obsessed with you, Enzo. And if she thinks you'll take her back, that you two will ride off into the sunset forever, then she'll do what we want. Otherwise...none of this will work."

He sighs, tugging on the roots of his hair. "How?"

"Tell her you love her. Convince her that working with me is the best chance for you two to be together." I swallow over the thick lump in my throat because saying this out loud is making me sick to my stomach. I don't want him to do this, but it's the best chance we have. "Do whatever it takes."

His chin stiffens, and he nods, leaning down and pressing a kiss to my lips.

"I'm doing this for us," he tells me. "So we can finish this and I can love you out loud. In this life."

Emotion swells in my sternum, and I nod, kissing him once more, and then I back away and watch him walk down the hallway to play the role and convince the princess she's won her prince.

CHAPTER 53

Venesa

THERE ARE A LOT OF PLACES I'VE IMAGINED ending my uncle's life.

His home.

His office.

The *Aquata*.

But in the end, I decided being on my home turf was the best choice. I needed somewhere familiar, somewhere that would benefit me if things didn't go as planned. Which it's highly probable they won't. The only thing you can count on in life is the unexpected, so you might as well play to your own advantage as much as possible.

Enzo played his role perfectly, and because of it, Aria came along willingly to the Lair, then allowed me to restrain her on the table she had me on two days ago before we went to the cabin, and flipped her to our side.

Uncle T was a little hard to find because he'd been out in

the middle of the ocean, and I didn't want to play our hand too soon.

But that's okay because it gave me time to plan.

I have Aria chained and ready to be "tortured," and if Uncle T doesn't show up alone to save her, then I'm going to kill her, and I'll broadcast my grandfather's documents to the world so he loses everything.

His fame. His fortune. His title as King of the Sea. He'd probably end up in prison for arson and murder too, but that'd just be icing on the cake, to be honest.

That's what Bastien's told him at least, because as far as my uncle is concerned, Bastien is still working with him and not against him. Using Bas as the way to get Uncle T here was the simplest option. We'll save the dramatics for later.

And now we wait.

Bastien and Enzo aren't far away, keeping an eye out on the Lair's parking lot so they can tell me when Uncle T shows up. I made them promise to stay out of things unless it was a life-or-death situation, because even though I know I don't have to take care of myself, some things are better when I do them. All the men in my life have this nasty habit of jumping in when they don't need to, and it's *tiring*.

My hand presses against the glass of my aquarium, my heart full as I watch my babies, Jack and Flora.

"I'm sorry I haven't been around much, pookies. Mommy won't leave you for so long again."

A scoff from behind me makes me bristle, but I don't turn around. "Something to say, sweet Cousin?"

"Oh, believe me, I have a lot of things to say. But I shouldn't waste my breath."

Her voice is cocky in a way that shows she carries the same gene as her father: overconfidence, which will end up being her downfall just as much as his.

As far as Aria knows, after this is over, I'll provide her with freedom and all the money she wants so she and Enzo can ride off into the sunset together.

Like I said, delusional.

Sighing, I tap the glass to Jack and Flora one more time and then stand before grabbing my black salt and walking around the perimeter, sprinkling it in a circle close to the edges of the wall.

"What are you doing?" Aria asks, trying to turn her head to watch me. It's difficult, since she's chained.

"A protection circle."

"Is this more of that witchy bullshit?"

"It's not bullshit. It's working with the elements, and nature, and the universe." I cut her a look. "I'd tell you to try it, but knowing you, you'd fuck up the cosmic order of things and we'd all pay the price."

After placing the salt container down, I move to the center of the room and close my eyes, visualizing bright white light spreading from above and filling the space. I point my finger, carving out a pentagram on the ground with my mind, taking a moment to appreciate each point like it's a compass. Top for spirit, then for air, bottom right for earth, bottom left for water, and the final point for fire.

It's a bit overkill to be doing both the salt and the pentagram, and I'm a bit out of practice, but I'm working with what I've got.

Aria keeps mumbling under her breath from behind me, and I shush her, focusing on grounding my energy to help strengthen the circle.

Finally, I open my eyes and smile. *There.*

"You know, I really hope you have more planned to protect us than some salt and a vision, or Daddy will kill you without a second thought," Aria says.

Spinning toward her, I lift my shirt and grab the gun I placed there before coming down here, raising it in the air. "No worries, I've got all my bases covered." I point it at her head, just to see if she reacts.

She does, her face paling, and I wink at her before moving the barrel away.

"It's sweet you care, though."

I didn't want to bring the Glock—it's still as big and blah as ever—but believe it or not, I have finally learned from my mistakes, and honestly, I'm tired of listening to Bastien chastise me every time he's proven right. And now he's got Enzo on my case too.

Besides, it's honestly embarrassing how often I was caught off guard, which allowed people like Jessica to get the upper hand.

The rolling table next to Aria is all set up, and I run my fingertips over the syringes, taking in the different vials I've prepared.

Venom for my uncle, because that's just my preference, and then one special…just for Aria.

Just in case.

Twisting until I'm at the head of the torture table, I look down at her. "Let's go over the plan one more time."

She sighs and fidgets, the clank of the metal making me wince. "You're going to hide and Daddy's going to walk in to save me. My job is to get him close so you can come up from behind." She fidgets, her left shoulder rising. "Can we loosen these chains a bit? They're chafing."

"No." I tilt my head. "And then?"

She rolls her eyes. "And then you do whatever you have to do, I guess." She cuts me a glare. "But you better give me immediate access to my trust."

I nod emphatically. "You have my word."

"And stay away from my man." Her eyes narrow before a dreamy smile takes over her face. "He doesn't want you anymore."

Grinning at her, I nod again, but I don't mean it. As much as I like to hold up my end of deals, there's no way in the world I'm holding up this one.

Even if I wanted to, Enzo wouldn't let me.

But feeding into her delusion is the best way to ensure she sticks to the plan.

I do intend to let her live. I'm not lying about that part. Despite her being the bane of my existence, I truly believe she's the unfortunate outcome of parenting, and really, can I blame someone for how they were raised?

She's a byproduct of toxicity, the same as the rest of us.

"Ugh!" she complains, pulling at her wrists again. "How much longer until he's supposed to get here? This is crazy uncomfortable."

I side-eye her. "Small price to pay for your life, don't you think?"

A burner phone Bastien gave me earlier buzzes where it's stashed in my bra, and without looking, I know what it means.

Uncle T is here.

Adrenaline pumps through my veins like espresso on a drip, and I close my eyes, picturing my momma's face, Fisher's hollow eyes, and all of my uncle's lies.

When I snap my lids open again, I'm hyperfocused on one thing and one thing only: taking what's mine.

I lean down and press my fingers against Aria's cheeks, gripping them tightly until my nails dig into her skin, just a little. "Showtime, my dear, sweet Cousin. Make sure to sell it, and remember… it's all in the body language, honey."

Rushing away, I grab one syringe of my pookies' venom off the rolling table and keep my gun ready in the other hand, moving to hide just behind the corner of the saltwater tank. Out of sight and out of mind.

Right on cue, the door bursts open, Uncle T storming in with his own gun held up.

"Daddy!" Aria yells out, what sounds like a real sob breaking free from her mouth.

She's good, I'll give her that.

"Where is she?" Uncle T asks, without moving toward her. But I can see his eyes from where I am, and they're looking over her, inspecting like he's making sure I didn't harm a single hair on her head.

Bastien walks in behind him, his gun also raised, and I let out a silent but shaky breath.

The plan is working.

"Bas, check the area," Uncle T demands.

Bastien nods and starts walking around the perimeter, his eyes flicking to Jack and Flora before landing on the rolling table and then on the salt placed strategically around the room to create the circle.

He rolls his eyes, like even in this tense moment, he has time to judge my practice.

Asshole.

When he walks by me, our gazes lock, and another hit of confidence swells inside me.

"All clear, boss," Bastien says, making his way back toward him. "She must be somewhere else. Want me to go check?"

"No, just stay on guard here." Uncle T rushes over to Aria, taking in the chains on her arms and legs. He sets his gun down on the table next to her.

Who's sloppy now?

"Are you hurt?" he asks Aria. "What did she do to you? Do you know where she went?"

Aria shakes her head. "No, Daddy, I'm okay, but you need to listen to me."

My spine stiffens because she isn't supposed to say something like that.

"Later, baby girl; we need to get you out of here. I'll take care of Venesa, but I…" He spins to Bastien. "How do we unlock these?"

"No, Daddy… Listen!" she yells, and that's my cue, because I don't trust her not to fuck this up, and I'm fairly confident the bitch was about to double-cross me.

Maybe Enzo wasn't so convincing after all.

So much for their true love.

I watch Bastien move closer to the table and pick up Uncle T's gun before slipping it into his waistband. Uncle T doesn't even notice because he's so focused on figuring out how to get Aria unchained.

Aria starts, "Daddy, she's right—"

Sighing, I stand and come out from the shadows. "Hello, Uncle. How are you?"

Uncle T spins toward me, his eyes blazing with anger. He reaches out to grip his gun, and only then does he realize it's missing. His face blanks, his eyes growing round as he looks at Bastien.

"You filthy rat," he spits before focusing back on me.

Bastien smiles and shrugs. "Learned from the best."

I tsk-tsk at Uncle T, pointing my gun at him as I walk over to Aria and stand next to my rolling table of poisons. "Now, that's not very nice. Bas has been nothing but accommodating." I look up at my uncle, catching his gaze. "Maybe you just need to learn how to treat your people better."

"I will kill you, Venesa."

Amusement at his words swirls through my stomach and curls up my throat, and I throw my head back and laugh. "It's adorable you think you have the power here, Uncle T. But I guess that's always been your problem, hasn't it? Thinking everything is about you."

"Isn't it?" he barbs back.

"No!" I smack my hand on the metal right next to Aria's face. "This is about me for once. And everything you stole."

His eyes widen, dawning realization hitting them.

"That's right, you absolute asshole. I know everything. So if I were you, I'd start figuring out how to beg appropriately, and maybe I'll spare your *poor* daughter's soul."

I move the barrel of my weapon, pressing it to Aria's temple.

She's shaking, small whines pouring from her mouth.

Good.

Uncle T's hands shoot into the air, his palms up like I'm the volatile one. "Let her go, Venesa."

I run the gun down Aria's cheek. Her eyes widen slightly, realizing that she didn't hold up her end of the bargain, so things have changed.

"Now, why would I do that?" I question. "She and I made a deal."

Aria tries again. "Daddy, I—"

I whip the firearm out and smack her cheek, the satisfying slap of flesh hitting metal resounding in my ears.

Cracking my neck, I breathe in deep. "God, I've been waiting years to do that."

Aria groans, pulling on her chains as she tries to focus her attention back on me. "You bitch!"

"What do you want?" Uncle T asks, stepping in farther.

I tilt my head. "What do you mean? I have everything I could want right here. The daughter of the great Trent Kingston—the girl who tortured and bullied me for years. She's quite the prize to have."

Lifting my nails, I look at the cuticles like I can't be bothered. "So I guess the question is, what are you willing to give me that's better?"

"Anything," he responds immediately.

I tilt my head, a hit of anger and hurt swimming through me like poison because he's giving up so easily.

For her.

He'd never have done the same for me.

A slow smile spreads across my face. "Well, then make me a bargain."

"If you let her go, you can have me," he barters.

"No, Daddy, she won't actually do it. Don't listen to her, I—"

"Deal," I interrupt. Nodding at Bastien, who has his gun aimed at Trent, I drop my weapon on the rolling table and pick up the syringe I made just for Aria.

"She's lying! Enzo is here and—"

Lunging, I press the syringe directly into her trachea. "That's about enough out of you."

"No!" Uncle T yells, surging forward.

Bang!

My ears ring from the loud blast, and I watch as Uncle T grabs at his side and falls to the floor. I look up at Bastien, who's holding his gun out, clearly having just shot it.

I groan, my hands going to my hips. "What is with men and always interfering? I had this handled."

He shrugs, waving his free hand in the air. "So handle it."

Sighing, I reach out, grab my Glock, and walk to my uncle, staring down at him.

Aria is sputtering and coughing, sucking in air as best she can behind us, but I ignore her. I didn't inject her with anything lethal.

"I had hoped to draw this out some, to make it more of an experience," I tell Uncle T. "But I've learned sometimes being quick and to the point is best. You taught me that, actually."

As soon as I crouch, his bloody hand shoots up from where it was pressing against his stomach, trying to rip my weapon out of my hands. I won't lie, even with him severely injured, his strength is a lot for me, and I fall backward as he rips the gun from my grasp and struggles to his knees, pointing the barrel down at me.

"You always were pathetic and a waste of space. Weak. Just. Like. Your. Momma."

Those words repeat in my head like a mantra and send fire blazing through me. He pulls the trigger on the gun at the same time I kick out my feet and shove him in the chest, propelling him backward.

His arm flies, and the bullet doesn't hit me; instead, it shatters the glass of my aquarium, water pouring out onto the floor, along with my babies.

"No!" I yell, jumping up and racing over to reach them.

Bastien is there before I can do anything, gripping Uncle T around the neck and placing him in a headlock. Uncle T grunts and tries to protest, but it's easy to see he's growing weak from the loss of blood.

I push myself up, drenched from the aquarium water, a new anger unleashing inside me. I stomp over to my syringes and grab the venom from my pookies before heading back to where Bastien is holding my uncle, who's wasting his precious energy trying to fight a man he'll never overpower.

"You tried to kill my babies," I spit, kicking his side and reveling in the way he flinches in Bastien's arms. I kick him again, just because I'm so angry and it feels good.

He grunts and grapples to hold his side, where blood is steadily seeping from his gunshot wound.

Luckily, stonefish can survive up to twenty-four hours without water, so as long as I can transfer them to a backup soon, they'll survive.

Still, it's the principle of the thing.

Uncle T stares up at me, growing weaker by the second. Bastien holds him down while I crouch and inject the venom into his vein.

"You'll never get away with this." He forces out each word.

I smile. "You fool. I already have."

Then I sit back and watch as the venom spreads, enjoying every second that his body physically shrivels and his eyes dim.

As I nod in satisfaction, a breath of relief escapes me, my shoulders relaxing and my victory reigning supreme.

Enzo comes bursting through the room a few seconds later, his eyes wide and his own gun drawn, only calming when he focuses on me.

"Christ, I heard gunshots and thought the worst." His hand goes to his chest.

"Everything's under control." I grin at him and then look at Bastien. "Can you take care of my babies? They need to go to their backup tank."

He nods and stands, cringing when he looks at his blood-soaked hands.

Uncle T's body falls to the floor with a slap.

Enzo looks around, taking in the scene before his gaze lands on Aria. His brow quirks. "What'd you do to her?"

I turn to see what he's looking at. She's stopped her gasping now, but her eyes are wide and panicked.

Half skipping, I make my way over to her, glee filling every bone in my body.

"Is it hard to breathe?" I ask, leaning over her. "You'll get used to that…I think. It's from all the swelling, you see."

She opens her mouth and tries to speak, but nothing comes out.

"Don't waste your energy," I coo. "That injection? It was a special mix I made just for you. A blend of arsenic and lead. You know what that causes? Vocal paralysis."

Enzo steps up next to me, looking down at her. "She won't be able to talk?"

I shrug. "Not well anyway."

"Now, about our deal." I focus back on her. "Considering it was made under duress—my duress—I'm afraid we'll have to renegotiate the terms."

Enzo wraps his arms around me, pulling me into his chest and pressing kisses up the length of my neck.

Aria's eyes flare, and I grin down at her.

"Don't look at me like that." I tilt my head, allowing Enzo to have more access. "You're smart enough to know I'd never let you have him."

Aria's eyes are wild, but they're dry—not a tear to be found—probably because she's a selfish bitch who doesn't care about anyone except herself.

Not even her dead father on the ground.

She tries to speak again, but only a hoarse rasp escapes. Her eyes grow round, and she tries one more time before sucking in what little air she can get.

"I'm going to let you live, Aria. That's my gift to you." I blink at her. "You're welcome."

Enzo chuckles into my neck, and I separate from him, even though Aria having to watch us together sends satisfaction racing through my bones.

What can I say? Spite fuels me.

I press my fingernails to her trachea. "And honestly, consider this a mercy. You may not have your voice, and I'm definitely not giving you any of the family fortune. But you still have your…looks." I lean in close. "That pretty face of yours should get you far."

Now a tear does drip down her cheek.

My fingers press on her esophagus, hard enough to leave a bruise, and I lean over her, pressing my lips to her ear. "Fisher's death is on your hands. And I want you to live out there, penniless, worthless, remembering the pain you've caused others every day." I stand and back away, looking at the single syringe left. "Or you can use that venom there and kill yourself. Doesn't really matter either way to me."

Bastien's still moving Jack and Flora into their smaller tank, so I know he'll make sure Aria doesn't escape until we're far enough away that she can't follow us.

Grabbing Enzo's hand, I turn around and walk out of the room, then pause to look back at her when I reach the threshold. "Consider this a mercy, sweet Cousin."

And I mean what I say. She'll have to learn how to make it on her own.

The way she's always wanted.

CHAPTER 54

Venesa

IT'S BEEN A MONTH SINCE EVERYTHING WAS upended in my life, and things are finally feeling like they're settling down.

Despite Enzo's protests, I gave Fisher a memorial service. Barely anyone showed up, and I honestly felt conflicted being there, but it was important to me because he was my best friend for years, and I refuse to let how things ended change everything he meant to me.

I didn't ask Enzo to go. Didn't feel right, all things considered.

There was one point where I could have sworn I saw Aria hiding in a back corner, but I brushed it off because I can't imagine she'd show her face in town ever again.

Not after what I did to her.

Besides, her *daddy* was disgraced once they found him shot on his yacht. Bastien took care of the nitty-gritty, because after Uncle T died, I didn't feel the need to keep hitting a dead fish. As long as things are taken care of, the vengeance in my soul is soothed, so I didn't ask many questions once I knew Bastien tied his murder to Johnston Miller. Something about them falling out after years in business together and the MC retaliating in the best way they know how: with violence.

I'll enjoy seeing that waste of space behind bars.

And if he doesn't end up there? Well, I'm always ready to enact more revenge when necessary.

Now I'm back home—in New York City, which still feels weird to say. Enzo gave me his private plane to use, and living in the lap of luxury is nice…definitely something I could get used to. But I want a house, not a penthouse where elevators open up at will and anyone can walk inside. My trauma from that won't ever heal.

Bastien is running Seven Seas Construction, reworking it from the ground up, and he's putting people in place to keep the Lair running smoothly. Unfortunately, it's just another thing that's been tainted after everything that happened.

I wasn't supposed to get back from Fisher's memorial service until tomorrow, but Scotty arranged the private plane to fuel early because I wanted to surprise Enzo. So even though I'm tired and it's late, there's anticipation buzzing beneath my skin.

It's been a week since I saw him. Granted, he's been busy setting up the new power structure and accepting all the gifts and pledges of loyalty that come along with being a Mafia don. Truthfully, he'd tell me anything I wanted to know, but I don't ask many questions. When we're together, I like feeling light, leaving the darkness of who we are at the door and letting ourselves just *be*.

Being in a relationship is new for me—for both of us, actually—and communication is something we were both taught to use as a weapon instead of as a foundation for something solid.

I even suggested therapy because every day I look at him and wonder if he secretly hates me for killing his brother, but Enzo was quick to say no; apparently Mafia men and their women don't *do* therapy. Something about ending up in prison and doctor/patient confidentiality not applying. But I'm working on him day by day. Maybe I'll have Gio sit down and listen to us instead.

The elevator pings open into the foyer of the penthouse, and the silence is overwhelming, so quiet that it almost has the opposite effect, making my ears ring with a high-pitched squeal.

Enzo is nowhere in sight, but it's late, so he's either out at work or maybe in bed, so I take my time, heading to the kitchen to grab something to drink before making my way back to wake him up.

I've just opened up the fridge and grabbed a bottle of water when the goddamn elevator pings back open and Scotty rushes inside, his breathing erratic and his eyes bulging out of his head.

"What is it?" I ask, immediately on alert.

"I saw…I heard… I mean, I didn't hear, but I saw that bitch—I mean, that *wench*, Aria! The doorman asked why she couldn't speak, and I—she's here—"

My eyes grow wide, my hand shooting out to grip Scotty's arm and try to focus him. "Take a deep breath, Scotty. What do you mean?"

Scotty presses a hand to his chest and follows my instruction, inhaling heavily. "Aria is somewhere in this apartment."

I'm off and down the hall before I can stop myself, Scotty's footsteps behind me, and I burst into the bedroom, my heart shooting into my throat when I see Aria with a knife raised high above Enzo's body.

He's passed out. *Did she drug him?*

I don't think; I just react, running toward her and tackling her. She fights, trying to yell, but the only thing that escapes is a hoarse shout. I smirk at her, slamming her body onto the ground and straddling her.

"Cat got your tongue?" I grin and wrestle the knife from her hand, spinning it around and forcing the blade onto her neck, my fingers clammy where they're covering hers. "Should have kept your fucking mouth shut and stayed away, you pathetic girl."

As I press harder, her eyes widen, her mouth opening wide like she's trying to beg for *something*.

But my mercy has run out.

"I'm going to enjoy this." I smile.

Then I plunge the knife into her chest and twist, reveling in the way she silently screams. I hold it there, my weight pinning her down and my fingers slipping from her blood.

And as her life flows out, every single hurt she's caused, all the years of pent-up animosity bleed away with it, and when she exhales her last breath, her body going lax and her eyes growing dim…I finally feel peace.

Because it's all over.

And now Enzo and I can live happily ever after.

EPILOGUE

Enzo

"HOW MANY TIMES DO I HAVE TO TELL YOU I hate my birthday?" Venesa asks as I steer her with my hand on her hips.

I smirk from behind her, although she can't see it because I've had her blindfolded since right before our plane landed in Atlantic Cove half an hour ago. And now we're here, at the boardwalk, and I'm determined to make her birthday a good memory again, just like it was when she was little.

"Enzo, hello?" she snips, her footsteps faltering. "You can't *not* answer me when I can't see either. It freaks me out."

Chuckling, I bend down slightly and press a kiss to the nape of her neck. "I'm sorry, piccola sirena. I know you hate them, but I don't."

Her bottom lip sticks out, and I have to bite back the urge to suck it into my mouth.

Focus, Enzo. Don't fuck this up.

"You're supposed to hate everything I hate." She pouts. "I thought that was a perk of being in a relationship."

"I could never hate the day you were brought into the world, baby," I reply. "You just have to trust me."

I prod her back until she starts walking again, and then, right before we get to the base of the Sea Wheel, her face screws up, sniffing the air. "Are we in Atlantic Cove? It smells like it."

Lightly, I smack her ass before gripping it in my palm, and then I let her go and take a few steps back, looking around.

My heart's kicking steadily but quickly against my rib cage, yet it isn't because of my fear of heights.

It's because of what else I'm about to do.

I've paid a generous amount of money to the city so the entire place would be closed to the public for the night. Not difficult to do when your woman is one of the most influential people in all of Atlantic Cove, even if her reputation isn't the nicest.

The Sea Witch, they call her.

Her uncle's protégé through and through.

She doesn't seem to mind the nickname. Besides, it's not like she's the one down here running the actual business anyway. She leaves the day-to-day stuff to Bas.

It's a beautiful evening, the sun having just set, and the clear sky opening up to millions of stars twinkling and the moon bathing us in its glow.

The second Venesa commented that her birthday fell on

the full moon this year, I knew it was my moment. I remember her talking about how she'd only get married under one. Something about it representing balance and harmony or some froufrou shit.

We're not getting married tonight, but…

Close enough.

Scotty went to that store A Rose by Any Other Name and picked up hundreds of white daisies and said he decorated the area himself. He did a good job—they're lining the makeshift picket fence that surrounds the Sea Wheel, and then overflowing vases of them are perched all along the perimeter. He also set up giant clusters of rose quartz crystals and white candles, just to set the mood entirely.

"Okay," I say, my voice surprisingly shaky. "You can take off the blindfold."

One thing I've learned is that life is never certain. Someone can spend their entire life searching for success, for happiness. Waste countless hours away from people they love, constantly searching for some unattainable thing that, in the end, won't really matter.

And then in one second—or in my case, one look—everything can change.

I looked at Venesa and my world tilted on its axis, altering my view forever.

There is one thing I'm certain of: her.

She's the only thing that matters.

Venesa reaches up, ripping off the fabric quickly, her back straightening when she realizes where we are and that there's no one else here. Her head tilts from side to side, and she slowly spins around.

I drop to my knees, gripping the ring I had custom made tight in my hand.

"I knew we were here. I could tell by the smell." She laughs as she's turning, and then her eyes meet mine, and they widen as she takes me in. "Enzo, what are you—"

She looks around again, her eyes taking in the display, and she grips at her seashell necklace, her mouth popping open as her gaze locks on me again.

"What is this?" she asks, her voice wavering, her eyes wide and soft as they stare at me.

"My entire life I've been told what to do and who to be." I lick my lips, swallowing around the sudden dryness in my throat. "What kind of path I'm supposed to travel. And I was always fine with it. Accepted it. I knew how my story would end from the beginning, because that's just the cards that were dealt. It's the way things were. And I was always fine with that…until I met you."

Reaching out, I grip her left hand in mine and bring it to my mouth to brush a kiss against the back. "You made me ache for a different life."

Her eyes widen, and I see the start of water lining her lower lids, emotion taking over her face, and a single tear dripping down her cheek.

"There are so many things I could say to you," I continue, brushing my thumb over the top of her knuckles. "But none of it would encapsulate the truth."

I take the ring that's in my right palm and slip it onto her finger, my heart skipping when I see it so perfectly on her hand.

She inhales sharply, glancing down at it.

There's a marquise diamond in the center, surrounded by rainbow moonstone set in a black platinum band.

"The truth is, Yrsa Venesa Andersen, my soul knew you were its other half the moment I laid eyes on you. You have changed me. Irrevocably. I don't want you in a different life. I *need* you in this one and all the ones we'll have after." Emotion clogs my throat and I clear it. "So marry me."

She laughs, a hand coming up to cover her mouth, tears dripping down her apple-shaped cheeks and off her chin. "Is that a question?"

"Not really." I shrug. "Let me make new memories with you every single day, piccola sirena. Do me the honor of allowing me to be your husband, and I'll love you so goddamn loudly, everyone will hear."

A bright white smile breaks across her face, the same way it did the first time I met her, and just like then, my stomach lurches forward violently; I'm transfixed like a moth to a flame.

Goddamn, she's gorgeous.

"Yes," she says. "I'll marry you. Now get off your knees, Lover Boy."

As soon as I'm standing, she jumps into my arms, wrapping her delicious thighs around my waist and peppering kisses across my skin. "I love you," she breathes.

I grip underneath her ass and squeeze. "I love you too, baby."

One of my hands leaves her ass and slides up her spine until I'm wrapping her perfect silvery-white hair in my fist, and I pull it harshly because I know that's what she loves. And then I claim her mouth with mine.

Fuck, I love kissing her.

She breaks away from me and looks around. "Are we all alone?"

"Of course. I didn't want an audience for this." I smirk. "Besides, we need to be alone for your birthday present."

"You mean there's more?" she asks, her left arm leaving where it's wrapped around my neck so she can lean back the slightest bit and stare at her ring. "It's beautiful, by the way," she says with a grin. "How'd you know I'd like moonstone?"

I palm her cheek, keeping her tethered to me with my other arm. "When are you going to realize I see you? Always?"

Pressing one more kiss to her lips, I slide her down my body slowly until she's standing again. Then I grip her hand in mine, and we walk down the boardwalk until we're in front of the game we played so long ago. Back when we were pretending not to want each other.

She squints as we approach the booth, her footsteps faltering.

"Is that—" she starts and then takes another step forward.

I press up behind her, wrapping my arms around her

waist and dipping my head into the crook of her neck to nibble on the skin.

"Did you really think I'd let anyone who would ever bring you harm go?"

She looks back at me, her brows raised like she's truly surprised, and then she grins before walking to me and slipping her tongue into my mouth.

I moan into her, gripping the back of her head and pulling her into me, because I don't think I'll ever get enough of her taste. There's something about her soft, pillowy red lips I just can't get enough of.

She releases me, and I grasp her waist, spinning her around and prodding her forward. The air is silent as she moves toward the booth. Goldfish swim around in their too-small bowls, and large squids and mermaids dangle from the ceiling. And right in the center of the bull's-eyes, tethered to them with rope, are two people.

One is Rusty…that stupid motherfucker who runs this game. He's broken and bleeding, barely hanging on to his pathetic life. His head is lolled to the side, and his eyes are so swollen, I can't tell if he's conscious. But I couldn't help myself when I saw him again. Not after learning the extent of what he did to the love of my life with Aria's help.

Then, right next to him, her eyes wide, her mouth gagged, and her body tied up with heavy-duty rope…is Jessica.

Venesa slips behind the counter and notices the lineup of her potions I had Bastien bring for the occasion. She runs her hands over them. "You brought me a gift."

I smile, happiness suffusing every piece of me.

"Happy birthday, piccola sirena. Now…go make a memory."

EXTENDED EPILOGUE

Venesa

"AND HOW DO YOU FEEL ABOUT THAT?"

I bite the inside of my cheek to keep from laughing as Gio tries to psychoanalyze Enzo from across the dining table in our new house.

Enzo groans, tugging on the roots of his hair. "Would you shut the fuck up?"

Gio shrugs and grins. "Just following orders from the boss." He points to me.

"Oh, no," I say, walking by and smacking him on the back of the head before I plop down in Enzo's lap. "You don't get to blame this on me. You trying to get me in trouble?"

"You wanted a therapist, and for obvious reasons, you can't just talk to any shrink out there… I'm just being the go-between guy because, honestly, you both could use some therapy, you know? Fucking weirdos out here torturing people as foreplay."

I beam over at him, and Enzo wraps his arms around my waist, bringing me more snuggly onto his lap and nuzzling my neck. "You smell so good, goddamn," he murmurs into my skin.

"Scotty!" Gio yells. "You didn't tell me their new house came with a show."

Scotty cackles from the open kitchen, where he's cleaning up the Sunday dinner he made earlier.

It's become a type of tradition, these family nights.

My heart fills with warmth as I look around and realize I have everything I've ever ached for right here. Who knew I'd wind up in New York with a bunch of mob guys at my beck and call, and my most trusted adviser, Bastien, back in Atlantic Cove, running my empire?

I miss him, though—Bastien, that is—and I wish he could be closer.

Enzo slides his hand up my stomach instead, teasing the underside of my breast in a way that has my cheeks flushing.

"Enzo," I admonish, but I wiggle on his lap, rubbing against him anyway. "Not in front of people, please be serious."

"They should get out, then," he complains, his grip on me tightening. "Because I'm about to fuck you right on this table."

Scotty waltzes into the room, grinning from ear to ear. "What's this about a show?"

I point my finger at him and Gio. "Leave. Both of you."

"Oh!" Gio exclaims. "That's the kind of love we get around here? I see how it is."

"It's because I love you," I admit. "Enzo may act like he doesn't care if you stay and watch, but we both know he'd kill you for seeing me that way."

"True," Enzo confirms, pressing soft kisses to the juncture between my shoulder and my neck.

Gio nods and stands. "You make some very valid points." He walks over to Scotty before clapping him on the shoulder and steering him toward the front door. "Come on, kid. Let's go find our own dimes."

I don't even hear them leave because, in the next second, Enzo has me off his lap and laid out on the dining table in front of him, my front pressed to the dark wood and my dress flipped up so that my ass is on display and my pussy is exposed for his viewing pleasure.

His mouth latches on to me immediately, causing a sharp breath of air to escape from my lungs. My arms fly out to try and stabilize myself, and my fingernails dig into the table, my body already soaring from how good Enzo's mouth feels.

I think he's obsessed with eating pussy.

And to be honest, I'm here for it. I appreciate the art of pleasuring a woman, and if he weren't so possessive over me, I'd introduce a woman into the bedroom and turn it into a competition of who can make her come the fastest. But he's too jealous, and to be honest, so am I.

The thought of him ever touching anyone but me sends me into a fiery rage that can't be tamed.

In fact, that thought, knowing he's mine and mine alone, makes me crazy with desire, and when his tongue moves in the way it does, and his finger slips into me and curls up, I'm already on the edge of oblivion and about to explode.

"Oh my god," I cry out, pressing my face harder against the table.

He stops suddenly, and the peak I was about to hit withers away. My body feels like it's on fire, though. Every single time he touches me, it's another electrical pulse that rages through my body and sets my nerve endings ablaze.

He's the only one who's ever done that to me.

"Don't move," he commands.

I sink into his voice, allowing myself to relax completely and let go of everything that I usually feel: the need for control and the sense of responsibility I have because everyone else defers to me in every aspect, especially now that I'm both the owner of the Kingston empire and Enzo Marino's wife.

Like he says, even though I can take care of myself, it doesn't mean I should have to.

And I think I really like being taken care of by my husband.

He's the first person who has ever shown me what it truly means to be loved unconditionally.

I gasp when he stands and slams into me from behind, his fingers digging into the meat of my hips and his sharp thrusts sending me up the table, my hands grappling for purchase. "Fuck, Enzo."

"That's right, baby—it's me who makes you feel like this. Goddamn, you take my cock so well."

Pleasure skitters through me at his approval, lighting me up like fireworks.

He's big—sometimes, I feel like he's almost too big—and at this angle, with these thrusts, it feels like I'm going to burst apart at the seams. It hurts so good, though.

Heat builds deep in my abdomen and spreads down my spine, collecting between my legs until the tension winds tighter and tighter. I'm going to either pass out or explode from the pleasure, and when his free hand wraps around my body and fingers my clit, I detonate, my body pulsing in time with my heart as I come undone around him entirely.

Enzo's movements turn jerky as he reaches his peak, and I say what I know will make him lose control entirely: "Come inside me."

He collapses on top of me, biting into my neck as he groans in my ear and unloads.

I know it gets him off to talk about making me pregnant, but we've both agreed that we won't have kids in reality.

It's just not something I'm interested in.

We have too much trauma from both of our parents, and I don't want to have the responsibility of making sure I don't fuck another person up for the rest of their lives.

I was worried that would be a deal-breaker, but he said "happy wife, happy life," and that as long as he has me, he doesn't care about anything else.

"Fuck, I love you," he murmurs, pressing hot kisses along the length of my spine, his cock still inside me, twitching as we both come down from our high. "I'll never get tired of you."

Emotion overwhelms me, my chest expanding as it fills with a gooey warmth.

I never thought I'd have this type of love.

One that's unconditional and all-consuming.

My throat swells, and I clear it before moving until he slips out of me, twisting around until I'm flat on my back and staring up at his perfect face. Reaching up, I ghost my fingers along his cheeks. "Thanks for being mine, Lover Boy."

He grins down at me before leaning down and capturing my lips with his. "Thanks for letting me love you out loud, piccola sirena."

"For the rest of this life?" I question.

"And every other one too."

Character Profiles

Venesa

Name: Yrsa Venesa Andersen

Age: 24

Place of birth: South side of Atlantic Cove, South Carolina

Current location: Atlantic Cove, South Carolina

Nationality: Danish American

Education: GED

Occupation: Manages the Lair and is her uncle's enforcer

Income: Modest

Eye color: Dark brown, almost black

Hairstyle: Long and usually curled or in an updo. Dyed a bright silvery-white blond. Naturally dark brunette.

Body build: Midsize curvy and tall. Five nine and a size 14 to 18 depending.

Preferred style of outfit: Sexy outfits that highlight her best assets

Glasses?: No

Any accessories they always have?: Crystals of some sort and her seashell necklace

Level of grooming: High

Health: Healthy

Handwriting style: Loopy and cursive

How do they walk?: Saunters. She's always highlighting her best features to draw the attention where she wants it.

How do they speak?: Slow, controlled, and sultry

Accent: Southern

Posture: Good

Do they gesture?: Yes, sometimes overly so

Eye contact: When it suits her

Preferred curse word: Doesn't have a favorite curse word, but she uses nicknames as an insult.

Catchphrase: "See ya later, Loverboy."

Speech impediments: None

What's their laugh like?: Deep, sultry

What do they find funny?: Watching other people be uncomfortable

Describe smile: Wide and proportionate, lights up face, causes dimples in her cheeks

How emotive?: Emotive, but it's usually being used by her as a manipulation tactic and not a genuine emotion

Type of childhood: Bad young childhood. Her mother was beaten by her extremely abusive father, who had a gambling and alcohol addiction and was in and out of their lives. Her mother was the heir to the Kingston legacy but cut off her family in favor of her husband. She put him before everyone, including Venesa and herself. Venesa always felt like she wasn't good enough to be chosen because of this. When her mother was killed and her father disappeared, she was given to the state, and her uncle, who was estranged from Venesa's mother, took her in. She had a better life but was still ostracized and made to feel like she wasn't good enough with her uncle. Because of this, she aches for her uncle's approval because he's the closest thing to a loving parental figure she has.

Involved in school?: No, she didn't like school.

Named in the yearbook: Most likely to be an outcast

Jobs: Always worked for her uncle

Dream job as a child: Didn't have one

Role models growing up: Her uncle

Greatest regret: Trusting the wrong people

Hobbies growing up: Learning witchcraft and the art of poisons

Favorite place as a child: Morgan's Ice Shack

Earliest memory: Trips with her mother to the boardwalk

Saddest memory: Finding her mother dead

Happiest memory: Going to the boardwalk with her mom on her birthday

Any skeletons in the closet?: Yes.

If they could change one thing from their past, what would it be?: Trusting her uncle

Describe major turning points in their childhood: Her father beating her mother in front of her until she stopped being able to cry. Her mother dying. Her moving in with her uncle. Her cousin humiliating her in school.

Three adjectives to describe personality: Manipulative, sensitive, sensual

What advice would they give to their younger self?: Believe in yourself.

Criminal record?: She's never been caught.

Any siblings?: No

Father:

Name: Harald Andersen

Age: Dead

Occupation: Who cares?

What's their relationship with character like?? Terrible. Nonexistent really.

Mother:

Name: Adrina Andersen

Age: Dead

Occupation: Waitress at the Lair

What's their relationship with character like? Venesa loved her mother but was never good enough. Her mom did her best, but was mentally chained to Venesa's father and always chose him over everyone, including Venesa.

Closest friends: Fisher and Bastien

Enemies: Aria

How are they perceived by strangers?: Sensual, mysterious, weird

Any social media?: No

Role in group dynamic: She's a loner.

Who do they depend on:

- **Practical advice:** Bastien
- **Mentoring:** Her uncle
- **Wingman:** Fisher
- **Emotional support:** No one
- **Moral support:** No one

What do they do on rainy days?: Catch the rainwater to use in rituals

Book smart or street smart?: Street smart

Optimist, pessimist, realist: Realist

Introvert or extrovert: Extrovert

Favorite sound: Aria's silence

What do they want most?: To be loved out loud

Biggest flaw: Not paying attention to her surroundings and thinking that blood = family

Biggest strength: Her loyalty and ability to use her sensuality to her advantage

Do they want to be remembered?: Only by the people she loves

How do they approach:

Power: Manipulates it

Ambition: Lives for it

Love: Longs for it

Change: Doesn't like it

Possession they would rescue from burning home: The Kingston family painting

What makes them angry?: Being lied to

How is their moral compass, and what would it take to break it?: Not a strong moral compass at all

Pet peeves: When people don't tell her things or she feels like she isn't included in decision-making

What would they have written on their tombstone?: Here lies Yrsa Venesa Andersen. She was unlucky in life, but fortunately, she had a bit of magic.

Their story goal: Venesa starts as a strong, very morally gray character who shies away from commitment in romantic relationships due to trauma from how her mother was treated by her father. She aches to be accepted and to have a family that's proud of her and chooses her first, always. Somehow, she never quite gets anyone's approval no matter what she does. She works for her uncle, and she tries to do whatever he asks, but her personality is strong, and she isn't able to always hold back how she feels, which can cause tension in their relationship. Especially since she doesn't get along at all with her cousin Aria, who is the apple of her uncle's eye. Throughout the book, Venesa will form an immediate connection with Enzo, who sees her for *her* and doesn't push or force her to do things for him, be any other way than she already is. Having that type of freedom and acceptance isn't something she's used to, and it will start to reveal the cracks in her other relationships, namely with her uncle. When she's betrayed by the people she trusted the most and was loyal to for years, it becomes her turning point where she becomes who she's meant to be: a woman who is strong enough to stand on her own but also is able to accept all the different facets/sides of herself, including the soft and vulnerable bits that she's always pushed away. Allowing herself to be taken care of and letting people in to let them love her fully and be loved in return is her character arc.

Enzo Marino

Name: Enzo Marino
Age: 29
Place of Birth: Trillia, Brooklyn
Current Location: New York, New York
Nationality: Italian American
Education: High school
Occupation: Mob boss
Income: UNWI (Ultrahigh Net Worth Individual)
Eye color: Blue

Hair Style: Dark brown/black. Slightly messy on top but styled well. Movie-star looks

Body build: Tall, six four, muscular and trim

Preferred style of outfit: Suits or Italian cashmere

Glasses?: No

Any accessories they always have?: His gun

Level of grooming: High

Health: Healthy

Handwriting style: Messy

How do they walk?: With purpose

Style of speech: Casual

Accent: Brooklyn accent

Posture: Good

Do they gesture?: Yes

Eye contact: Always

Preferred curse word: Fuck

Catchphrase?: Doesn't really have one, but calls his victims "sweetheart"

Speech impediments?: No

What's their laugh like?: Deep and raspy

What do they find funny?: People who are witty

Describe smile: Beautiful and straight. Movie-star smile

How emotive?: Relatively

Type of childhood: Got into fights a lot as a kid, always felt the weight of expectation of his father and being part of the family business. Teenage Enzo was always taking care of his mother.

Involved in school?: No

Named in the yearbook: Most likely to get a girl pregnant

Jobs: *Caporegime*, underboss, don

Dream job as a child: Always knew he'd be working in the Mafia

Role models growing up: His father until he saw how his mother was treated and then nobody

Greatest regret: Not being able to save his mom

Hobbies growing up: Cage fighting as an adult and fighting in general when he was younger

Favorite place as a child: The corner outside Max's Meats

Earliest memory: His third birthday where his whole family showed up and his dad gave him a water gun and taught him how to shoot it

Saddest memory: Finding his mom dead

Happiest memory: When he finally got to be with Venesa

Any skeletons in the closet?: Yes

If they could change one thing from their past, what would it be?: Saving his mom

Describe major turning points in their childhood: His father treating his mom badly and his mom being a drug addict and killing herself

Three adjectives to describe personality: Suave, lethal, dangerous

What advice would they give to their younger self?: Be careful who you trust

Criminal record?: Never been caught

Any siblings?: One older brother, Giuseppe (Peppino)

Father:

Name: Carlos Marino

Age: 52

Occupation: Boss of all bosses

What's their relationship with the character like?: It's tenuous because he is volatile and paranoid, but Enzo is very loyal to him both because that's how he was raised—it's the oath he took with the omertà—and it's also a promise he made to his mother.

Mother:

Name: Giulia Marino

Age: Dead

Occupation: Stay-at-home mom/wife

What's their relationship with the character like?: It was good when he was younger, and then parental roles were switched when she became a drug addict and he was constantly taking care of her.

Closest friends: Giovanni

Enemies: Many

How are they perceived by strangers?: Very handsome and dangerous

Any social media?: No

Role in group dynamic: Leader

Who do they depend on:

Practical advice: Gio

Mentoring: His father

Wingman: Gio

Emotional support: Gio

Moral support: Gio

What do they do on rainy days?: Work

Book smart or street smart?: Street

Optimist, pessimist, realist: Realist

Introvert or extrovert: Introvert but able to be an extrovert when needed

Favorite sound: Venesa's laugh

What do they want most?: To find true love

Biggest flaw: Believing the good in people he trusts

Biggest strength: The ability to think through situations rationally

Do they want to be remembered?: Doesn't matter to him

How do they approach:

Power: Commands it

Ambition: Always has it

Love: Aches for it but doesn't think it's in the cards for him

Change: Adapts to it

Possession they would rescue from burning home: He doesn't put much stock in material things.

What makes them angry?: Being disrespected

How is their moral compass, and what would it take to

break it?: Very morally gray, so it wouldn't take much at all

Pet peeves: When people don't give him respect, when people talk too much, people who are unnecessarily cruel

What would they have written on their tombstone?: Here lies Enzo "Lover Boy" Marino. He loved to kiss you before he fucked you up.

Their story goal: Enzo starts as a very loyal son to his father, the boss of all bosses in the Italian American Mafia. He has dutifully stepped into the role of being the underboss after his brother, Peppino, was murdered, but he doesn't enjoy the way his father runs things, and he also misses the freedom of being able to actually *be* in the streets and do things the way he wants. He has longed for true love his entire life but has realized that it's never in the cards for him simply because of who he is and who his family is, so he's okay with marrying Aria to please his father and strengthen his family's power. Throughout the story, Enzo will have to come to terms with the fact that sometimes blind loyalty isn't the answer, and although he's made promises to his late mother and feels a sense of obligation to follow through on his word, sometimes, he has to take the opportunity to rise up and take control, take the *real* power for himself. By the end of the book, Enzo will realize that love is the strongest and most important thing in the world, despite what happened to his parents, and he will find a better balance between who he's meant to be as a Marino in the Mafia and accepting love into his life, being able to love people fully and without restraint despite how scary it might seem. He will realize that although he thought he had power and control in the beginning of the book, it was all an illusion, and he will grow into a character worthy of running empires and being the man who gets to call Venesa Andersen his for eternity.

THANK YOU FOR READING!

Enjoy *Hexed*? Please consider taking a second to leave a review!

Come chat about what you read! Join The McIncult on Facebook by scanning the QR code:

JOIN THE MCINCULT!

EmilyMcIntire.com

Scan the QR code to subscribe to Emily's newsletter and never miss an update!

Acknowledgments

I wasn't sure this book would ever be written because I was diagnosed with breast cancer at the very beginning stages of writing it. During the most intense part of my chemotherapy, I wasn't able to work at all, and my muses left me entirely. I was worried I'd never be able to write anything again. But slowly, we got through it, and even though I'm still on chemotherapy because I'm stage IV, it's an easier type and my muses came flowing back, stronger than ever. Right now, I'm sitting here with radiation burns so bad that I can barely type from the pain, but through all of that, I am grateful.

So I'd like to acknowledge and thank myself first and foremost because I've been through some things this past year and a half, and cancer has a way of turning your entire world upside down until you don't know who you are anymore. I'm grateful to myself for not giving up and for showing up every day to write this book because the stories in my head still demand to be told.

To you, my readers: Without you, none of this would be possible. When I disappeared for over a year during treatment, you were there, shouting about my books to the world. You're the reason I was able to undergo treatment without worrying about bills, and you're the reason the McIncult grows stronger every day. Thank you for showing up, reading my words, and supporting.

To my editor, Christa; my marketing manager, Katie; and the rest of Team Bloom: Thank you for being the most flexible people on the planet with my schedule and for supporting me through every step of my journey. You push me to be a better writer, and your constant belief in me means more than I can ever express.

To my agent, Kimberly, and the rest of Brower Literary: Thank you for always having my back and for being my right-hand person when I need the support. I wouldn't trust my career with anyone else. You are invaluable to me.

To my publicist, Jessica, and the rest of Leo PRNY: Thank you for listening to me vent, for putting me in front of people, and for helping boost and support my career in ways I could never accomplish on my own. A person is only as good as their team, and you make my team the best!

To my PAs, Rae and Jackie: Thank you for keeping my life in order. Without you, team Emily would be a dumpster fire.

To my cover designer, Cat: Thank you for working on

this series with me: taking my ideas and bringing them to life in stunning ways.

To my best friend, Sav: Thank you for being my soul sister and for always supporting me, even when it's me crying to you at three in the morning. Thank you for driving to another state to take me to chemo when I need and for always being there through everything, no matter what.

To my husband, Mike: I always knew you were the one for me, but it's never been clearer as it has in the past year and a half when you've been with me through cancer. You are the most supportive, loving, incredible husband and father, and I am so lucky to have you in my life. I honestly don't know what I'd do without you. Thank you for loving me and for choosing me every day, even when I can't choose myself.

To my daughter, Melody: You are, now and always, the reason for everything. I love you forever.

About the Author

Emily McIntire is a *USA Today*, *Publishers Weekly*, and Amazon bestselling author whose stories serve steam, slow burns, and seriously questionable morals. Her books have been translated in over a dozen languages, and span across several subgenres within romance. A stage IV breast cancer thriver, you can find Emily enjoying free time with her family, getting lost in a good book, or redecorating her house depending on her mood.